Cobbler's Hill

The Misses Teachout, Volume 1

Laura E. Price

Published by LEP Books, 2024.

COBBLER'S HILL

First edition. October 15, 2024.

Copyright © 2024 Laura E. Price.

ISBN: 979-8227141811

Written by Laura E. Price.

Also by Laura E. Price

The Misses Teachout
Cobbler's Hill

Standalone
The Stars; the Silence

Watch for more at https://lauraeprice.com/.

Table of Contents

This book is for Scott, the girls' first and biggest fan.

PART ONE
CHAPTER ONE

"You hungry, little girl?"

Corwyn Teachout, ten years old and not quite sure she remembered not being hungry, for all that they'd only been without regular meals for maybe six months, found herself at a loss for words.

"You know who I am?" the lady in front of her asked. Corwyn nodded. Vadoma Hildago, the witch of Cobbler's Hill, with her long, black hair and her long, bony fingers, her muscles like ropes in her arms and shoulders. Everyone knew her. "Good. Come with me and I'll give you something to put in your belly."

Even at ten, Corwyn wasn't stupid. She'd been sat on the steps of St. Philomena's by Gwen with orders to stay, had been amusing herself watching a little girl she was pretty sure belonged to that Simcote lady case the dry goods store across the street (some newly-tattooed gangster kid had loomed over the girl like a threat, but when she'd rolled up her sleeve to show her own tattoo he'd backed off like a rat facing a dog), but Corwyn was more afraid of the witch than she was of her sister. So she stood up from the steps of St. Philomena's and followed the witch through the crowd down Fowler Road toward 34th Street. As they turned onto 34th the witch said, "I've seen you running round—ain't there two of you?"

"Gwen's my older sister. We ain't twins. Just one of her and one of me."

"She going to worry about you up and leaving?"

"Probably. But *someone* likely saw me leaving with you—you ain't the most ordinary of people. Anyway, I can always find her—if she don't know where I am, she'll just sit still until I can come back."

"That your knack, then? Finding your sister?"

"I can find lots of people."

They arrived at the witch's house. It was small, but like only a few houses in Cobbler's Hill, it wasn't stuck on both sides to another house. On one side of it was a large, sagging place that looked like it had been cut up into apartments; its windows were cracked and there were shingles missing off the roof. On the other side stood an empty store front with missing bricks and a roof that looked likely to cave in. But the witch's house was painted blue and had whole windows, along with a small porch covered in plants in pots. "Is it a spell that keeps it so nice?" Corwyn asked as they walked up the front path.

"Threats, more like. And punishments." The witch pressed her thumb to the metal circle above the doorknob, whispered a word into the dark red wood of the door. It opened, and Corwyn followed her inside to a tidy front room full of chairs and more plants, with rugs on the floor. Corwyn stood still in the middle of it, didn't dare touch anything with her dirty, snot-crusted fingers. Barely six months since they'd taken off after the Singleton Home fire, but cushioned benches and rag rugs seemed like items from somewhere far distant, like fairyland or India.

The witch was looking at her the way the Sisters had when they'd measure the kids for new uniforms. "First I think we'll clean the muck off. Then some food—you can't prove potions on an empty stomach, it'll skew the results. Come on."

"What's proving potions?" Corwyn asked. They passed through the tidy kitchen to a tiny, curtained alcove where a big washbasin sat. In the bottom of the basin was a puddle of water. The witch leaned over it, whispered to it, and it began to grow, filling the basin slowly but surely.

"You know what I do?" the witch asked.

Corwyn was again at a loss for words. Because the Cobbler's Hill witch was ... not mean, exactly, but she didn't take kindly to insults and was easily offended—also quick to revenge. "You do magic," she said slowly. "Sometimes healing stuff. Sometimes other stuff."

The witch murmured to the water again, which stopped growing. "I *sell* magic," she corrected. "I make potions. That's most of the 'other stuff.' And they're tricky things, with unforeseen effects, so I need someone to try them out, prove they work, prove they ain't got aftereffects that might prevent me getting paid for my efforts. Now, into the tub with you."

Corwyn shucked her skirt and shirt, then climbed into the tub—the water wasn't much more than lukewarm, but she hadn't had a bath that hadn't fallen out of the sky since the fire, so she wasn't inclined to complain. The witch gave her soap; she scrubbed her hair and self down roughly before climbing out of the now-gray water and back into her grimy, smelly clothes. They used to be a uniform, but half a year's street living had done them no favors. She wished she knew how to sew, or that Gwen had actually paid attention when the Sisters tried to teach her; maybe they could have made the skirt into trousers.

She got fed next, bread and cheese and milk. After, the witch handed her a small glass with a liquid in it that didn't look like much of anything—surely not the nasty green or brown sludge she'd expected to have to choke down. It smelled like ... a plant, maybe? Corwyn didn't have much experience with plants besides grass and whatever trees grew in Stolarski Park, so she couldn't say for sure.

I've already had the bath and the food, she's got me now anyway, Corwyn thought. She gulped the potion in one go.

It seemed to ooze down her throat of its own accord, but it didn't taste like much of anything and didn't make her throw up. She and the witch stared at each other, Corwyn standing and the witch on the settee in front of her, while they waited for the potion to do its work.

It took forever. The witch didn't seem much to mind. Corwyn stood with her hands behind her back like the Sisters had taught her to, shifting her weight from one foot to the other, her general wariness wearing down into boredom.

"You maybe want me to—I dunno, chop wood or sweep up or something while we wait?" she asked.

The witch thought about it, then said, "The broom's in the kitchen, by the bathing room."

Corwyn took a step toward the kitchen, but her foot didn't touch the floor. This left her off-balance; she windmilled her arms to stay upright as, leg flailing, she rose into the air. She didn't stop until her head bumped against the ceiling.

She pushed herself down and to one side with one hand to spare her head and the plants hanging from the ceiling. "I reckon it's a good thing we ain't outside, Miss Hildago," Corwyn said.

The witch's mouth twitched, and with a grumbling sigh she said, "I suppose you can call me Vadoma now. No, wait, *Miss* Vadoma. Yeah, that'll do all right."

"Any idea how long I'll be up here, Miss Vadoma?"

The witch answered over her shoulder as she walked into the kitchen. "Why would I need a kid to prove my potions if I knew every damned thing about them—weren't you listening, girl?" She returned with a watering can full to the brim and handed it up to her. "Everything wears off eventually, though. Make yourself useful up there."

SIX HOURS LATER, CORWYN stood on Miss Vadoma's porch stuffing two apples into her pockets. She was full, cleaner than she had been, well-rested—after having figured out how to balance her head on one of Miss Vadoma's plant shelves and hook her feet on another, she'd taken a nap—and the proud owner of three new bruises along her ribs and hip, gained by falling from the ceiling when the potion wore off.

She let her knack out to find her sister. It tugged her down the steps. With any luck it wouldn't get distracted by a lost kid or a drunk fancy-man; Gwen was likely worried and angry past reason at this point. The apples ought to placate her, but not if Corwyn got yanked after someone else before she got back to her sister.

Corwyn started down 34th Street, her stride quick. Evening settled over Cobbler's Hill: the bordellos and opium dens began opening their doors; kids scrambled back to their flats or squats; the bars tossed out their afternoon patrons to get ready for their evening rush. It was noisy and frantic, but easier to navigate with a full stomach and clean hair.

Six months on, she still didn't know if she missed the Home or not—she missed the regular meals and the bed, for certain, but the muted roar of the Hill's streets felt much more like home, for all that she'd been scared to death the whole time they'd lived on them before. She skirted round a pothole, ducked between two men on the corner drinking out of a shared brown bottle, and shooed a cat off into an alley before the gang of boys up the block could spot it and decide cutting its tail off might be fun. She got hissed at and a scratch on her ankle for her trouble, but it was still a good evening.

Her knack drew her along down Dunbar Road toward Rollins Boulevard and, eventually beyond that, the docks, passing the Collett house on her way. It hadn't eaten anybody recently, so the sidewalk in front of it stood empty save for a boy about her own age, olive skin and dark hair, who squatted, just watching, through the fence that went all the way round the house.

Well *that* surely did not bode well, and Corwyn, having already saved a cat, felt expansive.

"Up," she said as she approached the boy. "Or don't you know it's trancing you?"

The boy looked up, his face confused and cloudy. "It *likes* me," he said in a wistful, faraway tone that Corwyn didn't much like. "Nobody else looks at it like I do."

"That's 'cause everybody else looks at it like something as might eat them," Corwyn replied, leaning down and getting a hand on his arm. "Which it will. Ain't you got someplace to go?"

"My ma and sisters ..." he said, glancing over at the house once more.

"Here, take an apple, go home." Corwyn put the witch's apple into his hand and gave his shoulder a hard shove. "Don't make me push you down the street—I'll do it."

He stumbled three steps past the Collett house, took a bite of the apple, and wandered away toward the middle of the Hill. No *thank you*, for neither the fruit nor the life-saving, but Corwyn still felt like she'd done a good deed.

Her knack pulled her harder now. The streets were getting darker, so she picked up her pace—but not at all because she got the feeling that the Collett house was glaring at her, no. Just to get home to her sure-to-be-angry older sister before full dark fell and the more dangerous people and monsters who liked to work in it came out to do their business.

SHE SLIPPED INSIDE the unlocked alley door of an old office with boarded-up windows on Rollins Boulevard. One candle burned inside, illuminating Gwen near the front door where she could just barely see around the boards to the street. Her rucksack—which was actually a burlap sack they'd found in Shoemaker's Alley—was open behind her.

Gwen's prized possession was a truncheon she'd had the presence of mind to nick off one of the Sisters' desks during the fire that burned down the Home. She kept it carefully clean and hidden away when she wasn't practicing with it; as yet she'd never used it on anybody. The other weapons in her sack were more makeshift: a thick piece of wood, a couple of bricks, and a length of heavy rope that Corwyn didn't care to think about much after Gwen used it on one of the bigger boys who ran along the edges of the Goldberg gang.

Corwyn could find people wherever they might be; Gwen knew how to hurt them with whatever came to hand.

Tonight Gwen had half an eye on the door as she polished her truncheon with a bit of rag.

"And where have you been, Corwyn?" she asked.

To any of the kids from the Home, that tone of voice would have been ominous. Corwyn tossed the other apple at Gwen. It smacked her in the shoulder and landed in her lap. "You ask me that like nobody at St. Phil's fell over themselves soon as they laid eyes on you to tell you who I went off with today," Corwyn said.

Gwen picked up the apple and looked it over speculatively. Then she glanced at Corwyn. "Well, you ain't turned into a frog, so I guess you survived your encounter with the witch."

"She fed me and gave me a bath, even." Corwyn crossed over to sit next to Gwen, peering through the slight crack between board and door. People passed by, some staggering already, some with more purpose to their walks. Couple of hot corn girls, a street sweeper; the street noise just loud enough in here to be soothing. "Eat your apple, Gwen."

Gwen took a bite, chewed slowly. "What'd the witch want with you?"

"She gave me a job. Not regular or anything, just now and then. For food and a bath, mostly."

"What are you doing?"

"Drinking magic things and seeing what they do. Today I floated up to the ceiling."

Gwen took another bite of the apple, and Corwyn could tell she was turning this information over in her mind. "I suppose there ain't anything I can do to stop you."

"Well, you ain't my mother, so."

That got a dark look—there were things they didn't talk about, and Corwyn was skirting right to the very edge of one of them—but Gwen swallowed and said, "As long as she don't poison you."

"She'd have to find a new kid, then, wouldn't she?" Corwyn asked, lying back onto the floor.

"Don't do that—" Gwen reached out and grabbed her hand. "At least let me braid your hair up so it don't get nasty again so fast."

So Corwyn turned around and, as the candle burned lower, let her sister yank and plait her hair tight to her head. It hurt, but she kept quiet aside from the occasional smack to Gwen's hand when she was too rough. After it was done, they snuffed the candle and moved to the center of the room, using their Home jackets and a couple of burlap sacks—these found outside a fruit market, and so not quite so smelly—to fall asleep.

CHAPTER TWO

After their mother died, Gwen took them to the Sessionist sisters at the Charles John Singleton Home for Wayward and Feral Children because Corwyn wanted her to. They'd spent a month sleeping in Shoemaker's Alley. They'd both been tired beyond the telling, hungry, and Lars Hallstrom had cracked two of Gwen's ribs and wrenched her shoulder until her arm couldn't move after Gwen took exception to the nasty old bastard trying to buy Corwyn off her. Even Gwen had to admit that maybe a ten-year-old's knack for fighting wasn't what it ought to be when faced with a grown man.

"Yet," she'd said to Corwyn as they'd hobbled to the Home. She'd broken his nose and managed to kick him in the balls hard enough that he couldn't chase them; her face stayed lit up even as she took too deep a breath and winced. "Sooner than later, I will knock hell out of anyone who crosses me, and everyone is gonna know better."

Corwyn had watched her older sister turn uncanny and violently lovely in Lars Hallstrom's grip, had lost her breath at the graceful line of Gwen's wrist and hand as she smashed his nose. She had no doubts as to whether Gwen would be a legend someday. But Gwen needed time, and Corwyn desperately wanted to stop worrying so much.

The Home was supposed to be temporary. The Sisters taught them reading and sums and seemed to figure they'd be secretaries or nurses, but Corwyn never took that seriously. Gwen wasn't made for that kind of work, and really, neither was Corwyn. Not exciting enough.

The plan, worked out over many nights they snuck out into the back courtyard of the Home after lights out, was for Gwen to join a gang when she turned sixteen. Maybe Corwyn would join, then, too. Thirteen was younger than most gang lords liked their kids to be, but Corwyn's knack would be valuable once she grew into it a little, got it more under control. Most folks with knacks got better at controlling them the older they got. But if not, she'd wait it out at the Home and join the same gang as her sister once she was old enough.

Neither of them expected the damn place to burn down after only three years.

Corwyn, soot-stained, coughing, singed at the edges, found herself sick at the thought of another three years living wherever the nuns could find to keep them all. And then another two, maybe, without Gwen. Gwen, who was a better fighter after spending her nights practicing on a succession of bigger kids, was just as determined to keep eyes on Corwyn. So they bolted. And then they found they had connections.

Despite the vast lot of them being, indeed, wayward, not every kid at the Charles John Singleton Home was feral, nor were they, despite the old folk of San Xavier calling it the Orphanage, all orphans. Most of them were younger siblings who needed somewhere to go when the older kids joined a gang, or their parents couldn't feed them, or they'd been abandoned for rumors of gold up north.

(Not so many of them, now, were left there by alchemical engineers. There were fewer kids volunteering to apprentice to them, these days. Those that did, and ended up at the Home ... well, they were decidedly not useful to anyone anymore.)

This meant that there were people in Cobbler's Hill—older kids, and young men and women—who owed the Teachouts favors, whether for getting their kid sister out of the fire when nobody else could find her, or as payment owed for Corwyn's finding the person who set the fire, and Gwen's beating that person until he bled.

So they had places to stay, found or given by kids with connections or kids with good eyes. They had, if not protection, then a lack of harassment from a couple of the Hill's more notorious gangs. They didn't need to go selling themselves to Madame Tereza or Ben Brogan, or begging for shelter from the Simcote lady. Their ability to eat was hit or miss at best, but they got to stay together out from under the nuns.

A few weeks after Corwyn's first proving session with Miss Vadoma—there'd only been two more; one had involved fine, coppery-green hair growing all over her—each of them had an orange and a piece of beef jerky nicked from Mr. O'Shea's front cart while his son wasn't looking. Sleepy and resentful proprietors' children were one of life's special joys, particularly when your knack wasn't for thieving. Gwen ate fast, leaving a sweet-sharp scented trail of dropped orange peel in her wake. Corwyn put her peels in her pocket, as they smelled good and she did not.

They turned up Dunbar Road to find a crowd outside the Collett house, milling idly as they variously ate breakfast, passed bottles back and forth, and shoved would-be pickpocketing kids away from themselves. Corwyn and Gwen, being small, squirmed and wedged their way into a spot at the fence that faced the front windows of the house. There was a redheaded boy—Corwyn thought she'd heard other kids call him Bill, or maybe Fred—already there who made space with no fuss.

"Who'd it eat this time?" Gwen asked him.

The boy shrugged. "Some Italian kid. His mother and sisters were all out here crying earlier. It's been boring as hell since they shoved off."

"Heard any screaming?" Corwyn asked.

"Couldn't hear nothing over those women caterwauling. Hey, you going to eat that?" The boy pointed at the jerky in Gwen's hand.

"Nah, you can have it." She passed it over. Corwyn smacked her, hard, in the arm. "Ow! What in nine hells, Corwyn?"

"He don't need no damn food, Gwen—he's one of the Simcote lady's kids! He gets fed every day, don't give him your breakfast!" Miss Vadoma refused to feed Gwen because Gwen refused, bluntly and stubbornly, to go anywhere near the witch's potions. Corwyn could sneak half a sandwich or an apple out of Miss Vadoma's house, but that was about all; otherwise, it was whatever they could steal or scrounge. Gwen's knack sometimes pulled her into fights the way Corwyn's pulled her to people, would she or wouldn't she—though Gwen was usually 'would she' about it—and if Gwen was all skin and bones with no muscle between, what kind of maiming might she be in for?

The boy glanced back and forth between them before carefully holding the jerky out to Gwen. She looked from him to it with a face so full of disdain it could skin a cat.

Corwyn sighed, loud, and snatched the jerky.

"Um ... sorry?" he tried. Neither of them answered. They all turned back to the house. The grown-ups in the crowd, used to ignoring the scraps of the sundry kids running the streets in Cobbler's Hill, droned on around and above them:

"... maybe the gearwork factory—Harry Norton ain't keen on clockwork people."

" ... dunno, Ben Brogan gets wind of it, ain't just gonna be Tansa in trouble."

"... heard Beatriz hates the kid, don't trust him to do shit ..."

The curtains in one of the front rooms fluttered a little, like someone had walked past them fast, but nothing else moved inside so they could see it. Corwyn put her last orange piece in her mouth, breaking it open with her back teeth and letting the juice flood her tongue, thinking about the apple she'd given that boy: if he was just going to end up eaten by the damn house anyway, she wished she'd saved it for Gwen.

"Marcella still ain't back?" a woman behind them asked.

Another woman replied, "No, and I think Carl's about at the end of his rope; she ain't the kind to flit ..."

Had it been a person, Corwyn's knack would have sat up in bed and tossed the blankets off in one swift motion, grabbing Corwyn's chain from the wall hook and pulling it hard with both hands.

"What's wrong?" Gwen asked, frowning down at her, likely still mad about the jerky.

"We gotta go." Gwen's frown didn't disappear, but it softened when she saw Corwyn's face. Corwyn knew, dimly, that she looked glassy-eyed and sort of slack-jawed when her knack was running her—Gwen had told her—but now she just needed to get moving before her head started to hurt.

The redheaded boy was looking at them like they were a new kind of bug he'd never seen before. "You're that girl as finds things, ain't you?" he asked.

"Just people," Corwyn said, distracted. She glanced one more time at the Collett house. The front curtain, the one that had moved, was pulled back; the boy she hadn't actually managed to keep from being eaten watched the crowd in front of the house with a blank face and corpse's eyes.

THEY ENDED UP IN SHOEMAKER'S Alley before noon. Even with most of her attention taken up with the pulling of her knack, Corwyn remembered to keep her head down as they skittered past the actual criminals who squatted there in daylight, either so no-count or so notorious that even the bars wouldn't have them. They made their way carefully through the shadows the Alley held like treasure, the ground a sticky-wet ooze under their shoes, past the sick whores and drunks shaky to the point they couldn't move to puke no more. The whole place stank to heaven.

"It's a wonder this ain't where we found Mama," Gwen muttered. Corwyn didn't answer—her knack brought her up short in front of a pile of ... trash? Wooden slats, some cardboard and paper, canvas.

"Under there," she said. She dropped to her knees in the muck layered overtop the Alley's cement. Gwen sank down next to her, and they started pulling the pile apart.

Gwen jerked back, grabbing Corwyn's shoulder. "Stop, Wyn. We found her." She gently pulled some sacking away, so Corwyn could see the lady. Marcella. As soon as she set eyes on what was left of her, Corwyn's knack eased off.

"She ain't been dead as long as Mama was," Gwen said, thoughtful. Marcella lay in the pile of junk, arms akimbo and legs spread, though her skirts weren't rucked up or nothing. No shoes. Bruises and scrapes all over her face, her wrists. Eyes gone, maybe rats. Throat ripped open and blood all down her front, splats of it on her face and legs. Messy. Still somehow better than their mother had been, for all that Corwyn could smell shit and piss under the clean copper smell of blood—Mama'd already started to rot when they found her. *Putrefy*. The nuns had taught her that word.

"What do we do with her?" Corwyn asked.

Gwen's eyes widened; she had clearly not thought that far ahead, either. "I don't know." Corwyn glanced around; nobody was paying them any mind, but she surely did not want to call attention to herself here. "You know who she belongs to?" Gwen asked.

Corwyn looked back down at the woman's broken face. "No. Just her husband's named Carl."

Gwen snorted. "Oh, sure, Carl. The only 'Carl' in the whole of the Hill. God forbid something's easy."

Corwyn sat back on her heels, wishing for boots. She could feel the cold slop through the soles of her shoes. "I suppose there ain't any harm in leaving her here," she said slowly.

"I reckon not. Someone's bound to find her when she starts to smell."

They stood up, both of them reluctant. Maybe Gwen wasn't thinking of Mama as they kicked the trash out of their way, but Corwyn was. And wondering who it'd be who found Marcella and could do something about it.

CHAPTER THREE

Gwen was not, by her nature, much of a worrier, but she had a core of practicality running through her that insisted Corwyn learn to fight.

Corwyn wouldn't have known where to begin to teach Gwen to find people. Her knack was a cord she followed, not a procedure. And there were things Gwen couldn't teach Corwyn, either—how to look at a doorknob and know the best way of maiming someone with it, as an example—but how to throw a punch, how to use her size to an advantage, where to hit someone to hurt them long enough to run? Those were things Corwyn could learn.

And so, whenever they had space and few enough neighbors around to bother, they sparred. Corwyn didn't much enjoy it, but on this subject Gwen would not be moved. Corwyn needed to be able to protect herself. Good skill for future gang life.

Today Gwen was off.

She moved slower than she ought to, even just to give Corwyn a chance to land a punch. Hollows lay in her cheeks and under her eyes. They were both of them always tired, but.

"You feel all right?" Corwyn ducked the roundhouse Gwen aimed at her head and danced back.

"I'm good," Gwen said, but it wasn't long before she let them call off. St. Philomena's was having a breakfast social, so they made their way to the rear entrance. They collected a huge portion of leftovers without Sister Honore noticing and threatening to report them to the Jacks if they didn't go back to the Home. Never you mind that there wasn't a Home no more, just a bunch of bunks in a warehouse near the docks.

They ate on the wide front steps of the cathedral. Gwen ate slow, not kicking the pigeons as they tried to steal her food; one particularly cocky blackbird got a roll off her with nary a curse.

"Gwen?" Corwyn asked.

"*What*?" Gwen's eyes were glassy, her cheeks flushed red—she was redheaded and fair-skinned like Mama had been, though with as dirty as her hair and person were, you couldn't usually tell. She shivered, then coughed. "All right, maybe I don't feel so good," she said with a shaky laugh.

"You're bound for the liar's hell," Corwyn informed her. "Come on, we're going back to the room." Corwyn wrapped their food up in the napkins they'd filched and grabbed Gwen's very hot hand to pull her along, back to the squat behind the closed-down button factory. Gwen went without protest, let Corwyn sit her down and wrap her up in every bit of extra clothing, sacking, and rag they had between them, shivering as Corwyn added both their sad excuses for blankets.

"You sure you don't need this for sleeping, Wyn?" Gwen asked.

"No. You keep that right there."

And Gwen did, with no argument. Between that and the cough, which went wet and hacking toward the middle of the day and lasted all the night, Corwyn didn't sleep, anyway.

HECTOR, THE BARTENDER at Tanner's, liked Corwyn. He'd been at the Home their first year; she'd found his lucky charm for him one day while she and the other kids were playing "What Can Corwyn Find?" with her knack. He felt like he owed her one, even though the finding was an accident. Her knack didn't find things. It was just lucky Paddy Entwhistle, who was something she *could* find, liked hiding in the dumbwaiter. She'd sat on the floor while the bigger kids fished Paddy out and found the charm—a real charm, with *things* etched on it, as opposed to some nail he carried round in his pocket—wedged between the wall and the chair rail.

So Heck was nice to her, and when Corwyn got up the next day she made sure Gwen was no worse before walking the five blocks to Tanner's to beg Heck for some soup. The owner was there, so she ended up mopping floors for it, but Heck gave her a much bigger jar of it than, she was pretty sure, he was supposed to.

Gwen ate the soup, coughed, slept, ate more of it, coughed more. Toward the late afternoon she glared at Corwyn from inside her nest of cloth, hair a mess and cheeks hectic. "Get out."

"What?"

"Go do something, Corwyn. Quit staring at me. I ain't gonna die."

You don't know that, Corwyn thought, but she didn't say anything. Gwen coughed some more, then spat whatever she'd brought up into a scrap of rag. "I ain't gonna die while you're *gone*, anyway," she said, clearing her throat after. "So leave me alone a bit so I can hack my lungs up in peace."

Corwyn stood up. "Is it bloody?" she asked softly.

"No," Gwen said, her voice clogged and thick. "It's green, though. Go on. I can hear you worrying. It's irritating."

And so Corwyn went out and walked the streets of Cobbler's Hill by herself as the late afternoon light streamed down yellow and orange, illuminating the garbage and making the potholes into inky shadow pools. She didn't know where she was going to go, exactly—Stolarski Park was nowhere she wanted to go by herself, and the docks were too far away even if she thought she could head down there alone—so she just walked.

She wound up on Fowler Road, by Katsaros' Market. The windows and the door to the shop were all propped open. Old man Katsaros kept a fruit cart out front, usually watched by his son or his daughter. It was filled with oranges, today, with nobody behind it.

Corwyn took a quick glance around. No one was paying attention to her. More surprisingly, nobody was paying attention to the unattended oranges, either. In point of fact, people were hurrying past the cart like it might bite them if they stopped. And that was just stupid, because fruit didn't bite.

She sidled over to the cart, keeping an eye out for any of the Katsaroses—the boy more than the girl; the girl didn't care about much of anything past her hair, so far as Corwyn could tell—and started loading her pockets with oranges. She heard voices through the window as she worked.

"I don't know where the fuck she is—you think I *approve* this nonsense? I'm the one arranged the fucking thing in the first place—"

"Look, Allen is Mr. Brogan's only son," said a voice, calmer and without the Greek accent. "And Tansa said *yes*, and now ... well."

Her pockets full, Corwyn started shoving oranges down her shirt. "She ain't gonna come back here," Mr. Katsaros said, his voice getting a little higher. "She knows I'll beat her bloody if she shows her whore face around my house."

"Mr. Brogan don't care what you'll do if she shows back up. Mr. Brogan is *upset*, and you don't know who she took off with, so Mr. Brogan don't care who gets the worst of it." The not-Greek voice was quiet, the kind of quiet that made Corwyn drop the last orange back onto the cart and turn to leave, fast. She heard the younger Mr. Katsaros yell as she walked away, followed by glass breaking and the distinctive sound of someone getting punched, then kicked in the stomach.

GWEN WASN'T ANY BETTER the next day, but she wasn't any worse, either. Corwyn peeled oranges for her and left with their dented tin bucket to get water from the public pump up the street. Gwen waved vaguely at her, then went back to peering blearily at the orange piece in her hand like she'd never seen one before.

The pump had a crowd, as usual. Mostly women with small children hanging off their skirts and older kids with buckets like Corwyn's. Nobody paid her much mind as she waited her turn, swinging her pail back and forth, listening to the noises it made as it caught and let loose the air.

The corner of something interesting poked out from under the trash bin in front of her. Corwyn kneeled to work it out, fingers scraping on the asphalt. It proved to be a wrinkled, water-stained, somewhat smelly book. *A Treasury of Verse* was nearly worn off the front cover.

Corwyn could read—maybe not as well as she could have had the Home not burned down and taken her chance for further schooling with it, but passably enough for poetry, she figured. She and Gwen had liked verse quite a lot before their mother died: there was an English let-boy who kept a good-sized closet in their building for bringing his fancy-men to, and he'd taught them both some poems between appointments—oh, the book had an entire *section* of those poems, all Samson the Strong Man, look at that—

And so it took Corwyn by surprise when she was snatched by the hair and pulled into the alley. Whoever it was as grabbed her was good enough at it that she didn't see his face before he smacked her in the head with a heavy object and knocked her out.

CORWYN WOKE UP WHEN she landed on something lumpy. She recognized the smell of fish, alcohol, and stale, bitter sweat.

Somehow she still had hold of her book. Whoever dropped her was trying to get her shoes off.

She kicked her way backwards on the bed. It was hard to open her eyes, but she managed ... and found herself looking at Lars Hallstrom, who had one hand wrapped around her left ankle.

He was a big man, with the yellowy-gray hair and salt-scaled, weathered skin of a lifelong sailor, along with the red eyes and nose of a lifelong drinker. His teeth, when he smiled, were yellow and huge and looked very strong. "You're awake," he said, his voice as callused as his fingers.

He ain't brave, and he ain't that clever, Gwen had told her, three years ago and drunk to the gills on morphine after the Sisters wrapped her shoulder and her ribs. Corwyn swallowed, blinked to clear her vision, and said as evenly as she could, "You get the hell away from me, you nasty old man."

The room rocked gently under them. They were on his trawler, then. Degenerate though he was, Lars Hallstrom's knack told him where the fish were. Shrimp, too. That, and his willingness to rat out kids with knacks to various folks as had an interest, kept him in money.

"Now don't be like that," he said, hand tight on her ankle. "You belong to me, now. It'll be easier for you if you get used to it quick."

There weren't many certainties in Corwyn's life, but she knew as a fact that she did not belong to *anyone*. "It'll be easier for you if you let me go," she said, not thinking about Gwen, fever and cough-addled, trying to find her once she realized Corwyn was missing. *You can get out of anything if you keep your wits*—Gwen had told her that a month ago as they'd sparred, when Gwen's cat-calling made Corwyn lose her head and then the fight.

"Nah, that ain't true," Hallstrom said. He stroked her ankle bone with his thumb. Corwyn kept still. "Little girl your age by herself on the street, in the Hill? Anybody cared about you wouldn't leave you alone." Corwyn tried to scan the room for weapons without turning her head. "Now me, I won't do that." His fingers loosened but did not let go of her; he slid his hand up along her calf, stopping halfway to her knee before sliding it back down again. There was a box at the end of the bed—nothing in it but dolls and a stuffed rabbit that hadn't been new in a long time—and a set of boy's clothes hanging off a nail in the wall, a pair of boots on the floor beneath them. "I'll take good care of you. You'll be fed, and get candy and toys, and you won't have to do no chores—"

Corwyn's eyes snapped to him. "I know what you make your kids do, you pervert, and it is sure as all hells a *chore*."

That made him mad: he squeezed her ankle until the bones rubbed together. She breathed in sharp. "That is no way to talk to your Daddy," he said through his big yellow teeth. He yanked her off the mattress and pulled her upright by her hair. Corwyn caught a glimpse of a bed across the room full of bottles and dirty sheets, then clapped her eyes back to his. "You need to apologize, little girl."

This was familiar and unfamiliar at the same time; it was Gwen who'd always had to apologize to Mama. But Gwen had always done it, so Corwyn said, "I'm sorry."

"'I'm sorry' what?"

"I'm sorry, sir?" she tried.

His face was a mix of regret and enjoyment as he backhanded her, rocking her head back and sending her stumbling to the side, but apologies when Mama was alive were always followed with getting hit, so Corwyn wasn't surprised. A cricket paddle leaned up against the wall by Hallstrom's bed. She got her feet back under her and took a breath as the pain started up in her face. "I'm sorry, Daddy?"

"That's better. Good girl." He ruffled her hair. She swallowed hard to keep herself from spitting at him. The ruffling pulled the goose egg where he'd knocked her out, she could taste blood, and she was pretty sure one of her teeth was loose now. "Go change into those clothes—I'm sorry they ain't girl clothes, but we'll get you a dress in a few days." He moved to sit on the small mattress, leaned back across it to watch as she undressed.

Her hands flexed on the book in her hands. She looked over at the clothes. "You had a boy before me?" she asked.

"Yeah. His name was Isaac."

Corwyn waited, nervous, but her knack kept quiet. Good. That was a jar of complication that didn't need opening. "Where'd he go?" she asked. The shirt and pants looked nearly new. It occurred to her that the reason her knack wasn't kicking could be that Isaac, or what was left of Isaac, was still somewhere in the cabin.

"Never you mind. Get changed."

Corwyn surely did not want to take her clothes off in front of Lars Hallstrom, and with him all loose and lazy on the bed, she figured it was time to take her chances.

She threw the book of poetry at him. It went high, but she hadn't expected she'd nail him in the forehead with it, anyway. He looked up after it for a brief second, and she bolted for the bat.

His hand tangled in her hair and yanked her back, hard. Some of it came out as he reeled her into him and got an arm around her waist, lifting her off the ground. She thought she might puke for a minute; the sour, ugly smell of him wrapped around her as he turned so that she lost sight of the bat. Kicking got her nowhere.

He let go of her hair to adjust his grip. With a grunt, she slammed her head back as sharp as she could into his face. She felt *and* heard the crunch as his nose broke, even as her eyes filled with little black dots.

Hallstrom's grip loosened. Corwyn hit the floor and ran for the bat, every step jarring her nauseous. His punch, softer than it ought to be, landed upside her head; she staggered two steps and fell.

Gwen had taught her to roll out of a fall; luck rolled her toward the bat.

She got a hand on it, fingers around the handle, then used it to shove onto her feet. She was surprised she got that far, until she raised it up in front of herself and turned around.

Lars Hallstrom stood in front of her, hands on his hips, nose crooked and lips bleeding red all over his teeth as he grinned at her. Of *course* she wasn't the first kid to try this. He probably got real excited when he took the bat off them, all easy, and beat them with it 'til they called him Daddy and let him do whatever he wanted to them.

Yeah, well, those kids didn't have Gwen Teachout, high as a kite in the Home's infirmary three years ago, telling them, *His knees are bad, too.*

Hallstrom reached *up* for the bat. Corwyn twisted to the side and swung *low*, all her weight behind it as she smashed the bat into his left kneecap. It crunched with a noise not unlike his nose.

He hollered like a devil as his leg went from under him. The bat pulled her around a little; she came back and got him once good in the ribs before she tossed the bat across the room toward the door and ran to scoop up her book and grab the clothes.

He snagged her ankle when she passed him coming back, the same ankle as before, grinding the bones until she yelped and kicked—the kicking didn't do her any good, but pulling her foot back to try again got her shoe off. She left it, hopping back to get her balance until she could turn and run up the stairs.

"*You little bitch!*" he screamed after her—and thank you, Lars Hallstrom, for letting her know he wasn't right behind her as she burst onto the deck.

The gangplank wasn't out.

She made herself go as slowly as she could, hands shaking as she wrapped the shirt and pants around the book to throw them, and the boots, to the dock. Then she made a running jump herself, praying she wouldn't end up drowning next to Lars Hallstrom's trawler.

She fell on her face as soon as she landed, skinning both her knees. She got up again—nine hells and all attendant demons, she had spent a lot of damn time on the ground today—gathered her things, and made her way to the nearest quiet spot to put on the boots.

It wasn't even dark yet. The sailors ignored her, as did everyone else.

She let her knack out to take her back to Gwen.

Her face ached in time with her feet hitting the pavement. Her neck wobbled under her head like a piece of string trying to hold up a pumpkin. Her scraped knees stiffened so that both bending and straightening them hurt. The boots were too big and rubbed wrong at her sore ankle.

Her knack didn't hurt, though. Her knack was a smooth, silken, soothing ribbon in her body as it guided her through Cobbler's Hill to Gwen. She chanted poems to herself as she went, the ones she remembered from when their mother was alive, which she'd used to survive until things were quiet and calm again, when she could patch up her sister.

"OH, NO, NO, NO, STAND right the hell up, Corwyn, do *not* lean against the wall, you'll just slide down it and as soon as you're down you won't be getting up again." Gwen's voice was sandpaper-rough and squeaking; her hands hot against Corwyn's arm to pull her upright. She coughed, but it didn't sound as wet. "Come on. Keep moving while you can." Gwen pulled her to the side of the room where they kept their things, performing an awkward bending dance to keep Corwyn propped up while she snagged the side of her rucksack. The candle she kicked over and stomped on as they headed back through the door.

"Who did this, Corwyn?" Gwen's voice was grim; *Corwyn I need you to find Mama*-grim, which tone Corwyn hadn't heard in years now.

"Lars Hallstrom," she said.

Gwen swore for a while. Corwyn didn't pay much attention, being caught up in keeping her feet moving and not puking on the garbage in the street or any of the people lying in it.

"I smashed his knee pretty good with a bat," she eventually remembered to say.

Gwen paused in her colorful recounting of the Hallstrom family's relationship with their livestock. "Good girl, Wyn," she said, and then she swallowed hard enough that Corwyn felt it.

MISS VADOMA TOOK A sharp step back when she opened the door, before recovering herself enough to ask, "What hell'd the two of you crawl out of?"

Gwen shoved Corwyn at her. "Lars Hallstrom beat hell out of her. Just help her. I got some money." Then she started coughing.

"I kneecapped the bastard!" Corwyn crowed. Miss Vadoma caught her, gingerly, with just her long hands on her shoulders. The pain was bad, but Corwyn felt like she was floating over it, looking down at it. Now if Gwen could just stop *coughing*.

Miss Vadoma gave the lip-twitch that passed for a smile with her. "Good for you, girl." She frowned over Corwyn's shoulder at Gwen. "Keep your money for what I make you for that cough—this one can work off her debt, but you got nothing to deal with but coin."

"I think one of my teeth is loose," Corwyn said, trying to poke at it with her tongue.

"You're young enough still, you'll grow more," the witch told her.

They spent the night with the witch, Corwyn on a cot in the alcove off the kitchen, and Gwen on the settee in the front room. Miss

Vadoma wrapped Corwyn's ankle with a poultice, fed her some sort of bitter sludge, put a liniment on her cheek, cleaned the blood from her knees and hair, and bandaged her head. "Four provings, for free," she said severely.

"On your head be it if my bodily odor offends you, then," Corwyn replied, then laughed and said, "Oh, whatever you gave me oiled my jaw, now, didn't it?"

Miss Vadoma's mouth was a tight line as she asked, "Corwyn. He do anything besides beat you?"

Corwyn shook her head; it made the room wobble like Lars Hallstrom's boat, and she clenched a fist along the side of the cot to stop it. Despite what she'd implied to Lars Hallstrom, she had only the vaguest impressions—from her mother and the men she brought home, from the let-boy used to work in their tenement, from things the bigger kids at the Home said sometimes—of what Miss Vadoma meant exactly, but she knew the shape of it. "I got away from him before he got past telling me to take my clothes off." She heard Gwen, somewhere behind Miss Vadoma, let out her breath so fast it set her coughing.

Miss Vadoma's grin bloomed, crooked and closed-mouthed, across her face, and she said, "He had no goddamned idea who he'd grabbed. I'm going to put something together for your sister's cough. You rest. Or gab like a jay, makes no matter to me."

Gwen bought a good-sized bottle of that something for her cough, then fought awake through the haze of it to check on Corwyn throughout the night.

"Go sleep, Gwen," Corwyn told her.

"No. And shut up about it, Corwyn." But her hand was soft on Corwyn's forehead, careful as it smoothed her hair back.

CHAPTER FOUR

Now they were both hungry and moving a lot slower than usual. Mr. Katsaros and his son were still too busy looking for Tansa and her lover to pay attention to their goods, and one of the churches got ambitious and held an extra social, but Corwyn worried. Corwyn, as Gwen pointed out frequently, always worried. Then again, Gwen had been up in the night to reassure Corwyn the floor wasn't rocking under her (*just a nightmare, Wyn*), and had a couple of night terrors of her own that she refused to tell out loud. She hadn't let Corwyn go alone anywhere farther than around the corner to meet her with stolen apples, either. Between that and her thundery quiet—Gwen quiet was much a sight louder than Gwen yelling—Corwyn suspected she wasn't the only one worrying.

"Maybe I should join a gang *now*," Gwen said suddenly one morning. "You could go back to the Home a couple of years—"

"We don't split up," Corwyn said, alarmed. She glared, half-scared, from her seat against the wall of their squat. That was the agreement, the plan they'd decided on while they still smelled like smoke and the Sisters hadn't yet collected all the stray kids.

Gwen could maybe get in—she was undersized and only thirteen, but her knack was a thing of beauty—but Corwyn couldn't imagine they'd take her equally undersized ten-year-old sister who couldn't control her finding knack.

Gwen paced the floor, truncheon in her hand. She twirled it absently, like a Jack might, frowning at her feet. Outside, the fog hung onto the morning like it had claws, leaving the world damp and uncertain, but they were inside, Gwen wasn't coughing anymore, and Corwyn had a book to read. Corwyn had thought it was going to be a good day.

Gwen spun the truncheon with more intention. "I should set fire to his goddamned boat."

"With what?" Corwyn asked, though if she'd thought it would settle Gwen down, she'd have gone hunting some kerosene. "Not to mention he's a grown-up, and has a job—he might could set the Jacks on us."

Gwen rapped the truncheon hard against the doorframe of their current squat. "Someday, Corwyn, I will set fire to his goddamned boat." She set the bat down, leaned against the wall, and muttered, "Too many 'somedays' in my life."

Corwyn didn't know what to say to that, so she went back to reading her poems, unsettled.

"GWEN TEACHOUT!"

Gwen, in the process of shoving a handful of jerky down her shirt, gave a startled hop that nearly knocked over Mr. O'Shea's entire cart before she caught her balance and turned to see who'd called for her. He seemed familiar to Corwyn, older than they were and maybe Haitian, but she couldn't make out much more, standing as she was at the mouth of the alley across the street.

Gwen smacked him hard in the shoulder when he reached her, and he followed her when she started toward the church. Corwyn cut down the alley toward St. Philomena's.

She recognized him when she got there: Osian Lauredent, one of the older kids from the Home who'd also lit out after the fire. Osian was nice enough, not given to beating on the little kids nor stealing their stuff. He'd always been more interested in picking fights with the kids his age; he had a temper and a bit of a knack for fighting—if Corwyn remembered, he could usually knock someone out with one punch. Which was a decent knack, but not much good against Gwen's speed.

"Hey, Corwyn," he said when she got close enough. He had a little bit of an accent and a smile that always looked like he was keeping something back from you, even when he wasn't.

"Hey, Osian, how're you?"

"I'm just fine. I was asking your sister if she might want some money."

Gwen had her arms folded over her chest, smiling slanted. "Osian's running with the d'Souza boys, now." Osian shrugged and showed Corwyn the ornate *D'S* tattoo on the inside of his right wrist.

"Well, ain't he coming up in the world." Corwyn put her hands behind her back. "How much money?"

"A dollar here and there."

"To do what?" Gwen asked.

She'd moved more to his side; Osian had to turn to reply to her. Corwyn moved a little more behind him. "Running errands for us," Osian said.

"Errands?" Corwyn asked.

Osian turned again. This was fun. "Carrying messages, delivering packages. That kind of thing."

"How come you're asking me?" Gwen asked.

Osian looked at her, then back at Corwyn, then took two steps up so he could see both of them at the same time. They all three grinned at each other. "I'm asking you 'cause your sister pulled me out the fire, but I hear the witch already gave *her* a job."

Gwen looked to Corwyn, who lifted one shoulder. "I suppose I could," said Gwen. "I get paid up front or after?"

"Mrs. d'Souza's is always willing to pay up front. She'll find you if you don't finish your job."

IT WASN'T REGULAR WORK, and it surely didn't pay much, but it was fun to run around the Hill, it kept Gwen from being broody, and the nightmares tapered off. Maybe it would lead to something more permanent later on, too. Gwen hadn't brought up the idea of joining a gang again, but Corwyn—despite the knots in her stomach whenever she considered Gwen doing it without her—could see a cracked door Gwen could get her foot into.

And between money for food and Miss Vadoma feeding Corwyn the occasional regular meal again once she worked her debt off, things seemed downright luxurious.

GWEN COULDN'T STOP touching Corwyn's hair as they left the witch's house. "So is it really blue, or will it all run out if it rains?"

"Oh, it's blue all right—she made me wash it twice. It's blue and cleaner than any part of me has ever had call to be." Miss Vadoma had not been best pleased when Corwyn left, but after six hours with no sign of Corwyn's hair going brown again, she'd waved her out the door with a frustrated huff. Like it was Corwyn's fault.

Corwyn supposed the fact that it was just her hair—and her eyebrows, and her eyelashes—as opposed to the furry green pelt she'd sported the last time Miss Vadoma had experimented in this direction, was improvement. Of a sort: Corwyn wasn't fond of standing out in a crowd, and they got some curious looks as they approached the small crowd outside the Collett house.

"So when the potion wears off—" Corwyn shot her sister a grateful look that she said *when* and not *if* "—what happens?"

"Hell if I know. Maybe it grows out, maybe it falls out, maybe it runs down my head and I end up with a pretty blue shirt out of it."

They crossed through the crowd, dodging folk as weren't paying attention to anything but the howling noise coming faintly from inside the Collett house, like a wind down a tunnel. All the windows in the house were black, as though someone had hung dark curtains over them.

"That's new," said Gwen. They leaned up against the fence.

"Think it's tired of people staring—hey! Ow!"

The boy who'd pulled at Corwyn's hair jerked back as she smacked his arm away. He was grinning. "What in nine hells you do that for?" Corwyn demanded. "My hair ain't yours to play with!"

"I just wanted to see if it was real," the boy said, affronted.

"Ain't nobody taught you to keep your hands to yourself?" Gwen asked.

"Nope." The boy turned his grin to her. "Ain't like anyone can stop me."

There was a very particular way Gwen went still. It wasn't like a cat, muscles ready and tail switching back and forth, and it wasn't like a bird, eyes focused sharp on the thing it wanted to hide from. She could do both—still like a cat before she stole something; still like a bird when their mother started screaming. But when she decided to fight, Gwen went still like all the Gwen ran out of her, leaving behind just her knack and a sweet, sunny smile.

She cocked her head at the boy, who'd gone back to grinning at Corwyn, then, whip-fast, she punched him in the face hard enough that Corwyn heard something crack.

He recovered quick—maybe he had a bit of a fighting knack, too—and swung at Gwen, but she slipped in under his arm and grabbed it, yanked it forward, unhinging his shoulder. He howled. The group of people just in front of the Collett house cleared back away from them, watching, as Gwen swept the boy's leg and got him on the ground. She kicked him two, then three times in the ribs before leaning over him, into his face.

"The world ain't yours to go grabbing at, you hear me?"

He was mad as anything, red-faced and sputtering, but he held his disjointed arm and nodded.

"You touch my sister ever again, I will see you dead." There was a tone to Gwen's voice—a cold sound, like the dark gray stone of St. Philomena's in the fog—that Corwyn had never heard before. The anger drained out of the boy's face, and he tried to scramble back away from them. Corwyn touched Gwen's arm. "Come on," she said.

Gwen kept quiet as they started off, looking up over the buildings at the blue, cloud-streaked sky. Her voice was pleased when she finally spoke: "I ain't never pulled someone's shoulder out of joint like that before." She grinned cheerily at Corwyn and then bounced ahead of her down the street.

IN THE END, CORWYN'S hair fell out.

On the one hand, the amount of money they sold it for was a good sum: they bought sweets; a pair of trousers and boots for Corwyn, since Gwen had gotten Isaac's; real rucksacks with straps and buckles to shut them; a sewing kit; and two books each from the discarded bin at the library. They split what cash was left between them for safekeeping.

On the other hand, Corwyn's eyes itched like the very devil while her eyelashes grew back.

The witch, for her part, had very little sympathy for Corwyn, particularly given that they had no timepiece and therefore couldn't tell her how long it took the potion to wear off. She did, however, relent and give Corwyn a hat.

Corwyn liked her hair short: it kept her head cooler, and she felt light, as if her head might float away were it not tethered to her neck. She worried a bit that folk might think she was a boy, but no one did.

She half-expected Gwen to hack her own hair off, but she didn't; just kept it braided and wrapped around her head as usual.

She did give Corwyn's scalp a rub at every given opportunity. It made Corwyn squirm and duck away, but Gwen just smiled and rubbed some more.

CHAPTER FIVE

"So why do you think there's a cathedral here?" Gwen asked Corwyn.

Their plans to spar at Stolarski Park had been waylaid by a thick fog rolling through the streets. The damp and lack of a clear sightline sent them to spend a little of their last hair money on stuffed bread from a cart vendor who looked as miserable as they were. Now they sat on the steps of St. Philomena's to eat. The fog swirled around them, full of shapes and muted noises, but it seemed very much like they were alone with the cathedral. Corwyn supposed she ought to be more wary of this than she was.

" 'Cause the Hill was the first part of the town?" Corwyn answered. "It couldn't've always been so bad, neither. By the time it got bad, they likely couldn't move all that rock."

The spires and arches disappeared into the mist, but the bottom half of the broken clock in the top front face still showed. The gray stone was dark with wet.

"That's not what I meant—I meant, why did alchemical engineers build a *church*? It ain't like they're god-fearing men. And more than that, why can't they fix the clock?" Gwen glanced over at Corwyn and glared at the smile on her sister's face. "What?"

"Since when do you care why ... well, why *any* of that?" Corwyn asked. "Since when do you care why anything?"

Gwen looked insulted. "I got *some* intellectual curiosity, Corwyn. I ain't stupid." She bit into her pastry like it was the throat of an enemy.

"Didn't say you were stupid—I said you didn't care." She bit into her own pastry, which was still warm and full of meat and potatoes. Her hair was grown enough now that the wet plastered it against her skull; her eyebrows were grown out enough to catch the damp, as well. Her clothes stuck to her here and there, but she was happy with the warmth in her mouth and throat, the smell of her food in her nose, and the sight of her sister's wistful face in profile.

Gwen shrugged. "Sister Benedict, back at the Home—she said that years ago when the clock worked, every day at nine and noon and three, there were clockwork figures as came out of it and did things. Acted out parables, or danced, and one was a scene from St. Philomena getting martyred. They weren't regular clockwork, just wind-up dolls, but ... I dunno. Sister Benedict said nobody knows why none of the alchemical engineers ain't ever fixed it. Probably they don't care."

"Or the Church won't pay them," Corwyn said. The Sisters at the Home were always complaining about the Church being miserly.

"I guess it'd just be something to see. Don't you think?" Corwyn followed Gwen's eyes up toward the clock, stopped at twelve minutes past seven, surrounded by what she now reckoned were little doors for the clockwork dolls. Likely everyone on the street would stop to watch them. Likely some folk would gather round beforehand, a crowd on the sidewalk like at the Collett House, except to see something a sight nicer.

Well, maybe not—St. Philomena's martyrdom was pretty damn bloody. But it still sounded kind of nice. She wondered how they'd done the wolves devouring her guts.

"This can't be the only church in the world with clockwork dolls," she said, finally. "We'll just have to find one that works, someday."

"Someday," Gwen echoed, her voice flat, maybe from the fog. Then, "It's probably gotten late enough, we can spar at the squat and not bother anybody."

THEY'D HAD THIS SQUAT, a large empty room meant for storage overtop a closed-down restaurant, for nearly a month now. Gwen's job had some perks, and not being run off their flat looked to be one of them. Osian was outside their door when they got there, trying to slide an envelope underneath. He straightened and held it out to them when they came up the rickety outside stairs.

"This goes to Veigar Olafurson," he said.

"You got an address," Corwyn asked, "or are you hoping my knack'll kick?"

"Well, if it did, it'd save some time," Osian said with his salesman's grin, then rattled off a street and a couple of landmarks.

Gwen turned the envelope over in her hands. It looked flimsy. "That's in Pallasgreen, Osian."

"It is," he said.

"Ain't we a trifle raggedy to deliver something to the Olafurson gang? In Pallasgreen? Which is quite a long walk, Osian. In the fog." Gwen had her head tilted at him, her mouth pursed.

Osian rolled his eyes. "Not me who said to send two urchin kids to Veigar goddamned Olafurson—Mrs. d'Souza's grandson thinks this sort of task is beneath his dignity. It's me as thought you'd like the five dollars we're paying, and you're reliable, so, you want the job?"

They took it. And then they trudged through the fog—which lightened but did not disappear as they made their way farther from the bay—and the uneasily-quiet streets of Cobbler's Hill to the slightly better neighborhood that was Pallasgreen. Families lived in

Pallasgreen. Schoolteachers and bookkeepers and, rumor had it, one actual doctor lived in Pallasgreen.

But Veigar Olafurson, it turned out, did not.

What Veigar Olafurson had in Pallasgreen was an office: a large building with two stories and pillars along the front. It was nearly as out of place on its shabby street here as it would have been in the Hill. Corwyn, feeling small and dirty and very damp, climbed up the front steps and between two of the pillars with Gwen to pull the bell.

Corwyn's shoulders were twitchy. Gwen had been tense since they crossed Jersey Court Road. "It don't even look that different from the Hill," Corwyn said, her voice more fretful than she liked. "We ain't that far into it."

The door opened before Gwen could answer. A clockwork man in a dark suit stood behind it.

They'd both seen clockwork things before: Mr. Katsaros's clockwork arm; Sister Jonnson's clockwork leg; the tiny clockwork birds that were the only things that could keep Molly Coyer quiet on her bad days, which she showed the other children at the Home on the good ones. They'd been made for her by the alchemical engineer she'd been apprenticed to before her mind broke. If you touched them, they'd bite you; they were charmed to Molly's sweat.

But none of those were anything like a clockwork man.

He looked real enough from the neck down, despite the whining and huffing that always went along with clockwork. He wore a dark wig on his head. And like all clockwork folk, his face was made of a molded metal sheet, like a mask, with eye holes, a nose, and a mouth shaped to look pleasant.

Gwen swallowed. "This is from Mrs. d'Souza," she said, handing over the envelope.

The clockwork man took it, flipped it in his hands much like Gwen had—how did he *see* it? He must, somehow—and said, "Thank you." His voice sounded flat and far away, like it came from down a long alley, pitched like a man's, if stilted. He reached into his pocket and gave them each a quarter with cold, copper-filigreed fingers before shutting the door.

They both looked at the coins in their hands, wearing identical expressions of bafflement.

"You think he's ... *charmed* to do that?" Corwyn asked, befuddled.

Gwen shrugged. "What are we meant to do with these, you suppose?"

Corwyn grinned. "Why Gwen, I do believe we're meant to buy hair ribbons with them. Perhaps a sweet, if there's any left over."

Gwen snorted. Corwyn bit back a laugh. They pocketed their coins and started down the steps to the sidewalk. Partway there, Gwen glanced back at the building. Then she waved.

Corwyn looked back, squinting—the fog wasn't so thick, but it still swirled and slid round them and the pillars like a feral cat. On the second floor, in one of the windows, stood a boy. He looked to be about their age—or their size, anyway, and beyond that all she could really make out was a lot of hair and dark skin.

"What are you waving at him for?" she asked Gwen as they turned to leave.

"He waved first. I figure it pays to be polite to folk in a gang like that." Well, Corwyn couldn't argue, even if the Olafurson gang seemed a bit ambitious for the two of them.

Gwen said, thoughtful, "That's a big place for a kid to rattle round in."

"I suppose," Corwyn replied, but she thought he seemed just fine in that big place—like the Simcote kids, well-fed and above all the noise and dirt of the Hill and the world, for all it raged and spat around them. But even Mrs. Simcote's kids didn't see it from behind clockwork and glass.

THE FOG THICKENED ONCE more, and the sun went down behind it. The streets of Cobbler's Hill began to fill up. The hot corn girls who worked for the gangs began to appear on the sidewalk, arguing about who was going to work what streets with who, since nobody wanted to work in the fog alone. The let-boys and let-girls lit up the brothel windows to shine against the misty air, and the beerhall waitresses did the same for the bars. The men who ran the cockfights and the dice games in the alleys took up station on the corners, too; maybe they'd get better crowds tonight with the fog to hide them.

Corwyn stayed close to Gwen as they walked. The fog cut them off, kept them in their own small clearing, but it didn't feel safe the way it had on the steps of St. Phil's.

A big lug of a man with a deep-seated frown strode through their little space and between them, bouncing Corwyn off his arm into the street. She straightened up and looked around. The fog had closed between her and Gwen.

She heard two calls at the same time:

"Bert?!"

"Corwyn!"

Her knack started for Gwen, then tried to turn tail to whoever the hell Bert was. Corwyn, for a moment, thought her head might split into two and fall off her neck and yelped at the sensation. She wasn't sure if she actually heard Gwen's *goddammit* or not.

Then she felt Gwen's hand on her arm, and her knack shoved her toward Bert.

"Come on," she said to Gwen, who frowned until she twigged what was going on and followed Corwyn. They dodged grownups, street lamps, and an occasional dog or cat as Corwyn's knack drew them deeper into Cobbler's Hill.

"Who're we looking for?" Gwen asked.

"Hell if I know. Bert somebody."

This was a part of the Hill they hadn't been back to since they were little and still had a mother. Corwyn and Gwen avoided this side of it as much as they could. There were memories that found them easier here, and their old landlord might still be looking for them.

Corwyn came to a stop in a deep, shadowed corner between two buildings, a hidey-hole more than an alley, empty save for the body.

It was situated so that it couldn't be seen from the sidewalk, but once inside the man on the ground came clear enough. They both knelt down to get a better look at him, tucked away in the very deepest back corner of the little alcove. Corwyn's experience with corpses was perhaps more familiar than she liked to dwell on, but not as extensive as it could have been. Still, the shade of the blood on his clothes and skin made her think the corpse was fresh, if cooled off a lot.

It was pale, too; the tattoo on the inside of his wrist stood out against the skin, even in the half-light. It was two letters twined together, an O or possibly a D with a U or a V—maybe one of the dock gangs? He was white, maybe Irish, so not the Tongs. She thought for a minute of the lady they'd found in Shoemaker's Alley with her throat ripped open, but this guy's throat was more neatly done; much of the blood pooled under him and running down the pavement toward the street came from the gashes in his stomach.

Something scuffled behind them, up at the mouth of the alley.

Gwen turned on the balls of her feet, still crouched. Corwyn laid a hand on her arm, but Gwen didn't seem to be readying herself to fight: this was bird-still, not knack-still. The dark had crept up behind the mist, and Corwyn squinted, trying to see through it.

A figure crouched at the mouth of the hidey-hole. The fog and the streetlight conspired to hide any details.

Whatever it was, it was small—Corwyn's size or maybe a little smaller. Spindly in the backlight; bald, she thought. Corwyn sat frozen, hand on Gwen's arm, hoping the shadows and the fog would keep their faces hidden, smelling blood and piss, feeling the grit of the pavement under her boots as she shifted, oh so carefully, to ease her wobbly ankles. Gwen didn't move.

One long arm moved into the shadows, down toward the runnel of blood that must be right at the creature's feet. It crouched, and Corwyn held her breath, silently reciting "Samson and the Tyger Cubs," *For thirty days and nights, Young Samson fought the cur. The poison worked through blood and bone, And left his strength unsure.*

The thing drew its hand back and ran its fingers delicately over its head.

Out on the street, from the fog, someone shouted—yelling at a lazy child or possibly a mule. The figure didn't startle, but it did turn and move away, staying low.

They waited until the fog-flattened sound of bare feet slapping on concrete faded completely. Corwyn finished the poem. And another. Eventually, Gwen relaxed and stood up. With one last glance at the dead man behind them, they made her way to the mouth of the hidey-hole. The dark and the mist made it impossible to see more than a foot in front of themselves.

Gwen nodded, and they made their way as fast as they could back to their squat.

"WHAT D'YOU THINK IT was?" Gwen asked her later, as they sat with their backs to the wall of the squat, their eyes on its crooked door. The candle burned down low, but neither of them made a move to blow it out.

"Dunno," Corwyn said. "You remember the nuns talking about the weird things people find out on the prairie and in the mountains, out where monsters can hide?"

"Yeah?"

"I guess San Xavier's got its share of nooks and crannies, too. One more goddamned thing to worry about."

Gwen's head thunked back against the wall as she took Corwyn's hand in hers.

CHAPTER SIX

It started to end without their knowing it, as things tend to do.

Corwyn, after a morning spent waiting for her voice to change to something lower and ending up, instead, with no voice at all for an hour, opened Miss Vadoma's front door to find Gwen on the porch, rattling a box and sitting on top of a very thick envelope.

"You waiting for me?" Corwyn asked. She was still a little hoarse, but Miss Vadoma assured her it would get better as she talked more.

"I am indeed. Osian says this is to go to Mr. Cadogan Rentsch, alchemical engineer. I didn't think you'd want me to go without you."

Corwyn's knack tugged as soon as Gwen said the name, but she'd have gone, anyway—Chaffins Grove wasn't anywhere she'd been before, nor had she ever seen an actual alchemical engineer, either. And after meeting the doorman at the Olafurson place, she was curious.

Gwen had directions, so Corwyn's knack was more a nuisance than a help, buzzing in her head as she tried to look at the scenery changing from the run-down houses and beat-up shops of the Hill to the better-kept buildings in Pallasgreen. They made their way from shabby to nice to very nice indeed as they approached Mars Hill Road, the boundary of Chaffins Grove.

At one point, Chaffins Grove had been an actual grove—everyone in San Xavier knew the stories of the alchemical engineers toiling in tents and wagons under the trees and stars (if you went by the stories, nobody ever did anything approaching magic in the daytime), harnessing the eldritch forces contained in the particular rocks and dirt of this part of the world. Every place had them, but only San Xavier had so much of them.

Now Chaffins Grove was a neighborhood, the most important neighborhood, the whole of the city of San Xavier spreading out south from it.

They crossed Mars Hill Road, and where Corwyn had expected something grandiose, like mansions made from clockwork, or floating houses, or walking trees, it turned out alchemical engineers weren't quite so fancy as even the folks further into Pallasgreen. The houses were small, though most of them were maintained. A few of them had porches and yards full of *things*--things under tarps, gears, sheets of metal—but for the most part it didn't look that different from where they'd left. Sunlight glinted in flashes off the top of something to the east.

The small house Gwen's directions and Corwyn's knack finally led them to needed a couple coats of paint, but the front yard was clear and the porch didn't sag under them as they walked across it.

The man who opened the door looked neither dashing nor dangerous. He was short and narrow, with a wide nose and huge eyebrows. His skin had a sallow tinge of not going outside very often. He squinted at them through small square spectacles. A larger pair, with a magnifying glass attached, perched on his head amongst a mass of unruly, graying curls.

"Are you Cadogan Rentsch?" Gwen asked.

"I am." He sounded amused to find two stray kids at his door, but he frowned when Gwen handed him the box and the envelope.

"That's from Mrs. d'Souza," she told him.

"Oh, I see."

He didn't move much—shifted his weight, stilled his face—but suddenly Cadogan Rentsch seemed very, very dangerous. Corwyn wondered if he could teach her that trick; it seemed like something as could be handy. He rattled the box, then opened the envelope and read the letter inside quickly.

"I need to send a message back to Mrs. d'Souza. If I pay you girls, will you take it to her?"

Gwen bounced on her toes and said, "Certainly!" blinking innocently at the sideways glance she got from Corwyn.

They followed Mr. Rentsch into his shadowy front room to wait while he found pen and paper. The room contained shelves filled with clockwork: birds and musical instruments, music boxes and tiny clockwork-doll bands, jars and books that surely *looked* magical, even if they weren't. A table scattered over with tools and parts of things sat by the window, but other than that table and its chair, the room had no furniture. Mr. Rentsch stood at it, bent over and scribbling, then folded the paper and pulled open a drawer under the table to find an envelope.

"There." Mr. Rentsch handed Gwen the sealed white envelope. "Thank you, ladies."

Corwyn's eyes were still on the shelves, her brain turning something over. "How come the clock at St. Philomena's ain't been fixed?" she asked. "Your house looks like that'd be your speciality."

He looked at her, eyebrows raised just a little. "St. Phil's clock is Russian clockwork," he said. "Best in the world. But only blood will do to maintain it—over here, we use sweat or spit more, but not the Russians." He shrugged, one-shouldered. "You've seen how big it is. There's not enough blood to spare to keep it going. I don't know how the Russians managed to get enough blood to start it in the first place. Nobody does. They keep their secrets, over there." His grin got a little bigger; Corwyn didn't like the looks of it. "You looking to be apprenticed, Miss?"

Corwyn shook her head. "I got no magical aptitude," she said, thinking of the kids who'd stayed on the top floors of the Singleton Home—Molly Coyer and Archulus Daniels, and the others who hadn't had the sense left to run when the smoke started rising. Miss Vadoma certainly seemed a sight safer employer, even if she did give Corwyn rashes and make all her hair fall out.

"Pity. You seem a bright child." Mr. Rentsch handed Gwen five dollars and showed them to the door. "Be careful on your journey."

Back on the street, Gwen gave Corwyn an expectant look. "Well, then? Beatriz d'Souza?"

Corwyn's knack stayed quiet, but she considered Mrs. d'Souza, what little she'd culled about her haunts and her habits from offhanded things Osian said, the gossip on the Hill, and said, "Come on, then."

IT WAS JUST AFTER TWILIGHT when they arrived, footsore and irritable, at the tiny building off 35th that everyone called The Parlor. The lug at the front yelled for Osian, who came out to the street to listen as they explained.

"He gave you a note *back*?"

Gwen held the envelope up as proof. Osian looked over his shoulder at the doorman, who shook his head. "I ain't getting in the middle of that. They brought it, send them in to her."

Corwyn glanced over at Gwen, who suddenly looked a lot less tired, and hoped Mrs. d'Souza had rules against beating up little kids. They followed Osian in and down a short entryway to a dark room lit with lanterns and filled with armchairs and a few small card tables. The d'Souza boys played cards or leaned against the walls; in the very back, in a corner, was the table where Mrs. d'Souza sat.

At least, she assumed the portly lady with the short white cap of hair was Mrs. d'Souza. She played cards with three much younger men and drank something out of a coffee cup. Judging by the red in her nose, Corwyn would not have sworn to it being coffee. She glanced up at Osian before flicking her gaze, not unkindly, over Gwen and Corwyn.

Osian said nothing, just stood there like a lamp post. Gwen rolled her eyes, then stepped forward to hand Mrs. d'Souza the envelope. "Cadogan Rentsch sent you back a message, ma'am." Corwyn wondered whether, given the situation, the Sisters would be pleased that their lessons on manners hadn't gone completely to waste.

"Thank you, my dear. You're the girl Osian hired, aren't you? You've been very dependable—I appreciate that. And I remember good workers." Mrs. d'Souza's voice had the thick, broad accent of the lifelong Hill-dweller; she took the envelope, ripped it open, and started to read.

The shade of red that overtook her face eclipsed the red in her nose. "That son of a bitch."

Corwyn and Gwen, well-trained by their mother, stepped back simultaneously. Mrs. d'Souza stood up. "That whoreson fucking shithole—look at this!"

The girls kept still, eyes on Mrs. d'Souza and her two companions, who leaned over the table, heads together, to read the letter. "You see that number? The fuck does he think he is—goddamn clockwork-fucking—I will feed his fucking blood to his goddamned gears myself, and wrap his shit-stained intestines round that bitchshitting clockwork redwood!"

"*That's* what that metal thing was!" Gwen hissed to Corwyn, but Corwyn wasn't really listening. Mrs. d'Souza's attention had left them completely; it was a good time, Corwyn judged, to make an exit. She reached for Gwen's arm.

Fingers tangled in her hair.

"It ain't blue anymore," said a delighted voice, and the hand pushed to turn her head. The boy's arm looked all right, but his face was covered in fading bruises, and he grinned wide enough that she could see he was missing a tooth. He also wasn't grinning at *Corwyn*.

At the other end of the boy's grin stood Gwen, her face lit with the loose, bright smile that heralded her knack about to pull her into trouble.

"Gwen ..." Corwyn tried. Sometimes Corwyn could catch it in time, talk Gwen down—this was surely the worst place to let Gwen loose—but Gwen's eyes emptied out, she started bouncing lightly on the balls of her feet, and Corwyn knew they were well and truly fucked.

"You can't say I didn't warn you," Gwen sing-songed.

Well, in for a pound, Corwyn figured, and stomped hard on the boy's foot before dropping to the floor, some hair ripping from her scalp, and rolling to the side. He let out a yell and hopped, off-balance. Corwyn's head stung.

Gwen leapt at him.

Mrs. d'Souza stopped her ranting about Cadogan Rentsch's family in whatever Old Country they hailed from. The room stood silent as Gwen ducked under the boy's punch, hooked a bottle off a table, and spun to swing it at his face. The boy fell back and tried to sweep Gwen's leg; she danced out of his way and backed into a table. The boy closed in; Gwen caught her balance, dropped the bottle, braced her hands behind her and leaned back to kick him square in the face with both boots. His nose and lip sprayed red. He staggered backward; Gwen bounced to her feet and dove at him again.

Corwyn glanced round from her spot on the floor. Not a soul in the club had moved, save to get out of the way. When she looked back, Gwen was sat on the boy's chest, punching him on one side of the head and then the other. And again. And again. His head rolled back and forth. He tried to yell something as he struggled under her, but his voice was liquid-garbled and Gwen was long past noticing anything, anyway.

The stillness made Corwyn uneasy; it coiled tighter and tighter with every blow Gwen landed. The air smelled of blood.

"Gwen," she said. Gwen didn't stop punching the mess of blood and snot that was the boy's face; a tooth flew out of his mouth and landed on Gwen's knee. "Gwen you hear me? You're done. You made your point."

Corwyn pushed herself up and crossed the floor—trying to make herself as small as possible like that would keep anyone from noticing them—to her sister.

"Gwen. Come on." Her hand closed on Gwen's arm and, next second, Corwyn found herself on the ground next to the boy, unsurprised to be facing her sister with one bloody fist raised to strike.

Corwyn caught Gwen's fist as it came down. Relief spread out from the palm of her hand: there was no way she'd have been fast enough to do that if Gwen wasn't coming back to her. She let out a slow breath as Gwen's eyes cleared and widened.

"Pick him up," Mrs. d'Souza said. Gwen scrambled off Corwyn. They stood up. Mrs. d'Souza's companions from the card table strode across the room and gathered the kid off the floor.

Corwyn shot a fast glance at Gwen, who seemed to be staring very intently at a spot a couple inches in front of her nose. Corwyn turned her attention to the advance toward them of Beatriz d'Souza.

She looked from Gwen to Corwyn and said, conversationally, "Usually after a scene like that, and with you having been such a good courier, I'd offer you a real job. But that piece of shit kid you nearly murdered is my grandson Gad, and worthless as he may be, I'd never hear the end of it from my goddamned daughter."

Corwyn's stomach dropped to her ankles. Gwen said nothing, but her face looked like Corwyn's stomach felt.

Mrs. d'Souza shrugged. "Stupid little prick's not learned what fights to avoid, and that's a lesson he needs to get through his thick fucking skull so nobody manages to kill him an hour after I'm dead. So, young ladies whose names I will know before the day is out, because I think you have imparted a valuable lesson to my imbecile grandson, I'm not going to have my boys kill you."

Corwyn thought hard at Gwen to not say anything to make this worse, and for once in their lives it worked; Gwen kept quiet. She didn't even move.

"What *are* you going to do with us?" Corwyn asked.

"Well, you're fired, make no mistake. And we won't hunt you down, but the Hill's gonna know you're on my shit list." She paused and her face, jovial and almost kind 'til now, turned sharp. "You touch that boy again and all bets are off."

CORWYN WAITED A BEAT to make sure she was done before grabbing Gwen's arm to haul her out through the foyer back into the street. "The *hell* were you thinking?" she hissed, even knowing full well that Gwen's knack didn't really let her *think*. "That was a whole goddamned *future* you just beat into the carpet back there!"

Gwen turned to her with a face full of blood-spattered rage. "Shut up," she spat. Corwyn took a step backwards away from her, her own anger forgotten in the force of her sister's. "Come on."

Corwyn about ran to keep up, all the way back to their squat. Down the steps to the little root cellar they were sleeping in, and before Corwyn could light a candle, Gwen took a swing at her. She ducked, caught part of it on her shoulder.

"The fuck was that for?" she snapped. "Goddammit, I can barely see—"

"You didn't fight back!" Corwyn fumbled round for the candle; it lit up Gwen's tight-held jaw as she went on through clenched teeth, "I could have killed you and you didn't fight back—what the hell I been teaching you, Corwyn?"

Corwyn glared at her, wary. "I don't hit you," she said, her voice even and low.

"We spar all the time!"

"That ain't the same and you know it. I don't hit you to hurt you." Gwen frowned, and Corwyn set the candle on the box they were using as a table. "People. Mama. They hit you. To prove something or to shut you up or because you get between them and me. So maybe I'm the only one. So I don't."

"They hit me sometimes so I won't *kill* them," Gwen said, her voice thick. She stood slumped in the dirty, shadowed space where they'd slept the past two days and looked so tired. Worn. There were bruises, some fading and some fresh, on Gwen's face and arms. That wasn't anything so unusual that they ever made Corwyn think of their mother; Corwyn rarely thought of their mother anymore. But right now. Right now Corwyn thought of Mama's hand splayed across the splintering wooden floor where they'd found her the last time, the brass ring that made half the scars on Gwen's face set on her thumb because she'd got so skinny before she'd died.

"If anybody's going to kill me, I'd rather it was you," Corwyn told Gwen with a shrug.

Gwen hiccuped a laugh. "Nine fucking hells, Wyn. That's a terrible thing to say."

It was true, Corwyn thought, but didn't say. Instead she got their half-full water bucket from the corner and found a rag in her rucksack, gave them to Gwen to clean the blood off her hands.

CHAPTER SEVEN

It was downright astonishing, Corwyn thought, how many people forgot their goodwill when you'd incurred the wrath of a gang lord, even if she wasn't actively out to get you. The silver lining was that, now Gwen had a reputation for not caring whose heads she beat in, they were left alone; the cloud was how they were sleeping in alleys for the first time in years.

Gwen had absolutely no regrets about beating the hell out of Gad d'Souza. When Corwyn got back to telling her off about it, she merely replied, "He knew what he was gonna get," and went back to casing the Katsaroses' grocery for their breakfast.

There were other gangs, Corwyn supposed. Though Gwen seemed in no hurry to join any of them, which was both a worry and a relief.

"What d'you think about sleeping on a roof?" Gwen asked around a mouthful of stolen apple. Gwen had spent most of her breakfast looking up at the spires of St Phil's, sharp gray against a bright blue sky.

"I think that's a good idea," Corwyn said slowly. How'd they not already thought of this?

They spent the afternoon casing buildings, finally deciding on Madame Tereza's, the brothel on Fowler Road. It stood to reason that it must have *some* sort of roof access. They'd passed part of more than one morning in a jeering, cat-calling crowd on the sidewalk, watching one client or another try to get away across the rooftops from an angry Madame Tereza, who chased them with whatever had come to hand, demanding her money in a mix of Haitian French and plain old Russian.

They eyed the front door from across the street and a ways down the block. During the afternoon a steady stream of single people went in and out. Once the sun went down, the groups started arriving: pairs of older men, three groups of drunk younger men, a trio of older ladies who appeared to know the doorkeeper and made him laugh before they went inside.

"There we go," Gwen said, shoving at Corwyn's shoulder to make her cross the street.

These girls were young, a little drunk, nudging the girl in the middle of their party with their shoulders as they teased her. "You ought to ask for Harry," said one as Corwyn carefully caught up to the edges of the group. It was a tricky thing, trying to seem like a part of the crowd while also not looking like that was what she was trying to do if they noticed her. "Harry's got a talented tongue."

Corwyn considered what talents a person's tongue might have beyond insults and eating, because while she knew what people went to brothels to pay for, she surely had not known it involved *tongues*.

"No, she ought to ask for Veria! Veria's *lovely*!" The girls laughed, scandalized, as the one in the middle shook her head and blushed. "I just want someone *nice*," she said.

"You're paying good money—you'll get nice or not so nice, whatever's your choosing." The girls laughed again, and the one who suggested Harry said, "Madame Tereza's is a good one—I wouldn't bring you here otherwise."

They trooped up the front steps of the brothel, pausing in front of the doorman. He appraised them, eyes passing over Corwyn where she stood between and behind two of the girls. She saw his gaze move on, then catch. In the split second as his eyes began to move back to her, Gwen, one step down at the back of the group, pretended to trip and shoved the middle girl directly into the doorman's lap.

He laughed, jolly. She blushed and pushed herself up, apologizing. "A little eager, then, eh?" he asked, not unkindly, as Corwyn pulled the door open. She and Gwen slipped inside.

Madame Tereza's was decorated red and gold and silver; Corwyn shook herself to keep moving in the face of so much unimagined luxury. Cushions and overstuffed furniture sat occupied by ladies and gentlemen and their clients, paying no notice to the two ragged girls skittering through the front parlor. They wore such fine clothing, shiny stuff she didn't know the name for, lace in every color, and *hats*! Corwyn could never have said that she liked *hats* until now—the floppy, boring thing Miss Vadoma had lent her was *nothing* like these: hats with feathers on the ladies' heads, hats with colorful bands shoved back rakishly on the heads of the gentlemen. She knew that they weren't so much ladies and gentlemen as let-girls and -boys, but their *clothes* ...

The air smelled like flowers with sweat underneath. Corwyn and Gwen made their way to the back of the house, toward the kitchen. It wasn't nearly so crowded here, but the two cooks were busy at the stove and didn't turn around while Corwyn and Gwen crept past to the stairs. Gwen was sure they could get to the roof from inside, but finding the door was the trick.

They found it in the ceiling on the third floor, on the opposite end of the hallway. The hallway itself was deserted, their steps silent in the thick carpet. Corwyn could hear sounds from behind the closed doors as they passed. "It sounds like a lot of fighting," she whispered to Gwen, who snorted a laugh.

"*Wet* fighting."

Corwyn boosted Gwen up just a bit to grab the ring in the trap door. Gwen yanked on it, whisper-praying to someone *"Please be oiled, please be oiled."* The trap creaked as it opened, the ladder gave a soft whine as they extended it, but no one peered out of any of the rooms as they climbed up.

The attic space wasn't even tall enough for the two of them to stand straight. A window in the far wall let in a little lamplight from outside to silhouette the sheet-covered lumps of whatever Madame Tereza stored up here.

"Grab my legs," Gwen said, and leaned out to pull the ladder back in. Corwyn, feet set and arms straining, spent the time alternately praying for no one to hear them and wondering how in nine hells Gwen had gotten so heavy, considering how little she'd had to eat lately. Gwen kicked at her a little, so she hauled her back until the trap shut with a soft clunk. They headed for the window.

It opened easily; they leaned out of it together and looked up. "I think we missed the easier way up there," Gwen said with a puzzled frown.

"That or Madame Tereza's got a knack for climbing."

Gwen handed Corwyn her rucksack, then heaved herself out the window and onto the sill with the same fluid grace she used to kick out someone's knee. She gave a little jump that caught in Corwyn's throat, got hold of the edge of the roof, and, with a couple kicks of her boots, found a foothold on the top frame of the window to shove herself up and over.

Corwyn leaned out to pass her their rucksacks, then climbed out and balanced on the sill. The wind blew round her, smelling of tar and dirt and the vaguest hint of that flowered perfume from the parlor. She reached up and felt Gwen grab hold of her forearm; kicked herself a foothold on the top frame and pushed off as Gwen yanked her over the top.

They grinned at each other, broad and giddy, while they brushed off their clothes. Corwyn turned to look around for a good place to sit and heard, "I know you!"

They both spun round to find a skinny let-boy in trousers and an unbuttoned shirt, his jacket draped over the back of a chair, smoking a pipe. He squinted at them, trying to place their faces. His back was to a door—they *had* missed the easier way, dammit.

Gwen settled her weight and looked him over, puzzled, but Corwyn recognized him after just a moment. "Mr. Fritz? Is that you?"

His smile split his face turning it from sullen and haughty to much younger and just a little silly. He set his pipe down. "Corwyn and Gwendolyn, yeah? I haven't seen you since you bunked off on old man Doerr. Heard you've been getting into some trouble with Beatriz d'Souza's shiftless grandson—don't say I said so, but well done there."

"Thanks." Gwen sounded offended—likely because he'd called her Gwendolyn; his tone was admiring, Corwyn thought. She skipped over to him, pulling the rucksack off her shoulder as she went.

"Look, Mr. Fritz," she said, rummaging around to find the right book, "It's mine—I found it, and I thought of you—it has all the Samson poems!" She remembered Mr. Fritz, with his lovely hands and Limey accent, reading her the Samson poems from his own book when she was little, and the way his face lit up as she showed him her book, she guessed he remembered, too.

"Oh, now, look at that, that's lovely. Bit water stained, but you can read it." His smile at Corwyn was a bit wistful, the last little light of the day casting shadows along his face. He aimed his smile at Gwen, too, but she didn't smile back. "So what are you girls doing here, then? Madame T. won't hire you—even if you weren't on d'Souza's shit list, she don't take kids as young as you. I'd wait 'til fifteen or thereabouts, really, if you want to start careers in prostitution; safer for you if you've got most of your growth."

"We're looking for somewhere to spend the night," Corwyn said. "Somewhere that ain't an alley."

Mr. Fritz grinned. "Too good for the alley, are we?" he asked, and then, at Gwen's blank expression, added, "Too smart, I suppose. Well, you can't sleep up here—Madame T. will chase you off with a broomstick before the night's half over. But if you go down the block a couple of buildings, you should be able to find a spot." Both girls turned to look, and he said, "Oh, wait—hold on." Corwyn turned back to find him fumbling with the pocket of his jacket. He pulled battered, pocket-sized book from it and handed it to Corwyn. "Here, try that one."

She took it, uncertain. "But ... you're reading it, Mr. Fritz."

"I've read it before," he replied. "And high time you moved up from Samson, Miss Corwyn."

Corwyn rummaged around in her rucksack until she came up with a book she'd bought back when they were flush. "Trade you," she said. "It's in England, the story." Best not to owe anybody anything, even someone she remembered fondly.

Mr. Fritz looked impressed, maybe a bit like he might laugh. "Why thank you, that is quite sweet."

Gwen took Corwyn by the elbow, but gently. "Come on, Wyn, let's find our spot before it's too dark."

"Come back and see me—we can trade books again."

Corwyn felt shy all of a sudden, but she grinned and mumbled, "Yes," at her feet as Gwen pulled her away toward the edge of the roof. It wasn't a big jump to the next building. Gwen tossed their rucksacks across the gap, and then they leapt one at a time to the other roof.

They stopped two buildings down, across the street from Mr. Katsaros's grocery, and once they'd settled down Corwyn took her new book out and tilted it into the moonlight to read the title: *The Hawk and the Lark*. Birds, then? The moon shone bright tonight, but still not nearly enough to read by, so she'd have to trust Mr. Fritz's taste until morning.

"It was nice of him to give you a book," Gwen said, her voice grudging.

"I thought you liked Mr. Fritz," Corwyn said.

"He was all right, I guess. I know you liked the poems." Gwen was distracted, looking over the edge of the roof. Corwyn stowed the book away and followed suit.

"So," she said. "How are we going to get *down*, Gwen?"

Gwen shrugged. "I reckon we'll figure it out in the daylight."

THEY SLEPT THAT NIGHT in shifts, one of them keeping an eye on the other shadowy shapes spending the night on this roof. Which was how Corwyn came to be awake when the three men started loitering round Mr. Katsaros's grocery.

They acted like they didn't want to be noticed, but with exaggerated gestures and a casual air that all but shouted, *Don't look at us, we ain't doing nothing!* Not to mention the sheer amount of moonlight and the fact that the two clockwork street lamps on Fowler Road burned most of the night to accommodate Madame Tereza's clientèle. There were plenty of shadows, but hiding took effort.

To Corwyn's way of thinking, their half-assedness indicated they were either very bad at what they were doing or they were trying to make a point, so she shifted around to get a better view and elbowed Gwen awake. "Something's going on across the street."

Gwen sat up, leaned in warm and sleepy and close like they were watching a puppet show at the Home. They watched the men as they picked the front lock and slipped inside.

"I can't see anything now," Gwen grumbled.

"I don't hear nothing, either, so they ain't busting the place—oh, there it is." Something shattered inside the grocery, but after that everything went quiet again.

The men slipped back out the door and pelted down the street in three different directions as an orange flicker, and another, shone through the front windows. Both girls stiffened as the smoke curled up toward them.

"Nine hells," Gwen breathed, and then, top of her lungs, "Fire!"

The other people on the roof stirred; a couple of them took up the call. Windows ground open below as the folk inside the building heard the yelling and added to it with shouts of their own. Soon people emerged out of the tenements with buckets and pitchers, running for the public pump. Some of the let-boys and -girls, and Madame Tereza herself, came down the block in their night-clothes—Madame Tereza yelling "Arnim Katsaros!" as loud as she could.

Corwyn's knack pulled her up, even as Gwen tried to catch her arm to pull her down.

"Goddammit. *Corwyn*—" Corwyn was at the edge of the roof, her knack yanking at her; she slipped over the side and lowered herself gingerly to the top of the framed-out window underneath, then to the sill. The next window down had flowerpots outside; she crushed someone's geraniums as she crouched and worked her way down further.

She reached the ground shortly before Gwen did and strode across the street, dodging people with buckets, trying not to get brained. Finally she stood in front of the grocery; Gwen took her elbow. "Don't come in," she said, eyes darting around, looking for an entrance. "Stay out here, so I can find my way out."

Gwen shook her head once, sharp, and said, "No, now, hang on." She looked around, jerked her chin to the right. "That window, come on." Gwen kept a hand on Corwyn, lifting on her toes to peer through what was left of the glass. "I can see a ... well, it ain't a *clear* path, but it's a path to the stairs—if you go up, though, I'm coming in after you."

Corwyn's knack pulled her hard enough that she didn't argue, just pulled her shirt up to cover her mouth as best she could and climbed carefully over the bits of glass left in the window frame. It was hot inside. Shelves burned on the other side of the room; her eyes watered as she tried to pay attention to where her knack led her. Her shirt over her mouth wasn't nearly as helpful as she'd hoped.

"That's not enough water! The whole place will burn, why aren't you helping us?"—sounded like the younger Mr. Katsaros, outside, and he ought to get his ass inside to help her find his father. The smoke seeped down her throat and up her nose. That looked like a stairwell door, hanging open at the back behind the counter.

"—exactly what this is, your goddamned sister runs off and now the whole fucking street's gonna pay for it—"

The shouting helped Corwyn to remember, as she climbed over a collapsed shelf and stopped to wipe at her streaming eyes, that this was *not* the Home; the kids at the Home had screamed and cried, not argued with each other over who started the fire and why, all they'd wanted was *out*. Corwyn would not, as she clambered over the counter, suddenly find Sister Benedict's dead body—she'd known her knack could find corpses, but Sister Benedict was only the second time, and so much worse than finding their mother.

A jar exploded somewhere behind her with a pop and the sound of showering glass, startling her off the counter and onto Mr. Katsaros, who groaned as she rolled off him.

"Corwyn?" Gwen's voice from outside was faint. The air was clearer down here, and so was her head now she'd seen the grocer. Corwyn took a couple of deeper breaths, coughed a little, wiped at her eyes to peer at Mr. Katsaros. He was beaten pretty bloody, his face swelling up and his flesh hand bleeding, probably stepped on. His clockwork arm was maybe dented; she couldn't really tell in the flickering light.

It took some doing to get the old man upright. Corwyn hissed as she wedged her shoulder under his hot metal arm. He wasn't a tall man, but he was almost dead weight, and the arm didn't make him any lighter. He woke up, moaning, as she moved him.

"Where's my wife?" he asked, voice raspy and full of phlegm, as they came round the counter. "Zo—"

"*Don't*," Corwyn snapped. He looked at her, bleary and confused, like he wasn't much used to kids talking back to him. She glared at him and went on, "You say her name and my knack kicks in, you get left here while I get dragged off to find her."

For a minute Corwyn thought he'd say it, anyway, but he just closed his mouth up tight and leaned harder on her shoulders.

This fire wasn't near as bad as the Home fire. There was a difference, Corwyn thought, between wanting people dead and wanting them alive after to suffer. Practically, it meant that, this time, Corwyn didn't have to follow her knack to Gwen in order to find her way out, though she let it, anyway.

Gwen leaned in the window to help Mr. Katsaros maneuver through the frame and into the street. Corwyn watched until he was through, then scrambled to follow.

She hit the pavement next to the old man, who was bent double, holding his hands to his chest. His dressing robe hung off him crooked. His clockwork arm was dull with soot, indeed dented, Corwyn saw, as he coughed and spat gray phlegm.

A crowd had gathered across the street in front of the store, but they weren't looking at the dirty people emerging from it; the younger Mr. Katsaros grappled in the middle of the street with another man, both of them bloodied and bruised.

"Idiots," Gwen muttered. "Weapons all around them and they're wrestling."

The elder Mr. Katsaros straightened up and didn't even glance in his son's direction. Instead he looked at Corwyn and said, "My wife. Zola."

"You son of a bitch," Gwen spat at him, taking a step, but Corwyn grabbed her arm to pull her along as Corwyn's knack did the same to her.

"You ain't beating up an old man, Gwen," she grumbled. "Come along, old man!" she called over her shoulder, then coughed and spat on the ground without breaking stride.

They made their way to a small knot of older women at the edge of the lookie-loos watching the fight—nine hells, *Corwyn* could have ended that fight faster than those two fools—with their fists in front of their mouths and their eyes wet. In the center of the group stood a short, round woman with gray hair who was flat-out sobbing. Corwyn's knack let go at the sight of the crying lady, so she waved Mr. Katsaros over.

He called her name, his voice choked with smoke or tears or something, and Mrs. Katsaros turned and saw him, moved toward him with a wail of relief. Mr. Katsaros opened his arms to her. When she got near enough to close the embrace, she hit him, hard, in the shoulder.

"Gods damn your eyes, Arnim, I *told* you this would happen—we're *ruined*—"

Mr. Katsaros took a step toward her. "Hush, Zola, hush, it'll be all right ..."

"It will *not* be all right—you *spoiled* that girl and now look at what she's done to us!"

Gwen shifted her arm in Corwyn's grip to take Corwyn's wrist. "Come on." They turned and moved down the street—it looked like the brawl was a draw; the younger Mr. Katsaros now crying into the shoulder of his opponent—passing the Katsaroses' neighbors, all of them keeping a wary eye on the fire and soaking their walls and roofs with buckets of water.

"Where we headed?" Corwyn asked.

"St. Phil's. It's late enough, and you look pathetic enough, we should be able to sleep in the doorway for a few hours. Ain't no way we're getting back up on the roof, now." Gwen pulled Corwyn closer, which made it awkward to walk, but Corwyn didn't pull away. Her stomach and legs felt loose; it was nice to have an arm around her waist. "Maybe you should see if the witch will spot you a bath tomorrow," Gwen went on.

Corwyn grinned a bit, then coughed. "Let's get some water first?"

From the pump, they could see sparks shooting up from the green grocer's that then drifted back down through the air like snowflakes. Corwyn drank straight out of the pump-stream and fell asleep in the doorway of the cathedral with her head in her sister's lap, smelling smoke and chased by screams.

A WEEK OR SO AFTER the Katsaros fire, Corwyn sat on Miss Vadoma's floor and waited for the potion she'd drunk to do something. She considered Miss Vadoma's puddles. Every basin, tub, and sink in Miss Vadoma's house had a puddle in the bottom, waiting to expand as she whispered to it. And it wasn't fancy *magic* water or anything; on the rare occasion that the puddles went dry, Miss Vadoma sent Corwyn to the public pump.

"Can you do that with blood?" she asked the witch.

Miss Vadoma paused in whispering to her watering can and said, "I don't work with blood."

"How come?" Corwyn pulled her knees up to her chin under the witch's assessing gaze. "Is it getting smaller?"

"Can't tell." Miss Vadoma shrugged, then went on to answer Corwyn's question. "Blood's tricky. It belongs to someone, and it carries echoes of other people in it. Lots of things can go wrong when you mess with it, for the person the blood belongs to and for the person doing the messing—you'll find more lunatic alchemical engineers in the world than you'll find lunatic witches." Miss Vadoma stretched to water a hanging plant, sending it gently swinging on its creaking chain. "It just ain't worth the trouble."

All of that was terribly interesting, but it didn't answer Corwyn's question. "But if you wanted to, could you do the water spell with blood?"

Corwyn could tell Miss Vadoma was thinking about it; her eyes got the same faraway cast as when a potion went wrong. "I suppose, in theory. It's a liquid—and I've done it with oil, though blood's a good sight more complicated—"

It suddenly became a good sight harder for Corwyn to breathe, and when she said, "Miss Vadoma," her voice sounded strangled.

"Well, look at that, we managed to shrink your nose after all." Miss Vadoma's mouth twitched a smile as Corwyn felt at her face. Nothing else felt smaller, but her nose was downright tiny.

"How big id the lady's nose as wands this?" she asked.

"Ain't a lady. And bigger than yours was. Let me get the calipers again."

Corwyn breathed through her mouth and kept her head still as Miss Vadoma measured her nose and went to her little table in the far corner of the front room to calculate how much it'd shrunk. Miss Vadoma distracted was much more likely to answer questions.

"So you're nod an alchemical engineer 'cause you don' like blood?"

"That's one reason."

"Was id also 'cause you're a woman?"

"Not so much that as I don't like having people watching my work over my damn shoulder. But being a woman had something to do with it, yes."

The Russians guard their secrets, Corwyn remembered, and though, so far as she knew, Miss Vadoma wasn't Russian, she supposed everyone had secrets to keep.

EVENTUALLY, SLOWLY, Corwyn's nose returned to its regular size, and she left Miss Vadoma's house thoughtful and very glad of being able to breathe. Maybe that distracted her, because she got the bucket of piss straight in her face.

She wiped her eyes, blinking at the blurred, smirking figure in front of her.

"So," Gad d'Souza asked, bucket swinging from his hand, face swollen and shaded yellow to green to purple to black, nose particularly lumpy, lip and right cheek split, "What you gonna do to me?"

Corwyn could taste the piss, even with her mouth shut. She smelled it in her dripping hair, felt it sticking her shirt to her, but she said nothing because what *could* she say, that threat from his grandmother hanging over her? The other people on the street—a pair of hot corn girls and a group of the Simcote lady's kids carrying big burlap bags—walked past without more than a couple glances; whatever this was, kids' stuff or something worse, nobody wanted a piece of it.

But then. "Your grandmama keeps saying you're dumber than a box of goddamned hair, Gad, and you just keep on proving it, don't you?" Osian Lauredent pushed himself off the wall across the street where he leaned and ambled toward Gad and Corwyn.

"The hell you doing here?" Gad demanded.

"Playing nanny to your sorry ass—Mrs. d'Souza's got a guy following you wherever you go to protect you from your natural proclivity for idiocy and self-harm."

"This ain't idiocy, this is shoring up my power."

"You think she ain't going to run back to whatever hidey-hole she and her sister's squatting in to tell on you? Hell, the way she smells, you think she's got a choice?"

Gad glanced at Corwyn, then back to Osian. "Don't matter. They don't dare touch me or they're dead."

"And Gwen Teachout cares?" Osian asked. "That girl's knack is spiteful, bloody mayhem. Who we got's gonna manage to kill her before she kills you? Then it won't matter what power you think you've shored up."

Gad's face was red under his bruises. "You're out on your ass as soon as that goddamn hag dies, you fucking golliwog." He threw the bucket into the street, prompting a yell from a guy that looked to be a sailor, and stalked off.

"Sweet bleeding St. Phil, the battle-axe really leaves him in charge, I'm going back to Haiti." Osian turned to Corwyn. "You all right?"

"Do I look it, Osian Lauredent? Get the hell out of my way." She shoved him to one side and started walking.

"Hey! I *helped* you!"

"You should have helped me earlier!" she hollered back, throwing a gesture over her shoulder that one of the Italian kids at the Home had taught them both.

HER RUCKSACK HAD KEPT everything pretty well dry. The bag itself was nasty, but her food and the books were all right—except for the one she'd stuck in her pocket on her way out of Miss Vadoma's house. The poetry book she'd found under the trash bin was wet and would likely stain yellow-brown round the edges of the pages, assuming they even came apart again.

Corwyn rinsed her hair and skin at a public pump, dumped water over her boots, and went back to their squat: a tiny room off the back of a storefront that was open only haphazardly. Neither Corwyn nor Gwen could tell what was sold out of it, neither. Gwen was gone, so Corwyn changed her shirt and thought of asking Miss Vadoma for clothes-washing as payment for her potion proving next time instead of a bath. She'd tell Gwen she fell in the wrong puddle on her way back.

She didn't cry over the book; considering where she'd found it, she reckoned it'd been through worse. But she tried not to look at it as it dried in the sun, ignored the sick, hot feeling she got whenever she caught a whiff of piss from her pants. She was mad, she told herself. Just mad.

CHAPTER EIGHT

The Collett house, in a fit of apparent desperation, had swallowed a dog. It barked every so often from inside. Corwyn and Gwen sat propped against the house's front fence to eat the pastries Mr. Fritz had given them earlier that morning, when he and Corwyn had traded books. He'd let her keep *The Hawk and the Lark* so she could learn "The Ride of the Hawk In the Netherworld" by heart, like she'd done the Samson poems, so she'd given him another book for the new one that currently sat balanced on her knee. She paged through it slowly with her pinky to avoid getting sugar glaze on it.

"Is this one more poems?" Gwen leaned over her shoulder to peer at it, breath warm and her neck smelling sweaty.

"It's poems and stories about a pirate—a *lady* pirate."

Gwen carefully flipped the pages back to the title page and read, "*The Sad Whore's Privateer?*"

"That's the name of her ship."

"So a privateer's a kind of ship?"

Corwyn frowned. "I *think* it's another word for pirate." She took another bite of pastry—stale, but still sweet—and talked round it. "Maybe it's just for lady pirates?"

"Hold on, then—her *ship* is named 'pirate'?" Gwen looked unimpressed and skeptical.

"You thought her ship was named 'ship' a minute ago," Corwyn pointed out.

Gwen licked sugar icing from her fingers with a thoughtful air. "So the boat is named after a pirate who belongs to a let-girl."

"A sad let-girl."

"I suppose it makes more sense than a let-girl owning a ship."

Corwyn swallowed the last of her pastry. "I bet Madame Tereza could own a ship." She set to licking her own fingers.

Gwen shook her head. "A ketch, maybe. Or a fishing boat. Not a whole ship—those are *huge*."

"I can't see Madame Tereza on a boat, anyhow. She ain't never in anything more than a nightgown, and they're all fancy. She'd just get messed up on a ship."

Gwen reached for the book again and flipped through it. "So are the stories any good?" she asked.

"I dunno—I only read three lines of one of them before you were flipping the pages and asking me what words mean."

"Shut up." Gwen sounded distracted, her brows drawing together as she looked at the book. "Pirates just sound interesting."

Corwyn smiled, but Gwen didn't see it, drawn into the story as she was. Gwen'd make a pretty good pirate, Corwyn thought. Maybe they ought to start spending time at the docks. "You can borrow the book," Corwyn offered. "Mr. Fritz won't mind."

Gwen's head pulled up and she shook it, handing the book back to Corwyn. "No, he's *your* special friend—"

Corwyn was about to ask what that meant when a shadow fell over them. They looked up to find the younger Mr. Katsaros, shifting from foot to foot. He first addressed the sidewalk, then, seemingly, the Collett House.

"My father wants to speak with you. He has a job to offer."

CORWYN COULDN'T THINK what sort of job Mr. Katsaros was in a position to offer anyone, but she knew she and Gwen weren't in a position to turn down hearing about it. The Katsaroses had a connection to the Brogans, as frayed as it might be, and the Brogan gang had no love for the d'Souzas. Couldn't hurt to try and get on their good side.

Two weeks since the fire, the Katsaroses were living in one room of a tenement off Drury Avenue—very similar to the one Corwyn and Gwen had shared with their mother, but thankfully on the other side of the Hill. The lower floors smelled of garlic and onions and old sweat. The noise of too many people in too little space followed them up the shabby stairs.

The upper floor smelled less of food; instead, sweat, smoke, and char stench hung in front of the crooked door, which the younger Mr. Katsaros pushed open.

The elder Mr. Katsaros was somewhat cleaner than the last time they saw him, his ankle bandaged, sitting in a wooden chair with his flesh hand cradling the elbow of his clockwork arm, thumb tracing over and over round a bolt. Mrs. Katsaros stood behind her husband's chair, still wearing her nightdress but now with the addition of cloth shoes. They kept their eyes on Corwyn as she and Gwen came into the room.

Corwyn didn't like their expressions. They reminded her of some of the Sessionist nuns—the ones who always called Gwen "Gwendolyn" and told her having a fighting knack was a test of her moral strength, so using it would displease God.

The younger Mr. Katsaros stayed near the door; once both Corwyn and Gwen were inside, there wasn't room for him to come in much farther. Corwyn tried to avoid stepping on the jumbled pile of blankets on the floor that she reckoned was the Katsaroses' bed. Really, knowing company was coming, they could have rolled them up.

"You," Mr. Katsaros said. Corwyn looked up from the bedding. "You got a knack for finding people. I need you to find my daughter."

Corwyn tilted her head. "And what are you gonna give me to do that?"

"I'll give you the food what's left in my inventory."

Gwen snorted. "That ain't much."

"It's enough."

"No, it ain't," Corwyn said. "I pulled you out a fire, now you want me traipsing all over San Xavier looking for your girl, nobody's seen her in months, she could be shacked up with the Right Reverend Root for all anybody knows, and you're gonna offer me charred cucumbers and some busted jars of jam to do it?"

Mr. Katsaros drew himself up in his chair. "I don't got to give you nothing, little girl. All I got to do is say her name and Cristos'll follow you when you run."

"Cristos is welcome to *try,*" Gwen said with a glance over her shoulder that showed how little impressed she was with that threat.

Corwyn rolled her eyes at the old man. "People been saying 'Tansa Katsaros' all over the Hill since the day she ran off—it ain't sent me running yet."

"Then you cannot help us," Mrs. Katsaros said. Her voice was soft, her accent thicker, but she didn't sound much nicer than her husband.

Corwyn grinned at her; it was a mimic of Gwen's *let's see how much damage I can do with* this *thing* grin. "I didn't say that. I said you'd have to pay."

The kids at the Singleton Home figured out Corwyn had a knack for finding within two weeks of the Teachouts' arrival. Within another two, the favored game amongst the wayward and feral occupants of the Home was "What Can Corwyn Find." Nearly everything Corwyn knew about her knack came from those games: what she could find, what she couldn't find, an idea of how far away someone could be and still set her off ... and the ways she could coax it if merely hearing a name wasn't enough.

"I need something that smells like Tansa," she said to Mrs. Katsaros, after negotiating with Mr. Katsaros for free run of his green grocery, once it was in business again, plus occasional delivery of goods.

"Everything we have smells like smoke," Mrs. Katsaros said.

"Up to you if you want me to try," Corwyn said with a shrug. "I'd think, were I you. What more you got left to lose, Mrs. Katsaros?"

IT TOOK A COUPLE OF days, but eventually Cristos Katsaros found them on the steps of St. Phil's. Gwen lay on her back, looking up at the clock tower while Corwyn finished her pear and watched people go by: a couple of dirty kids had wandered by counting coins they'd clearly pinched; Heck from Tanner's had waved at her; Sister Jonnson had given them an exasperated look as she came out to sweep the steps but hadn't said anything to them; a couple of kids she thought belonged to the Simcote lady had sat on the steps below with some sort of clockwork contrivance held between them, poking it and waving it around.

That had been the highlight of the morning, especially when it made a whistling noise and produced something from a tiny door that looked like a pinwheel. They'd both jumped and left shortly after.

Corwyn licked pear juice off her fingers and watched the younger Mr. Katsaros as he approached, his arms full of cloth. She jumped when he dumped his armsful of soot-spotted ivory dress into her lap. It slid, made of some smooth fabric, and overflowed to spill down the steps in a wash, the late afternoon sunlight turning it almost orange against the dark gray stone. Gwen sat up and reached out a finger to trace the line of buttons over Corwyn's knee, then sat back to look up at Mr. Katsaros.

"It's not as dirty as everything else," Mr. Katsaros said. "She'd shoved it under the bed. But she sewed most of it herself."

Corwyn had never seen anything so pretty so close up. The tips of her boots, dirty and scuffed and sturdy, peeked out from under a froth of lace. She grinned down at them, liking how they clashed. Corwyn plunged her hands into the cool, slick material—it was heavier than she'd expected—and lifted it to her face.

She smelled smoke first. Then sweat—her knack lurched and subsided immediately, so that must have been Mr. Katsaros's, from hauling the dress around the Hill. Under that lay someone else's sweat, laced with something chemical that reminded her of Cadogan Rentsch's basement, and a scent like the tree in Stolarski Park that grew the black berries.

Corwyn felt it, then, her knack waking up to pull at her. She stood up, dropping the dress. Her feet tangled in it, sending her almost down the steps head-first, dragging the dress with her.

"Whoa—" Gwen caught her by the arm and pulled her up before she landed. Corwyn shook her boots free, then shifted to take Gwen's hand. Down to the street and west toward the Park. "Come on," Gwen shouted over her shoulder, and Mr. Katsaros jolted after them, leaving his sister's wedding dress spilled down the steps of the Cathedral.

IT WAS A LONG WALK, a couple hours winding west through the Hill, past what was left of the grocery then up through Stolarski Park. "Where we headed?" Mr. Katsaros asked eventually.

Corwyn shrugged. "Toward the docks," she told him, though he could likely tell that himself.

The farther west they walked, the stiffer Gwen's shoulders got. She pulled her arms up around herself, ducked her head. They were approaching the far western side of the Hill, between the docks and the part of Pallasgreen where all the actors and other well-paid degenerates lived—along with the orphans and the nuns.

The hunched bulk of what remained of the Charles John Singleton Home for Wayward and Feral Children emerged from the rest of the Hill, crumbled brick and charred wood jutting into the sky, the whole thing surrounded by scaffolding. Shouts and hammering echoed down the block, not sounding at all like the screams of children that Corwyn knew were only in her head.

Corwyn felt Gwen's hand on her wrist. "She ain't in there, is she, Wyn?" Gwen's voice was strange; timid. Corwyn wondered what she was hearing in *her* head.

It wasn't likely—Tansa Katsaros and her lover would have to be pretty damn stupid to hide out somewhere with that many people around—and Gwen knew that. But Corwyn's stomach was knotted and rolling, too, so she didn't say anything beyond, "No, Gwen, she ain't."

They finally drew abreast of the Home. Corwyn could at least blame the lingering smell of char on Mr. Katsaros, so that was something. She glanced across the street as they passed.

The huge redwood doors still stood, though the walls around them had crumbled to half their height. She remembered tugging Gwen up the front steps, trying and failing to keep from hurting her, knowing that as much as Gwen told her it was fine, the Home was the last place in the world she wanted to go. Corwyn had kicked at the door because she didn't want to let Gwen fold to the ground.

She wondered what Gwen remembered, but decided not to ask.

It was Mr. Katsaros as broke the silence. "It's a wonder the Reverend Root doesn't tear it all down and rebuild it in Pallasgreen."

"It ain't his choice," Gwen said, shoulders lowering as they put the sight of the Home behind them. "The Home's got its own money."

"But still, why keep it in Cobbler's Hill?"

Gwen smiled a slanted smile and gave him an off-center little curtsy. "Because here's where all the feral kids are, Mr. Katsaros."

CORWYN HAD NEVER BEEN to the docks in the daylight.

She found herself keeping half an eye out for Lars Hallstrom as gulls screamed overhead and sailors swore at each other. Boats creaked, the smell of salt and fish, tinged with tar, swirled in the air all round, and no one paid the slightest bit of attention to them. She wondered if she'd feel more uneasy if her knack wasn't taking up three-quarters of her skull.

"There," Corwyn said, pointing across the Bay, toward Dieujuste Island. She settled and resettled her feet. Her knack was growing insistent; if she didn't get moving again soon it'd pull her off the seawall and into the water that slopped up against it not a foot down from them.

"Ain't nothing out there but Bishop's Light," Mr. Katsaros muttered, shading his eyes from the glare of the sun off the water. Then, "Goddammit. I told them Tansa's smarter than she looks."

Gwen was looking around them, turning almost in a circle before pointing. "That one."

"That one what?" Mr. Katsaros asked.

Gwen grinned. "That rowboat's the one we steal."

STEALING THE ROWBOAT was so easy that Corwyn wondered if Mr. Katsaros had a knack for theft. Then again, if you were going to steal something in San Xavier, the docks were the one place everyone was guaranteed to mind their own damn business.

Corwyn climbed in gingerly and sat in much the same way, knuckles white on either side of the boat. The only seafaring vessels she'd ever been on were Lars Hallstrom's ketch and a retired Navy ship the Sisters had taken the Home kids to tour. Neither of them had rocked this alarmingly under her, nor had the water been so close to her. She tried to remember what Sister Benedict had told them about how boats floated, but she was too equally amazed and appalled that they weren't *sinking*.

She shifted to keep both their rucksacks between her feet and kept her eyes on Gwen, who sat in the front of the boat with her head back and her eyes closed. Leave it to Gwen to enjoy this. Corwyn looked at the dirty rings round her sister's neck and tried to relax her fingers.

Mr. Katsaros rowed them, slowly but steadily, across the Bay toward the island and the deserted Bishop's Light lighthouse.

"How come the lighthouse ain't used anymore?" Corwyn asked as a means of distraction.

Mr. Katsaros was out of breath, but he answered, "The alchemical engineers put up a new one, farther out in the water—it's full clockwork, don't require a keeper. One of them's supposed to go out and maintain it once a year, but we'll see if they do it."

The Bishop's Light came clearer with each lurching stroke closer; it was a tower, broad at the base and narrowing at the top where the light sat. The boat's bottom scraped the shallows around the island, close enough for Corwyn to see the wooden door and wide windows set into the base of the lighthouse.

Mr. Katsaros stepped out of the boat and pulled it up on shore. His boots squelched as he and the girls began their trudge to the lighthouse.

"I don't want her to see me," he told them. "You two knock on the door and look pathetic so she'll open up, while I stay on the side."

"Well, that'll work if she don't wonder how two kids got out here," Gwen said cheerfully. "And you already said she's smarter than you thought, so ..."

Corwyn gestured to the lighthouse itself. "Likely she's seen you out the windows already. She's probably barricading the doors right now."

Mr. Katsaros looked from them to the lighthouse for a long minute, then stalked toward the front door, his shoes squeaking and slapping as he went. After a bit they followed him; Corwyn's knack wouldn't ease until she had eyes on Tansa Katsaros, anyway, though the urge to take the rowboat back to San Xavier proper was nearly as strong.

Mr. Katsaros arrived at the front door and tried the knob, then pushed at it—it gave only so much and then wouldn't move any more. "I guess she did look out the window," Gwen said with a grin. "She's got the most sense out of any of you people."

Mr. Katsaros, aggravated with the door, moved to a window. He picked up a rock from the many scattered on the ground and heaved it through the glass, then broke the rest out with his elbow before climbing through. "Tansa, you bitch, I know you're in here!" Corwyn heard him fumbling around inside.

"What's that?" Gwen asked. She was looking toward the same side of the lighthouse as Mr. Katsaros had been on, but more to the right. A twisty-stumped tree clung to the rocky soil there. Under it slumped a figure.

"Is he dead?" Corwyn asked. Somebody who didn't twitch during the ruckus of Mr. Katsaros storming the lighthouse—the sound of thumping boots came faintly through the broken window—was either dead or dead drunk, and liquor seemed a lot less likely out here.

"Dunno," said Gwen. "Let's go find out."

Corwyn's knack still tugged her toward the lighthouse, but she ignored it as best she could and followed Gwen to the figure under the tree.

"Oh!" said Gwen. "He ain't dead—he's clockwork!"

They stood over the clockwork man. This one looked a lot less fancy than Veigar Olafurson's clockwork doorman. He had no wig and no clothes; both feet, half his right leg, and his left hand were missing; and his mask was warped and pitting, turning green round the edges of the eye holes and mouth.

"Lighthouse keeper?" Corwyn asked.

"I suppose so," Gwen said. She squatted down next to him and poked at his mask. "I wonder if this comes off?" She gave it a yank, then pulled back with a yelp, her finger bleeding a little.

The clockwork man half sat up with the hissing and grinding noise all clockwork made, but with an additional loud clunking all his own. Corwyn stumbled back a step; Gwen just leaned back on her haunches.

"This automata is in need of repair," he said in a voice that didn't sound entirely like a man or a woman. "Please contact Mr. Fraley Bishop of Chaffins Grove, in San Xavier. Malfunctions are extensive and require the attention of an alchemical engineer."

By the end, the voice had slowed and slurred to the point that, when the message repeated, it was garbled and almost beyond understanding. A crash of something—not glass, Corwyn wasn't sure what—and a long string of swearing that ended with "—nobody cares about your fucking *toys*, Tansa!" from Mr. Katsaros in the lighthouse turned their attention away from the broken clockwork man. Running footsteps, a slammed door, some muffled yelling back and forth, then pounding like fists on wood.

Corwyn shifted her weight back and forth between her feet, staring at the lighthouse. Her knack wasn't happy: *she's right there.*

Gwen spared another glance at the clockwork man, then asked, "You got a book in your rucksack you can read me, Wyn? A body can't appreciate the beauty of creation with all that racket going on."

"Sure," Corwyn said through the haze of *there there there, go there.* She followed Gwen over to the steps of the lighthouse, where they sat. Corwyn pulled out *The Sad Whore's Privateer.* "All right, so ... she's been thrown overboard and cleverly made her way back onto her ship. She climbed the mast."

There was a loud, long scream from inside, and Corwyn twitched as her knack tried to pull her after it. She took a breath and read:

"*Arenthia Sans Souci, queen of the pirates, stood atop the Privateer's mast, her hat in her hand and her smile ablaze in the light of the setting sun.*" Another yell, this one presumably from Mr. Katsaros. Corwyn took a steadying breath against the *get up and find her get up and find her* insistence in her head.

"*'Did ye think tossin' me overboard would stop me, milady?' she called to the creature on the deck. 'There be not a thing in the ocean I've not beaten, after all.'*" Gwen reached over to still Corwyn's jumping knee with a hand.

"*'I had my hopes,' said the witch. With a wave of her scaly, clawed hand she pulled up the winds and drew the clouds to obscure the sunset, but the pirate queen merely grinned harder and placed her hat back on her head with a flourish before sinking her clockwork hook into the canvas of the mainsail.*"

Corwyn dropped the book and stood up, pacing. Gwen watched her from her seat on the steps, then said, "Tell me some of that Hawk poem you've been getting by heart."

Corwyn felt through her head, past the banging of her knack, trying to find the bits of "The Ride of the Hawk in the Netherworld" she knew were in there.

"*The lake was still as glass and full,*" she began, voice unsteady but improving as she went on. She kept pacing; that seemed to help, too. "*Of Death's unending dark. Upon this shore did light the Hawk; he turned and sought his Lark.*"

A couple heavy thumps, another scream, and then not much other noise of any kind until they heard a stumble of footsteps and the loud scrape of furniture being pulled away from the door.

Corwyn let out a harsh, silent breath as Tansa Katsaros appeared in the doorway and her knack dropped away, so fast it set her off-balance. Tansa was pretty—long, tangled brown hair falling out its braid; big brown eyes with a bruise round the side of the right one; a delicate nose with a smear of blood beneath it. Crooked teeth, but they might have always been that way. She held one arm close to her as she limped down the steps.

Mr. Katsaros limped, too. He also had a black eye and a split lip, but he was sight bigger than his sister and thereby better off, Corwyn thought.

They all climbed into the boat, Mr. Katsaros taking up the oars again. Corwyn sat in the front; Gwen shoved them off the shore and climbed aboard to sit next to Miss Katsaros in the back.

The sun dropped lower in the sky. Corwyn turned to look over at San Xavier, where lights came on aboard the ships and in the buildings across the water. It looked ramshackle and thrown-together, but peaceful in a way she knew was a lie. The boat rocked a little, but the water didn't seem as frightening now they'd been across it once.

"I hope you're proud of yourself." Corwyn turned to see Miss Katsaros glaring from her to Gwen, the last orange light of the sunset sharpening the planes of her face and catching in her eyes like tears. "You're sending me to hell, you know that? You have any idea what they'll do to me?"

"Nine hells, Tansa, ain't you put us through enough shit yet?" Mr. Katsaros asked. "You fuck this up, *Mama* will kill you—"

"Mama's got no idea what—"

"—and ain't *nobody* interested in your idea of hell."

"The fuck you know about it, any of you?" Miss Katsaros turned from her brother to glare at Corwyn, since Gwen was paying her no mind. "Stupid little bitch, how'd you even—"

Gwen didn't shift her gaze from watching the twilight roll in over the water as she reached over, wrapped her hand around the upper part of Miss Katsaros's bad arm, and gave it a solid pull.

Miss Katsaros *screamed.* Gwen let go with a shove. "Don't talk to my sister again or I'll knock all your teeth out and let you see what Allen Brogan does with you *then.*"

Corwyn kept her mouth shut and didn't say any of the things she'd been thinking, like three meals a day and never sleeping on a roof in the rain. Miss Katsaros hung her head and cried, quietly, as they lurched closer and closer to the docks.

CHAPTER NINE

"You got a sale on I don't know about, Miss Vadoma?" Corwyn asked. This was her third potion proving in a week, and she hoped there wouldn't be any swelling this time. A body needed to be able to completely bend her knees, she'd discovered.

Miss Vadoma was unamused. And just the slightest bit harried. "You sure you can't sweet talk your sister into a square meal and a bath now and again?" she asked.

"Gwen does what she wants," Corwyn said. "Ain't nobody can talk her into anything."

"Yes, that surely is the *story*," Miss Vadoma said darkly, her lips twisted into a wry scowl. "And look at that, now."

Corwyn glanced down at herself, but it took a minute to see—all her freckles (and they were numerous) were gone, faded away into her skin. It made her feel a little odd, something of herself that she saw so often she didn't anymore, disappeared like that. Like they'd been more than brown spots.

Well, Miss Vadoma stayed in business because everything wore off eventually, so the freckles'd come back. Corwyn pushed the odd, pinpricked feeling away and rummaged in her rucksack for her book to pass the time.

"You're getting bigger," Miss Vadoma said suddenly, just as the pirate queen was beheading the sea witch—and the pirate queen seemed sadder about it than Corwyn would have been; she'd have to ask Mr. Fritz about it. Stories were always hinting round at stuff and Corwyn never saw what they meant, so she didn't know what in nine hells was going on and why the pirate queen was crying into the witch's seaweed hair.

"I ain't *that* big," she said to Miss Vadoma, shifting a little in her seat.

"How long you two been out in the Hill, now?"

"I dunno—you're the one's got a calendar." The weather in San Xavier stayed middling year-round; it varied into chilly and wet, foggy and wet, and sometimes clear and warm. And then there was rain. Corwyn lost track of the days a while ago, but she had other concerns about this conversation. "You fixing to fire me, Miss Vadoma?"

The witch shook her head. "No. Well, not 'til you're full grown. There's things kids shake off easier than adults can. No, I just noticed that you're currently made of knees and elbows." The witch's voice had gone funny, like she made it when kids snuck onto her porch to filch her plants, or grown-ups tried to stiff her on a payment ... but emptier, an echoing space in the middle of it.

"You're not the only thing that's changing," she said in that deeply hollow voice. "There's forces gathering all round you and in you, impossible to miss, waiting for their moment. You won't be able hide behind your sister forever, not from them or from you."

Corwyn, having never seen an aboding before, blinked at her, mouth agape. *That* was the downright spookiest thing she'd ever seen, and she couldn't wait to tell Gwen about it.

"So what the hell does that *mean*?" she asked the witch.

Miss Vadoma shook her head, whipped her hair back over one shoulder with a shudder, and said, "It means you should have a care, Corwyn Teachout. Matters are about to complicate, but I can't quite see how."

Corwyn raised her eyebrows, unimpressed. Matters were always complicating, in her experience; that seemed a pretty easy prophecy to make, like *you're going to die.* 100% accuracy if you gave it long enough.

"Your freckles are back," Miss Vadoma said briskly, brushing her hands off on her skirt. "Damn, that was fast. I'll need to recalibrate."

Corwyn sat as she did so, looking at her freckles with relief and considering what forces might be gathering round her, biding their time. Really only one stood out, the phantom scent of piss in her nose as she thought of him.

THE BASKET HIT THE steps of St. Philomena's right in front of their feet. Three apples fell out of it and rolled away to their own adventures. The rest stayed where they were. Cristos Katsaros was already striding back to the street, leaving Gwen to yell after him, amused, "You're aware we got nothing like a storeroom, Mr. K?"

"We pay our debts," he called back, not turning. "You girls have a good lunch!"

"How's your sister?" Corwyn yelled.

"Married!" And he was off down the street, slipping into the crowd. Corwyn turned her attention to their payment.

"What in nine hells are we going to do with a whole basket of apples?" she asked.

Gwen, now on her second one, said, "Eat 'em?" around a mouthful. She chewed and swallowed, rather grotesquely, and went on, "When we're full, we can stuff as many in the bags as can fit, then give the rest away."

Corwyn's stomach rumbled. It wasn't a bad plan.

Once every spare inch of space in their bellies and their bags contained apples, once they'd given away the rest to whoever wanted one—Shrimpy Jackson and his sister, a couple of kids who belonged to that Simcote lady, a hollow-cheeked man and a very pregnant woman, all of whom had been side-eyeing them the moment the basket hit the ground—they took the basket to the back kitchen entrance of the cathedral and knocked. Sister Jonnson opened the door.

"We've a donation, Sister," Gwen said, her diction as perfect as they'd forced them to make it in the Home. The nun gave them an up and down look, her face severe, as Gwen held out the basket. "You look worse for wear, but you're not dead yet, which is more than I would have expected," she said.

Corwyn kept her mouth shut, which had always seemed to her the best course with Sister Jonnson. Gwen had no such qualms. Or sense. "This is why you were my favorite, Sister," Gwen said. "You speak your mind. Now, you want this basket or not?"

Sister Jonnson put her hand out, and Gwen passed her the basket. "It's been a while, you're both bigger, but you ought to be back at the Home," she said to them both as she turned to head back into the cathedral. "The Hill is no place for children. Mark me." She shut the door with a thud, and Gwen rolled her eyes.

"'Mark me.' Like she's the witch in some play."

Sister J. had the voice down better than Miss Vadoma did, Corwyn thought, but just said, "You want to spar at the park today?"

Gwen had that look in her eye. The *what kind of trouble can I get into with* this? look. She smiled winningly at Corwyn. "It's a nice day for a long walk," she said. "And we've provisions ... and I've heard tell of a clockwork redwood in a neighborhood where we might, perhaps, have some business to conduct due to the solid moral upbringing given us by the Sessionist Sisters ..."

Now it was Corwyn's turn to roll her eyes. "Just say it, and we'll see."

"Want to go find Fraley Bishop, Corwyn?"

And, as it turned out, Corwyn's knack did.

"I WAS THINKING ABOUT the lighthouse," Corwyn said as they made their way up Foreston Street toward the north end of the Hill. Her knack was distracting but easier to ignore as they walked in the direction it wanted her to go.

"Hard not to, everyone talking about it," Gwen replied. Tansa Katsaros's return to Allen Brogan was news round all of Cobbler's Hill, though so far nobody was bothering Corwyn over it. There'd been people looking, though, which she wasn't exactly happy about. "What are you thinking, Wyn?" Gwen went on.

"It's in pretty good shape," she said. "And it's deserted. We could go out there."

Gwen's eyes were full of care as she looked sideways at Corwyn. "We ... could. Yeah. You really want to, though? Live out on Dieujuste Island in the Bishop's Light?"

She'd go, if Corwyn really wanted her to. Corwyn knew that like breathing, no matter what she said to anybody else. But Corwyn also knew better than to think Gwen would want to, no matter what *she* said to anybody else. So that hadn't been what she'd meant. "No, not *live* out there. Stealing a boat to get back and forth's just asking for trouble, and it ain't like we could farm it." She nudged Gwen with her shoulder. "But it'd be a place to keep stuff. Food and water and maybe extra clothes."

Gwen nodded, looking impressed. "A bolt-hole ain't a bad idea," she said. They turned onto Dunbar Avenue and found a gaggle of little kids gathered round the gate of the Collett house.

Gwen sped up—"Oi, you lot!"—and waded into the middle of them, shoving them up the road and away from the house. Corwyn pushed a couple along with a, "Take off home!" as they went like cats: in no hurry and looking back the whole time.

After that they walked in silence for a while, then Corwyn said, "You know, everybody thought Tansa ran off with some man, but she was alone when we found her."

"Huh," Gwen said, thoughtful. "I guess, my family was like hers, I'd have been hunting a lighthouse, too." Gwen aimed a real smile at Corwyn, who smiled back, the sun on her head warm and her steps lighter.

THEY CROSSED JERSEY Court Road into Pallasgreen and stopped to eat apples by the mouth of an alley. Corwyn's knack protested, but she resolutely chewed and swallowed. *I pass out from hunger, we ain't going anywhere*, she thought at it.

Behind them, suddenly, came a wet, heaving noise—the distinctive sound of someone puking. They turned, dropping back a step, and peered into the shadows of the alley.

The puker was a kid. A boy, maybe about their age, but small and in shadow so it was hard to tell; dark skin, a head of ringlet curls that likely had puke in them now, and good luck washing *that* smell out—

"What the hell you looking at?" he snarled from his knees, hair swinging and face twisted. Corwyn couldn't place his accent: not quite regular San Xavier, with a little bit of Creole to it.

"You," Gwen answered placidly.

"Well, quit it." He wiped at his mouth and watering eyes with his sleeve.

"You *sick* sick, or'd you just see a dead cat or something?" Gwen asked. Corwyn shot her a look—her knack was still pulling at her, and it was Gwen's fault it was going in the first place; she wanted to be moving, not talking to some strange, weak-stomached kid—but Gwen ignored her.

"None of your goddamned business." His voice was shaky.

Gwen's was kind. "You need us to walk you home?" she asked, and this time Corwyn put her hand on Gwen's arm.

"What are you—"

"No!" The kid clambered to his feet; he swayed a little, eyes wild. "I can't come home escorted, that'll—" He stopped, looking green again. His throat worked once, then twice.

"Breathe slow," Corwyn advised him despite herself. She'd been a puker when she was smaller, back before the Home. "Come away from the smell."

Once he was at the mouth of the alley he looked better. Sometimes all you had to do was take a few steps away from a bad minute and get yourself into the next one, Corwyn thought.

They looked him up and down: puke spattered shoes and what Corwyn was pretty sure was blood in splats and drops all over his clothes. A couple of red smears decorated his cheeks, though his hair seemed to have only caught vomit. Small mercies.

They were all three quiet for a long moment, then Gwen, with the air of a decision gravely made, said, "You should stop at a pump on your way home. Rinse out your mouth, splash water on your face."

Corwyn's eyes caught on his fingers. "Maybe scrub your hands," she added

The boy looked down to his fingernails, outlined in rusty, drying red, and replied, "Can't do that," with a twisty smile. Corwyn thought for a second he might cry, but he just shook his hands out like Sister Benedict before she played piano for the kids and took a long, slow breath through his mouth.

"Thanks," he said, grudgingly.

"It's all right," Gwen replied, her voice thoughtful. "You take care." They watched him go until he turned a corner and Corwyn's knack wouldn't let her stand still anymore.

THE NUNS AT THE HOME hated the clockwork redwood, and Corwyn never knew why. Waste of money? Idolatry? No one said.

But the fact of it making them so mad meant she never doubted its existence, even though she didn't know anyone who'd ever seen it.

It wasn't in a park; the square of grass in which it stood was small, considering the size of the tree—and the tree was *enormous*, wide enough around that it might take ten kids to circle it in a chain—stretching up into the sky, taller than the roofs of the houses around it. The trunk was wide strips of greened brass, bronze, and rusted iron, twined together into branches that moved, some up and down, some back and forth, their leaves—tarnished silver and gold and some other shiny metal—spinning and flapping even in still air. Corwyn and Gwen stood behind the knee-high fence that surrounded it.

Corwyn's knack pulled her closer; without thinking much about it, she climbed over the fence. Gwen followed close behind her. Corwyn stopped a foot or so away, but Gwen kept moving until she was nearly nose-to-trunk with the tree, dwarfed by it so she looked like a little girl again. She cocked her head as if listening to it whisper—which made Corwyn grin, because the tree was loud: it clanged and wheezed, creaked and chimed.

Her knack subsided. She took a deep breath and smelled copper and dirt and grass, looking around for someone who looked like he might be Fraley Bishop. Why didn't they have a bigger park? The clockwork redwood was a symbol for Chaffins Grove and the alchemical engineers of San Xavier, you'd think they'd have some greenery and a couple of benches under the thing. Though the ground was so uneven, the benches wouldn't sit right ...

Corwyn looked down at her boots, dirty and covered with odd bits of grass. *Oh*.

All the bodies she'd found so far, and not a one of them'd been *buried*.

She opened her mouth to call to Gwen—at least she didn't have the urge to dig him up—when from behind them came, "Hey, get out of there!"

Neither of them ran, like they usually would have at the sight of a grown up clambering over a fence to get to them, because neither of them had ever seen a uniformed Jack before. He had a badge and a truncheon and everything. And then he stood in front of them, face a little red. Gwen made her eyes wide and her eyebrows surprised as she asked, "We're not allowed in here?"

"There being a fence around it didn't give you pause?" the Jack asked. "Which engineer you bunking off from?" Corwyn glanced at Gwen, before looking blankly back at the Jack, who sighed and asked, "Who you two 'prenticed to?"

"Rentsch," Corwyn blurted.

"*Cadogan* Rentsch," Gwen clarified.

For a minute, Corwyn thought it would work and they'd get shooed off so they could scarper back to the Hill, day spent, tree seen, Fraley Bishop found, more or less. She was ready for the Hill and its lack of policemen. But the Jack gave them a long look and said, "Come on, then."

They climbed back over the fence; once over the Jack took them both by the elbows. Corwyn sent Gwen a panicked glance, only to find Gwen's face going still, looking the Jack over with an appraising expression Corwyn did not like. "I don't remember how to get back," Corwyn said, loud enough to make Gwen look at her and see her shaking her head.

"Uh-huh. Lucky for you I do." The Jack yanked them down the street, almost pulling Corwyn off her feet, and Gwen's face went even stiller. Corwyn thought, not for the first time, that she'd give every apple in her rucksack and all of her books to be those two kids from the Home who could talk to each other with their brains and not their mouths—because she did not want to get arrested for attacking a policeman in goddamned Chaffins Grove. Instead she had to settle for warning looks and vigorous head shaking, neither of which was consistently effective.

Gwen seemed to get the message this time, thankfully—she clenched her jaw and stumbled along on the Jack's other side as he moved them briskly along the street.

After a fairly short walk they reached Cadogan Rentsch's little house, the Jack rapping on the door with his truncheon while Corwyn watched Gwen. She stood still, mostly. Corwyn could just about see Gwen's muscles straining under her skin. Gwen's fingers twitched in and out of fists as her breathing came quicker than usual.

The door opened. Cadogan Rentsch looked quizzically from the police officer at his door to Corwyn, then Gwen. Corwyn only hoped he remembered them. Well, not *only*, but it seemed a place to start hoping. His hair was wilder than the last time they'd been here, but this time he only had one pair of glasses on, riding low on his nose. He shoved them up with a finger wrapped in a brown-stained bandage; part of his forearm was bandaged, as well. "May I help you, officer?" he asked.

"Your *apprentices*"—the way he said the world left no doubt that he didn't believe them—"were up past the fence, Mr. Rentsch, getting a good look at the redwood."

Mr. Rentsch didn't pause. He did raise his crazy eyebrows and look at Corwyn over his glasses, though. "I give the two of you a day off and *that's* what you do with it?" He glanced back at the Jack and asked, "Do you need to arrest them, officer?"

The cop blinked at him uncertainly. "Do you *want* me to arrest them?"

"Not particularly, but the law is the law, and I did want them out of my hair today. 'Take on girls,' they told me, 'they're easier than boys.' Never again." Mr. Rentsch opened the door wider, and Corwyn reached around the Jack to grab Gwen's wrist and jerk her into the house as Mr. Rentsch went on, "All right, miscreants, you're cleaning gears in the lab today, then. Silently."

Corwyn paused in the front room to peer at Gwen's face. "You okay?" she asked.

Gwen nodded; that almost-unseen twitching had gone quiet again, mostly, but Corwyn didn't much like the glassy look in Gwen's eyes. "I'll be all right, Wyn," she said softly. "It just got riled up when the Jack was jerking you around like that. It'll fade."

Corwyn sighed through her teeth, wishing she could have talked to Gwen before—it helped. But nothing to be done. "Now what do we do?" she muttered, looking round at the music boxes and clockwork dolls that filled Cadogan Rentsch's front room.

"Run at the earliest opportunity?" Gwen asked with a weak grin.

"*Now* you're going to clean all the gears in my lab as repayment for my saving you from arrest." Mr. Rentsch leaned in the doorway of the front room, a grin on his face. "The officer is barely around the block, well within distance for me to call him back here."

CORWYN POLISHED CADOGAN Rentsch's astonishingly large collection of gears—big ones, small ones, iron and silver and brass ones, loose and attached and, in one case, melted together in either an accident or the name of art. It didn't take much thinking because she wasn't concerned with doing a good job. Mr. Rentsch was distracted by poking around at some project on the other side of his basement lab—he hadn't even suggested they stop for lunch, hadn't let them bring their rucksacks downstairs, and she was hungry. Gwen was twitchy.

"I'm *fine*," Gwen whispered to her when she caught Corwyn looking. "Are *you* okay? We didn't find Fraley Bishop—"

Mr. Rentsch, clad in a heavy coat and gloves, his regular glasses traded for his stranger ones, had his back to them. They could likely creep away—wasn't like he knew their names or anything. "We found him," Corwyn whispered back, considering the exit and whether Gwen was too nervy to be sneaky.

"What? What d'you—"

"*Goddammit!*"

Mr. Rentsch jerked back and around; his blood, in little droplets, arced through the air from a bit of uncovered skin between his sleeve and his glove to spatter on a dinner plate-sized metal disk he'd been poking at. He swore some more and scrabbled around on the table it sat on. Corwyn took a step toward him. Something blurred off the table, and she was shoved between the shoulder blades.

Corwyn dropped to her knees; something *chittery*, like a rattle made of metal, flew over her, landed with a thump, and skittered away somewhere behind her. She scrambled to the table, locking eyes for a minute with Mr. Rentsch before the two of them shoved it on its side and crawled behind it. Mr. Rentsch unrolled some bandaging he'd found to wrap his arm. There was more chittery noise and a lot of thumping and crashing. Mr. Rentsch wasn't having much luck with bandaging his arm, possibly due to the fancy glasses he still wore. Corwyn batted his hands away and tied it off for him.

The sounds subsided. With another look at each other, Corwyn and Mr. Rentsch eased themselves up onto their knees to peer over the table.

"What in hell ... ?" Mr. Rentsch muttered, shoving his fancy glasses up onto his head.

The metal disk now looked more like a beetle—it had semicircular wings and one antenna extending from what Corwyn assumed was meant to be its head. Somewhere it had found six legs, as well, which were now spread out so it could turn to follow Gwen, who hung from one hand, one foot braced, from the shelving that lined the wall next to the tiny basement window. Gwen swung gently back and forth, eyes on the metal thing on the floor, head cocked and wearing that calculating look she got before she punched someone. She surely wasn't twitchy now.

"It ain't much of a flyer," she said, and then, "Say something."

"Something?" Corwyn said. The metal bug-thing didn't turn away from Gwen and her gentle swinging.

Gwen nodded and swung harder, catching a higher shelf on the other side of the window, twisting back around with one foot on the window sill. The bug scrambled forward a couple of chittery, frantic steps and stopped, its wings sliding open and shut with a slicing noise, followed by a click that made Mr. Rentsch stand up. Corwyn pulled him back down.

Gwen pushed off from the wall, landed just in front of the beetle as it rose up on its legs, and with a high, wide step, *slammed* her boot heel-first just between the beetle's wings with a clang, then another, and, at last, a loud click.

It froze after the first hit, then gave a shuddering heave before collapsing with a wheeze. It caught Gwen along her calf with one skinny metal leg as it went. She hissed and stagger-jumped away from it, cursing.

"You okay?" Corwyn called.

"Yeah, it ain't deep. Bleeding all over, though. These pants are almost new."

"You maybe want to come over here away from the clockwork knife-monster, then? Just because?"

Gwen stepped over the bug. "It's *off*, you big baby. There was a button. Is it clockwork?" she asked Mr. Rentsch, who was watching the two of them in a way Corwyn didn't entirely like. "It ain't like any clockwork I've seen before."

Mr. Rentsch shrugged. "So far as I can tell, it is—but it's not the work of anyone in the Grove. I found it down by Jersey Court Road."

Gwen whistled, slightly distracted as she checked her now-scabbing cut. "I wouldn't expect an alchemical engineer to be down that near the Hill, Mr. Rentsch."

"Well, that's apparently where all the interesting things come from," he said, and now Mr. Rentsch looked like Miss Vadoma, sizing Corwyn up to calculate ratios for her potions.

Corwyn didn't have very many mottos, rules of thumb, or guiding principles, but among her few she numbered *don't trust anyone who forgets you have to eat.* Thus, despite his smile and his willingness to lie for random urchins who showed up at his door, she did not trust Cadogan Rentsch. Truth be told, she didn't trust Miss Vadoma or the Sisters that much, either, but the point stayed the same.

"All right, we're going, then," she said, standing up and hauling Gwen—"Ow, ow, ow!" as they went—with her.

"Wait, what? This place is a mess—and I could call the Jacks—"

Corwyn didn't stop, just yelled over her shoulder, "My sister made that mess cleaning up yours, so you go ahead and call the Jacks. Tell them you had two little girls in your basement with something you stole."

"Something you stole that has knives attached," Gwen added as they reached the stairs.

"Thanks for the help, though!" Corwyn called. She wasn't sure, but she thought he might have been chuckling behind them as they pelted up the steps.

THEY FOUND A ROOM TO squat in on the first floor of a tenement that Corwyn was pretty sure didn't have a landlord, judging by the state of its windows and roof. They'd have to sleep in shifts to keep an eye out for rats, but at least they wouldn't get rained on if they stayed along the inside walls. Gwen and Corwyn sat leaned against one of them, eating apples.

"Do you think," Gwen asked out of nowhere, her mouth full, "that the kid—the puking one? With all the blood?—you think that's who we saw in the alley, the one as ripped up that gangster?"

Corwyn hadn't quite forgotten that night, but it wasn't at the front of her mind, so she had to stop and consider. "No. That thing was bald. And it moved funny."

"Wonder what trouble he got in, then," Gwen mused.

"That much blood on a person, I figure we're better off not knowing," said Corwyn darkly.

"Eh." Gwen's tone was noncommittal. "All right, now explain how we 'found' Fraley Bishop."

Corwyn swallowed her own mouthful of apple and said, "We were standing on him. Or I was."

It took Gwen a minute. "Wait, he's *dead*?"

Corwyn shrugged. "He's *buried*."

"'Cause that ain't creepy at all, god's *sake*, Corwyn!" Gwen shoved at her with one foot. Then, after a few minutes of thoughtful chewing, she said, "You think they bury all their dead at that tree, or was he just special?"

Corwyn didn't know. What she remembered was what Cadogan Rentsch had told her, about the things that made clockwork run, the sparkling, spinning leaves of the redwood, and the uneven ground under her feet.

"I'm glad I got no knack for magic," she said, knocking her boots into Gwen's.

"You and me both," Gwen agreed. She leaned her head into the top of Corwyn's. Gwen's jaw ground into her scalp as she chewed, the sound of it echoing in Corwyn's skull. Gwen smelled of sweat, gear oil, blood, and apples, and Corwyn thought this might have been a perfect day.

CHAPTER TEN

"You the girl with the finding knack?"

Corwyn wiped the rain out of her eyes to peer, somewhat blearily, up at the boy who asked the question. No, not a boy, a young man—the rain ran off his braids and dripped over the too-large coat he clutched around himself; she could see his wrists, thin as bird's bones with darker bruises ringing their dark skin. Gwen shifted slightly closer to her as she said, "I can only find people. Not things."

Let-boy, maybe? The coat was too nice for a shopkeeper's kid or the Home, and those skinny wrists didn't say much for regular meals, so he wasn't one of the Simcote kids. He pulled the coat closer to himself and said, "I lost my little sister. Fritz said maybe—you think you can find her?"

"You think you can pay us?" Gwen asked. The rain made her cross: all their usual hidey-holes were full up with people, and nobody who owed them favors was anywhere to be found. That left them on a roof without cover, getting soaked through.

"I got some money," the boy said. "Not much, but. Some."

"You pay up front," Gwen told him.

"You pay if my knack kicks," Corwyn said with a sigh and a sharp look at Gwen, standing up and shoving her hair off her face.

The boy took a step back and said, in a rush, "Her name is Zoreah, she's five, and I went to see her and my dad ain't seen her in nearly a week—but why's he care when that bitch he's shacked with likes

103

it better when she's not around—and now *I* can't find her, and I should've taken her to the nuns, I knew it when I left—"

Corwyn started walking, knack tugging hard in her head, across the roof to the stairs. She heard Gwen get up behind her. "Payment's due now, please."

CORWYN STOPPED DEAD on the sidewalk outside the Collett house, because not even her knack was going to get her to walk in there without pause to think about it first. She heard Zoreah's big brother—Jericho, his name was—take a hitching sort of breath and blow it out hard when he realized where they were. Gwen shook her head, trying to flip some of her wet hair out of her face, and said, low, "You ain't leaving me outside, Wyn, don't even try."

"I ain't going in there alone," Corwyn said, affronted. The rain poured steady from the roof of the house, down the gutters and the front walk, out onto the pavement like a river past their toes. Corwyn, knack howling at the back of her skull, put a hand on the gate and pushed.

"You stay here," Gwen told Jericho.

They made their way up the uneven walkway, boots splashing through the puddles. A cold, wet drench poured from the roof down Corwyn's neck as she stepped onto the sagging porch. It was hard to breathe, between her knack yanking at her and every other instinct for self-preservation she had wanting her to turn around and run.

"You think we're the first people to come up here of their own free will?" she asked Gwen.

"I reckon whoever Mr. Collett was, he probably did," Gwen replied.

Corwyn didn't think that had to be the case, actually, but she was caught again and moving through the rain-shadows on the porch to the door.

Except the door had vanished, between one echoing step and the next. "Where's the door, Gwen?" she asked.

"It's right—wait, hold on ..." The rain smelled of salt and sulfur and other metals Corwyn couldn't put a name to, and the door was back, over by the corner of the house. But when Gwen stepped toward it, it was gone again—in a blink, disappeared, just wood siding and peeling paint left where it was.

Her knack got worse, pulling at her, narrowing her vision down to just *inside, inside, inside.* Corwyn took a step to the side to try to ease it just a little while she looked for the door. It was nowhere she could see. She took three long, blissful steps toward the house, reaching out to touch the space between the front windows where the door ought to have been ... nothing. Just splintery wood and the tacky feel of paint.

Her knack gave another hard pull; she gasped like she'd been hit. "To hell with this," Gwen muttered, and stalked to one of the windows. Corwyn rubbed a hand through her wet hair—not long enough to braid yet, but not short enough to not be an aggravation—trying to breathe, her head full of *inside, inside, inside* so she couldn't think how to help Gwen; she had a wild idea that she might end this day walking into the wall, over and over again.

"*Goddammit!*" Gwen hissed, rubbing her elbow and glaring at the unbroken window.

"The door's *right there*, you stupid twat!"

Now Gwen glared back at the sidewalk. "Lovely, we've got an audience," she remarked, voice grim in the way it got when she was scared, but Corwyn couldn't do anything about it. She felt like she had a leash in her skull; she hunched, trying to keep from being pulled along like a reluctant dog. She heard Gwen yelling, "You come up here and try to find it, you think you can do better!" and shut her eyes, just for a minute, just to maybe get a moment, one second to take a breath as Gwen's boot made an echoing thud against the window—

—and she didn't remember taking even one step, but her own boot hit something that made a hollow sound and trembled, just a little. Her fingers drifted down and caught a splinter before finding a cool, metal knob.

"Gwen, stay out here so I can get back out!" she called, squeezing the knob to keep herself from turning it; the dark under her eyelids was easier now, her head was easier now, Gwen's boots thumped across the porch, "Goddammit, Corwyn—"

Corwyn took a breath, turned the knob, and opened the door.

THE POUNDING STARTED as soon as the door shut behind her; Corwyn felt it shaking under her sister's fists as she opened her eyes.

The gray light of the weather outside filled the front room of the Collett house. It hung round the dusty, tattered furniture and caught in the swags of cobwebs that dangled from the ceiling, the mantle, the windowsills. Darkness pooled in the corners, so thick it seemed more silk than shadow. Faint sounds in the walls snuck in between Gwen's door-beating and the droning of the rain to chatter softly at her, maybe warning, or fearful, or taunting, but too wispy-thin to be understood.

It was just noises, she thought. She and Gwen had spent nights with rats in the walls and the roof and the floorboards under them—this wasn't so different.

Corwyn let out her breath. "All right," she said, her voice pitched low, "where d'we go from here?" Her knack gave a gentle pull—maybe it felt intimidated by the house, too. Upstairs.

She glanced across the room to the foot of the staircase. "Oh look," she said aloud, failing utterly to sound careless and jovial and thereby calm her nerves, "a pile of *bones*. I suppose that's to be expected."

The bones knocked softly against each other as she waded through them. The whispers sped up. It sounded like Gwen had started kicking the door. Corwyn sneezed and took the first step. The stairs creaked under her, and the carpet exhaled a dusty, moldy smell with each footstep.

"The door disappeared, but the stairs stayed in place," she whispered to herself, or maybe to her knack. "I don't like that."

The stairs emerged onto a hallway carpeted the same as the staircase. The dry mold smell got stronger up here, layered under a wet, sweet stench that reminded Corwyn of Shoemaker's Alley and deep fog so to set her heart to pound. The whispers faded further away. Her knack pulled her *this way, this way, down there.*

The pounding on the door downstairs stopped abruptly.

"Gwen?" Corwyn turned. She wouldn't see the door from up here, but she turned anyway.

The stairwell was pitch black dark.

Thunder rumbled low, softly rattling the windows in their frames. Corwyn watched the black stairwell. It moved, like water underneath the boat when they'd rowed out to the Bishop's Light, not even a tiny shimmer in it to tell her where the first floor was. Her knack gibbered at her—*this way, this way*—and so, slowly, with a drawn breath, she turned her back on the stairwell and its slowly-roiling dark to start down the hall.

Her back and scalp prickled, warning of something behind her; she wasn't sure if she actually felt cold or if her imagination wanted to give her the willies. Better cold than another goddamned fire, she told herself, fighting the urge to pant like a dog, swallowing to shove her heart back down to her chest.

She saw herself reflected ghostly in the window at the end of the hall, the mass of pure black behind her. The rain drummed harder.

The thrice-damned hallway was getting longer.

The rage that flashed sudden as lightning through her shoved all the fear aside: she'd kneecapped Lars Hallstrom; she'd stood on the grave of an alchemical engineer and stared at the clockwork redwood; she'd found *corpses*, one of them her mother. She'd be damned if she was going to run down this hallway in a goddamned panic.

"You got no idea who you're dealing with," she said aloud, then shut her eyes and let her knack pull her down the hall.

SHE MANAGED TO NOT slam the door behind her, though she did stumble over the threshold. The room was as dim and full of dust as the rest of the house, with a rocking chair and a bed on one wall, a dead fireplace on the other. Corwyn decided she didn't want to look very closely at the things in the fireplace.

She decided, instead, to investigate the still lump in the bed, which hadn't moved despite the noise she'd been making. The blanket covering it wasn't a color anymore, barely a step better than threadbare.

Corwyn's knack shut up completely as soon as she got close enough to see the puff of hair on the pillow.

The little girl lay curled in the bed, eyes screwed shut like her stomach hurt. She looked strange—unevenly gray, even her eyelashes. When Corwyn reached out to touch her shoulder the gray flaked off like dried mud; the girl stirred and shed more in a dust shower.

"You Zoreah?" Corwyn asked. The girl's eyes opened slowly, big and brown and dull as paving stones. She frowned at Corwyn and nodded.

"Your brother asked me to find you," Corwyn said, glancing around the room and crossing to the window. "I'm going to take you to him, okay?"

The window looked out onto Dunbar Road and the crowd at the fence. She could see where Jericho stood, but no sign of Gwen. Corwyn imagined she was sitting on the porch, waiting to yell at her when they emerged.

"I shouldn't go." Zoreah's voice was tiny, high and hoarse. "It loves me. An' it ain't safe out there, neither. My step-mother ain't so nice. It loves me, in here."

Corwyn tried the window, but it didn't budge. She glanced back across the room and saw shadows seeping in under the door. Right, then. She had left Gwen outside for a reason. She crossed back to the bed and got Zoreah under the shoulders to haul her up. "It ain't that safe in here, and your brother's going to take care of you—there's lots of places in the Hill you can go." The girl didn't weigh much, but she wasn't being a lot of help and she wasn't that much shorter than Corwyn, so lifting her was awkward. She wasn't fighting, anyway—she didn't seem to have the strength for it.

"You know the best part?" Corwyn asked, grunting as she arranged Zoreah. "A lot of those places have food." Zoreah's dress and hair shed dust back into the drifts on the bed; Corwyn kept chattering to avoid thinking about where all that dust might have come from. "I'll take you and Jericho straight to Sister Jonnson. Maybe that'll get her off my back. When's the last time you ate anything decent?"

"It tries," Zoreah murmured, snaking her arms round Corwyn's neck. "It really tries."

Corwyn staggered across to the door; her feet, through her boots, grew cold as she waded into the pooling shadow. "I'll bet it does," Corwyn replied grimly, shifting her grip to reach the knob.

The hallway was black, no light to be seen from the window, not even a hint of a window, or other doors, or a floor. A hot gust of air blew into Corwyn's face, carrying a smell she'd only experienced once but immediately, sickly, recognized.

"Zoreah, I need you to keep your eyes shut," she said, using her voice for the little kids she'd led out of the Home fire. Then she shut her own eyes, let her knack loop out to find Gwen, and stepped into the hallway when it tugged.

THE SCALDING DRAFT blew Zoreah's hair into Corwyn's face before burrowing down the neck of her shirt. Zoreah whimpered and wrapped her legs around Corwyn's waist, which helped with the lifting but sent Corwyn staggering to hit the far wall with one shoulder. Her eyes popped open.

The dark swirled like the world swirled when you'd been hit in the head with something hard, but slow and lazy. The whispers came back, louder but not any clearer. She could hear the softest sort of screaming, and a sobbing noise, but over that, breathing. Light and fast, like a scared cat. Rhythmic, a counterpoint to the slow rotation of the dark. Both the breathing and swirling drew at something in her, made the dark close in to surround her, but her knack—steadier when it took Corwyn to her sister, never as urgent, pulling but never yanking for Gwen—chanted *Gwen, Gwen, Gwen,* and gave her a gentle, insistent tug.

She could feel the fire. She pushed off the blistering wall and lurched a few steps forward. The hallway was made strange by the smoke and the detours she had to make around the flames she encountered, rising up ahead of her so that she nearly dropped the girl in her arms—*Mercy?* she thought, *too heavy for Katrina.* She reeled backward down the hall, her knack pulling harder now; she could get lost in it, back out to Gwen and then back into the Home to find more kids, she had to, they were screaming, she could hear the Sisters screaming for each other and for the kids, and Gwen would be scared—she'd not have beaten that little firebug Gino Sanna half so bloody if she'd not been scared.

The girl in her arms squirmed, whining, and dazedly Corwyn's brain offered up that Gwen beating up Gino wouldn't happen for three days yet.

Corwyn's wits snapped to with a violent pull from her knack. She wasn't in the Home, she was in the Collett house.

"Goddammit," she muttered into Zoreah's hair.

She shut her eyes so she wouldn't get lost and began walking. The screams seemed to muffle, though the breathing sound remained. The heat receded and a new smell, more living but still unpleasant, began to waft around them.

She shuffled her feet to try and avoid it, but still nearly tumbled them both down the stairs. Corwyn overbalanced. Zoreah let out a yelp and clutched at her. Corwyn lurched herself backward as hard as she could to fall back a step and catch her balance. At least this time she kept her eyes closed.

"Dammit, dammit, dammit." Corwyn carefully, carefully sank to the floor, settled Zoreah, and hitched her way with her heels to the first step. Then she hitched herself to the edge, put her boots down, and bumped her way down to the next step. And again. And again.

You're a big girl now, and I can't keep carrying you to the washroom, Wyn.

Corwyn had snorted, because there was no way to imagine the two of them were in any wise big, but she'd known what Gwen meant. So she'd done what Gwen told her, because their room was up in the attic, the only toilet and sink in their building were on the first floor, and Mama got really mad at Gwen when Corwyn made a mess of herself.

Sometimes Gwen would hustle her out of their room, tell her to go downstairs—when Mama was drunk enough and looked to be winding up real good—but those times Corwyn would stay where she was and listen, just in case Gwen needed her.

Bumps and thuds, and maybe a sob, muffled by a door, then Zoreah's tiny voice asking, "Miss? We at the bottom yet?" and Corwyn realized they weren't bumping downstairs no more.

"I don't think so," she said, and hitched forward again. Now she felt hard for the familiar sensations of her knack, of the particular shape it made in her head for Gwen, and held tight to it so she wouldn't get fooled again by memories held up like pictures from a book.

The bottom step came as a surprise—she hitched forward and off, hit the floor, hit things—*bones! You landed in that pile of* bones!—and fell over. She managed to keep Zoreah on top of her, but her eyes opened again.

The grayish, rainy-day light still filled the whole bottom floor of the house. The bones scattered across the threadbare rug; a rib, she thought, and maybe a leg bone, and some tiny ones she couldn't place, strewn like pebbles. Corwyn shoved all of it away into the same part of her brain where Mama lived with the corpse of Sister Benedict and that strange, shadowy thing they'd seen in the fog once.

She rolled Zoreah off her, sat up, and took the little girl's hand, then pulled both of them upright. Zoreah swayed rather alarmingly. "Come on." She ignored the hollow noise of her boots kicking the bones out of their path.

When she walked toward the door, her knack pulled her to the right. *Gwen, Gwen, Gwen.* Corwyn frowned—maybe she had found the door, come in after them? Where was she, then? Behind the staircase?

Corwyn pulled Zoreah with her after her knack: past the front window next to the door, past the staircase and the shut door under the stairs. Her knack led her right up to the wall next to the window, turned her to it, and dropped away.

"WHAT IN NINE HELLS ..." Corwyn ghosted her free hand over the peeling, faded orange wallpaper, then banged on the wall. "*Gwen!*"

Zoreah twisted her hand in Corwyn's, trying to squirm out of her grip. "Let me go—I wanna go back to my bed, let me go."

Corwyn pounded on the wall one more time, as hard as she could without letting go of Zoreah, who was putting her weight into it now without much luck. "Gwendolyn Teachout, *you answer me right now, goddammit!*"

"Lemme *go—*"

" ... Wyn? ..." The voice was faint, and it was Gwen's, but it surely did not sound right.

Zoreah gave a mighty pull that nearly toppled Corwyn over, but she got maybe half a step before Corwyn snatched her by the wrist and hauled her back, banging her up against the wall. "I will break your *goddamned* arm, you ain't going anywhere but out that door, you got me?" The little girl nodded with wide, angry eyes; Corwyn yelled at the wall, "I am coming back here to get you, Gwen, don't wander off!"

" ... where would I go? I can't see nothing, Wyn ..." That last sounded almost wounded. Corwyn bit her lip. No way in hell was this bloody house getting her tears.

"You just stay there. I'm coming back." Then she yelled to the ceiling, "You got no idea who you're fooling with, do you?"

She hauled Zoreah to the door by the wrist, but the girl set her heels and pulled back. This was not the first time Corwyn had dealt with a recalcitrant child; the older kids at the Home were always in charge of the younger ones, and weren't a three year old nowhere wanted to go to chapel after a puppet show. Corwyn put all her rage into her arm to drag Zoreah along. Zoreah lost her balance and twisted down to her knees in an ungainly flip, but Corwyn kept on even when she started screaming and crying. This wasn't Corwyn's first tantrum, neither.

The door didn't want to open, but Corwyn gave it a solid kick right under the doorknob and it slammed wide. She picked Zoreah, kicking and screaming still, up again, and heaved her over her shoulder. "I will drop you on your head if you don't quit," she said, which didn't do a damn thing. She loosened her grip. *Then* there was a scrabble as Zoreah grabbed her belt.

Jericho was still waiting, as was the crowd. There was noise—maybe people clapping, certainly people talking; someone told her her sister had just disappeared into the wall; someone else repeated it—but Corwyn ignored everything as she dumped Zoreah into her big brother's arms. Zoreah started bucking again, but he held her tight and blinked at Corwyn like he was scared. "Go to St. Phil's and ask for Sister Jonnson."

She didn't wait for him to thank her, ignored the people gathered round. Corwyn shoved her way through them, pushing her wet hair out of her eyes because it was *still raining,* and turned toward 34th Street and Miss Vadoma's house.

CORWYN STALKED DOWN the road, heart hammering and knack—knowing where Gwen was but not knowing how to get to her—spinning in her skull like it didn't know what to do with itself. But Corwyn had an idea, and she kept her mind on that, kept her anger up in front of her eyes so she wouldn't have to notice the cold place where Gwen's voice—*I can't see nothing, Wyn,* not like Gwen usually, not at all—was living.

"I need a sledgehammer," she said as soon as Miss Vadoma opened the door. "You got one I can use?"

It was rare that anyone caught Miss Vadoma flat-footed, but she stopped with the door half-open and blinked a few times before saying, "I do."

Corwyn dripped everywhere as she followed the witch to the kitchen and waited for Miss Vadoma to find the hammer in a broom closet. She handed it to Corwyn. Its weight staggered her a little as she took it, but climbing all those buildings must have done her some good because she was fine once she got the right grip on the handle.

"And what are you planning to do with that, Corwyn Teachout?" Miss Vadoma asked.

"The Collett house ate Gwen," she said, hefting the hammer in her two hands. "And it's gonna give her back."

Miss Vadoma's eyebrows raised. "That house don't give things back."

"It's gonna give my sister back," Corwyn replied, teeth clenching around the words.

"You think you're the first person gone up after that place with a hammer, girl? Grown men ain't managed to knock holes in those walls."

Corwyn's teeth ached, and she shoved the hammer, two-handed, at the witch, managing not to scream as she said, "Then you *do* something to it, Miss Vadoma. I'll work the rest of my life to pay it off, but you *witch* this fucking thing for me."

Miss Vadoma stood still, her face impassive before it softened into the look she wore when a potion went wrong but she had an idea how to fix it. Corwyn said nothing, just dropped her arms to let the hammer hang. She knew she'd get what she wanted now.

"Blood," Miss Vadoma finally said. "We'll use blood." She reached over with a long, bony hand and took Corwyn by the wrist, pulling her to the table and pushing her down onto a chair.

"You don't do blood work," Corwyn said. Miss Vadoma took the hammer from her and set it on the floor next to Corwyn's chair. Then she flipped Corwyn's right hand palm-up on the tabletop.

"*Don't* ain't the same thing as *can't*. You seem hellbent to create mayhem, and even I make exceptions sometimes." Miss Vadoma turned away to one of her drawers. She came back with a small, sharp knife and a piece of fine cheesecloth.

Corwyn swallowed hard but didn't flinch as the witch sliced delicately along the lines of her palm—not deep enough to keep her from using her hand, but enough to hurt when she moved it. Miss Vadoma mopped up the blood in Corwyn's palm with the cheesecloth, overturned the bowl of potatoes that sat in the middle of the table, then dropped the cloth into it.

She stood up, gathering the bowl to her side like it was still full of potatoes and not just a bloody piece of cloth. "Clean yourself up. There's bandaging in the washroom." Then Miss Vadoma turned to the counter and started doing things to the bowl.

In the washroom, Corwyn rinsed the blood off her hand with some water from the basin. It was hard, wrapping the bandage around it, but she managed.

She did not think about what would happen if she couldn't get Gwen out of the Collett house wall. They took care of each other because there wasn't another soul in the world going to do it for them, and she was going to get Gwen back and not have to figure out what to do without her. She would not have to find out if she could *bear* to be without her sister; she would not have to think about Gwen alone in the dark and the cold, sounding so strange because Gwen was never scared—

No, Corwyn wasn't going to have to do *any* of that, because she wasn't leaving Gwen in the dark. She would tear down the Collett House, Cobbler's Hill and the rest of San Xavier, too, but Gwen was coming out that thrice-damned wall.

Corwyn yanked her sleeve over her hand and wiped at her eyes, hard. Crying wasn't going to do her a bit of good, and god knew she didn't want Miss Vadoma catching her at it.

She was dry-eyed but still thinking furiously when she went back into the kitchen. The bowl rested on the kitchen table, now full of some kind of liquid. Miss Vadoma straightened, holding the hammer and laying it on the table, too. She picked up a paint brush set next to the bowl, dipped it in, then brushed the head of the hammer with it. The light was too dim to really make out the color of the liquid, but it smelled bitter: the metal smell of blood; some sort of herb that made Corwyn's stomach swoop like when she'd gone floating to the ceiling; another scent like the stuff Miss Vadoma had sold Gwen for her cough.

"So what's this do, exactly?" she asked. "Make the hammer stronger?"

"Yes." Miss Vadoma sounded distracted. "And it'll make the hammer lighter for you. Your blood'll give it a little bit of your finding knack, for specificity. You want to let your sister out, but there's some things as needs to stay inside that house." She swirled the brush around in the bottom of the bowl to gather the last dregs of the potion and applied it. "It's blood magic, though—who the hell knows if it'll do what it's told." She put the brush down and leaned in to whisper something to the hammer—or maybe the potion—and the liquid sank into the hammer head like water into dry soil.

It was lighter when Corwyn lifted it off the table. She looked at Miss Vadoma and asked, "What do I owe you for this?"

"A big favor," Miss Vadoma drawled. "Likely an inconvenient one, too."

Corwyn figured as long as it wasn't *now* she was asking, it wasn't going to put her out much, and Miss Vadoma wasn't dumb enough to ask her anything now, Corwyn standing in front of her with a sledgehammer in her hands. "You coming?" she asked as she turned toward the door, but she didn't wait round to see if the witch followed.

It had stopped raining. A cold wind blew down the street, making Corwyn's step hitch before she steadied and stalked back down the street toward the Collett house, gathering a collection of curious looks and smaller kids as she went. The crowd at the Collett house was a little bigger when she got back, and she saw a few of the Home kids there—Shrimpy Jackson and Heck from Tanner's bar—but she didn't talk, just shoved through to the gate, her knack practically singing Gwen's name up the porch steps.

"Gwen?" she called.

There was a long moment of standing there, swaying a little while her fingers reworked and readjusted her grip on the handle of the sledgehammer, listening as hard as she could.

" ... Wyn?"

Nine hells and all attendant demons, what had made Gwen's voice so small? Once she got her out, Corwyn would burn this goddamned house to the ground.

"Gwen!"

She moved closer to the wall, and heard Gwen's voice, muffled, "*Sorry,* I didn't mean to, I'm sorry ..." She sounded like she was crying.

Corwyn put a hand on the wall, forgetting everything else as she said, "You got nothing to be sorry for, Gwen—"

"I'm supposed to take care of you ..."

"You do, stupid—"

"You're *dead,* how in hell is that—"

"I'm not dead!" Corwyn felt the rage run up her throat; she pulled her hand off the wall and said, "I'm going to get you out of there, because we got churches with clockwork dolls to find and Lars Hallstrom to beat hell out of, and you're the scariest goddamn thing in the Hill, no thrice-cursed haunted house is going to scare *you*, so watch out."

"Why?" That sounded more like Gwen—wary.

"Because I'm gonna knock a hole in the wall with a sledgehammer."

"Who gave you a sledgehammer, Corwyn?" and Corwyn could have fallen over with relief at Gwen's suspicious big sister voice.

"Miss Vadoma. She witched it for me, too."

"Corwyn Teachout—"

"Yell at my face, Gwendolyn," Corwyn said. She swung low and slammed the hammer into the wall, heavy as when she first picked it up. The glass rattled in the windows; she felt the wall shake. The hammer left a dent when she pulled it back, but felt light again.

"Not a thing in here liked that, Wyn." Gwen's voice sounded just the littlest bit shaky, though nobody else but Corwyn would have noticed.

"I don't care," she said, readying her swing. "It don't want a hole in its side, it needs to let you go." She swung the hammer again, and this time the wood cracked around its head. The house shuddered. Corwyn grinned broadly; Gwen swore but sounded more impressed than scared. There was a hole—not a big one, but a hole nonethe-less—when Corwyn brought the hammer back again, cracked brick and dust and a scuttling noise that could have been a rat.

She couldn't hear Gwen at all, now, as she settled her grip on the handle, but there was a pounding behind the front door—not like a knock, more like someone kicking it.

"Corwyn, open the door, my hands are too stiff to get it!"

Corwyn shot a grim look at the hole and dropped the hammer. The door stayed where it was supposed to this time, and opened eas-ily when she pulled at the knob.

Gwen stood covered in dust like Zoreah had been, her hair and skin and clothes all gray with it, but Gwen was tinged blue underneath. Her hands were icy when Corwyn yanked her out the doorway and onto the porch.

PEOPLE CLEARED A PATH when the girls emerged through the front gate, Gwen leaning in toward Corwyn if not directly on her; Corwyn glaring down anyone who might look her in the eye. They all looked funny. Kind of scared, kind of wary, but something else, too, that Corwyn couldn't name and did not like. Eager, maybe. Not wary enough.

"Oi!" she heard, and Mr. Fritz, in an undershirt and suspender-trousers, a hat askew on his head, shoved through the crowd. *He* didn't look at them any different. Maybe more tired; Corwyn couldn't tell in the half-lit street. "Come on," he said with a jerk of his head. "You're staying with me tonight."

He turned and headed off toward Fowler Road. Corwyn followed with a quick glance at Gwen, who had her hands stuffed into her armpits and looked likely to fall over if she didn't find a place to sit soon. She came along without a word, just a yawn and a jerk of her shoulder to get her rucksack settled on her back. Corwyn wished the light was good enough to see if her skin still had that blue tone to it.

"How'd you know to come get us?" Corwyn asked, pulling her eyes away from her sister.

"Jericho came and found me. Though I'm willing to bet half the Hill knows what you did by now." Mr. Fritz was walking slower now they'd turned off Dunbar. He gave Corwyn half a grin. "Madame Tereza told me to go fetch you, give you a room." His grin fell to only a quarter as he went on, "Just for a night, though—she won't cross Beatriz d'Souza quite so much as to let you stay longer."

Corwyn shrugged and shifted the hammer from her left shoulder to her right, used a finger to adjust the strap of her bag where it cut into her neck. Gwen kept plodding along with her hands under her arms, quiet and biddable and worrying in the extreme. She didn't say anything until they started up the back steps of Madame Tereza's, when she paused at the stoop to ask, voice so careful, "You got any rats, Mr. Fritz?"

"No," he said, puzzled but gentle. "No rats. Bad for business."

Gwen nodded. "Okay, then," she said, and hauled herself up the half step to the door.

THE NOISE OF MADAME Tereza's foyer, buzzy and excited, filtered back to the stairs Mr. Fritz led them up. Corwyn wondered if it was early or late in the evening. The clouds from the day were all rained out, but they still covered the sky.

Mr. Fritz's room was halfway down the second floor hallway Corwyn remembered; he opened the rather plain door to reveal thick carpet and mirrors hung all round on the walls, with an enormous bed in the middle like a colossal carnation. The room came alive with movement as soon as she stepped inside: a girl in all the mirrors, sallow-skinned and hollow-eyed; wispy hair escaping her braid and waving all round her head; dirty, with thick gray smears of dust across her forehead and all over her clothes. Skinny, scrawny, short little girl; she didn't look like she ought to be able to heft that sledgehammer over her shoulder. Tired little girl. Then the mirrors flowed with movement again, and Corwyn saw Gwen's skin, pink under her coating of dust, and felt some fear slide out of her.

"It's not like seeing yourself in a shop window," Corwyn said softly. Gwen shrugged one shoulder, uninterested; her eyes were on the bed.

Mr. Fritz started untying curtain-sashes so that red and gold drapery fell across the mirrors. "Sorry. The mirrors are one of my specialities." He finished covering them up and crossed to the bed, peering down at it. "She's had the sheets changed; that's a kindness."

Gwen dropped her rucksack to the floor and said, tired and monotone, "I am far too filthy to sleep in that bed, Mr. Fritz."

Mr. Fritz looked at her in that same puzzled, gentle way he'd spoken before. "I've a wash room." He stepped round the bed to a door in the wall behind it. "I can only offer you a basin, not a bath, but the water runs and it can be hot, when it's got a mind to be. My bedroom's through here, but I'll likely be downstairs most of the night."

"This ain't ... ?" Corwyn frowned, shook her head, looked at Mr. Fritz and noticed that his pants were a deep, rich purple. "We keeping you from working, Mr. Fritz?"

"I'm playing host tonight. Don't you worry, Miss Corwyn."

Corwyn did not have the wherewithal to make herself wonder why his voice sounded strange, a little too jolly. He gave her a smile as he headed back to the door, and paused to put a hand on her shoulder. "I've a new book for you, if you come knock on my door in the morning. But clean up and sleep, now, girls." And with one more odd, gentle smile, he slipped out the door and was gone.

GWEN KEPT CLOSE TO Corwyn as they cleaned up, which wasn't that unusual, but the cloud of quiet she'd been moving in since they left the Collett house's porch was unnerving. There was no jostling at the washbasin, no flicking water at Corwyn, no use of Corwyn's face for a hand towel. Gwen just washed her face and hands, took off her boots, and shook out her trousers and shirt before putting the shirt back on to sleep in.

It wasn't just Gwen. The room was quiet, everything muffled by curtains and rugs. Corwyn felt small next to the bed, engulfed by fabric and silence, tired and put out, prickly like she might crack if touched. She sat down next to the bed and pulled their rucksacks closer, opened them up and emptied them. Gwen paused at the side of the bed for a long moment as Corwyn inspected her books—damp round the edges, mostly; she stood them up with the pages fanned and hoped they'd dry overnight—before sitting down next to Corwyn, their sides touching.

Bit by bit, Corwyn pulled everything out of both bags: weapons, extra bits of clothes, books, some dried-up apples, sewing kit, odds and ends. Gwen leaned on her, temple pressed to her shoulder, head growing heavier and heavier. Corwyn tried to move smoothly to keep from jostling her awake. Finally she spread the bags out on the carpet and hoped they'd dry all through.

Corwyn sat back. Gwen stirred and mumbled, "Carpet's soft."

"I bet that bed's softer," Corwyn said. "Come on, Gwen."

"Don' wanna move."

Corwyn let her breath out carefully, like it might be dangerous. "Now, how long's it been since we slept in a bed? And I bet Madame Tereza's are a sight softer than the Home's."

In the end she manhandled Gwen up and gave her a boost into Mr. Fritz's mad red and gold bed. Corwyn waited as Gwen got the bedclothes back and herself under them, wondering if all beds at Madame Tereza's were tall and ornate like this, or if it was another thing special to Mr. Fritz like the mirrors, but once she scrambled up next to Gwen she found she didn't much care—nine hells, maybe she'd apply to be a let-girl when she got old enough, if the beds were all heavenly soft like this.

Gwen rolled over and slung an arm around her; Corwyn took Gwen's hand and pulled it up by her chin, rested her cheek on it, concentrated on the feel of the fancy, fine sheets against her feet until Gwen's breath evened out again, until her arm went lax and heavy over Corwyn's ribs.

And then, just as she thought Gwen was asleep: "Wyn? It wasn't you in the dark, right?"

"I wasn't ... no, Gwen. No."

"It—the dark, maybe? It said things, and it sounded like you. But not—you don't ever say things that way ..."

Gwen was drifting off, but her voice was so small and so tired. "Whatever it told you," Corwyn said, "it was lying."

Gwen didn't answer, asleep and gone to the world. She didn't even move as Corwyn, finally, started to cry.

CHAPTER ELEVEN

It seemed Allen Brogan was feeling generous, and that mood had infected Mr. Katsaros, who handed Corwyn a paper bag full of jerky, four grapefruit, and a bunch of carrots. He stood puffed up like a pigeon behind his grocery cart and paused mid-shout at the carpenters to ask her, "What's the hammer for? No—do not tell me, I don't care. Where's the other one?"

Corwyn glanced behind herself to find Gwen gone again, not a glimpse to be had in the crowd on the sidewalk.

"Goddammit," she muttered. She folded the top of the bag over and left to hunt down her sister for the third time in as many days.

CORWYN WAS NOT SURPRISED to find Gwen in the midst of a fight with two boys, both of them bigger than her. She'd been picking fights with anyone as looked at her or Corwyn sideways since they'd snuck out of Madame Tereza's place. The d'Souza tattoos on these boys' arms were unexpected, though. One already crouched at the side of the road, not quite in the gutter, cradling a broken nose; Gwen swung round to face the other one with a rolled-up newspaper in her hand. She smacked him hard in the face with it a couple of times, darting in and out like a dragonfly until, with a roar, he rushed her.

After all those dragonfly stings, he really ought to have known he wasn't fast enough to catch her unless she let him. As Gwen, grinning loopily, worked her way out of the boy's grip, Corwyn sat down on the curb behind his broken-nosed companion. She settled the sledgehammer between her legs and began packing their new food stash into her rucksack.

"Did Mrs. d'Souza send you two?" Corwyn asked without looking up. "She trying to kill us for real now?"

Broken Nose turned ponderously to look Corwyn over. "You the sister?" he asked.

Corwyn put a hand on the still-witched sledgehammer and lifted it just off the pavement. "I am entirely willing to let my sister thrash the both of you, but you make one move toward me and I'll crack your skull wide open."

The boy gaped at her for a moment, then said, "No, it ain't the crone. Gad sent us out, he—"

The howl of someone who'd just had his balls crushed with a boot-tip drew both their attention back to the fight; Broken Nose up and sprinted into the fray to defend his friend's honor. Gwen ducked under his roundhouse, skipped to Corwyn, and dipped her hand into Corwyn's bag. She came up with one of the grapefruit. She spun, moved a half-step into the kid's reach, and smashed the fruit into his ruin of a nose.

The metal smell of blood faded under the sudden bloom of grapefruit scent in the air. Broken Nose staggered backward, crying now, as Crushed Balls tried to stand up. Corwyn looked at Gwen—breathing hard, cheeks flushed, the empty expression her knack gave her gone and replaced with a real smile. "You about done?" Corwyn asked.

Gwen dropped the remains of the grapefruit and shook juice and pulp from her hand. "I think so, yeah," she said.

"Well then, let's go eat something. I got carrots today."

Gwen retrieved her own rucksack from behind a trash bin, shooing off the cat nosing at it. Corwyn slung her bag over one shoulder, the sledgehammer over the other, and the two of them headed off to St. Phil's.

"Third fight this week," Corwyn observed.

Gwen shrugged. "My knack's sparky, lately."

"I guess. What'd they even do?"

"Said something rude." Gwen's mouth was stubborn.

Corwyn just sighed. "Apparently Gad d'Souza sent them out after us."

Gwen's voice was distant and lacked care. "Wonder how long it'll take him to grow a pair of balls and come after us himself."

THEY ATE CARROTS ON the steps of St. Phil's. Gwen leaned on Corwyn, the sledgehammer balancing between Corwyn's legs. Gwen touched Corwyn more lately, keeping close and careful eyes on her, but also going off fighting more and talking a lot less. Corwyn didn't mind being leaned on like Gwen was a cat; she didn't even mind the fighting so much. The quiet and the watching she wasn't so keen on.

"Wyn," Gwen said, tilting her chin toward the street and the squared-off blond boy coming up it, eyes on them. He wasn't much older than they were, but he was a good sight cleaner and less raggedy. He didn't have that same air about him as the Katsaros kids, though—he moved through the Hill like he didn't like it, not like he didn't know how.

He fetched up in front of them and sat down. Corwyn could feel the tension in Gwen's muscles, though she didn't move.

"Which of you's Corwyn?" the boy asked.

Neither of them answered, though Gwen shifted to stare at him straight on instead of sideways. The boy rolled his eyes heavenward. "Look, I don't rightly care which of you's Corwyn. I'm here because Mrs. Simcote sent me." Mrs. Simcote, Corwyn thought. That explained a lot. "The old lady has seen fit to take an interest in your particular talent, whichever one of you is Corwyn."

"She make you learn that speech by heart?" Gwen asked.

His expression—not too happy but otherwise calm—didn't change. "Yeah. She said to tell you she's willing to take both of you in. She's got fighting knacks to spare, but she's aware you're two or none."

Gwen's face didn't change, but *fighting knacks to spare* raised Corwyn's hackles. She put one hand on the handle of the hammer. "No," she said.

The boy raised his eyebrows at her, ignoring Gwen now he knew who she was. "You sure? We learn a lot about our knacks, in the Volary. And the old lady takes good care of her kids. You look like you could use some caretaking."

He wasn't wrong, Corwyn thought, even as she refused to acknowledge the memory that rose up round her of sleeping in an actual bed.

Gwen leaned all the way back on Corwyn again, far enough so the boy couldn't hear her. "You sure, Wyn?" she asked.

Corwyn heard, buried at the bottom of her voice, a trace of that smallness from inside the wall of the Collett house. Corwyn hadn't heard it since that night at Madame Tereza's. The hint of it still made her want to set fire to things.

"I'm sure," Corwyn said, keeping her voice down. She didn't need to make another grown-up enemy, but, "Fighting knacks to spare' my ass, the woman's clearly stupid."

Gwen scoffed and shrugged one shoulder. "Fighting's a dime a dozen knack."

"Yours ain't," Corwyn said. It was true. She'd never seen another person with a knack like Gwen's—her speed, and the way she used weapons so easy. She turned back to the boy. "No," she said again.

"All right," the boy said, standing up and stretching. "You change your mind, come to Wickham Street, north end of the Hill over by Jersey Court Road." He turned and walked down the Cathedral steps.

Gwen sat up and popped the last bit of her carrot into her mouth.

"So," she said, her mouth full, "we've turned down shelter and regular meals—what d'you want to do now, little sister?"

"Errands," Corwyn said, her fingers playing along the handle of the sledgehammer. She'd been hatching a plan to shake the quiet out of Gwen. Time to put it into action.

"OH, BUT DO WE HAVE to?" Gwen asked, bouncing next to Corwyn with her hands clasped under her chin. Gwen was grinning her bright, sunny grin, not a half-smile like she didn't have the wherewithal to smile with both sides of her mouth; that bouncing, swaying Gwen-walk hadn't been around in a while, either. So Corwyn had to grin back even though the witching had worn off and the sledgehammer was heavy again.

"We have to," Corwyn said. "I owe the witch enough without stealing her sledgehammer."

Gwen's grin fell away, and Corwyn's stomach dropped because she hadn't meant to do that, but then Gwen put the smile back on again, just as bright. "Fine. But be warned, Corwyn, one day I aim to have a sledgehammer of my very own."

"So long as you carry it around, I agree to help you achieve your fine and lofty goal, Gwen."

"It's good to have dreams," Gwen observed. Corwyn told herself that she didn't notice them turning down Drury Road to avoid Dunbar.

THE WITCH TOOK THE hammer without letting them in the house, just a, "I'll have provings for you in a week or so, Corwyn," and shut the door.

"She is always so personable," Gwen remarked, hands in her pockets, leaning on the porch railing. "So what else are we going to do?"

They went from Miss Vadoma's to Madame Tereza's, where they traded books with an exhausted Mr. Fritz. Then sparring in Stolarski Park for awhile, which Corwyn quite clearly needed to do if the way her arms and shoulders ached afterward was anything to go by. On their way back toward St. Phil's, Heck stopped them outside Tanner's.

"I'll give you a dollar if you take this note to someone."

Gwen was cheerful after a day of tasks, and Corwyn was eager to keep her that way. "Yeah, all right," she said. She squinted at Heck—his cheeks and the tips of his ears were pink, like he was feverish. "Who's this 'someone'?"

Heck turned even pinker. It was pretty, which was funny because Heck had gone from a skinny scarecrow of a kid at the Home to a slab of muscle and calluses working at the bar. He still had the scarecrow hair, though, tufts sticking up all directions. "Her name's Charlotte. She works doing the fine stitching over at the tailor shop on 26th."

Corwyn ignored her waking knack for a minute to ask, "Heck, are you *courting* this girl?"

"Just take the note, Corwyn."

"Payment up front," Gwen chirped. Heck shot her a look. "We're not gonna steal your money—Corwyn's knack's gonna drag us there, now, anyway."

"Okay, fine, just ... be nice to her, okay?"

Corwyn started walking before she called back, "We'll tell her all about the time you got stuck in the chimney in Sister Benedict's office!"

"I hate both you Teachouts!" he yelled back, but he was laughing and Gwen was cackling next to her.

SO THEY KEPT BUSY, or Corwyn did her best to keep them that way. Heck and his lady friend looked to be conducting an entire courtship by letter—"Bet you're glad the Sisters taught us to spell, now, ain't you?" Gwen asked him, dancing away from the half-hearted swat he aimed at her—so they had something to do most days, even if half the time they did it for free.

And Gwen seemed happier, by and large. Her knack was still sparky: Corwyn kept on finding her gone and tracking her down to a fight in an alley, or the street or, on one memorable and frightening occasion, at a bar near the docks. But that, too, looked to be settling down. Corwyn thought maybe the echoes of whatever had claimed to be her in the walls of the Collett house were fading from Gwen's ears. She hoped, anyway.

CORWYN'S WORK WITH Miss Vadoma had an odd feel to it now; they'd never been chattery with each other, but lately they were both quieter. Corwyn didn't feel much like asking questions, and Miss Vadoma didn't seem much like she'd answer, anyway. Finding the witch's porch empty when she'd expected to find Gwen waiting for her didn't do much to help the strange, off-center feeling as had lodged in Corwyn's chest. She ran a hand over her face and yanked at her still-short braid, then let her knack out with a sigh to find her sister.

Gwen slouched on the steps of St. Philomena's, gazing at the broken clock, not fighting nor twitching nor anything else, just one foot propped off the other knee, head back on one arm, hair escaping her braids, mouth relaxed. She was grimy and bathed in sunlight; Corwyn smiled as she climbed the steps to her.

"You best not fall asleep, the nuns'll be out here like crows."

Gwen blinked at her and grinned, lazy. "I ain't sleeping."

"Yet." Corwyn weighed how much trouble she'd get into if she nudged Gwen's side with her toe.

"So what'd the witch have you—"

"You know everyone in this goddamned city is talking 'bout the two of you?"

Two steps below them stood Gad d'Souza. He looked as rough as the well-fed grandson of a gang lord could: messy hair, red eyes, clenched fists, skewed clothes. His breath hitched like he'd been crying, shoulders heaving up and down all shuddery.

Gwen sat up and put her forearms on her knees. Corwyn's back tensed even as Gwen's ran looser. "I can't say as I'm surprised; we are *fascinating* creatures," Gwen drawled.

Gad turned to Corwyn. "You ain't never brought no little girl out that house," he said. "Nobody ever comes back out that house. You didn't bust no hole in that wall, neither."

Corwyn took one step down, still a step above Gad, as Gwen stood up and towered over them both. It wasn't just the steps—her pants were up round her ankles. She'd grown without Corwyn noticing.

"I wasn't aware you saying things made them true," Corwyn said to Gad, her voice even despite the panic in her chest. She glanced around, hoping one of Beatriz d'Souza's boys was nearby to keep this from getting stupid, but she didn't see anyone looked the part.

"Used to be. Used to be people listened to me 'cause of who I am," he said. Gad turned to glance at Gwen, and Corwyn shifted slightly so he'd have to really turn to look at either of them. Maybe it would keep him off-balance. "Not anymore. Now the thinking's that maybe a girl with a finding knack and a sister as fights like a monster is somebody we should take on. Maybe I need to shut my mouth and keep my place. Maybe I *got* no place, if I can't get nobody to respect me." He was furious and sulky, his eyes full of tears when he spun back to Corwyn. "There ain't nothing special about neither of you," he spat, voice thick and shaky. "You live on the fucking street; you got no family—"

"The hell you think a sister *is*, stupid?" Gwen asked, but Gad didn't look away from Corwyn. She slid her rucksack off her shoulder and into her hand; it wasn't as heavy as Gwen's because Gwen had a brick in hers, but it did have two books and a bunch of apples in it. That was heavy enough to stun him.

"You got a witch on your side, you maybe got an alchemical engineer—'those girls got respect,'" he spat in a high-pitched voice Corwyn guessed was supposed to be his grandmother. "You're nothing, but everyone knows who you are." Corwyn felt a sharp stab of fear at that, and in that distracted second he grabbed her.

She shoved at him and twisted to get away—fear abruptly replaced by rage—but when the knife pressed up against her ribs she stopped short.

Things went very, very still in Corwyn's head; her heart even seemed to pause. She held her breath, trying to hold the rage—as much at herself as at him, he'd grabbed her *again*, the bastard—down under it. She'd managed to turn Gad more toward Gwen, at least.

"What's the plan, Gad?" Gwen asked. Her eyes moved all over him, always flicking back to Corwyn, who waited to see what Gwen was going to do. "Kill us so your grandmama will let you take over?"

"You can shake down candy stores, you mewling infant," Corwyn muttered. He jabbed at her with the knife, breaking the skin but not quite stabbing.

"Don't need to kill both," he said.

Gwen smiled. Corwyn could see her knack in it. "Yeah, you do. And you should have just done it. I told you not to touch my sister again." Whip-quick her arm flashed out and caught Gad's knife-hand. The knife dragged across Corwyn's skin, white and sharp, as she stumbled down two more steps. She pressed her hand against the wound and turned to watch. She didn't think Gad d'Souza was that good a fighter, but she wanted her eyes on that knife.

He must've got himself with his own blade along his forearm—it bled all over as he sliced at Gwen. Gwen moved away easily and kicked him in the side of the head, sending him stumbling toward Corwyn, who hauled herself up some steps away from him. He shook the kick off—yeah, his recovery time was his knack, all right, because he hadn't learned a damn new thing about fighting—and charged up at Gwen, knife raised like to stab her.

Gwen got a good kick to his knee. He lost his balance and threw his arms out to get it back. Gwen darted toward him, plucked the knife out of his hand, and buried it where his neck and shoulder met.

Gad looked surprised.

Corwyn forgot about her side. She lunged for Gwen, seized her arm just as she pulled the knife back out. Blood spurted out the wound all over everywhere.

"Run," Corwyn snapped. Gwen, blinking like she'd just woke up, turned and did. Corwyn saw Gad try to climb up a step and fall, but she didn't stick around to see more.

THEY RAN A COUPLE OF blocks, then Gwen pulled Corwyn into a side-street and rummaged around in her bag for a piece of rag. She wrapped the knife in it and stowed it with shaking hands before looking around them, covering her mouth with one hand. She took a deep, wavering breath.

"Wyn—" she said as she turned back around. Corwyn tried to stand up straighter because Gwen's voice had gone small again. She shoved her hand harder against her side and bit back a whimper at the pain, but Gwen caught sight, anyway.

She looked Corwyn up and down, once, and when she spoke her voice sounded like Gwen again. "The Alley," she said. "This time of day, nobody as sees us will remember we were there. We'll get you cleaned up and figure out what the hell we do next."

Corwyn nodded and followed Gwen down the street. Her side hurt like a demon, so she distracted herself by considering their situation. She didn't know if Gwen had killed Gad d'Souza or not, but she was pretty sure stabbing him with his own knife was bad enough, even if Beatriz d'Souza didn't seem to like her grandson much. Mr. Fritz had to answer to Madame Tereza, so that was right out. Miss Vadoma might, in the right mood, find it amusing to face down Beatriz d'Souza's boys ...

In Shoemaker's Alley, Gwen cleaned Corwyn's wound with water, swearing over it and wrapping it with bandages they'd kept from Corwyn's run-in with Lars Hallstrom. "Here, swallow this," Gwen told her.

Corwyn took the little bottle from her hand and shook it. "What is it?" It looked like one of Miss Vadoma's bottles.

"It's the last of the cough syrup the witch sold me. It made my chest stop hurting when I was sick."

Corwyn drank it—syrupy-sweet lemon and ginger with something bitter underneath. Gwen began to almost vibrate, arms around herself and eyes darting across the opium-dazed figures who dotted the Alley. "You think—the Brogans owe us, don't they?" Gwen asked. "We found Tansa for them, you think they'd help?"

The pain dissipated slow out of Corwyn like fog in the sunlight. "Maybe," she said. It was a bold move to approach the Brogans, but there wasn't any better time than this to be bold. "Let's see what they say."

CORWYN'S KNACK DIDN'T kick, but it hardly mattered: unlike Art Goldberg, who kept where he lived as secret as he could and ran his business out of his gentlemen's club, or the Tongs, whose headquarters nobody could get a bead on, Ben Brogan lived out on Jersey Court Road in one of the biggest houses in the Hill, with his name carved over the front door. The girls went to the back, though. No sense in drawing extra attention.

The Brogans' cook was an old man, maybe Mexican, Corwyn thought; he spared them one long, appalled look before leaving them to wait outside on the stoop while he went to get Mr. Brogan.

Corwyn worked to breathe steady as they waited. Her side didn't hurt as much, but her heart still pounded fit to gallop and her head raced with thoughts and half-formed plans that skittered away when she tried to look at them straight on. The smell of onions seeped round the door. This might work—the Brogans and the d'Souzas had hated each other for years; maybe the Brogans would help just on the strength of that. Even if all they did was give Corwyn and Gwen a place to hide for a night or two, give them a chance to think.

A man opened the door. All the onion smell spilled out past him. The man was too tall, too thin, and too young to be Ben Brogan. Looked like they'd got Allen.

"Mr. Brogan," Corwyn said, "I'm Corwyn Teachout—"

"I know who you are," he said. His voice was rough, like he was losing it, as he went on, "You're the one found Tansa for my father."

"And the hell do you two want?" Tansa Katsaros Brogan peered over her husband's shoulder before moving to stand in the doorway herself. Allen stepped aside smoothly, giving her room.

Tansa stood tall, a hand on one hip, dirt or grease or something smeared across her neck, her hair tied up in a messy knot atop her head.

Gwen glared at her. "We were hoping to speak to your father-in-law," she said.

Tansa snorted half a laugh. "Well, you got us. More's the pity."

Gwen's jaw clenched. "We need help," Corwyn said.

Tansa smiled: it stretched tight across her face and revealed a couple missing teeth along the right side of her mouth. "Trouble enough to send you running here?" she asked.

"Your husband owes us a debt," Corwyn said, jerking her head toward Allen.

"My *in-laws* owe you a debt, maybe," Allen said, his reedy voice grown dark. "What *I* owe you ... well, it ain't a debt."

Tansa looked sideways at him, clearly displeased; he returned her look with one that seemed to ask if she cared to argue the point.

It appeared she did not. "So when we tell you no—and we *are* telling you no," she said to Corwyn. "—consider it the word of the entire Brogan family." The smile faded a little; Tansa's face went grim. "Good fucking luck," she said, and shut the door. Her footsteps echoed from behind it, moving away, followed more slowly by her husband's.

"Guess marriage worked out better for her than she expected," Corwyn said.

"Nine goddamned hells," Gwen whispered through her teeth. "Now what?"

But Corwyn had an idea, now. She didn't want to say it out loud, not here, so she reached for Gwen's hand. "Come on."

THEY RAN DOWN THE SIDEWALKS, keeping to alleys and back streets, two more dirty kids among the mass of urchins in Cobbler's Hill, until they found a building with a door half-hanging off its hinges. They took to the rooftops then and got quite a ways toward the docks, even if the jumps were a little wide in places. Corwyn bled through her bandage and was panting by the time they found a rowboat to steal. Gwen made her sit still while she rowed them across the water.

The sun started to dip lower in the sky. Corwyn watched it, catching her breath, not thinking much, now. Just listening to the water and the wind.

Gwen dragged the boat with them toward the lighthouse. She didn't complain, but her mouth tightened as she got tired.

Not much had changed since the last time they'd been here. The door was still partway open, dirt and rocks drifted in the entry as they stepped inside. With a clockwork keeper, Corwyn supposed that the little bit of furniture—two chairs and a couch—was meant for whoever came to maintain him.

The first floor smelled of rotting vegetables; they found them in a box under the metal staircase that curved up the wall and away through the ceiling. After they tossed the food out the front door and took a quick look round the bottom floor, they climbed the stairs to check the other rooms, too tired to talk.

The middle two floors under the light looked to be storage. One of the rooms directly under the light held a door, flat on the floor, and some sawhorses. Rusted, green-tinged tools and gears, along with fine metal wire, lay scattered across the floor. None of it looked particularly useful to them, so they left it and continued upstairs.

The light room was bare, aside from the light. The sky had darkened. It surrounded them up there, deep blue all round, mist rising and rolling far below, glimmers of gold from San Xavier across the black bay.

Each of them nearly fell down the stairs on their way back. Gwen shoved Corwyn onto the couch and covered her in a blanket that must have been Tansa Katsaros's, since it was neither as faded nor full of dust as the couch. Gwen pulled the cushions off the chairs and made herself a little nest out of them with her rucksack as a pillow. Corwyn watched her sleepily; her last thought as she slipped into sleep was that it would've been smarter to shove the couch in front of the door.

CORWYN WOKE WITH A jolt, like she'd fallen into her own body out of the dark. She lay still on the couch, breathing the dust-mold-salt-blood air of the lighthouse, watching the sunlight filtering down from the stairwell and through the windows while her heart slowed down.

Gwen still slept, an arm thrown up over her head. Corwyn looked at her for a little while, her red eyelashes and big hands, dirt under her nails and in the creases of her neck. Corwyn's side started to ache, and she suddenly felt desperate to get her boots off her hot, sticky feet.

She got up quiet, wincing as the bandage—dried to her skin with blood—tugged at her ribs, and crept out the door, pulling it to. She sat down on the steps to work her laces. It was still morning, she thought: the air was wet and cool against her neck and her white, wrinkled feet, the sunlight still shaded the bluish-yellow that it lost in the afternoon. Gulls' calls and men's voices carried over the water. The tearing thunk of Gwen's knife sinking into Gad d'Souza's neck sounded again and again in the back of her mind.

By now, Beatriz d'Souza's boys would have been scouring the Hill for them for hours; Osian knew most of their haunts, so they'd be pounding on doors and shaking folks down—though Corwyn wished them luck getting anything out of the nuns or Miss Vadoma.

Being barefoot made the stiff rub of her shirt and the way she smelled a little more bearable. Some of the stink was the rotten vegetables they'd thrown outside, but she was still pretty rank.

Corwyn wiggled her toes against the grit on the steps and regarded the undulating water in the bay. It'd be nice if they could stay here, but aside from their lack of supplies it wasn't entirely safe. Tansa Katsaros being married to Allen Brogan might keep the d'Souzas from talking to the Katsaroses for a while, but eventually they'd get there. Corwyn didn't think it likely that young Mr. Katsaros would think of Dieujuste Island as a place they might hole up, but she thought Tansa would. And odds were good that she'd say something if asked. Hell, odds were good she'd say something without being asked.

Corwyn pushed herself up off the step and started walking. Her head felt stuffed with thoughts, all simmering away, none of it useful and not much of it clear. So she left it to simmer, stepping gingerly over the rocks toward the twisted tree and the figure under it.

The clockwork man remained green and rusty as the last time they'd been here. His voice was more slurred when he noticed she was there and began his speech: "This automata is in need of repair. Please contact Mr. Fraley Bishop of Chaffins Grove, in San Xavier. Malfunctions are extensive and require the attention of an alchemical engineer."

Corwyn sat down near his hip. Scraps of cloth clung to his frame. Where his mask didn't cover his head she could see the scratched-cloudy glass. A tiny scrub tree grew between his remaining hand and his hip. He droned his distress message a couple more times before falling silent.

She pulled her knees up to her chin and looked at the keeper, the way the sun caught on the few bits of him that still reflected light. The shadows of the tree flickered over his body.

"We did try to find him for you," she told him. "Mr. Bishop. He's dead, though." The clockwork man, silent, reacted in no way she could see. Corwyn wondered if he'd been made to say anything else—who would he have to make comfortable with talking, out here?

The breeze carried the reek of blood and sweat off her up toward the lighthouse. Corwyn ducked her head a bit to catch the scent—she stunk, but it was her smell and still comforting—as she thought about the Home, such as it was. But even Sister Jonnson wouldn't be able to keep Beatriz d'Souza off their backs.

Nowhere to go, forwards or backwards, just the sound of that knife going into Gad d'Souza, the heat from the blood spray, all of that spun in her head like webbing.

The front door of the lighthouse scraped open. Corwyn waited. Gwen eventually crunched her way down to where Corwyn sat and dropped down next to her, unlacing her own boots.

"How are you?" Corwyn asked.

Gwen, still puffy-eyed with sleep, shrugged. She didn't look at Corwyn. "A trifle sore, but all right. How's your side?"

"Hurts. Ain't bleeding, I don't think." The bandage pulled whenever she moved.

"I can change the bandage for you," Gwen offered. She still wasn't looking at Corwyn.

"I ain't mad at you," Corwyn said.

Gwen paused in the middle of peeling her sock off her foot to take a quick glance at Corwyn before stripping her foot bare and digging her long toes into the dirt. "Dunno why not. I spoiled every plan we had."

Corwyn considered this. She was a trifle surprised to find she meant it when she said, "Eh. So we make a new plan."

"You scared?" Gwen asked, still not looking up.

"Not of you. Little of Beatriz d'Souza—woman's got a temper."

Gwen put her socks into her boots. "You think Gad's dead?" she asked. The light caught in her hair, half fallen out of its braids, and let free the red and gold that Corwyn rarely saw because Gwen's hair was rarely clean or loose enough to catch the light.

"I dunno," said Corwyn. "Odds're good, though, it *was* you as stabbed him."

That got a small smile. "I ain't sorry about it," Gwen said. "Even if I did kill him. And maybe I ought to be?"

Corwyn wasn't sorry. Aside from how it got them in the middle of a mess she hadn't yet thought a way out of, Corwyn thought the twat likely had it coming. Mrs. d'Souza was right: picking on folks and counting on his name to keep him safe wasn't no ways smart; someone would have killed him eventually just because he was too stupid to know he'd have to stop them. "I don't think you need to be," she told Gwen.

Gwen said nothing, just rested her arms on her knees and watched the water.

THE WATER WAS COLD, and Gwen working the bandage off her side was decidedly uncomfortable, but both sensations had the benefit of clearing some of the cobwebs out of Corwyn's skull.

"We should have done this last night," Gwen said grimly as she worked at the cloth.

"Yeah, half-blind with being tired and no light to speak of, it would have been so much easier," Corwyn gritted. She bunched her trouser legs up in her hands, breathing in and out until, finally, the bandage came away and Gwen got to work cleaning the wound.

"It ain't too deep—mostly just a scratch." Gwen prodded at it gently with a finger and frowned, then started re-bandaging with a new one. "Sorry, Wyn. I thought ... well, I figured I should get you away from him. Even if you got a little hurt it'd be all right, not as bad as what he wanted to do—"

"Would you quit saying you're sorry? You didn't cut me."

Gwen tucked the end of the bandage in and looked at Corwyn's bloody, torn shirt. "Well, we'll have to wash and mend this."

In the end, they washed and mended just about every piece of cloth they owned, Gwen kneeling in the shallows of the bay in her underwear while Corwyn sat on the shore in hers with their sewing kit to fix holes and frays. Fiddly work that demanded her focus, while things continued to simmer in the back of her head. She cleaned the knife, too, leaving it to dry on a rock next to Gwen's rucksack.

Corwyn was squinting at her own bag, calculating just how much thread she might need for *that* job of sewing, when Gwen said, "Even if he ain't dead, I think we can't live on the street anymore."

Corwyn bit off a piece of thread and stuck it through the needle's eye. "No, we likely can't. I think ... well, the Simcote lady's our best bet. Nobody messes with her kids."

Gwen nodded, shaking out the shirt she held and looking it over. "We're a lot of trouble, though. Or I am. What if she don't want me?"

"Well, only other people I can think of ain't troubled by Beatriz d'Souza's temper is Cadogan Rentsch and Miss Vadoma."

"We still owe Miss Vadoma, though," Gwen said, and now Corwyn nodded. The favor she still owed the witch nestled alongside rules that were vague and dark, more than Corwyn was willing to chance Gwen's life on. Maybe her own, she might trust the witch that far, but not Gwen's.

"We can go apprentice Cadogan Rentsch," Corwyn said. "I think ... if we told him our knacks, he'd take us on." It wasn't something she'd ever thought about, nor was it an idea she especially liked, but it was an option to consider.

"Probably he would," Gwen agreed. "But there's the 'drive you mad or blind you' risk of being an alchemical engineer's apprentice." She let out a long sigh. "So. Simcote lady first."

"And if she won't take us both, we go get 'prenticed." Corwyn swallowed, nervous, and added, "Both of us or neither of us, Gwen, okay?"

Gwen paused, crouched in the water with her hands tangled in a shirt beneath its surface. Her face was soft, easy, and her eyes were wide and clear, clear brown on Corwyn's as she said, "I ain't leaving you, Wyn. Don't worry yourself about that."

"Okay. Good," Corwyn said. They went back to their chores.

THEY SPENT THE REMAINDER of the day and that night in the lighthouse, resting and letting their clothes dry, not talking much. It was fine, so long as Corwyn didn't let herself consider the next day. When it crept into her head she got nervous. Maybe the Simcote lady wouldn't want them anymore. Maybe their last resort would be their only choice, and maybe they'd end up losing fingers or eyes to the gears and strange magic of alchemical engineering.

Or maybe the Simcote lady would still want them. Corwyn thought of how her kids all looked well-fed, clean, always on odd errands. Rumor was she sent some of them all over the country, out of the city, and when they got to be grown she set them up with some money and work. Corwyn pushed those thoughts away as hard as she did the ones about lost fingers.

Her side ached and itched a little, but she'd had worse.

You look like you could use some caretaking, that boy had said.

As the afternoon and evening wore on, Gwen's quiet changed from broody to easy. The bounce and sway of her walk hadn't returned, but the trudge that replaced it after the Collett house didn't come back, neither.

They went to bed with the sunset and got up with the sunrise, which made for decent cover after they rowed back to the Hill: nobody was out besides sailors. They made their way toward the north end of the Hill and Wickham Street unremarked.

"Somehow this ain't what I pictured a finishing school for street urchins to look like," Gwen said when they approached it.

Corwyn had expected something big and brick, like the Home; the fact that she couldn't remember a big brick building on this side of the Hill didn't trouble her, as she'd been little when they scarpered out of their attic apartment and had avoided the north end ever since. But the Simcote lady's place was just another building, likely a warehouse, all wood and shingles, no better looking than the ancient, boarded-up building next to it.

The streets were starting to populate as people woke up and got on with their day. Corwyn took Gwen by the elbow and pulled her along across the street. They found a bell pull in front of the door; Gwen gave it a hard, two-handed yank.

A kid their age, shorter than Gwen and wearing a hat so big Corwyn couldn't tell if she was looking at a boy or a girl, opened the door. "Yeah?" the kid asked.

"We're here to see Mrs. Simcote," Corwyn said.

"Who are you?"

"Corwyn and Gwen Teachout."

The kid didn't respond beyond letting them into a small room with a couple of chairs and a street-view window. The kid disappeared through a door in the opposite wall without a word, closing it firmly. Corwyn sat in one of the chairs. Gwen fidgeted, moving round the room even though there wasn't anything to look at and barely enough room to pace in.

Finally the inner door opened again and the kid, her hat stuffed into her back pocket, stuck her head through and said, "She'll see you. Come on."

Through the door, the building opened up and down. They stood on the middle level. Doors stretched down the walls beside them. A balcony hung above them connected by crisscrossing catwalks and ladders, and a wide staircase on the eastern side of the building connected the middle and bottom floors. Mrs. Simcote's kids moved round the place on whatever business they had when they were home, some carrying odd contraptions, some muttering under their breath; a small knot of boys and girls played some sort of complicated game of cards, slapping them down and either swearing or crowing at the results.

Their guide took them down the staircase, then behind it. Corwyn knew that the bottom floor must be under the street, but she felt dizzy over it, like her knack wasn't happy with this place.

Tucked behind the stairs was a wooden door with a shiny metal knob. The kid knocked and opened it, waving them both past her with a flourish.

The wide room had no windows and was made snug by the crowding shadows cast by clockwork lamps. A rug lay on the floor; dark wooden bookcases stood along the walls. In the middle of the room sat a desk, a vast surface covered over with papers, ledgers, odd objects—was that a hand?—each in its place. In the middle of the desk lay two folders, brown and bearing their names—they looked to be the files from the Singleton Home, though how Mrs. Simcote might have gotten them from the nuns Corwyn couldn't fathom. A pipe lay in a dish just off-center from the folders, a magnifying glass next to that.

The woman behind the desk owned a face made up of curves and wrinkles, not a sharp edge on them, for all that she was a skinny old lady. She looked at the two of them over her half-circle spectacles, grinning crooked and close-mouthed. "I heard about you girls killing Gad d'Souza," she said. Her voice sounded like worn-down cobblestones, with the Hill accent. Gwen relaxed, just a little, at the news that Gad d'Souza was, indeed, dead; Mrs. Simcote went on, "That is quite a peck of trouble."

"Enough so's you're taking back your offer?" Corwyn asked, her voice steady. Her heart pounded and her hands were sweating, for all that this reminded her of negotiating terms with Mr. Katsaros.

The old lady sat back in her chair. "No, no. Just trouble enough to make things interesting. I like things interesting." Her grin widened into a smile that showed her teeth—yellowed, the front two crossing each other a little bit—and she gestured at the two chairs in front of her desk as she flipped both the folders open.

"Welcome to the Volary, my dears. Have a seat, and we'll discuss the terms of your staying."

PART TWO
CHAPTER TWELVE

"Nine hells, but I'll be happy to be rid of this *hat*." Corwyn Teachout, now fifteen years old and smelling like the inside of a train car, ducked the pins that flew from her sister's hair as Gwen yanked what had been, three weeks ago, quite a fetching hat from her head. "The damn daisy's been poking me in the ear for the last two hours."

Tired and footsore, they lugged a small trunk up the bridge from the second floor of the Volary to the third floor and their room. Mrs. Simcote wanted the item inside the trunk, but as it was currently wrapped in their dirty socks and the trousers they'd gone hunting for it in, unpacking took precedence over immediate delivery.

Gwen dropped her handle. The bridge swung back and forth. She tied the hat by its ribbons to the belt on her dress and sighed. On the second floor other kids scampered between rooms; some climbed up the ladders and ropes connecting the second floor to the third. Nobody headed downstairs to the old lady's office, though, and Corwyn wondered how that boded.

They hoisted the trunk between them again and started along the gallery toward their room. Mattie Singh, singed round the edges and with her own huge hat stuffed into her pocket, emerged from the washroom in the corner and yelled, "She wants to see you soon's you're back!"

"She in the washroom, then?" Gwen called back as Mattie walked toward them.

"She's been telling us for days now."

"Yeah, well, things went sideways," Gwen said darkly.

"Should have sent a message," Mattie sang to them as she passed. Gwen rolled her eyes. Corwyn refrained from pointing out that she'd suggested this, a number of times, as it became clear they'd not be back when expected. Corwyn had a hard time anymore figuring out what Gwen would set her heels about, and she'd got stubborn about this. "She's more worried than angry!" Mattie called from the bridge.

"That won't last," Gwen said.

"Come on," said Corwyn, swinging the trunk a little to get Gwen's attention. "Let's make sure it don't smell like feet when we hand it to her."

THEIR TINY ROOM SMELLED stuffy, which told Corwyn nobody'd been in it since they'd been gone, but Gwen went looking anyway. Most of the Volary kids knew better than to snoop in their room, but sometimes Jouanna liked to show her ass. Corwyn unloaded the trunk. The dirty clothes went into the corner; the jeweled skull went onto Corwyn's bed; the instruments Mrs. Simcote gave them for the trip went on the bed next to the skull. Corwyn's book went on the table between their beds, while Gwen's rucksack and everything she carried in it went onto the other bed.

The three glowing rocks they'd found on their way home were stuffed into one of Corwyn's work boots. She pulled them out one by one. In the daylight they were white; smoother than a normal rock, maybe, but otherwise unremarkable. In the dark, they glowed green, pulsing just a little with enough light to read by. Their room had no windows, and the lamplight was just too dim.

Corwyn looked at them for a long moment, two in one hand, one pulsing faintly in the palm of the other, then she leaned over to push them under her pillow, so the glow wouldn't show under the door once they left.

"WELL, AT LEAST YOU brought me back the money you didn't spend on a telegram," Mrs. Simcote said, eyeing the pile of cash sitting on her desk next to the jewel-decorated skull, all the contraptions they'd returned to her, and assorted notes and schematics of buildings one could only assume were in San Xavier.

Corwyn shifted in her chair. Gwen, still as a pond and three times as murky, merely replied, "We ain't *that* late."

"Late enough to be of concern," said Mrs. Simcote. She reached over and pulled the skull closer. "Considering how hard you fought to be allowed to go on this assignment with your sister, Gwendolyn, I'd have expected you to mind the rules."

Gwen's jaw went tight, the first ripple of anything Mrs. Simcote said striking her clear, quiet surface. Corwyn said, "Sorry, Mrs. S. If you send us out again, we'll do better."

Mrs. Simcote gave Corwyn the slanted smile that meant the chewing-out, at least, was over. "We'll discuss the consequences of your lack of consideration tomorrow, Gwen. Go get some dinner. Corwyn, stay. I have some questions for you." The old lady didn't look at Gwen, just turned her prize over in her hands for a few minutes, examining it with a critical eye. It was a gaudy thing, Corwyn thought, as she felt her sister pass behind her to leave the room.

"We didn't *know* we were going to be so late," she said when the silence went on for a while.

"This is why I so rarely send you anywhere with your sister," Mrs. Simcote said, implacable. "She leads you astray."

"If by 'astray' you mean 'out the way of that crazy old man's rifle,' then she surely did, yes." Corwyn kept her hands still on the arms of her chair and didn't fidget. Backsassing Mrs. Simcote about Gwen took focus.

Mrs. Simcote remained unimpressed. "At least she knows what her job is." She let out a long-suffering sigh and waved a hand in the air in front of her face. "Now. Tell me about the crazy old man."

There wasn't much to tell past the way he changed his mind about selling the skull to them and tried to kill them both, so it didn't take long to relate. Corwyn added the way the skull caught and cast light in long, fingerlike shafts of bright rainbows across whatever surface it rested on, and if she perhaps made it sound like they'd used the skull to find their way out of the old man's warehouse, well, it wasn't *exactly* lying; more like good practice.

A long, chattery noise came from somewhere in the depths of Mrs. Simcote's office before Corwyn was entirely done, but the old lady waved a hand at her. "Out—I got something to do, and I don't need you here while I do it. Go find something to eat."

As the old lady slipped through one of the side doors of her office, Corwyn left through the front and around the stairway to climb to the second floor. The charms that allowed the Volary its basement set Corwyn's knack out of sorts, like something was missing in her head, so she was surprised to find Gwen on the steps, waiting. Gwen let out a long, angry breath and got up to climb the rest of the stairs with Corwyn.

"You didn't tell her about the rocks?" Gwen said.

"No," Corwyn replied. "She'd just have taken them and we'd never get them back." Corwyn liked them. They'd been right handy when the old man doused not only his warehouse lights, but every lamp in the vicinity, including the clockwork ones they'd had in their bags.

"Maybe you ain't so much her pet as I thought," Gwen said. Corwyn bit back the reply that came up into her throat. She didn't have any experience with pets, but she was fairly sure they got scratched behind the ears on occasion for bringing their master his slippers, instead of whatever *that* conversation had been. But *Mrs. Simcote don't have pets* was an old fight between them, and Corwyn didn't feel like getting pulled around by it today.

ONCE THEY'D EATEN AND peeled out of their traveling clothes, Gwen left to see if any of the other fighting knacks wanted to spar on the roof with her. Corwyn settled into her bed to read. No doubt tomorrow would be kitchen work or cleaning the water closet; she'd not have time to read again until later in the week.

She was less than pleased not fifteen minutes later when Jouanna Upright came knocking on doors and yelling at everyone to get downstairs, because Mrs. Simcote had a new kid for them to meet.

Nils's feet appeared dangling at the top of the doorway just as Corwyn opened the door. She waited for him to jump down to the floor before she went through. He had a hammock-type bunk strung up in the rafters over their corner of the third floor; sometimes he banged on their ceiling at night to get them to shut up sniping at each other and go to bed.

"How was Arizona?" he asked as they walked to the bridge. He was still blonde and still mostly squared-off, but he'd gotten lankier in the past few years. He was, like they were, just a year or two away from taking his endowment to light out from the Volary on his own.

"Hot," said Corwyn as they made their swinging way down to the second floor. "And all the mountains looked melted."

"Maybe they were—there's strange stuff out in the desert," Nils said. "I think half the reason she sends us out there is to make sure we never want to leave San Xavier again." Corwyn snorted; Nils grinned. They got along together, and not the "got along" of the uneasy truce Mrs. Simcote insisted on and enforced through making everyone suffer for any fight, prank, or backbiting between her kids. In the face of that rule, Gwen had got much better at sneak attacks and ambushes—nobody called Corwyn Mrs. Simcote's little bloodhound anymore—which she felt was true to the spirit of the Volary and its rules, if not their letter.

But Nils never called Corwyn anything but Corwyn—maybe because Corwyn never called him Bloody Nils like the rest of the kids did—and the two of them rubbed along in ways that reminded Corwyn of the way she'd once got along with Mr. Fritz.

"What'd we miss?" she asked him.

"She's got a new con getting started, with some of the littles. Some fancy clockwork whatchamahoozit she's got her eye on."

"Just the littles? How's that work?"

Nils shrugged. "I'm never in on these things 'til there's blood to clean up." Corwyn couldn't argue; she herself was rarely part of the old lady's long cons unless someone needed finding. And Mrs. Simcote never asked Gwen to be muscle for them, either.

They reached the floor and joined the growing group of kids at the head of Mrs. Simcote's staircase until the last of the stragglers—Gwen among them, unsurprisingly—arrived. "This ain't how she did it with us," Corwyn said. Their own introduction to the Volary had been Mattie Singh showing them a room, the water closet, and the kitchen, followed by two days of trying to figure out where they were going when they were summoned to lessons, and months of near-constant interrogation by the other kids. "She do this with you?"

"Nope," said Nils. "I never seen this much ceremony out of her before. But maybe she was more fanciful in her youth." They all talked about Mrs. Simcote's youth; not a one of her kids believed she'd ever had one to speak of.

Corwyn shifted her weight from one sock-clad foot to the other, longing for her book—it was a good one, adventure in the mountains, snow everywhere, wolves and a witch. Alas.

Dark ringlet curls emerged from the gloom of the stairwell before the soft waves of Mrs. Simcote's updo followed. She was a short lady when she stood up, and the boy with her wasn't much taller. He was dark-skinned, sullen, his nose crooked, bruised under one eye and dirty. He glowered round the crowd of kids, but not right at them; his eyes seemed more to skim over the tops of their heads.

He seemed familiar, but Corwyn couldn't place him. Maybe it was just the attitude, or the bruising—most kids came into the Volary with one or the other, though not usually both.

Mrs. Simcote's glare took in each of them. Corwyn occasionally thought that Mrs. Simcote's knack wasn't sensing other knacks so much as it was being able to look at all of her thirty-odd kids at once. She dropped her skirt with a flourish, the signal to pay attention, and the group went silent.

"The Misses Teachout are the only ones of you with reason to be ignorant of Veigar Olafurson's death," she said. Corwyn's eyes snapped to Gwen's, *we've been to his house!* strung between their gaping expressions. "Life in the Hill ain't going to be a picnic for anybody for a while—you've all already been told to be careful, keep your damn heads down, don't get caught. Well, that's doubled now because this—" she put a hand on the boy's shoulder and gave it a small shake; the kid shot her a sideways look of pure black hate that was impressive in its audacity, "—is Ioren Gudrunson, Veigar Olafurson's grandson. He's under our protection, now. Treat him as one of our own. Nobody get killed." She gave Ioren a push towards the group and, grabbing her skirt in one hand and the bannister in the other, descended to her office.

He looked directly at them, finally, assessing like he thought he might have to fight them all. Jouanna, their forger who could never keep her mouth shut, spoke up. "What's your knack?"

"I ain't got one."

The group was silent for a long, stunned minute, then he whispered outrage began like cracks in a frozen puddle. Mrs. Simcote only ever took in kids with knacks.

"What the hell'd your grandpa have on the old lady that she'd take you in knackless?" asked Frank Klied. *His* knack was being able to make poison out of just about anything. He never got kitchen duty.

Ioren Gudrunson ducked his head and grinned all twisty at his hands, shaking them out like maybe he was going to play piano, and said, "I guess I got my uses."

Corwyn knew where she'd seen him before: bloody and puking in an alley in Pallasgreen.

Gwen knew, too; Corwyn saw it in her face when she piped up, "Come on, we'll find you a bed."

THEY NEITHER OF THEM said anything to him that night; just asked him if he wanted a room with a door, or just a bed, or one of the hammock-cocoon contraptions like Nils had, where you could hear the world even though you needed to hide from it.

"A room," he said. "With a door, for preference."

"We got an empty one," Gwen said, leading him round the terrace to the other side from their room. "Things get crowded, though, you may end up sharing."

"Oh. All right, then," he said, distracted, peering down to the second floor. The other kids were drifting upstairs or going about their business down there; Corwyn saw Mattie Singh disappearing into one of the laboratory rooms and decided to stay up late so the explosion later wouldn't scare her awake.

She wondered how the Volary looked to Ioren Gudrunson, after growing up in his grandfather's big house in Pallasgreen with pillars on the porch and a clockwork butler inside. Following Mattie to their room, tired and tense and uncertain, this place had looked like heaven to Corwyn—or a haven, anyway. Someplace safe, finally. Someplace she didn't have to watch her back. Well, past the stupid shit kids always pulled on each other, but the old lady kept a tight lid on that, too.

Ioren eyed the crisscross of catwalks and rope ladders and just plain ropes that connected the third and second floors. Eulala Hosse and Rufus Tominey, both fighting knacks, scrambled up them like spiders. "You all right?" Corwyn asked him.

"It looks like a ship," he said, his voice far away.

"You and your grandfather sail a lot?" she asked.

"No—my mum was a sailor. And my dad. I grew up in rigging 'til I was six or seven."

Corwyn, uneasy in the face of two parents, even if they were both probably dead, said, "Go ahead and climb it all, if you want. It don't belong to anyone in particular, no matter what anybody says."

"Thank you," he replied, still distracted.

Gwen waited by the door of the empty room. "It don't lock," she said when they joined her. "Nobody'll steal your stuff, though, because Gertie Penzik has a knack for sussing liars."

"I ain't got much stuff," he said, and then, "Am I—she makes you, the old lady—you work, yeah? Do I start now, or ...?"

"She'll leave you be tonight," Corwyn said. "Whatever she's got planned for you, it'll start tomorrow."

"Probably lessons," Gwen said with an eye roll. "You'll recite every blame thing you know a thousand times, and show what you can do twice that."

"Kitchen's on the second floor. There's usually some kind of dinner round dusk, breakfast round sunrise. Otherwise you fend for yourself. Water closet's over there—" she pointed.

"Thank you," Ioren said, and with a last assessing look at the two of them, he slipped into his room and shut the door behind him.

Corwyn and Gwen exchanged a glance, then walked back around the terrace to their room as fast as they could without giving it away by running.

"WE HELPED VEIGAR OLAFURSON'S grandson when he was puking in a goddamned alley!" The grin on Gwen's face as she leaned against their closed door was huge; Corwyn hadn't seen that kind of a smile on Gwen in a while.

"D'you think he recognized us?" she asked.

"Dunno—we were filthy back then. He was covered in blood and puke, and he was still cleaner than we were." Gwen sat on the bed and pulled off her shoes, tucking her feet up under herself. Corwyn did the same. "You think we ought to do anything with this information?" Gwen asked.

"Dunno there's much to do with it besides shame him with it at some point, maybe."

"Yeah," said Gwen, nodding. "Keep it for later in case he's a jackass."

"Think he will be?" Corwyn asked. She felt giddy, a little like she remembered floating felt in her stomach; she wanted to keep Gwen talking.

"He's Veigar Olafurson's grandson, I bet the odds are pretty good," Gwen said. They fell quiet; Corwyn pulled her knees up to her chin and leaned her head against them, thinking as the silence stretched out that Gwen would likely leave or fall asleep soon, but then Gwen said, "I wonder who managed to kill him? Olafurson?"

It was a good question. Veigar Olafurson was as powerful a gang lord as San Xavier had ever seen—even Mrs. Simcote owed him favors, it looked like. Killing him would be like Vadoma Hildago dying: the larger city would pause; the Hill would come to a stop; and the chaos that followed would fall on everyone with a crash like a pillar collapsing out from under the roof of St. Phil's.

Corwyn grinned into her knees. "Osian Lauredent," she said.

Gwen let out a loud snort. "If Osian Lauredent managed that, I'll drown myself in the damn bay."

"Maybe Allen Brogan—Tansa told him she wanted Olafurson's head for an anniversary present."

Gwen made a skeptical noise. "Tansa Brogan wants someone's head, she'd go chop it off herself, cranky bitch." Corwyn laughed at that, and Gwen went on, "No, you know who might've done it? Madame Tereza!"

"In her fancy nightgown!" Corwyn crowed. "With that fireplace shovel she chases people off with in the morning!"

"She's a damn terror," Gwen said, giggling and defensive. "And you know Mr. Fritz knows where to hide a corpse."

Corwyn had no actual idea if Mr. Fritz's talents extended to corpse disposal, but she was too delighted by Gwen's smile to say so. But then it dimmed, the smile, though Gwen's eyes didn't. "You know who'd know," she said.

Corwyn nodded. "Miss Vadoma."

MISS VADOMA, IN THE end, knew very little. Corwyn waited until she was only half-paying attention before she asked.

"What the hell you want to know that for?" Miss Vadoma asked.

"Why the hell wouldn't I want to know that? I'm nosy. And his grandson's at Mrs. Simcote's now."

That got a surprised expression from the witch. "Really? Well, someone's thinking."

"So you don't know who did it," Corwyn said. She flexed her hands, her fingers swollen and stiff.

"There be a surfeit of possibilities," Miss Vadoma said, most of her attention still on Corwyn's hands. "Every gang lord in the Hill wanted him dead, but not a one of them, so far as anyone knows, has the wherewithal to have done it, between his people and that nasty thing he kept as a bodyguard."

"The what now?"

"Some bloody creature. Literally. He swanned 'round with it when he first got started, years ago. Mostly he used it for intimidation, but sometimes he let it rip someone's head or arm off."

"Nasty."

"As I said. Anyway. Veigar died messy. Someone cut him up like dinner. Lift that."

Corwyn followed Miss Vadoma's pointing finger and frowned at the bucket. It looked to be cast-iron. "What is it?"

"Heavy." Corwyn obediently hefted it and put it back down, easy.

"So it's been bad, now he's dead?" Corwyn asked.

Miss Vadoma took her hands and looked them over, front and back, then her forearms. "Was it heavy?"

"It was hefty, but not too bad. My hand hurts now, but I reckon that's the swelling."

Miss Vadoma dropped Corwyn's hands and cast about for her notebook. "It's not been bad. Yet. This is the indrawn breath as everyone takes a good look round. The Tongs and the Dockworkers' Union have been living on the kindnesses of the Goldbergs, the d'Souzas, and the Brogans, so they're looking at a chance to get their own territory. Ain't nobody's gotten any new turf in the Hill in thirty-odd years ... you tell me what you think, Corwyn Teachout. You ain't stupid."

"What about his grandson, though? He's the heir, right?"

Miss Vadoma didn't look up from scribbling her notes. "He's neither old nor white enough to hold the scrobs together. Veigar's folk, the ones he trusted? They double down and keep him alive a couple years, maybe he's got a little bit of empire left to build on. His grandpa put that gang together with fish paste and spit, so. Could happen. Likely not, but it could." Miss Vadoma fixed Corwyn with a glare. "You keep your head down and an eye on your sister—there'll be plenty of blood sport to get her in trouble."

YES, WELL, KEEPING an eye on Gwen wasn't as easy as once it had been. Their different knacks meant they had different lessons and different duties, and while Corwyn's knack was unique amongst Mrs. Simcote's current crop of kids, Gwen had other kids with fighting knacks to spar with and talk to. But Gwen'd been sneaking out through the attic before they took their trip, looking for trouble with the bigger boys in the Hill, so Corwyn would make sure to warn her.

Miss Vadoma was right, though: as Corwyn made her way back to the Volary, it seemed all of Cobbler's Hill was holding its breath.

"SO YOU'RE HERE ON PITY, then," Corwyn heard as she closed the entryway door behind her. She saw a gang of kids in the middle of the floor and heard Cyrus Blackburn over them. "You got no knack, just the old lady's guilt or something."

"You don't know a goddamned thing about me," Ioren Gudrunson said. He was barefoot and looked not entirely awake, which was a bit scandalous at this hour of the morning. The fact that he'd gotten to sleep that late was probably what got Cy on his case. "I don't need a fighting knack to beat your sorry ass."

"That ain't saying much; Cy fights for shit." Gwen's drawl came from overhead; she was sitting on one of the catwalks overhead, legs dangling.

Ioren and Cy both started, then glared up at her. "You got any skills to speak of?" Ioren asked.

The group got quiet. Gwen swung her legs. "I might," she said. She looked Ioren over and said, "You want to find out?"

WELL, OF COURSE HE did, so they all of them trooped to the third floor and up the stairs to the roof. Corwyn got a good spot at the front by dint of being Gwen's sister. The air up here was cool and the day sunny; her stomach showed no ill-effects from Miss Vadoma's potion, and the wind kept any nasty smells from the roof next door away from them.

Ioren tied his curls back with a piece of string while Gwen checked the laces on her boots. There was something—gang tattoo?—behind his ear, but Corwyn couldn't quite make it out from this distance. Gwen and Ioren nodded at each other and started circling round, sizing each other up.

Gwen was more patient, now: her muscles loosened as she looked at Ioren from her slowly-emptying eyes, her knack waking up, but she watched and waited to see what he'd do. Ioren was patient, too; he grinned a little when he realized she wasn't going to rush him.

"You planning to bore each other to death?" asked Nils from somewhere behind Corwyn.

Ioren glanced at the crowd, then back at Gwen. He gave a little shrug and darted in—quick, quick—to kick her. She caught his leg—nobody was as fast as Gwen—and tossed him backward. He regained his balance right away and stood bouncing on the balls of his feet, smiling. Gwen smiled back, the lunatic grin she got just before she gave in to her knack, then with a skip she went after him.

They were both fast: not many punches landed as they ducked away from each other; when a blow did land they bounced away from it. They couldn't fight too hard—Mrs. Simcote had rules about damaging each other for fun—but Corwyn had never seen Gwen fight this all-out since they'd come to the Volary. She was sweating, starting to breathe heavy, and so was he, sure, but ... nobody'd held their own with her sister since they were little kids and Lars Hallstrom broke her ribs.

The other Simcote kids cheered, but Corwyn pulled her knees to her chin and just watched.

Ioren danced back out of the fight, shaking back the hair that had fallen out of its string. Maybe only Corwyn saw the flash of calculation on his face before he dove for Gwen and got her face-down in the grit and tar of the roof with both hands pinned and his knee in her back. He put a hand around her neck, then, and in the sudden silence of the other kids' shock, said, "See? You're dead."

"Yeah, but so're you," Gwen said cheerfully as Corwyn, silent but not slow at all, herself, put both her hands around Ioren's sticky, sweaty neck.

MUCH LATER THAT EVENING they sat in Corwyn and Gwen's room, attempting to teach Ioren how to play Dilly-O.

"You can't use an ace against a four like that," Corwyn said, leaning over to adjust Ioren's card. "You play it sideways for defense or upside down to show you're traveling."

"What if I want to attack?" he asked.

"Can't attack with an ace," Gwen said equably.

"You used an ace to assassinate my King!"

"No, my Jack used an ace to protect himself in a duel."

"That's what I'd call a vehement defense, then," Ioren said darkly. "And I still can't decide if you were cheating or not, before on the roof."

"That ain't cheating—that's using every advantage you got," Gwen said. She frowned over Ioren's cards and put down a six of hearts. "The four is now a three and the eldritch phantasm is manifesting."

"What if your sister's not there, then?" he asked.

"I'd have been dead, maybe, but I'd've taken you with me." Corwyn's back went straight, but Gwen's voice was light.

"Not much of a victory, everybody dead," Ioren observed, tentatively setting a seven of clubs upside down over Gwen's six, glancing a question between them. Corwyn nodded stiffly and he pulled his hand back. "It won't fully manifest for three more turns."

"Two. But fine. And I take whatever victories I can get," Gwen said. She sat back, assessing Ioren over her hand. "You ain't been in many fights, I don't think."

Ioren didn't answer, but Corwyn reckoned his hand would've been in flames if looks could have set cards on fire. "I've seen my share of violence," he said quietly.

Corwyn thought of his red-ringed hands when they'd met and said, "We've no doubt of that, no."

"I know who you are, you know—the Teachout girls."

Corwyn and Gwen exchanged a look, but neither of them said anything. Finally, Ioren looked up at them both and said, "You're the ones as killed Beatriz d'Souza's grandson, few years back."

"That we are," Gwen said to her cards. "Or I am, anyway."

"You're infamous, the two of you." Ioren had a sweet, sly grin that Corwyn didn't much like the looks of.

"How'd you manage to get the better of me?" Gwen asked; she sounded honestly curious, but also still calculating. "Ain't nobody here ever managed to beat me before."

"I've no doubt of that, no," he echoed slowly, wary. "You're really fast. But you get in thrall to your knack and you leave yourself open in spots. There were a couple other times I could have got you at the knees, but I waited to see if it was a pattern."

Corwyn didn't say how fast Ioren must be to have seen that; Gwen grinned and said, "I think ... you and me could have a very mutually beneficial relationship, Mr. Gudrunson, if you're interested."

The wariness eased out of Ioren's face—Corwyn felt it take up residence in her neck and the small of her back as he smiled at Gwen. Corwyn took the Queen of spades out of her hand and put it down sideways over the pile in the middle. "The Empress of Air and Darkness. Dilly-O," she said, and scooped up the cards as Gwen's grin went wicked sharp and Ioren's head snapped around, his mouth open to protest.

THAT NIGHT CORWYN HAD the dream again, the locked room on the second floor of the Volary and her fingertips bloody from clawing at the door, her ragged breath and the scratching inside the walls as her knack howled to haul her through them.

She woke with a jerk that brought her halfway up off her pillow, silent, then fell back onto the bed and rubbed at her eyes with one hand. She could still hear the scratching, then a thump, from the direction of their baseboards—something in the walls along the second floor, she reckoned—before it subsided. She'd forgotten she'd even heard it by the time all her muscles unclenched.

There'd be no sleeping for a while, so Corwyn turned over to reach under her bed for one of the glowing rocks, and got her book from the bedside stand.

Gwen slept on in the other bed, the glow from the rocks casting her face green. Corwyn watched her for a while, reminding herself they were both here, both safe.

CHAPTER THIRTEEN

The door creaked and Memno Busignani's voice broke over the near-silent dark: "Corwyn, the old lady wants you."

Corwyn pulled the blindfold off her face. She used it to wipe the sweat from under her eyes before putting her lockpick kit back together and sliding both into her pocket.

She stepped carefully around the other kids in the room. Some wore blindfolds and some didn't. All of them picked locks of varying difficulties—mechanical, alchemical, charmed—under the watchful eye of Ruby Mulligan, who could fix anything they broke, and Bolivar Crespo, who was likely the best lockpick in the Hill and had been one of Mrs. Simcote's kids before the rest of them were born. He looked almost as old as the old lady did. He watched Corwyn leave with mild interest, then turned back to Ned Shuluk, hissing, "If the Greek don't work, use Latin, you idiot child."

The Volary sat quiet, as it usually did this time of day: kids were doing lessons or out in the Hill on errands for Mrs. Simcote. A few of the smaller kids sat in a corner, frowning over a map. Corwyn's footsteps echoed as she made her way downstairs, mingling with some muffled clanking from inside one of the workshop rooms she passed.

She knocked on Mrs. Simcote's office door and went in right after—the old lady wanted a warning, but she also wanted you in front of her right away when she called—to find her sitting behind her desk, looking over a piece of paper while smoking her pipe.

"You called me, Mrs. S?"

"I did. Hold on a minute, the other one'll be here momentarily." The pipe-smoke smelled of tobacco and apples; it permeated the room. The fresh tendrils of it stood out sharp against the muted ghosts of pipes past.

There were boot-sounds on the stairs, then a knock. Ioren Gudrunson came through the door.

"Corwyn, there's a boy with a knack, and I need you to find him for me." Mrs. Simcote gave Ioren a severe look. "You're to go with Corwyn. Watch her back." Ioren asked no questions, just nodded, his face impassive.

"Find me the boy with the knack for finding things," the old lady intoned. She didn't need the dramatic voice, but she always used it, to Corwyn's amusement and Gwen's annoyance. It did the job to wake Corwyn's knack up, anyway. It felt groggy, off-center, sharpening the farther from the basement she got.

Once they reached the street with the Volary door shut behind them, Ioren asked, "Why do I have to watch your back, now?"

"Things go a little fuzzy round the edges when my knack's pulling," Corwyn replied absently. "You come back with a black eye and a goose egg a couple times and you're never trusted to find someone without a bodyguard again."

She paused at the corner and felt the pull south. They turned to follow it.

"So ... your knack's finding," Ioren said.

"People," Corwyn said. "Not things." Which was why a kid with a knack for finding *things* would surely be valuable for Mrs. Simcote.

"Oh." Ioren fell silent. Corwyn followed her knack.

They walked up Wickham Street, the faint briny scent of the docks giving way to a duller, earthier smell as they neared Jersey Court Road. Ioren kept up with no complaints; they passed the Brogans' warehouse and the tiny patch of brown grass that was the orphans' graveyard. He kept an eye out as they went, though whether that was for the sake of Corwyn's skin or his own she couldn't have said.

"How come she didn't send your sister with you?" he asked after awhile.

"She don't send us out together much. She says it's unhealthy and we need to learn how to work with other people," Corwyn recited. Ioren didn't respond. He kept looking over his shoulder and up toward the rooftops as they walked. "You nervous, being out in the open?" Corwyn asked.

"I confess to some concern as to whether Mrs. Simcote's protection will be taken seriously on my account," he said dryly, and Corwyn laughed.

"Ain't no way she'd feed you if she thought she couldn't keep you alive," she said. "She'll want you to pay back the investment, no matter what she owed your grandfather."

He didn't say anything in response, leaving Corwyn to trudge along with half her head taken up with her knack and the other half wondering what Veigar Olafurson had over Mrs. Simcote. That led to other wonderings, and she thought maybe she could get an answer for one of them, so she said, "How come your last name's Gudrunson? I didn't think your dad was Nordic."

"He wasn't." Ioren sighed, then said, "It's a thing, from the old country. Tradition—your dad's first name's your surname. Olafur's son. Veigar's son. I didn't know I should have another name when I got here, and then Grandfather sure wasn't going to let me have my dad's name, and *his* name, well. *I* wasn't gonna take that. My mum was Gudrun. I figured Veigar couldn't argue if I told him I wanted my mum's name instead."

There was something more there, hidden in how he held his mouth crooked and grim. "Did he?" Corwyn asked. "Argue?"

Ioren shook his head. "No. He cried, point of fact."

Corwyn had a hard time imagining that, but it may have been because, since she didn't know what Veigar Olafurson looked like, her imagination put Mr. Katsaros in the role. She shook her head, then asked, "How'd you not know your last name? Hell, I knew my last name and I just barely had a mother."

He shrugged. "We were aboard ship. Everyone knew who I was."

THEY FOUND THE KID in an alley next to what was left of his father—well, presumably it was his father, based off the crying he was doing and how he hadn't moved away from the corpse yet. Corwyn was surprised the Jacks patrolling Pallasgreen hadn't found them, the alley being this close to Jersey Court Road.

"Is it usually like this, finding kids for her?" Ioren asked, eyebrows raised.

"Sometimes," Corwyn said, her knack appeased now. "But usually when their parents are dead it ain't quite so recent."

"This is going to suck," Ioren muttered. *Suck* was a new one on Corwyn, but she didn't ask, just followed Ioren into the alley.

It smelled of shit and blood. The wind blew the stench mostly away from the two of them, but that sent it right into the kid's face. He'd puked at least once. Corwyn and Ioren picked their way around the vomit and bits of corpse. Ioren lowered himself next to the boy. "You the kid with the finding knack?"

The kid glared. "Who in hell are you?" His voice was wet and squeaked.

"You know who Mrs. Simcote is?" Corwyn asked.

"My dad did. He didn't like her." The boy wiped the back of his hand over his face and sniffed hard.

Ioren glanced at the corpse, then back to the kid. "You see what did this to your dad?" Ioren asked. Corwyn idly looked the body over as Ioren talked: eyes open but rolled up into his head; looked like his throat had been hacked at with a dull knife, all ragged edges and lots of blood; stomach wide open and spilling out onto the cement.

"Not—it was fast, and it—" The boy coughed, but he didn't puke. "It had claws. And it was a thing, not a person, I ain't—"

"Mrs. Simcote would like to offer you a place to stay," Corwyn interrupted. Ioren shot her a look, maybe because she was using her posh-but-not-too-fancy Pallasgreen accent to keep her voice steady. "She's taken an interest in your knack. We learn a lot about our knacks, in the Volary. And Mrs. Simcote takes good care of her kids. You look like you could use some caretaking."

The kid couldn't have been much older than Corwyn had been when she and Gwen came to stay at the Volary, but the way his mouth pursed at the offer was the reaction of an old man. "Well, I got nowhere else to go, do I?" he asked. Then he did retch, threw up some bile, and climbed to his feet.

He swayed, looking down at his dead father. He clenched his jaw before leaning over to dip both hands into the blood-soaked pockets of his dad's pants, coming up with a battered, stained handkerchief that he stuck in his own pocket. "Lead the way," he said.

None of them spoke on the way back. Sometimes kids had questions about the Volary or the old lady, but the boy cried silently as they walked, his hand bunched in his pocket.

"We need to tell anyone about the body?" Ioren whispered.

"Mrs. Simcote. She'll take care of it. We got rules about corpses we find."

"I do not doubt that," Ioren said in a dark tone.

Corwyn made herself not think about some clawed thing roaming the Hill where Gwen ran around alone at night looking for more training than Mrs. Simcote provided her.

They dropped the boy, clutching his handkerchief and still leaking tears, at Mrs. Simcote's office. They left at her nod.

"I guess she don't mind crying," Ioren said quietly when they reached the stairs.

"Rumor is she saves the tears to bathe in," Corwyn said, her voice not as light as she'd have liked.

Ioren stopped on the stairs, one hand on the banister, the other picking at something on his neck. Corwyn paused. "You all right?" she asked.

"You ever find people for anyone else?"

"Sometimes. When they can pay me. And if it's a fast job."

"I got some money." Ioren's eyes rested steady on her face. "D'you think you could find whoever it was killed my grandfather?"

Corwyn's knack, unsurprisingly, didn't so much as fidget. "You got anything more than that?" she asked carefully.

"Someone uses blades, but more than that, no."

"Likely not, then," she replied, as kindly as she could. People got funny sometimes when she told them no, and he was a match for Gwen in a fight. "Most times I need a name, or a smell, or a knack. Something specific." She paused, then asked, "You looking for revenge, Ioren Gudrunson?"

He snorted and shot her a look she couldn't read. "Of course I am. I took a blood oath." He swept his curls up off the side of his head, revealing a small, bloody brand mark behind his left ear. "It'll bleed 'til I'm done, or it'll kill me."

Corwyn stared, fascinated by the way the blood oozed out of the wound but never dripped down his neck to call attention to itself. "Killing you seems contrary to the goal," she observed.

Ioren let his hair drop. "Usually you know who you're after," he sighed. "And they can charm it, you know. As long as I'm trying Veigar's people won't let it kill me."

"There ain't, say, a charm to aim you in the right direction or something? They just cursed you and that's that?"

Ioren shrugged. "They don't trust me not to run off to sea and let them all hang. I made no secret of wanting to be a sailor."

"Well, that's your first mistake—never tell people anything unless you have to, and then only half of what they want to know." Corwyn took a step up. "Does it hurt? Make you sick?"

"It hurts. It's not making me too sick yet. You get used to it."

Well, that was true enough of anything. "If you find out more, come see me and we'll talk."

"Yeah, all right," he replied, and sat down on the steps as she turned for her room.

CHAPTER FOURTEEN

Gwen had usually spent her free time—what little of it they got, and some of it skivving off chores—picking fights in the Hill and getting paid by kids from rival gangs to rough each other up without the gang lords knowing. But now she spent that time on the roof, sparring with Ioren. Which was a relief, on one hand, considering the variety of ways, from monsters to gangsters, Gwen could get into trouble. On the other hand, which Corwyn didn't want to think about because it made her spine clench up and her brain feel sour, it was not. When she could, Corwyn slipped up to watch the sparring, along with whichever Volary residents who weren't out on errands for the old lady or in on her current long game.

"You missed a good opportunity to get the high ground!" Ioren told Gwen from where he'd landed on his back.

"I rushed you and knocked you on your ass—why would I need the high ground?"

"I dunno, a concussion would have kept me from getting back up and breaking your arm?"

"Is *that* what you were trying to do?" Gwen asked, rubbing her forearm absently. "Look, my knack kicks and I don't see the high ground, I just see the easiest way to hurt you."

Ioren looked skeptical. "I don't believe that—your sister ate falafel and told me the history of that orphan's home you lived in while we were following her knack to that kid who can train dogs."

"Ginger Schwetje," Nils provided. "It's any animal, too. Not just dogs."

Ioren spared Nils an unamused glance as he brushed off the back of his pants. "I'm just saying, if Corwyn can think through hers, you can think through yours."

"To be fair, Gwen's usually got a number of pressing concerns when her knack kicks," Corwyn said. She pulled her shirt over her nose to filter out the smoky smell from the next building.

"No, he makes a good point," Gwen replied, thoughtful. Corwyn rolled her eyes and settled in to hate Ioren's face as he and Gwen started back throwing punches. It was slower this time. Gwen seemed clumsier somehow, even as she deflected and ducked and landed her hits. She was *thinking*, Corwyn guessed sourly.

"Corwyn, the old lady wants you!" Jouanna called from the roof door. Ioren and Gwen didn't seem to notice as she got up to leave.

"AND HOW IS IOREN SETTLING in?" the old lady asked Corwyn, peering over her desk. It wasn't completely out of the usual for Mrs. Simcote to ask Corwyn about the other kids when she summoned her downstairs, but it startled Corwyn to realize that Ioren Gudrunson was now part of the pack Mrs. Simcote thought she ran with.

"Fine, I guess?" she said, thinking about it. He didn't seem *happy*, but who did? Especially considering his death seeping blood behind his ear. But the fighting knacks had claimed him as their own, which made the other kids stop their hazing. So, fine.

"Your sister seems fond of him," Mrs. Simcote said, distractedly, turning to search her desk drawers for something.

"I guess," Corwyn said again. It didn't seem a good idea to tell Mrs. Simcote that Ioren Gudrunson was more of an education in Gwen's knack than the old lady had ever seen fit to provide her. Or the other fighting knacks, for that matter. So she shrugged. "As fond as Gwen gets of anyone, anyway."

"Oh, it looks a sight more than *that*." Mrs. Simcote found what she'd been looking for—an envelope and a key—and placed them on the desktop. She either did not notice or ignored the way Corwyn's back had gone straight. "Not a bad alliance to make, though, assuming he can get his grandfather's revenge sorted. Smarter move than I'd expect from Gwen, really, and 'twould surely make *my* life easier when the time comes for her to leave, so keep an eye on her, Corwyn. Make sure she doesn't fuck it up."

Corwyn said nothing, just ground her teeth together. She felt too warm, anger and shame and some other emotions she didn't have names for roiling behind her ribs. And who were they about, all those feelings? She couldn't separate that out, either—Gwen, Ioren, Mrs. Simcote, herself; it was just a tangle of feelings and people that she couldn't tease apart while she sat in the old lady's office.

Mrs. Simcote pushed the envelope and the key across the desk to Corwyn. "Take this to DeKalb, please," she said, her voice gentle. "Time to brand my new chicks."

WHITTINGTON'S TATTOO parlor was just over Selwyn Avenue, but not quite at the docks. It kept a certain neutrality, tattooing all the gangsters in the Hill save for the Tongs, who maintained their own tattooists.

Dekalb Vickery was the most recent of Mrs. Simcote's kids with a weak talent for magic and a strong knack for intricate designs. Like the others before him, the old lady set him up at Derrick Whittington's tattoo parlor with the understanding that he would ink Mrs. Simcote's kids for as long as he tattooed in the Hill.

Corwyn met Dekalb outside the front door and handed him the envelope and the key Mrs. Simcote had given her. "This is from the old lady," she said, probably unnecessarily; Dekalb, having tattooed her, knew who she was and who she belonged to.

"How many new kids she got?" he asked, looking at the key curiously.

"Just two," Corwyn replied.

"What's the key for?"

"I figured you'd know—she gave me both."

Dekalb looked confused. "She's never sent me a key before." He opened the envelope and scanned the note inside. "This is just names. No mention of a key."

He handed it back. Corwyn pocketed it, stomach turning uneasy. But she feigned unconcern. "On your head be it, then, if I have to schlep back out here with it."

"She ain't gonna be mad at *you*, Corwyn," he called after her. Hell and damnation, *everyone* thought she was Mrs. Simcote's pet—Dekalb Vickery'd been out of the Volary for years now, lord.

Corwyn swiped an apple from a grocer's cart on her way back. The day was gray and the streets were crowded, so she meandered home while eating her lunch.

Nils met her at the door in the foyer, face set in a very particular way that made her think she ought to have rushed back.

"Is it Gwen?" she asked.

Nils shook his head. "Come on."

He led her to the second floor and the far-back corner closet that was Corwyn's least favorite place in the Volary. Hell, in the Hill. It was too small to do much more than store stuff or keep kids in when Mrs. Simcote wanted to test their knacks.

It had to be Antoine in there; Ioren had no knack to test.

"She told him to find the key to the room." Nils sounded a little sick, a little scared. After Corwyn's testing, when Gwen was being punished for rushing the old lady, Nils had been assigned to keep an eye on Corwyn. He'd told her he'd been the one to clean the entire room, including the floor. "I ain't sure what half those stains were from," he'd said, with a half smile that looked more ill than kidding.

Corwyn dug in her pocket, hearing the swish of long skirts behind her and smelling the distinctive scent of Mrs. Simcote: tobacco and apples, with a trace of blood at the edges. "He really needed to be locked up, ma'am?" she asked without looking.

"Between your testing and Mattie's, I lock everyone up," the old lady replied. Mattie'd apparently blown all the windows out of the building with her test. Mixed water and alcohol or some nonsense.

Corwyn gave the key to Mrs. Simcote, who unlocked the door and opened it. Corwyn didn't know what to expect. Her time in the closet had ended with a bloody forehead and torn up fingertips. She remembered smelling puke. She refused to remember smelling anything else.

Antoine sat in the corner closest to the tiny, high window that let in the only light the room got, his hands flat on the floor and his eyes shut. He'd leaned his head into the place where the walls met, his face aimed at the ceiling. He muttered something—from the rhythm of it, maybe the Prayer for Intercession from Saint Therinetta—and didn't move when Mrs. Simcote approached.

Mrs. Simcote held the key out to Antoine. He opened his knack-fogged eyes before slowly lowering his head. Corwyn saw his knack recede once his fingers touched the metal, his muscles dropping loose and the clouds clearing from his eyes.

The old lady took his hand to haul him up standing. She smiled and ran her fingers through his hair, which he allowed but did not look happy about. Corwyn didn't remember if Mrs. Simcote had done that for her when she came out of the room. All Corwyn remembered was Gwen's frantic, angry expression and her trembling hands skipping and grazing the unbruised bits of Corwyn's face, holding Corwyn's fingers to see if they were broken, and the sweet smell of apples and salt blood in the air around them both.

CORWYN WALKED ANTOINE to the ladder of his hanging bed. She'd spent two days in the infirmary after her testing, but Antoine seemed unhurt.

"What were you reciting?" she asked as he put his hands on the ladder. "When we opened the door?"

"Oh. Directions. To get to the key."

He still seemed off. Not quite there. "You all right?" Corwyn asked.

He looked over at her, face slightly puzzled, and said, "I'm fine. My ma used to like to play with me like that, when I was little, ask me to find stars or unicorns or that kind of shit. She thought it was funny. Or sometimes it'd go sideways like it was just trying to find something to fit, and she could sell some of that stuff. So she kept doing it." He let out a long, tired sigh. "I knew the key would show up sooner or later—the old lady don't want me dead or nothing. So. Just had to hang on 'til she brought it in."

Corwyn thought about poems, then, all the ones she had tucked away in her head for when she needed them. She thought maybe she'd recited some in the closet, before it got too bad, but she wasn't sure.

Antoine shrugged. That was the most he'd said to her or anyone since he'd gotten to the Volary; he'd been sulky and silent since he'd walked through the door, and Corwyn couldn't blame him much for it because he wasn't taking it out on anybody. She watched him climb into his bed-sack, thought about going to her etiquette lesson, but decided in the end to go read her book instead.

When Gwen came in later, sweaty and grinning from a sparring session with Ioren, Corwyn answered that her day was fine, nothing exciting, she'd swiped an apple off a cart and delivered mail to Dekalb Vickery.

A COUPLE DAYS AFTER Corwyn delivered his list, Dekalb showed up at the Volary with needles and ink in a bag, and everything went to hell immediately.

A door slammed underneath the floor of the kitchen, where Corwyn and Nils peeled vegetables. Mrs. Simcote snapped, "Ioren Gudrunson!" in a carrying voice such that they dropped their knives and ran for the stairwell to see the bloodshed.

Thus they heard Ioren's, "It's not going to happen. I already got my grandfather's mark on me." His tone was adult and almost conversational, not like anything Corwyn had heard out of a kid before.

Mrs. Simcote's tone, to her amazement, matched Ioren's. "Without my mark on you, I can't guarantee my protection," she said. "I owe a debt to your grandfather—"

"I *know* that," he replied, and now he sounded like a boy again.

"He's got balls," Nils said, admiringly.

Not for long, if he's not careful, Corwyn thought, but she didn't say it because Ioren's voice had gotten softer. "I have my own debt to Veigar, and it's likely the same size as yours, Mrs. Simcote. I can't repay it if his people think my loyalties are divided."

"Yours," she said. "Your people. Not his. If you're going to take over Veigar's empire, Ioren, you'd best start thinking of it as yours."

They heard Ioren's boots on the stairs and hightailed it back to the kitchen, even though they knew both Ioren and Mrs. Simcote would hear them and know they'd been eavesdropping. Appearances were important.

"She made Memno and Eulala hold Jouanna down for her tattoo," Nils said. "I can't believe she let him out of it."

"He's an exception to a lot of rules," Corwyn said, not sure if she meant it admiringly or resentfully.

"You think he'll do it? Take over his grandpa's empire?"

That bleeding brand might kill him before he got the chance to try. There'd been a few days he'd looked peaked and gray; his grandfather's people—*Ioren's people*, she corrected herself—showed up regularly and seemed to improve things, but their patience wouldn't last forever. And if he managed to find the killer, well ... Corwyn thought about what Miss Vadoma had said—*He's neither old nor white enough to hold the scrobs together.* "If he does, it won't be easy, tattoos or not," she finally said, glad it was none of her affair.

They peeled and chopped in silence for a while, then Jouanna came swanning into the kitchen. She stood across the table from Corwyn, deliberately caught her eye, and pronounced, "*Antoine Gre-goire.*"

Corwyn rolled her eyes, irritated. "You know it don't work like that, go do your own damn chores." Corwyn's knack rarely kicked for anyone in the Volary without more coaxing than just a name.

"Can't fault a girl for trying," Jouanna said, turning to leave.

"Like hell I can't!" Corwyn called after her.

Corwyn could remember, vaguely, the first couple weeks they'd lived at the Home, her knack lurching and receding often enough to make her sick. This was coupled with the far more visceral memory of frantically trying to force it to kick during the fire. Gwen, the other fighting knacks, most of the kids in the Volary, seemed like they could turn their knacks on like a faucet—getting them back off again once they'd kicked was more the problem. The only thing Corwyn could do on command was find her sister, and nobody seemed to know why.

"I guess Antoine ain't keen on being tattooed, neither," Nils said.

"I guess not."

After they passed the peeled vegetables onto Cyrus Blackburn, whose cooking knack meant he got to oversee dinner every night, Nils went to diction lessons with Lucy Adair, and Corwyn, not due at comportment for another hour, found herself at loose ends. She stood beneath the criss-crossed ladders and bridges to the third floor considering whether or not she could make it to the falafel cart and back again before lessons.

Jouanna, looking aggrieved, stepped back through the third floor door to the roof. It'd been at least an hour since she'd annoyed Corwyn in the kitchen, and she still hadn't found Antoine. Corwyn was likely about to get summoned to smell Antoine's pillow and go find him. If she wanted falafel, she'd have to go now.

But as she stood there, she got a hunch.

Next to the Volary stood an abandoned, boarded-up boarding-house that took up the rest of the block. Its roof was riddled with odd vents and chimneys that occasionally belched rotten-smelling smoke or steam, but that didn't deter Mrs. Simcote's kids from using it as a road. They'd strung a bridge between the buildings.

Corwyn found Antoine next to one of the vents—it smelled of sausage and almonds—as bitter-faced as he'd been sitting next to what remained of his father. He looked resigned and unsurprised when he saw her approaching his hiding spot.

"Dekalb's waiting to give you your tattoo," she said.

He rubbed a hand over his face. "I know."

She thought about leaning against the vent, got another whiff of it, and decided to sit down next to Antoine instead. "I was thinking about running away," he said.

Corwyn considered this abjectly terrible idea and decided on a circumspect approach. "You could, I guess. Art Goldberg'd probably take you on, kid or not—he buys and sells fancy rare stuff, bet your knack'd be something he could use. I don't think the old lady would send anyone after you or nothing." Corwyn was mostly sure this was true. It had been the other three times someone had left the Volary. Those kids didn't have finding-things knacks, though.

"I don't think I got it in me to be a gangster," Antoine said morosely. "My dad was an apothecary. I ain't like the rest of you, fighting and all." He looked at his forearm, where the tattoo would go. "I keep hearing how she sets us up when we're grown and just asks for favors now and then, and it seems like a good deal, but. I dunno."

Corwyn said nothing, just like she did when Gwen complained about Mrs. Simcote's long leash. Corwyn was always on a leash, it felt like, so the idea that there might be folks without one seemed strange beyond her ken.

Antoine finally sighed. "My dad took me away from my ma, and she's dead now. I got no other family, nobody else to take me in. I got no choice, really."

"Well, none of us do, or we wouldn't be here," Corwyn said, relieved that he'd figured it out himself. "Might as well make the best of it."

She got up when Antoine did, brushed off her pants and started back to the Volary roof with him.

"Corwyn, you ever hear noises?" he asked suddenly.

"Oh yeah," she replied. "This place is haunted or something. Cy thinks somebody's locked up down there, but between the boards over everything and the seven layers of keep-out charms, nobody can get in to see, not even the Jacks."

"No, not here—in the Volary, in the walls. You ever hear weird noises over there?"

She remembered her turn in the closet, leaning on the wall and banging her head against it. She remembered the voice—*Sister. I'll find your sister*—small, creaking, like maybe it came from the wood of the walls itself. She thought most times it did, kind of—her tired, frantic head trying to calm her from under her knack by making creaking boards into a voice.

Still. "Maybe?" she said. "The old lady keeps lots of strange stuff, so ... I suppose there could be clockwork in the walls or some such."

"Clockwork don't whisper or scratch," Antoine said, but Corwyn didn't reply.

LATER, AFTER GETTING high marks for moving silently while keeping a book on her head, Corwyn went to the kitchen to get something to eat. Cy'd been wanting those turnips and carrots for stew tomorrow; it'd be cooking overnight in the clockwork cook-pot Mrs. Simcote had given him to use. Allegra and Chilo had just made sandwiches for tonight, which was not the same—she cursed herself for not getting felafel when she had the chance.

Sandwich in hand, she made her way to the third floor via the bridge. Glancing down she saw Ioren, framed by ropes and netting, talking to an older woman Corwyn had never seen before. He still didn't seem happy. He rubbed at the spot behind his ear. The woman looked haggard; Corwyn thought she saw a bruise along her neck.

Gwen sat on the landing in front of their room, watching the scene. Corwyn sat next to her. "That one of his grandfather's people?" she asked, then took a bite of her sandwich. Tomato. Kind of slimy.

"I think so," Gwen said. The woman leaned in and prodded at the mark, whispering something and rubbing it. Ioren tolerated this stiffly. She pulled her hand back and said something else to him, then turned to leave. He watched her go.

Once the foyer door shut behind the woman, Ioren let out a long breath and glanced around. He smiled when he saw Gwen and Corwyn, grabbed a rope and scaled it like a squirrel to to join them.

"Any news from the underworld?" Gwen asked him as he swung over the rail and sat down between them in one fluid motion.

He grinned wider. "I can't tell you that, I took an oath."

"The gangster's oath, sure, that sounds like it's real," Gwen said, matching his grin with her own.

"There's one thing—you remember that island that disappeared a while back?"

Gwen shook her head, but Corwyn nodded—she remembered, distantly, hearing a couple of sailors talking about it when they were kids. "Do they know where it went?" she asked.

"Nope. But it's back. And wherever it was, the water there was red—they say the water around the island is purple now."

"Oh, now, no way that's true," Gwen said. "Water's clear. It's light and reflections that turn it colors."

Ioren shrugged. "It don't sound likely, but then, there's enough in the ocean *here* that ain't likely."

"Your parents ever sail there?" Corwyn asked.

"I don't think so. *The Ocean's Scorn* wasn't all that superstitious, but they still thought that patch of water was cursed."

"Wait ... *Ocean's Scorn*? Your ma and dad crewed for Josué Holophene? The pirate?"

"My dad *was* Josué Holophene the pirate," Ioren said.

A whole lot about Ioren suddenly made sense, Corwyn thought—his curly black hair, his speed. They called Holophene the Whip.

"That's the one'd send the rowboats into the Bay, right?" Gwen asked. "Raid the docked ships. Hell, the Dockworkers Union find out who you are, you'll need protection for who your father was as much as your grandpa."

Ioren was trying to look careless of it, but his eyes were proud, if still a little wary. "Don't matter for who, if they all want me dead."

GWEN'S KNACK WASN'T made for stealth.

"No," she said, letting Ioren out of a headlock. She wiped some blood from his brand off the heel of her thumb, "it ain't kicking when I just grab you from behind like that. I don't think it knows I'm looking to fight."

"You sound like it's got its own mind," Ioren said.

"It does," Gwen said. Corwyn, Nils, and Gertie Penzik chorused along with her from across the roof, where they were playing Dilly-O while Ioren and Gwen sparred. The wind blew the right way to keep the smells from the old boardinghouse from them, so it was actually quite pleasant on the roof today.

"Maybe you can coax it, Gwen," Corwyn suggested, frowning over her cards.

"With what, though?"

"Smell of blood?" asked Nils.

"So I ought to cut myself up before creeping up on someone? That ain't particularly stealthy, Nils."

"She can take you along everywhere to clean up after her," Corwyn said to him; Nils shoved her. Gertie put down a Jack of Diamonds and turned him upside-down.

"Maybe work yourself up into a righteous fury," Ioren said. "Surely you carry a grudge *somewhere* on your person."

Corwyn wasn't sure that was the best idea, but she kept her mouth shut as Gwen thought about it, then continued as Gwen proceeded to sneak up behind Ioren and kick his ass.

There were similarities in their fighting styles. They were both stupidly fast—though Gwen was just that touch faster—and they both of them liked fighting and violence in ways Corwyn didn't think too closely about.

They moved different, though.

Gwen about to fight was bouncy, swaying as she made her way in the fray if she wasn't leaping or running full-tilt. There was a savor to the way she moved into chaos, and a sinewy, bounding beauty once she was in the center of it.

Corwyn watched Ioren walk into a fight, be it to break up a scuffle between a couple of Volary kids or a sparring match with anyone, and it was like he flipped that switch he had, that turned him from a cocky boy to a man ready to murder someone. And she wasn't one to judge, all things considered, but she felt pretty certain everyone else who saw him stalking toward them had the same thought. Maybe that was why he liked being sneaky.

Gwen looked like she was headed to a party, and it threw folk off because they didn't know what to make of her (unless they knew her, and then they knew she *was* going to a party). It was maybe the one way Gwen was sneakier than Ioren Gudrunson.

Gwen's violence flowed from her like water down a gutter. Ioren was self-contained; his violence came abrupt and eruptive, even when you knew to expect it.

Gwen kicked the practice knife Ioren held from his hand. He lunged after it, and she used his bent leg as a step to kick up and get her legs around his shoulders. He lurched forward a step; Corwyn couldn't tell if that overbalanced Gwen or if she always meant to swing down round his neck to hang like a pendant, but it was surely why *Ioren* overbalanced. He fell; she pushed away. They rolled in opposite directions and came up breathing hard and grinning at each other.

"Where in hell did you learn that?" he asked, rubbing at the back of his neck.

"I dunno," Gwen replied, pushing herself to her feet. "Wasn't it impressive, though?"

"You ought not be allowed to play the Mad Queen," Nils told Gertie. "It ain't fair that you can lie and the rest of us can't."

Gertie looked smug as she scooped up all their cards.

"You can't always sneak up on folk," Gwen told Ioren later that day; the two of them sat on Gwen's bed. She dabbed at Ioren's bloody forehead with cotton-wool. Her knack had taken her under his legs; he'd expected her to sweep his knees, but she'd kicked him square in the small of his back instead. "You got a disadvantage, having no knack, and eventually you'll have a reputation, assuming you live."

"Reacting is weakness," he said. "Action's where the strength is. Get the high ground, have the advantage."

"That ain't realistic, or your forehead wouldn't be bloody and ready to scar," Corwyn told him from her own bed.

"You think it'll scar?" Ioren asked, sounding hopeful.

"You should only be so lucky," said Gwen with a smile.

Corwyn left them, debating different ways to kill someone with a nail, shortly afterward. She felt unhappy but couldn't exactly say why.

CHAPTER FIFTEEN

Corwyn traced her initials with her forefinger, smeary and wide, onto the shiny top of Mrs. Simcote's desk. The old lady said nothing, just watched and waited. She was pretty good at waiting her kids out, usually, but Corwyn had no plans to talk first. She'd been right, and she was still mad about being in trouble for it.

The old lady finally heaved a sigh and said, "You know what I've had done to people from outside the Volary who have hurt my kids, Corwyn Teachout. So what ought I do with you, who's broken Lawrence Boothe's nose?"

Corwyn met Mrs. Simcote's eyes. "He refused to really spar, so I figured maybe he needed to learn how to duck." The old lady looked unimpressed. "How'm I supposed to get better if they're all afraid to hurt their hands on my face? And how're they supposed to improve, either? Come to that, how come Lawrence's got to learn to fight, anyway? His knack's all languages. You'll set him up in a shipping business or something where the only chance of getting hurt'll be on a pen."

Mrs. Simcote's knobbly forefinger tapped sharply at Corwyn's smudgy initials. "You all learn to fight. Just like you all learn comportment and accents and geography and any other skills I see fit to stuff in your little skulls." Corwyn's heart stuttered for a moment at Mrs. Simcote's tone, but another part of her, that she thought might be lodged in her fingers, dug in fast as the old lady went on. "You're one of the few kids I have who can fight but doesn't have a knack for it, which means you are one of the few I can trust to work with the others. Or so I thought."

"There's Ioren," Corwyn pointed out. "He ain't got a knack, and he's not bad at teaching."

"Oh, yes, an excellent suggestion; he's got even less patience than you do and only marginally more self-control," Mrs. Simcote replied. "Now then, Miss Teachout, bearing in mind what I would do to an outsider who broke one of my children's noses, and considering the rather significant part Mr. Boothe has to play in the plans I've currently got in motion, what do you think I ought to do with you?"

Corwyn's fingers pressed hard into the desk, and she didn't look away. "I don't rightly know, ma'am—it's pretty clear I got some value to you, so like as not you don't want to kill me. I reckon cutting my hand off or similar would learn me."

Mrs. Simcote sat back in her chair, eyebrows raised just slightly. "That kind of mouth's usually on the other one," she observed. "What's wrong with you, then?"

Corwyn went back to her initials, because she didn't have an answer for that.

Mrs. Simcote sighed. Again. "Well, I hope you take great pleasure in your basic fighting classes, because you're staying put there. And you're on nursing duty until I decide you're not. Start today, get to making an inventory of our medical supplies—surely we need more bandages." She snapped her fingers; Corwyn stood up. "There had best be an improvement in you—"

A sudden teakettle shriek from behind one of the closed doors farther back in the office cut Mrs. Simcote off. She stood up, waving Corwyn out with one aggravated hand. Corwyn took to her heels before the old lady changed her mind and started yelling at her some more.

She ignored Mattie Singh on the stairs, and Agnes Doty and Gertie Penzik, who were friends with Lawrence and glared a hole in her head as she went by. The infirmary was empty, which suited her fine, so she got to work counting bandages and aspirin, sutures and ether bottles—wondering for a moment if those were still good and who she might try them on in order to find out.

The door opened. Gwen swept in smelling of sweat and the Hill. Out with Ioren again, shaking down shopkeeps or gangsters or who knew what.

"You broke Lawrence Boothe's nose?" Gwen asked, bewildered.

"Well, I'm here counting ... whatever this thing is, what d'*you* think?" She held up a set of metal instruments that looked to be made for grabbing things, but that were shaped, for some ungodly reason, like a frog with its legs stretched out straight. She handed them to Gwen, who immediately opened the legs, making the mouth gape wide.

"You got more control than that, though," Gwen said. "What'd he do to piss you off?"

"He left his guard down again, and it just made me mad."

"He *is* a crybaby who don't want to learn," Gwen said. She shut the frog with a snap and placed it on one of the shelves.

Corwyn tossed another bunch of bandages into the bin with the rest of them. "They're all just so slow," she said.

Gwen sat on the bed. "You're used to me," she replied with a shrug. "We could spar a little, still."

"In the great swathes of spare time we got," Corwyn said. "You're always busy doing something. It's against the rules, too."

"You just broke Lawrence Boothe's nose," Gwen pointed out.

"Yeah, and see what that got me." Corwyn threw more bandages into the bin, then thumped it all back into place on its shelf.

"Please, the old lady loves you—"

Corwyn grabbed a basket of rags and dumped them out on a table. "If she loves me so goddamned much, how come I'm on baby-sparring duty—"

A loud screech, then a noise like a gong from the clockwork grille set in the corner of the ceiling. A puff of dust and the smell of hot oil came from it, followed by Mrs. Simcote's rasp. "Do not leave the Volary until further notice. Corwyn and Gwen Teachout, report to my office immediately."

They looked at each other. "What'd we do now?" Gwen asked. "This is the first time we've been in the same room all day."

Corwyn dropped the rags and followed Gwen out the door. The entire place buzzed, whether from behind closed doors or kids upstairs wondering why they had to stay inside. Corwyn couldn't recall a time they'd been told they couldn't go out. Leaving at night was frowned upon, but it wasn't expressly forbidden so long as you came back. And they were always in and out during the day.

Esma Innovil landed in front of them with a thud from the third floor, then sprinted down the staircase.

Halfway down, around the time Corwyn could feel her knack going funny, Gwen asked, "Who are you so mad at, Wyn?"

She didn't answer until they made it to the bottom of the stairs, because she thought the answer was *You*, but she didn't know why. "Guess I'm just moody," she said. Gwen looked skeptical, but there was no time to say anything before they were through the old lady's door.

Esma stayed off to the side. Mrs. Simcote stood behind her desk, looking over one scribbled paper while making her own note on another one. She started talking at them, distracted, as she flipped the paper over, "The Dockworker's Union is making a move on the Olafurson territory, and it's a damned mess. Looks like they're fighting on some of Art Goldberg's turf, too, which ain't going to make it neater. Who the hell the Olafursons have left to send fighting I do not know ..." She looked up over her glasses at Corwyn and Gwen and said, "I don't want any of my kids out there in this—nobody's paying a damn bit of attention to who belongs to who. But we've got two still out on errands, so I need you to find them, Corwyn, and bring them back."

Corwyn shared a look of confusion with Gwen—the old lady was sending them out together, without conditions or an argument?—as Mrs. Simcote pushed her piece of paper across her desk, then said, "Move quick, don't get distracted. Keep your heads down."

Corwyn took the paper and read the names: *Antoine Gregoire and Nils Hulslander.*

SHE'D NEED SOMETHING of theirs to prompt her knack. Gwen took Antoine while Corwyn climbed into Nils' bed-cocoon to find a shirt or snatch a pillow. Her knack, sluggish and irritable, took notice of the distinct and not very pleasant scent of sweat, feet, and boy that signaled Nils surrounding her. The cocoon swayed, its wooden frame creaking, as her knack got hold of Nils and began to pull at Corwyn, pushing everything else—anger, tiredness, nerves, the muffled buzzing of the kids outside—out through her arms and legs. She took a deep breath, letting the pull grow more insistent before she slipped back out of the cocoon onto the roof of their room.

Gwen, stuffing something of Antoine's down the front of her shirt, met Corwyn as she climbed down to the floor. "You ready?" she asked. Corwyn nodded, her head full. Gwen handed her a knife, which she slipped into her right boot like clockwork.

ST. PHILOMENA'S ROSE, serene and broken as ever, above the mass of bodies fighting below and around her. Corwyn from her rooftop perch imagined the nuns inside praying in that scolding, hectoring way that always made her wonder how they got anything but "no" out of their god.

"They got clockwork fighting down there," Gwen observed.

Corwyn squinted and saw a couple of clockwork men—she thought, maybe—toward the middle of the crowd. "I guess they'd be fighting for the Dockworkers' boys," she said, "I can't tell who's who—how do they know not to kill their own?"

"Charms in their tattoos, Ioren says. I mean, they *can* kill each other, but it ain't no picnic."

Corwyn was saved from saying anything about Ioren by some gunshots from the brawl. The other people watching drew back from the roof's edge at the sound; Gwen bounced a little where she stood. "Where do we go from here?" she asked.

"Toward the middle of all that mess," Corwyn said.

"Like to know how you call it a middle when we can't barely see an edge," Gwen said as they backed up to run and jump to the next roof. None of the other lookie-loos on this one spared them more than a quick glance; some of them had bottles and some had food. They passed a couple leaning on each other, watching the fight with their hands entwined and her head on his shoulder.

They were coming right up on St. Phil's, about to lose the tall buildings, when Corwyn stopped short and grabbed at Gwen's arm. Her knack turned her round to face the tenement across the street, where Nils Hulslander, face bloody and clothes torn, had just emerged onto the roof.

"Well, Mrs. Simcote don't raise us stupid, I suppose," Gwen sighed. She cupped her hands round her mouth and yelled, "Nils!"

The noise—and smell—from under them was getting worse, so it took some frantic jumping around, waving from Corwyn before he noticed them.

He pointed to himself, then to them, and Gwen shook her head. "He don't need to traverse the damn street with a head wound."

Corwyn gestured at him to stay put and glanced round for a door; soon they were moving down through the building toward the street, Gwen pulling her truncheon from her back pocket.

A lady poked her head out her door. "It bad out there?" she asked. Something outside and downstairs crashed loud enough to rattle the floor and walls; the lady shut the door fast, apparently taking that as an answer.

They spared a moment at the door to take a breath. Corwyn's knack was quiet, now she'd laid eyes on Nils. Gwen's eyes were bright and a little mad. She turned the knob and opened the door.

The wall-rattling crash had been a cart that lay smashed up by the side of the building. They picked their way over the debris scattered across the steps—bits of wood, some sort of gourd—and plunged into the crowd.

The stink of sweat, blood, and shit hung over everything, combining with the heat of all the bodies to settle over Corwyn like a nasty-smelling blanket. She shoved a man out of her way with both hands; Gwen lurched into her as a man not much older than them crashed into Gwen's side. He came to his feet swinging. Gwen slammed the truncheon into the side of his head and sent him a-stagger. Gwen's hand bunched Corwyn's sleeve as they climbed across someone—knocked out or dead, Corwyn couldn't tell—and kept going.

The crowd itself moved them farther down the road than they wanted; Corwyn kicked knees and shins with her iron-nailed boots while Gwen broke noses with her elbow, and elbows with her truncheon. After a while it got almost like a dance, the rhythm of thuds, wet smacks, breaking sounds, yells—and then a metallic clang.

"What in nine bloody hells?" she heard Gwen ask. Corwyn turned to find her sister facing a dented, raggedy clockwork man who reared his arm back and punched Gwen square in the face.

Well, not square—Gwen dodged at just the last second, so the fist glanced off the side of her head. She pitched into Corwyn, who caught and shoved her back on her feet. Corwyn glimpsed a fist coming her way from the side and twisted around. Gwen ducked under the clockwork man's—a sailor, he looked to be a sailor—arm as he swung again, and Corwyn smashed her own elbow into the bloody-nosed face of the flesh man long before his fist connected. He swore, tried to back away, and swore a lot more when she planted her boot in his balls to the tune of Gwen's truncheon hitting metal.

Lord, it was hot—the clockwork sailor spewed steam and radiated heat. Corwyn shoved her hunched-over attacker away and spun to find Gwen, with a solid hold on the clockwork man's shoulder, hauling herself up his torso. He grabbed at her, but she swung herself onto his shoulders, ripped his mask off and tossed it aside in one motion, before commencing to bang the heel of her hand around on his head.

Someone tangled a fist in Corwyn's hair to yank her backward—she went with the motion, felt the person behind her lose balance, took two steps rearward and smashed the back of her head into someone's nose. "Gwen, truncheon," she shouted; Gwen tossed it in her direction without looking, focused on banging and shoving at the plates on the clockwork sailor's head with both hands, now. He lurched side to side and pawed at her legs like a drunk, but she held on stubbornly.

Corwyn careened round and hit the woman whose nose she'd broken in the back of the head with the truncheon, then did it again when the woman fell to her knees. Blood spattered over Corwyn's hands; she turned to Gwen only to find herself with a faceful of clockwork chest and her sister's legs. The three of them stumbled, landing in a tangle on top of the woman Corwyn had just knocked down.

Corwyn lay pinned under god alone knew how much weight of hot metal. Hot water soaked through her clothes, scalding her, but she couldn't catch a breath of steaming air to howl. Not a soul cared to watch their feet during their riot, so Corwyn was going nowhere as those feet connected with her ribs and arms.

Gwen scrambled off the top of the clockwork man, shoved folk away, and crouched to work her hands under the clockwork sailor's shoulders. "I'm willing to admit that shutting him off might not have been my best plan," she said, breathless.

Corwyn, herself breathless, didn't answer. A boot connected with the back of her head. She felt sick and wondered how she'd manage to puke if she couldn't breathe. Gwen swore as she scrambled round and braced her back against the body of the woman under Corwyn, got her boots on one of the clockwork sailor's shoulders, and shoved with both feet.

Corwyn heaved a breath as the body budged up. Gwen let out a teeth-clenched yowl as someone trod on her hand while Corwyn muzzily scrambled out from under. They both clambered to their feet, and even dazed with concussion, Corwyn could see Gwen's knack in her whirling, empty eyes and lunatic grin.

"Watch the hand," she warned as Gwen turned round, and then they were off.

IT WAS MOSTLY A MATTER of nudging Gwen in the right direction whenever she veered off-course. Bruisers and boys fell around her; the ones that didn't fall got a truncheon to the head from Corwyn to help them along. Gwen disarmed two different thugs carrying knives, used another one's hat to gag and lay him up, then tangled a woman in her own jacket sleeves before sending her flying with a boot to her back. Really, it was a shame Gwen's knack hadn't kicked as soon as they stepped out the door, Corwyn thought; it would have saved them some time.

Finally they emerged onto the sidewalk—which was marginally more open than the road—about two blocks down from where they'd been aiming for. Corwyn put a hand on Gwen's arm to keep her close to the buildings, and also to keep her balance as her head wound reasserted itself.

"Wyn?" Gwen asked.

"I'm all right," she said. The world seemed ringed with brown, but Corwyn could see just fine through the middle of it. "How's your hand?"

"Likely I oughtn't have punched anyone with it, but it'll heal," Gwen said. She sounded like herself, Corwyn thought, but didn't dare turn to look and take the chance of puking or falling over. She felt Gwen take the truncheon from her. Then Gwen grabbed Corwyn's elbow and shoved her, nauseatingly, to the side and up some steps. Once she had Corwyn by the door, she grabbed the rusty railing on either side to brace herself as she kicked someone in the chest. "Ow, goddammit!"

Corwyn leaned over the rail and puked before trying the door, which wasn't locked, but only opened so far before it hit—something. Furniture, more than likely. Corwyn leaned against it, skin stinging. She turned her aching head in time to see Gwen shoving her fingers into the eyes of some unfortunate, scrawny sailor. "I'm gonna need some help, Gwen."

"Hang on," Gwen grunted, pushing the sailor down the steps. Corwyn heard a scrape of something heavy dragging inside the building, then caught movement out of the muddied side of her eye—she turned, her back to the door, Gwen already between her and the woman who fetched up at the bottom of the steps, grinning with teeth filed to points.

Gwen shifted her weight back; Corwyn gave the door as subtle a shove as she could. It opened a little more, but not much—how the hell much furniture was stacked against it?—as the pointed-tooth woman just stared. Her hair was braided tight to her head; her brown eyes had the same wild emptiness as Gwen's got.

The woman took two quick steps up. Gwen grabbed the railings again, bracing herself. Corwyn held her breath.

The sharp-toothed woman snaked a hand out quick as a rattler to muss Gwen's hair with a face like pure mischief. Then she bounded off the steps, back into the fray.

Gwen stared after her like god himself had come down to mess up her braids. "That was Tammy the Squid," she said, her voice soft. "*Tammy the Squid*, Wyn!"

The last piece of furniture must have been moved: Corwyn fell sideways through the door.

Landing on the floor sent small squiggly starbursts across her eyes and a sharp lurch of nausea through her head. When her eyes cleared she looked up to see Nils, literally bloody, grinning down at her. "Hallo, Corwyn."

Gwen slipped inside and shut the door. She started pushing the furniture back into place using her left hand and her right forearm. "Wyn?" she asked. "How's your head?"

Nils looked a question at Corwyn, who shrugged and regretted it. "How'd you find us?"

"Your sister leaves a visible trail; it ain't hard." He gave her a hand up and ducked round to peer at her head. "That ain't good."

"It feels wonderful," Corwyn told him. "And what happened to your face, Nils?"

"Got nicked by a bottle." He pushed his hair back to show her the cut near his hairline. Something or someone banged up against the door, then away again. "Back to the roof?" Nils asked.

It wasn't a pleasant thing to climb a ladder with a dizzy head and blurred vision; it was even less so when her ribs decided they didn't want anything to do with said activity. The air up here was cooler and smelled a sight better, though. Gwen made her way to the roof's edge to get a look at the fight.

"Damn, we are right in the middle of it," she said, bouncing a little. Maybe her knack wasn't riding her, but Corwyn wondered if maybe it wasn't quite back to sleep all the way, either. "What the hell is that?" Gwen asked, pointing.

Corwyn and Nils moved closer. It was hard to focus past the headache, but Corwyn saw ... something—a flash of light off metal, skittering and low, before the crowd closed over it and it was gone.

"There's another one," said Nils, pointing to a closer section of the mob. A man took something to the leg and fell to block the view.

"More clockwork," said Gwen.

"I ain't seen nothing like that before," Nils replied, thoughtful.

"Me, either." Gwen sounded thoughtful, too, which didn't bode well for anything. The way that thing moved as it tunneled through the mob tugged at the back of Corwyn's mind, but she couldn't focus enough to figure out what the tugging meant.

"Get Antoine's shirt," she said instead.

Gwen rummaged down the front of her own shirt. "It ain't clothes," she said. She came up with the threadbare handkerchief Antoine'd taken off his father's body, unstained now probably thanks to Nils, and gave it to Corwyn.

Lemon and pepper, something under that that Corwyn shied away from because it wasn't the right scent; the one she wanted was the lemon and pepper and sweat ...

Corwyn's knack didn't wake up so much as slide through her aching head like a cool, silky snake. "That way—" She pointed north away from St. Phil's. "You think he's headed home?"

"As if that'll make it any easier," said Gwen.

CORWYN PAUSED EVERY so often to puke, which slowed them down a titch, but her knack pulled her steady without yanking. It was like after her brawl with Lars Hallstrom, when her knack was the only thing that didn't hurt her.

The farther along they got, the more Corwyn thought that Antoine was headed to the Volary, so their speed didn't much matter: eventually they'd catch him up. She let herself sink into the knack-fog further than usual, ignored Gwen's steadying hand on her arm and Nils' side-eye, passing the last straggling edges of the brawl, into the streets again, along Sorenson Road and down a side street, just following her knack until it took her to a dead end.

This was an alley. It appeared to be empty. Corwyn's head throbbed. "Where is he, then?"

"I swear to all nine hells, if he's dead after all this—"

"I ain't *dead*!" Antoine's head emerged out of a rubbish bin, angry and glaring them down. "What're we supposed to do when someone's following us, Gwen Teachout?" He tried to climb out of the bin, hampered by his funny-hanging arm. Nils went to help him. It must have been a trial for him to get in there with his arm like that, Corwyn thought.

"What happened to you?" Antoine asked Nils. His hair was matted with what Corwyn sincerely hoped were coffee grounds.

"Nicked by a bottle." Nils looked the situation up and down, then wrapped an arm around Antoine's chest. "Lift your legs up," he instructed. Antoine did so, hissing with pain, and kicked the bin out from under himself with a hollow clang.

"What happened to *you*?" Nils asked as he set Antoine on his feet.

Corwyn had never seen Antoine look so very ten years old before, not even when she'd met him over his dad's corpse. He hunched over his dislocated arm and said, "Something hurt me," in a small voice.

"Something?" Gwen asked.

"It was—I dunno. Not a person. Not clockwork." He looked at Corwyn and said, "It was like the thing that killed my dad. I was in Saints' Alley when the brawl started, and I figured I'd bolt for the Volary … and it grabbed me. It had long arms. Long fingers. And it … sniffed me? Maybe? Didn't have much of a nose. I thought it was gonna kill me. But it … I dunno, the fight got loud and it just threw me. Kept hold of my arm too long, though. Then it let go and ran off."

"What did it—"

Gwen stopped talking when Corwyn turned away, retching up bile and spit.

"Okay, everyone gird your damn loins so we can get home in what pieces we got," Gwen said. She got an arm around Corwyn in much the same way as Nils'd got Antoine and set off.

ONCE HER KNACK WASN'T pulling her along and keeping the worst of the pain at bay, Corwyn didn't have much choice but to let Gwen take over. She remembered very little of getting back to the Volary. She noticed when they all stumbled through the door; she noticed being stripped to her underwear and put into a bed in the infirmary while some Simcote kid or another complained about the mess, but she couldn't rile herself to say anything about her part in that mess.

At some point a lady who had likely been a Simcote kid but was now a nurse bandaged her ribs, her head, and put a nasty-smelling ointment on the worst of the burns. Then she left. Corwyn took as deep a breath as she could, sank into the mattress as far as she could, and slept.

SHE MOVED THROUGH A sickly dream of rocking floors and sour sweat stink that faded into the tearing sound of a knife into a neck before it became creaky-wood whispers, blood in her eyes, smeared across her raw fingertips. Corwyn jerked awake.

The bed shook before Nils said, far too close to her face, "Corwyn, wake up, Mrs. Simcote says I've got to check your eyes."

The nausea hit as soon as her head cleared from the dream. "D'you *want* me to puke all over you?"

His voice seemed farther away; he must have pulled back. "Your breath is *foul*. Open your damn eyes, Corwyn."

Corwyn cracked her eyelids open. Nils leaned in with a lamp in his hand, which he thankfully did not shine directly into her eyes. "Everything hurts, so I must be fine," she groaned.

"Well, your eyes look normal, anyway."

"So you can go, then?"

"I ain't going out there," he replied. Corwyn frowned, listened.

"—mistake, I didn't know the thing would fall on her, for god's sake, Mrs. S—"

"You do not *think*, Gwendolyn—this is your primary and most egregious fault, and while it will very likely be the death of you, I would prefer it *not* be the death of your sister."

Gwen said nothing for a long time, and Corwyn could see, in her mind, the set of Gwen's jaw and the curve of her neck as she glared at her boots. Gwen's voice was thick when she asked, "May I please go back in, ma'am?"

"Is your hand seen to?"

"It's splinted. It's fine."

"Very well. Bear in mind what I've said, Gwendolyn." The old lady's careful steps and swishing skirts moved away from the door.

Corwyn shut her eyes as it opened, but she caught Gwen's muttered, "My name ain't *Gwendolyn*," before sleep swept over her again.

THE NEXT TIME SHE WOKE, it was to Gwen climbing into the bed. "Nudge over, Wyn, there's a girl."

"There is a bed right there," Corwyn grumbled as she shifted, much to the outrage of every bit of her body.

Gwen was serene as she bounced and jostled herself comfortable. "That one's lumpy."

"*You're* lumpy." Corwyn poked at her. "How's your hand?"

"Broke a finger, the rest's just bruising." She held her left hand out—the smallest finger was splinted up, and the rest was, indeed, all bruises.

"That's gonna be pretty," Corwyn said around a yawn. She settled her head on Gwen's shoulder, feeling far away from the world, now she was comfortable. Something moved in the walls, making a rustling noise, but aside from that and Gwen's breathing, all was still. "How come Antoine ain't in here with me?"

"Antoine wants nothing to do with us, because it seems nobody's allowed to touch his fucking handkerchief."

"Well ain't that just precious." Corwyn yawned again and rubbed her cheek on Gwen's shoulder. "What'd she have him out looking for?"

"Some kind of rock. Looked old. Had something carved on it."

"He tell the old lady about the monster?"

"He didn't have much choice—that shoulder ain't easy to hide." "And?"

Gwen rested her head, gently, on top of Corwyn's. "Mrs S. got that stern look, like she was going to throw the lot of us out on our ears; I ain't sure Antoine cared, but."

Corwyn snorted, which made her face hurt. "I guess she don't know what it is, then."

She felt Gwen's smile. "That's what I thought, too."

They were quiet for a while, then Corwyn said, "You don't hear much about monsters in towns—they're all out in the country or up in the mountains. In the ocean."

"I reckon city-dwelling monsters are a different breed, is all," Gwen said softly. "Maybe just people acting like monsters."

Corwyn was falling asleep again. "Or monsters who look like people," she said. She reached for Gwen's battered hand and slipped her own underneath it, cradled it gently. "How would you tell who a monster was, they looked like just anyone?"

Gwen kissed her temple before whispering, "I guess by if they got anyone as loves them," and Corwyn slid back into sleep.

GWEN WOKE HER UP EVERY few hours to check her eyes and make her talk; Corwyn didn't mind this much, but groused about it anyway so Gwen wouldn't worry. Sometime nearer to dawn, Corwyn felt Gwen roll herself out of the bed and cross the room to the infirmary door. Corwyn opened her eyes; Gwen let Ioren into the room. He carried a parcel.

"I hope you weren't expecting change, 'cause she took all your money."

"'Course she did," Gwen said, taking the parcel and untying it, setting out its contents on the table near the foot of the bed. Corwyn could make out a bottle and a lump of … something. "Did she send instructions?"

"She drinks half this now, half same time tomorrow. Poultice goes on the lump. Or the crack. Is her skull cracked? It don't seem to make a difference, but—"

"No, she's just concussed," Gwen said. "Anything else?"

"Um. She also suggested that 'perhaps you might work on your forethought, Gwen Teachout.'" Ioren made his voice deep and creaky as he spoke.

"That's a pretty good imitation," Corwyn said, startling them both. "You two are loud. What'd you bring, Ioren?"

"Weird, witchy hoodoo," he replied. "You know she made me stand on her porch the whole time she made this?"

"Miss Vadoma ain't much for guests," Corwyn said. Her head felt heavy, but her back seemed pleased to be sitting up.

"I've only ever been in that house once, myself," Gwen said, distracted by measuring the potion into a small glass jar. "This smells nasty."

"Why're you spending money on medicine from Miss Vadoma, anyway?" Corwyn asked. "Mrs. Simcote got a nurse in."

"Yeah, well, I know Miss Vadoma's witchery works," Gwen said, reaching the jar over to Corwyn. "Drink."

The potion tasted nasty, too, but she'd downed worse from the witch. At least this wouldn't turn her bald or give her spots. She expected the poultice to smell like the potion tasted, but it had hardly a scent at all beyond the clinging roses and fish smell of Miss Vadoma's house.

Her brain went muzzy again as Gwen stacked pillows against the headboard of the bed and eased her back to sit against them. The poultice made leaning her head straight back uncomfortable, so she turned it to look at the dawn light edging round the curtain in the window. Gwen and Ioren talked over by the table, their voices murmuring-soft until Ioren's crept up: "—the *Squid*?"

"Yup." Gwen sounded smug *and* thrilled. Corwyn smiled sleepily, ignored the way her heart twitched. "Did you ever meet her?"

"I saw her from a distance," Ioren said. "Grandfather hustled me out the room whenever she was around."

"Can't believe she rubbed my *head* ..."

"'Course she did." Ioren's voice was fond. "Like calls to like."

Gwen sounded, of all things, bashful. "Shut up." Then, " ... You feeling okay?"

"I ain't dying today, if that's what you're asking, Miss Teachout."

Corwyn shifted herself a little lower under the blankets, cold now without Gwen. Her head felt lighter, somehow, and itchy—but itchy on the inside more than the out. She couldn't quite bring herself to much care. She did wonder, as she drifted off to sleep to the sound of Gwen and Ioren laughing together, if she'd ever be able to stay awake for more than half an hour at a time again.

CHAPTER SIXTEEN

"I can't stay any longer," Corwyn told the witch. "I got elocution this morning."

"And you surely do need it," replied Miss Vadoma; she did not look happy. She turned Corwyn round by the shoulders to inspect her from all sides. "All right, anything happens, you note the time, you hear me, girl?"

"I hear you," said Corwyn. She also heard the resigned sigh which meant Miss Vadoma did not believe her one whit.

Corwyn left the witch's house and started running to the Volary. The sun was up, the gangs were fighting on the south side of the Hill today, and Corwyn's bruised head felt normal for the first time in weeks. It was nice thinking at the usual speed again, even if all she was thinking was *hurry up, don't be late.*

"PARDON ME, MA'AM, DO you have a moment to spare to learn of the Joyous Missive?" Corwyn recited, half her mind on her accent, the other half irritated that she'd run all the way back just to practice *Pallasgreen*, which she'd had cold since the first day they'd been taught it. *Bellsbridge* was harder. And Scots—she and Gwen had been up nights working on Scots accents.

"Good." Lucy Adair, whose knack was accents and who worked in the Coroner's office now, nodded and moved onto Ginger Schwetje with a lingering, almost puzzled glance at Corwyn.

Corwyn frowned after her. Lucy cast a quick look sideways at Corwyn and smiled again, sort of sly, before setting the recitation for Ginger. *What on earth?*

And she realized: Miss Vadoma's potion must have finally kicked in. *Took long enough*, she thought.

She swiped at her face to feel if anything strange might have sprouted on it. Nothing. The other kids in the room were looking side-eyed at her, too. Maybe her eyes had turned color again—that got lots of furtive stares because people knew something was off but couldn't decide what.

Ginger slid out of her accent halfway through reciting and tried to recover, ending up with a mouthful of mish-mashed Spanish-by-way-of-Cobbler's Hill. Lucy told her to practice and went on to Memno Busignani.

"Corwyn? Could you maybe help me?" Ginger asked. She bit her lip shyly and shifted from foot to foot, arms held loosely behind her.

Ginger was older than Gwen, older than Nils, and had never really talked to Corwyn before; she'd never had a reason to. Usually she was stuck to Memno like they shared limbs.

"Um." Corwyn thought back over what she'd only been half-listening to a minute before. "Sharpen your endings."

"What d'you mean?"

"Make sure you pronounce your ending *t*s and *d*s. If you have to, hit them too hard to start and then back off as you practice. Pallas-green's not *that* much posher than the Hill, but they don't swallow their endings."

Ginger pursed her lips, then whispered a little to herself as Lucy worked through Memno, then Eulala Hosse, before coming back round to them.

Ginger recited, and Lucy smiled. "Not perfect, but much better."

Ginger beamed. "Corwyn showed me," she said, reaching over to take Corwyn's hand.

Ginger's hand was very different from Gwen's—smaller, and rough in different places—which froze Corwyn for what seemed like minutes. "She's so good at accents, isn't she? My prize pupil." Lucy reached out to rub her shoulder; Corwyn jumped. Lucy Adair had never said more than the name of an accent and a phrase to recite to Corwyn before.

Oh, she thought. Twigged to. *Oh, wait. This ain't good.*

"Is ... class over?" Corwyn asked, her voice as stiff as her spine.

"Hm?" Lucy seemed startled, but she stepped back—hand still on Corwyn's shoulder—and said, "Oh, yes, class dismissed!"

Corwyn took the excuse to pull away from both Lucy and Ginger, bolting for the door and ignoring the calls of "See you later, Corwyn!" that followed her.

"*Gwen*!" she roared as she hit the landing. She let her knack out and hoped to hell Gwen wasn't off on an errand or doing one of her under the table jobs.

"D'you need something, Corwyn?" Nils came up next to her. She turned to him, wary.

"No," she said, "I need to find—" Gwen was in their room. Nils was looking at her funny.

"Corwyn ..." Nils tilted his head and reached out to brush her hair off her forehead. Corwyn flinched back from his fingers.

"Nils ..." she said, warily and, she might as well admit it, despairingly.

His voice sounded marveling. "You look like art."

"I most surely do *not*. And you like boys! Gwen!"

"What are you yelling about?" Gwen leaned over the rail of the third floor landing, hair and clothes askew.

"Were you *sleeping*?" Corwyn asked, appalled.

"I—no. What is your problem, Wyn?"

Corwyn gestured to Nils with one hand; the gesture led her to noticing how many other kids were now staring at her, so she widened it to include them all, eyebrows raised at her sister.

Gwen's voice was suspicious. "Why're they all staring at you?"

"She's lovely," Nils answered in that same frightening, awestruck voice.

"Hey, Corwyn." Cy Blackburn slid up next to her, followed by Antoine Gregoire and Allegra Taft.

"Any one of you touches me and I put you on the ground," Corwyn said. From the corner of her eye she saw Gwen reach over for a rope, which she used to swing to the second floor with a muted thud. She wasn't wearing her boots, Corwyn noticed absently.

"All right, loverboys and girls and in-betweens and neithers—and whatever the hell animal you are, Cy—back away from my sister."

"Aw, Gwen, how come you get all the fun?" asked Cy, shrinking away from the look Gwen turned on him.

"How do you get your hair so pretty?" asked Antoine. "Can I have some of it? Your hair?"

"I will break your goddamned fingers, you touch my hair," Corwyn snapped.

"Come on." Gwen steered Corwyn by the arm toward a rope ladder, snarling, "Not a one of you follows us, you got me?" over her shoulder. There was an audible moan from the group as Corwyn began climbing the ladder, which she hoped to all nine hells was disappointment and not some sort of comment on her ass.

Gwen followed her up, shoved her into their room, and shut the door.

"Why, Miss Corwyn, you're beautiful today."

Ioren Gudrunson sat tailor-style on Gwen's bed, which was made up neater than any time since the two of them had moved in. He looked a little drawn, dark circles under his eyes, but his face lit up like everyone else's when they landed on Corwyn.

"What are you doing in our room?" she asked—today was shaping up all kinds of off-balance—as he stood up and moved toward her.

"At the moment, I'm admiring the look of your eyes in the lamplight."

"Well ain't you just a smooth-talking bastard?" Corwyn asked.

Gwen took a quick two steps around Corwyn. "Out."

"Oh, come on, Gwen, I won't hurt her—you know I'm gentle as—"

"Nope. Out." Gwen put her hands on Ioren's shoulders and turned him—Corwyn turning, too, to keep Gwen between them—then walked him backward. Corwyn darted an arm round Gwen's side to open the door, and Gwen shoved him through before shutting it again.

"So, proving potions this morning, then?" Gwen asked, leaning back against the door.

"Yes."

"You know, Corwyn, you could ask Miss Vadoma what the damn things are supposed to do!"

"She usually tells me! Sometimes." Corwyn ran her hands over her face, then dropped them with a loud exhale. "Do I look like me?"

Gwen, bless her, stood up straight and took a long, serious look at Corwyn. "You look like you always look," she said, finally. "To me, anyway."

"I don't always look like 'art,'" Corwyn said darkly.

"Neither of us knows a damned thing about art," Gwen said. "Nor magic, neither. We can hole up in here, I ain't leaving you alone without a lock on the door—"

Said door was rapped with two sharp knocks and then opened by Jouanna, who promptly stopped halfway through to stare at Corwyn.

"You got a reason for opening that door, Jouanna?" Gwen asked, voice tight. "Because if not, I feel obliged to warn you that I'm gonna break your nose."

Jouanna started. "I—um. Sorry. Corwyn's just—I mean, they said, but. Um." She took a breath, fixed her eyes on her hand clutching the knob, and said in a rush, "The old lady wants to see you, Corwyn."

"*Just* what we need to add to this mess," muttered Gwen.

"Scat," Corwyn snapped at Jouanna, who turned and fled down the landing. Corwyn put her hands on her hips, breathing deep with her face aimed at the ceiling, trying to imagine how she was going to walk through the Volary with everyone staring at her like she was the night sky strung with stars or the curve of Gwen's wrist as she landed a punch to someone's face.

Gwen reached out and took her left hand, swinging it between them. "Let's go," she said. "Don't want to keep her waiting."

"You're coming with me?"

"Well, I ain't leaving you alone right now, especially not with the old lady."

"She won't do anything."

"Unless she gets curious what might happen and locks you in a room with Nils or Rufus Tominey." Gwen pulled Corwyn out the door; Corwyn let the argument pass. The last time Mrs. Simcote locked her in a room to see what would happen was, Corwyn thought, justifiable. Everyone ought to know their own limits, and the limits of the things they invested in. But she couldn't argue Gwen's suspicions about the old lady's curiosity, and she had no hankering to be locked in a room ever again, with or without ... company.

"SAINTS BE FUCKED, THEY weren't kidding." Mrs. Simcote's eyes were wider than Corwyn had ever seen them. Corwyn paused at the door.

"Could you maybe tell everyone to go back upstairs?" she asked. Gwen's back was pressed up against hers as she stared down what appeared to be the entire population of the Volary, including two adult kids come to teach today and a lady who'd been hired to remove the birds' nests from the rafters.

Mrs. Simcote shook her head like she was trying to toss her hair from in front of her eyes and stood up. "Yes," she replied, rounding the desk. She pushed Corwyn to the side, yanked Gwen through the door by her collar, and leaned out. "Get back to your tasks, you lot! Now!"

It seemed fear of the old lady trumped however Corwyn looked, much to Corwyn's relief. The crowd dispersed. Mrs. Simcote shut the door. She looked from Corwyn, to Gwen, then back to Corwyn. "Ain't no way you can blend into a crowd looking like that," she said. "Your hair alone—and damn if I know what she did to your eyes ..."

The old lady stretched out one finger to trace Corwyn's left eyebrow. Gwen flinched like she'd stopped herself from moving, but Corwyn leaned into the touch, just a little. It wasn't often Mrs. Simcote touched one of her kids, and it was nice. The tobacco and apples smell of her was stronger this close; her eyes had gone soft, hazel colored and, she fancied, like their mother's might have been if she'd actually cared for them.

"Gwen," Mrs. Simcote said, smiling fondly at Corwyn, "it ain't turning you odd? You've no sudden urge to sculpt your sister's face from marble or anything like that?"

Gwen's voice came from between clenched teeth. "No, ma'am."

"Good. Take her to the witch, see if she can get it off quicker than just waiting round. If not, tell her she's to keep Corwyn 'til she's back to normal." She dropped her hand from Corwyn's face and looked at Gwen. "You keep her safe through the city, you hear me?"

Gwen looked murderous. "That's not something you have to tell me, Mrs. Simcote."

Mrs. Simcote said nothing to that beyond a skeptical expression. She turned back to Corwyn. "You tell Vadoma Hildago that I do not appreciate your employment with her—which I have generously allowed to continue—disrupting my entire house."

"Yes, ma'am," Corwyn said, wondering how the hell she could phrase that in a way that would end well. The meeting between the two of them to decide Corwyn's continued employment had been long, and as nobody else had been in the room when it happened, nobody knew what sorts of agreements, threats, or magic might have been used to get the witch what she wanted. Corwyn didn't relish the idea of giving either of them an excuse to be in a room alone again.

"Gwen, drop your sister and come back here—I want to know what the witch says."

"Yes, ma'am," Gwen said, reaching for Corwyn's hand. "Come on, I think we still have that hat Miss Vadoma leant you when you were bald."

AS THE HAT DIDN'T COVER her whole face anymore, they decided to take to the roofs for as long as they could manage it. They took the bridge across to the old boardinghouse, which stunk of rotten fish tonight, and jumped to the next building from there.

Corwyn had never realized, before, how much she took it as given that she was in no way remarkable, nor how much she counted on it. Gwen's red hair had always been something folk noticed—at least when it was clean—but there were Irish all over the Hill, so "redhead" was less helpful a description than it might have been otherwise. There were always people on the roofs—not so much the roof of the old boardinghouse; people mostly avoided staying up there with the smells and the charms—whether tenants or folk come up for some air or some snogging, kids or grown-ups needing a place to sleep, or people traveling through the city with no wish to be seen. The people clumped in the corners and middles of the rooftops stared as the Teachouts passed; they'd remember seeing them go by, if anybody asked them.

Nobody followed them, but Corwyn kept looking back all the same. People stared at her the whole time.

34th Street, where the witch lived, was a street of houses and little storefronts, not tenements and warehouses, so as they got close to it they had to return to the ground. As they emerged from the front door of the building, a man got up from his stoop across the street and came closer, peering at them with red-watered eyes. Gwen glared at him 'til he froze, but when Corwyn glanced back, he was following.

They added a lady, two kids, and a dog that seemed to belong, more or less, to the kids. Nobody spoke. The noises of the street seemed to fade away as they passed, as the people stopped to stare and sometimes join their little parade of supplicants.

Every time Corwyn looked behind them she found the crowd bigger. Some of the faces looked awestruck, like Nils's; some of them looked afraid. The ones as looked hungry made her nervous.

Three houses down from Miss Vadoma's, about the tenth time Corwyn looked back, Gwen grabbed her round the waist and shoved Corwyn's head into her neck. "Keep walking, I'll guide you," she whispered.

Gwen's neck smelled of sweat, with something musky underneath that Corwyn thought was familiar, but wasn't Gwen and was therefore unpleasant. After a few steps, Corwyn asked, "Is it helping?"

"Nobody's gone, but nobody new's joined up, neither."

Not a one of the crowd dared follow the girls up to the witch's porch. Gwen pounded on the door and, when Miss Vadoma opened it, shoved Corwyn at her. The witch caught Corwyn by the shoulders and kept her at arms' length as Gwen stalked in. "You need to take it off her or keep her 'til it wears off," Gwen said.

Miss Vadoma set Corwyn back solid on her feet, then went to the door and peeked out. She turned to regard Corwyn like a painter finding a work in progress wanting.

"I imagine that *is* inconvenient at the Volary," she said with a sly grin. "I don't suppose you noted the time when it took effect, like I asked you?"

"It was during elocution, toward the end, so late morning?" Corwyn offered.

Miss Vadoma merely sighed. "How're *you* feeling, girl?" she asked Gwen.

"Irritated," Gwen said.

"No blood relatives—I got that much right, anyway," Miss Vadoma said, philosophically.

"Mrs. Simcote wants me back—*you* ain't gonna go all moon-eyed on us, are you, Miss Vadoma?" asked Gwen.

"What sort of witch would I be, if I got caught in my own magic?" Miss Vadoma asked. "Go on back, I'll keep your sister safe. You been fed, Corwyn?"

Gwen didn't pause on her way out the door, just yelled, "Don't eat a goddamned thing she gives you, Wyn—I swear to hell, I come back here tomorrow to find you blue or grown a tail I will disown you!"

She slammed the door as she left. Corwyn, for the first time since the potion had taken effect, grinned and felt all her body relax.

THE POTION WORE OFF sometime during the night; Miss Vadoma checked on her every half hour until it faded. This was certainly better than the witch watching her *all* night, but still made it right difficult to sleep.

"What were you dreaming about?" Miss Vadoma asked her once, when she came awake gasping.

Corwyn was too bleary to not respond. "Locks and blood," she said.

"Those ain't gone yet?" the witch asked, but she didn't seem interested in an answer.

And so Corwyn was tired, fuzzy-eyed, irritable, and queasy when Gwen knocked on the witch's door the next morning. She wasn't alone: Ioren stood squinting at Corwyn through the doorway. She squinted back: he looked better this morning, but he was still getting skinnier and skinnier, for all he ate his weight every day. He might not die tomorrow, but the curse was working steady.

"She looks like Corwyn again," Ioren told Gwen. Then, sweeping a bow, "I apologize, Miss Teachout, for any discomfiture I may have caused you yesterday."

"Your accent needs work," Corwyn replied. She recognized that musky scent in Gwen's neck, now, and was not best pleased.

Ioren's mouth twitched in a way that seemed amused. "As you say. My diction's a thing of beauty, though."

Miss Vadoma, information recorded, was still abed, so Corwyn stuck her hat upon her head and made sure the door latched on her way out. "So did the old lady send you to babysit me the whole way home?" she asked. A couple of people on the street glanced at them, likely because they'd emerged from the witch's house, but nobody stared.

"Not only—we've got an errand to run," Gwen said. She stole the hat off Corwyn's head and put it on her own. Gwen steered the three of them in the direction of the docks, while Corwyn took a breath of the not-very-fresh Hill air to try and ease her stomach back toward normal.

THEY WAITED ON A CHINESE sailor with a black and red Tong gang tattoo on the side of his neck, who'd disappeared into the holding shack next to the dock. There was no ship at the end of it, which seemed odd since they were, Corwyn thought, picking up cargo, but it wasn't her place to wonder much. Besides that, she'd caught sight of Lars Hallstrom moving round the quay to talk to people, a kid with a black eye following behind him with his head down.

This meant Corwyn had to keep an eye on Gwen to be sure she didn't go off. Lars Hallstrom kept Mrs. Simcote supplied with kids and leads on them; in return, nobody killed him. He got to keep the kids he wanted who didn't have knacks. Nobody much liked it. Corwyn tried not to think about it, but whenever she couldn't avoid it—like now—she took some solace in the fact that in all the times he'd come to the Volary with a lead on a kid for Mrs. Simcote, Lars Hallstrom had never bothered Corwyn beyond a wink in her direction. When she looked at him she could feel the smack of the cricket bat hitting his knee, and it seemed to her he remembered it, too, from the other direction.

Ioren was useless, mesmerized by the boats. Every bit of him seemed to lean toward the water. The breeze blew his curls back, and the brand, pink and seeping blood, flickered in and out of sight behind them.

"That son of a bitch," Gwen muttered, never taking her eyes from Hallstrom.

Corwyn was saved having to respond by the Tong sailor's return with his arms stretched out in front of him. A burlap sack dangled from his hands, dripping what looked like blood out the bottom. That got all of their attention.

"What in actual hell ...?" Ioren murmured. Even Corwyn, as used to blood as she was, swallowed and forced herself to look at the sailor's face as he made to hand the bag to Gwen, who turned her deeply unimpressed gaze on him.

"You expect us to carry a blood-soaked sack through the streets? Even the Hill ain't that apathetic."

"The *docks* appear to be that apathetic," Corwyn muttered—not an eye lingered on them for more than a few seconds at a time, the sailors and merchants and other denizens surrounding them studiously ignoring the entire exchange.

"You find us a box, we'll take it with us," Gwen said.

"I got a trunk, but it cost you."

"We go home to the Volary empty-handed because you were too stupid to make Mrs. Simcote's package unremarkable, it ain't us going to be blamed," Corwyn piped up. "And I dunno what she's paying you, but she'll be wanting it back."

The sailor glared at her, then shoved the sack into her startled hands before vanishing back to the holding shack.

The bag wasn't as heavy as she'd expected, given what she figured was in it. A smell of blood and something sweet, like raspberries or apples, rose from it. Corwyn held it far away from her body. The blood dropped onto the wood of the boardwalk, *spatter spatter*, the light catching strange in it, reflecting colors back up at her.

The sailor dumped the trunk at their feet. The lid sprung open with a metallic shriek. Then he walked away.

Corwyn looked from the sack to the trunk. "Should we just throw the whole thing in, sack and all?"

"I want to see what's in the bag," Gwen said.

"Because 'something bloody' ain't enough?" Ioren asked. Gwen glanced at him like she hadn't known 'til now just *how* dumb he could be, and he sighed.

Corwyn looked the bag over, spinning it a little so it splattered blood in a circle on the ground. "This is a lot of blood. And I'm not sure how—"

"Lord, the both of you are a sight to behold." Ioren grabbed the bag from Corwyn, dropped it into the trunk, took hold of both sides of its open top and ripped it along the seams.

The contents of the bag collapsed into the trunk with a squelchy series of thuds, so Corwyn was not the least bit surprised that those contents were bits and pieces of a body. She wasn't even that surprised that the body wasn't human, though the fact that it also didn't look like any animal she'd ever seen, even the weird ones in Arizona, was a trifle disconcerting.

What she could see of its skin was wrinkled and red-brown; it'd been cut up into pieces and the pieces were all over blood. Or, no—she leaned in closer the same time Gwen did—more like those pieces *were* blood. The arm on top—long fingers, long claws, some of them broken—was melting into a pool of blood. So were the rest of the pieces. And not blood like anything Corwyn'd seen before; this was deepest red, other colors caught in it where the light hit, and the source of the sweet smell.

"Ain't that intriguing?" asked Gwen just as Corwyn murmured, "Well, what are you?" They caught one another's eyes, grinning, before Gwen went back to looking at the dead monster and Corwyn took a look around the docks.

Nobody paid them any mind, save for Lars Hallstrom who looked at her over the shoulder of some bartering sailor. He winked. She gave him her fingers with a cheerful smile and turned her attention back to the trunk. Gwen reached in and moved the creature's head so they could see its face.

Its eyes were open, a clear blue with flecks of yellow caught in them, huge like a kitten's. Its lips were drawn back over three rows of teeth. Its nose was a lump with a couple of holes in the bottom. No hair, just what looked like smooth jelly all over the top of its skull.

"Goddammit," Ioren muttered.

Gwen went to poke the top of its skull with a finger, but Ioren batted her hand away and shut the trunk practically on her arms. "Come on."

Ioren barely waited for Gwen to take a side before he got the other and started for the Volary at a pace as brisk as his tone of voice. Corwyn followed at a trot. Ioren held his jaw tight. Corwyn sent Gwen a questioning look that got a mystified shrug in return.

It wasn't a long walk from the docks to the Volary. Ioren pulled Gwen in the foyer doors and through the building, which caught the attention of every kid in the place. They made their way through a tangle of stares down the steps toward Mrs. Simcote's study. Ioren sent Gwen stumbling about halfway down; the trunk tipped, some blood spattered on the boards, but Ioren barely noticed.

Corwyn ran ahead and rapped on Mrs. Simcote's door, then held it open for them. She ducked inside just as Ioren wrenched the trunk entirely into his own hands and—he didn't shout, didn't raise his voice at all, but it gave the feel of a shout all the same—asked the old lady, "How in hell did you get this?"

For one tantalizing, terrifying moment, Corwyn thought he would tip the bloody, dismembered monster onto her desk, but he just slung the trunk onto it and opened the lid.

That metallic, sweet fruit smell filled the room. Mrs. Simcote eyed Ioren before turning her gaze to the trunk. "My contacts are none of your concern, Ioren Gudrunson."

"That—" He pointed, then paused. "I don't actually know what that is, but it belonged to my grandfather."

"Did it, now?"

"Don't play dumb, we both know you ain't stupid. That thing was always around and you never knew where unless he wanted to scare you to death—" Corwyn found herself impressed, because the look Mrs. Simcote had on her face was one that did not bode well for Ioren's continued health, such as it was, but he either didn't notice or gave not a damn about it. "Who killed it?" he asked. "Who in nine hells *could* kill it?"

The two of them stared each other down. Corwyn rather desperately wanted to know what Gwen's face was doing, but she didn't dare look away from the silent spectacle in front of her.

"Why, pray tell, am I giving you all this damn free time if you can't make your own progress in your revengeful endeavors?" Mrs. Simcote finally asked, her voice even. "What on earth are you doing, beyond wasting my resources and goodwill?" The old lady stood up and shut the trunk. "I suggest you get off your idle ass and fulfill your familial duties, Ioren Veigarson, whilst keeping your nose out of the business of the person protecting you as you gad about the Hill after dark."

Ioren's face grew thundery. He turned and stormed out the door—without an answer to his question, Corwyn thought but did not say.

His steps echoed up the stairs before resolving to silence. The smell permeated the entire room now, and somewhere in the back, behind the doors that ringed the office and led to what everyone supposed were Mrs. Simcote's living quarters, there came a thud and a shuffle. Mrs. Simcote didn't react to it, just contemplated the lid of the trunk.

"Could you girls send Antoine to me, please?"

"Yes, ma'am," they said, not quite in unison. Mrs. Simcote pulled the trunk off her desk and set it on the floor as they left, shutting the door behind them.

Partway up the stairs, Gwen stopped and turned, head cocked, her blood-stained hand on Corwyn's wrist. "Do you hear crying?" she asked.

Corwyn listened. Sure enough, she could hear, faintly from behind Mrs. Simcote's office door, sobs—harsh and barking, sounding not at all like Mrs. Simcote.

"NILS! WE NEED YOU to clean up a mess!"

Corwyn opened her door to find Lawrence Boothe and Agnes Doty yelling up at Nils' sleeping sack. "He ain't up there, you're the third pair's come looking for him, what the hell'd you idiots do, and why can't you learn to tell each other where you've already been?"

Lawrence, who hadn't ever gotten over Corwyn breaking his nose, blinked at her while Agnes reported, "Antoine got into a fight with Ioren, there's blood and puke all over schoolroom three, and I don't know, I just live here. Where's Nils, then?"

"Hell if I know, maybe he found a nice boy to kiss. Antoine got into it with Ioren?"

"I thought you and Nils kissed," said Lawrence, frowning.

"Corwyn don't kiss anybody," said Agnes. "Will you tell Nils if you see him?"

"Probably," Corwyn said. The two kids turned away from the door, and Corwyn stopped short of shutting it when she saw Antoine Gregoire climbing down from his own sleep sack across the way. She could see the swelling in his face even from this distance. He wasn't moving very steady, but he had a pillowcase over one shoulder and a good pair of boots on.

She got to the roof door before he did, and slipped inside to sit on the steps just behind it. The drama of addressing him from the shadows as he edged the door open pleased her.

"Now what are you planning that needs a distraction like Ioren Gudrunson kicking your ass until you vomit, Antoine?" Disappointingly, he didn't startle, just let the door close soft behind him so the shadows enveloped both of them.

"I'm leaving, Corwyn."

"You ain't got nowhere to go," she said, astonished.

"I can't stay here. I don't wanna."

"What're you gonna do?" she asked. "You said yourself you can't live on the streets."

"I'm gonna take your advice and sell myself to Art Goldberg." He paused, looking like he was fighting with himself, then said, "Corwyn, you know there's things she ain't telling any of you. Things she does, to get what she wants. I … I just want to go, all right? I ain't happy here. Just let me go."

Corwyn said nothing. She leaned away from him to let him pass up the steps. There was scratching in the walls; she could hear the usual noise of the Volary from behind the door, but she sat in the dim until the other roof door closed overhead.

The old lady told them a couple days later that Antoine had decided to leave them. It was big news; not many kids ever left the Volary without Mrs. Simcote's say so, a job she got them set up in, and a little bit of money. In fact, Corwyn didn't know the names of any kids who had, though she spent a lot of time trying to remember.

CHAPTER SEVENTEEN

It felt like her knack, a little, except it pulled harder, made the world go black, and seemed centered in her liver. It didn't last as long, neither; she'd only managed one verse of "Valloise's Last Remarks" before it faded off.

A wet, rhythmic noise—squeaking, slapping, a mechanical wheezing she couldn't place, with the occasional grunt for punctuation—made Corwyn aware of three things, almost at the same time: she was on her side on the floor, said floor very likely belonged to a brothel, and she was about to puke spectacularly.

There was nothing for it. Perhaps, she thought fleetingly as her stomach turned itself inside out, the patron and patronized of this fine establishment would be too involved in their activities to notice her being sick on the floor. They didn't seem to have noticed her arrival. Surely she could throw up all subtle-like.

In fact, she soon discovered, she could not.

The rug on the floor looked much more expensive than Corwyn's lunch, now covering it, had been—falafel and coffee and an apple stolen from the Katsaroses' food cart for old times' sake. Once it was all up and out, Corwyn pushed herself into a more seated position, wiped her mouth on the back of her sleeve, and looked around her.

An old, oddly familiar-looking gentleman lay tied to the bed, a clockwork person wearing nothing but work boots and brandishing a very large wrench poised at its foot. The clockwork person stood uncanny still. The man in the bed stared, aghast, over his shoulder at

Corwyn, who took a couple of seconds she likely oughtn't to try and work out how she knew him.

When he started to struggle against the ropes—and judging from the state of the back of him, *that* was highly uncomfortable—Corwyn scrambled to her feet, dropped a quick, absurd curtsy, and bolted for the door.

The old man didn't shout after her, but that didn't mean he wouldn't. And when he did, her best bet would be to have gotten out of the building and lost in a crowd. Corwyn skipped down two sets of stairs—how many floors was this place, she wondered—garnering amused smiles from a let-boy and an older lady draped in fur and pearls before she heard footsteps behind her.

If the damned staircase didn't turn on a landing, she would have gotten away, but it did and whoever was behind her got a hand on her arm over the banister. Not for the first time, Corwyn wished she had her sister's quick brain in a fight, but she swung round with the grab, ready to scrap.

"Mr. Fritz?"

"Come on," he said, pulling her back up the stairs.

It had been years since she'd seen him last, certainly before the Volary took them in; Corwyn barely recognized him in clothes this fine. His hair was swept up elegant, and he wasn't as ropy-scrawny as she remembered. He glanced up and down the now-empty hallway before shoving Corwyn into a room full of fancy underwear on racks.

"All right, then, Corwyn Teachout, what are you doing here?"

"Potion proving for Miss Hildago?" Corwyn ventured. Mr. Fritz looked angry, which was intimidating in those clothes. "I just ended up here. Weren't my plan." Mr. Fritz took a deep breath. "You appear to have moved up in the world since I've seen you, Mr. Fritz," she said, attempting charm.

"Yes, well, I suppose I have." Mr. Fritz let his breath out, resigned. "You even know where you are?"

"Someplace swank, if that clockwork whore upstairs is anything to go by."

"Of course you've been upstairs, fuck everything. All right, let's get you out quick, then." He put a hand on her shoulder to steer her toward the windows of the little room.

"Clockwork folk ain't even got *bits*, how can they—"

"There's not a thing on this earth that ain't being used for fornication by somebody, Miss Corwyn," Mr. Fritz interrupted calmly. "Humans is an astonishingly creative animal." He reached to the wall and opened a door she hadn't seen, revealing a much less respectable set of stairs. "All right, down these and out through the kitchen. Anyone asks, you act proper outraged and tell them you never agreed to *that*—"

"What would 'that' be?"

Mr. Fritz grinned. "Leave something to their imagination, right? They won't press; we hear it a lot."

Corwyn could hear footsteps in the hallway—purposeful ones, which did not bode well—but she didn't move. "Mr. Fritz—did we get you fired from Madame Tereza's, staying with you that night? After ... you know, the Collett House?"

Mr. Fritz's mouth twisted. "I got m'self fired, but that was why, yeah. I made Tereza cross the patron saint of the Hill's brothels, got her in quite a bit of hot water. But worry not, young Corwyn, it led to better things once the bruises healed."

Corwyn nodded, turned toward the stairs. "Also, sorry about the puke," she said.

"Wait, the what?"

Corwyn grinned sunnily at him over her shoulder before bounding down the stairs.

"NINE HELLS, I'M IN fucking *Bellsbridge*," she murmured as she emerged onto the street. This was not a part of San Xavier Corwyn had even a nodding acquaintance with—the streets were clean, the buildings whole, the people well-dressed as they openly stared at her. It even smelled decent this far south—well, aside from the faint scent of puke coming from her sleeve.

Corwyn took a breath of the rarefied morning air of San Xavier's richest neighborhood. Airships docked even farther south; she could see them from where she stood, dark against the sky. Music played from a restaurant across the street, too, and the air sat lightly against her skin like it was made of something different from the air in the Hill—sunlight and gossamer and wind, not soot and cobwebs and fog.

There'd be no blending into the crowd down here; best thing to do would be head home fast, if she knew which way to start. If she was careful she might be able to lift a couple wallets on the way. She let her knack out to find her sister with a sigh, let Gwen pull her up the street.

CORWYN NEEDED TO GO to Miss Vadoma's and report, not to mention give Mrs. Simcote her cut of the idle larceny in which she had indulged on her way home, but her knack demanded she lay eyes on Gwen before it would leave her alone. And Corwyn had a good story to share, especially once she twigged to the old codger in the bed being the man whose portrait had hung in the dining room of the Singleton Home. So she swung up the Volary ladder and bounced to the door, speaking even as she reached out for the knob, "You will not *believe* where I just saw the Right Reverend Root—"

Gwen and Ioren were in Gwen's bed, Ioren's face buried between Gwen's legs, Gwen's hand knotted in Ioren's hair, her head thrown back and eyes shut.

Unlike during the earlier encounter, neither Gwen nor Ioren noticed Corwyn as she stepped back out the door and closed it quietly behind her. She leaned against the wall next to the door for a moment. Her knack had calmed, at least.

A noise—Gwen, she thought; it was higher than Ioren's voice and not muffled—seeped through the wall. Corwyn pushed herself up to standing.

The noise was troubling. When Gwen had been fucking Memno, she'd been pretty damned silent, much to Corwyn's dismay: the number of times she'd walked in on them had been horrifying for all three of them. It would have been nice had Gwen remembered the damn signal they'd agreed on back then, though, because even the calming of her knack wasn't worth the sight of Ioren Gudrunson's bare brown ass in the air.

She stalked down the stairs and back out the door toward Miss Vadoma's. The air hung thick and foul, the buildings were crumbling, and not a damn person on the potholed street spared her a glance. Corwyn breathed deep to calm her churning head, because she couldn't rightly put a name to why she was mad.

It wasn't like Gwen was chaste—hell, she'd screwed around with Ned Shuluk and Eulalia Hosse and once with DeKalb Vickery, mostly hands and mouths and rubbing on each other because Miss Vadoma's potion to keep her from catching pregnant was expensive. Gwen said it was fun, like fighting a little, and so long as she'd been hanging a sock on the doorknob and making sure she didn't make Corwyn an aunt, ever, Corwyn'd had little interest in what she got up to.

Corwyn had little interest in copulation at all, come to that. She allowed, to herself, that maybe it was something uncommon about her that she didn't want to get off with anyone, that she didn't understand any sort of love beyond what she had for Gwen. Probably people were supposed to love more than one person, but loving Gwen was hard enough to manage, the two of them fighting all the time.

Corwyn didn't think she had the wherewithal to love anybody else, and, in the end, it didn't trouble her overmuch. Spinsterhood suited her fine.

It dawned on her slowly; she stopped walking when it came clear. *Ioren* could love Gwen, too, maybe. He was always around now, either sent on errands with Corwyn by the old lady, or haring off into the Hill with Gwen at night to look for whoever killed his grandpa.

So ... what if Gwen loved him back?

None of the other ones had been in love with Gwen. Gwen had never loved them, either. What the hell did people do about love? Got married and had kids, she guessed, walking again now while her brain whirled with thoughts of babies—*Gwen don't even like the little kids at the Volary*, a small part of her tried to say, *and they ain't even in diapers*—and Ioren Gudrunson as a constant presence at Gwen's side.

If he got the Olafurson empire back, it'd keep Gwen safe from the d'Souzas, even safer than Mrs. Simcote could keep her. She wouldn't have to stay at the Volary. Ioren'd let her fight. She'd get a nickname, like Tammy the Squid.

And Corwyn ... not much difference. Take the job the old lady would find for her, keep Mrs. Simcote's protection, live in the apartment she'd be given, maybe in the Hill or Pallasgreen.

All to herself, and what in hell would that be like?

If Ioren didn't get his empire. If he failed and died, well, they'd be no worse off than now, but Gwen—what would she do if she lost somebody she loved? What would she feel, or be, or become?

Goddamned Ioren Gudrunson. Fucking bloody hell and demons.

In this supremely foul mood, Corwyn reached the witch's house.

CORWYN HAD NEVER BEEN allowed to look at the notes Miss Vadoma kept on her; today the witch pored over a stack of them after draining both Corwyn's rage and will to live with five dozen questions about her unexpected jaunt to Bellsbridge. It seemed she hadn't been meant to go that far south.

"Once you puked, you felt all right?" Miss Vadoma asked.

"Yup." Corwyn rubbed a hand over her eyes and wondered if she might be able to get her book out of her rucksack, which she'd left in the corner when she took the potion. Miss Vadoma stacked her notes and put her pencil down, fixing Corwyn with a long, considering gaze.

"Well, Corwyn Teachout, the day has finally arrived."

Corwyn tensed. "What day?"

"The day you're of no use to me anymore."

Corwyn sat up and leaned forward toward Miss Vadoma. "Why?"

"You're too old," she said. "The potions are taking longer to work. They're making you sick. I don't aim to kill you, so."

Corwyn couldn't rightly understand why it felt like the floor had shifted under her; she'd known this would happen eventually. "You could have warned me, Miss Vadoma."

The witch ignored that. "Come along, girl. I'll feed you once more before you leave."

CORWYN LEFT MISS VADOMA'S house with a full belly and no earthly idea where she wanted to go, beyond not the Volary. Maybe St. Phil's, she thought. Sit on the steps and read or stare at the broken clock before heading back nearer sundown.

The street in front of the Collett house was empty. Corwyn squinted at the house; she could just barely make out the dent she'd left in the front wall.

Something moved in the shadow by the house—close to the ground, skittery. She whipped her head to look straight on, half-expecting a monster like Antoine had seen, all blood and teeth and eyes.

But it was a dog. A spindly, scrawny thing that moved funny on three legs with the other pulled up by its body. It crossed the street without looking back at her. She sighed, loud. The dog made her think of Antoine, again, running off from the Volary bruised and unsteady with nary a glance back.

As she turned away, she felt it—her knack seemed almost to stretch, lazy as it woke up, before giving her a jolting tug. At least it was aimed in the direction she'd already been heading.

The closer she got to St. Phil's, the fewer people she saw and the more noise she heard: goddamned gangsters fighting in the street again. Rochester Boulevard was plunged into shadow—somebody'd barricaded the end of it. Two kids hung out a second story window, eating apples, high enough to peer overtop the piled junk and see the fight.

"Is it bad?" she called up.

The older kid shrugged. "You ain't gonna want to plow through it," he called back. "They got guns and knives."

Corwyn stood there for a while, feeling out her knack to work out whether or not she'd be climbing the barricade.

Halfway up, the noise got louder—gunshots, glass breaking, the distinct thud of implements hitting flesh—and it occurred to her that this might likely be the stupidest thing her knack had ever gotten her into, even including taking her into an alley to find a corpse before its killer was completely on its way. The barricade was sturdy, but its foot and handholds were uneven and treacherous. Her rucksack banged against her back, threatening to fall off her shoulder, because her knack hadn't given her a moment to think of securing it better, and it wasn't going to happen now.

Finally, she reached the top and paused to glance over the mass of people fighting below. No silvery flashes or scurrying movement; no clockwork sailors, either. She readjusted her bag before starting down the other side. At least if she got killed out here, her tattoo would mark her as one of Mrs. Simcote's.

She hit the ground with a thud she felt in her jaw. Her knack led round the edges of the fray, past suspicious-looking women and young kids holding ammunition to run into the crowd, past wounded men being patched up. One bloody-faced man grinned at Corwyn with a mouth full of broken teeth, then her knack turned her down an alley.

Someone had strung laundry across it, which cast oddly-shaped shadows, but the air felt cool. The noise of the fight receded as she walked, replaced by the strong smell of blood.

Two half-crumbled walls, one of them attached to the side of the tenement, created a strange little space farther along the alley. Maybe it'd been a mud room once. Corwyn walked to it, slow and watchful in the emptiness and the shadows.

Then she heard something. She stopped moving, unable to name it. Chittering chiming, underscored with a wheezing, grinding clockwork noise. Kind of familiar. It came from the corner where the crumbled wall met the building.

Corwyn's knack tugged her away from the noise to a pile of trash and boards deeper in. For a moment she felt much younger, standing in Shoemaker's Alley. She knelt—the ground dry and warm under her knees—and pushed the trash aside.

What was left of Antoine Gregoire's face looked up at her. Her knack receded. The bruises Ioren'd left on him had almost healed, she noticed. His nose was gone, but he had both eyes. One cheek lay open in a flap. When she uncovered his body, she found his stomach ripped open, and his arms untouched except for blood spatter.

On his right forearm was a blue and gold Goldberg tattoo that didn't quite cover the purple of Mrs. Simcote's.

Corwyn rubbed her eyes with the heels of her hands and did her best to box away thoughts of monsters and Mrs. Simcote and the other kids she'd heard of but couldn't name.

The wheezing clockwork noise went off again. Corwyn pushed herself to her feet. She could occupy herself with whatever that was, she thought, and left Antoine where he was, in the pile of trash.

Half her muscles moved forward and the other half tensed to run if she needed to. The noise surged, then dropped back down again. The feel of the gravel under her boots changed; rocks and bits of shell stuck to her bootsoles with blood.

It was turning into a bang-up day for corpse-finding; this body was tattooed on the inner elbow with the dark blue Dockworker's Union mark. It was one of the few bits of him not bloody; he'd been cut up pretty good. Corwyn thought it likely the blood loss was what killed him.

The cuts were too clean for whatever killed Antoine, though. This didn't rip; it sliced.

She heard the noise again and looked around.

She found it on the ground, behind a lost pair of pants and a couple of rags: an oversized clockwork bug. A wasp, maybe, with a touch of dragonfly, glinting silver in the uneven sunlight. It reminded her of the wrought-iron gates in front of some of the houses in Pallasgreen, only more delicate.

It heaved itself upwards, gears grinding and wings trying to move—both of them were bent, the right one also twisted—then fell back again with a long wheeze.

Corwyn knew that thing.

Well, not that thing in particular, but she had a sudden, dusty memory of a beetle in Cadogan Rentsch's basement and Gwen pushing a button to turn it off. She certainly hadn't felt sorry for the beetle, but she did find herself pitying this little clockwork monster, struggling to get off the ground. She could turn it off, at least.

The segmented body was solid, but it wasn't very heavy. It tried to get loose of her grip, the grinding noise growing alarmingly louder—then it twisted so its left wing sliced her across the back of her wrist. Corwyn hissed and swore. She flipped the bug over as it tried to cut her again. She found a tiny lever hidden under the right wing; she pulled it with her thumbnail.

The bug died immediately with a fading whine. Blood ran down the back of her hand from her wrist, sliding down the twisted silver wires that made the bug's wings. It was pretty.

CORWYN GOT BACK TO the Volary near dark, the bug wrapped in the rags she'd found and stashed in her rucksack. She wove round the gaggle of little kids coming in to report to Mrs. Simcote about the latest developments in her game, ignored Jouanna's shout of her name, and walked up to her room.

She listened for a moment at the door before opening it. Nobody was in there—Gwen's bed was made, which was not a normal occurrence, though now she thought of it, it had been happening for a while—so she crossed to her own bed and pulled the bug out of her bag.

The kids at the window, when she'd come back and showed it to them, had called it a Jersey Devil—"That's what the gangsters call 'em," the older one had said—and Corwyn considered Cadogan Rentsch, all those years ago, finding interesting things down near Jersey Court Road.

She carefully pulled the rags away, revealing the finely-wrought body and delicate wings. It shone where the light struck it.

She had a little money. Sometimes kids or adults in the Hill paid her off the old lady's books to find someone quick. Sometimes she skimmed off the top of what she lifted for Mrs. Simcote. Hell, she'd pick-pocketed a bunch of rich folks in Bellsbridge today and nobody knew about it. Maybe she could pay Cadogan Rentsch to fix the bug and let her keep it. She was unemployed now; if all else failed, she could work for it.

She'd never had anything really pretty before, she thought, running a finger along the twisted wire of its wing, rubbing her blood off it. It would be nice to have some protection.

CHAPTER EIGHTEEN

Corwyn snugged her socked foot into Gwen's left armpit and laced her hands around Gwen's wrist. "You ready?"

"Yeah." Gwen clenched her jaw. Corwyn leaned back slowly, pulling Gwen's arm steadily to try and get her shoulder back into joint.

"Now how'd this happen?" Corwyn asked.

"You know that Mexican gang's ever only in the Hill for six months out the year? They stay over by the Home?"

"You beat up Miguel Suarez?"

"No—" Gwen let out a clenched growl and went on, "He paid me to go beat on some of those jackass Irish kids—I guess they been running his street and pissing him off. It's beneath his—ow, ow, *ow*!—dignity to beat up kids or something."

"No way in nine hells some kiddie gangster did this to you," Corwyn said, irritated. Steady, firm pulling. Her foot was threatening to slip, though.

"Of cou—*goddammit*!" The shoulder popped into place and Gwen relaxed back onto her pillow, panting. "I beat hell out of three of them and then fell off the thrice-damned balcony we were fighting on." She rubbed her face with her good hand. "I got paid, though, so it's all good."

"Until the old lady wants you to do something and you can't because of your busted-up shoulder." Corwyn got up and crossed the room to her own bed. She hadn't expected Gwen back so early; she'd been wanting to turn in and get the day over. She'd spent a lot of it brooding, and some more of it trying to *not* brood over ... well, a lot of things, when it came down to it. Antoine Gregoire. Jersey Devils. Ioren Gudrunson. Her lack of outside employment.

Gwen shrugged with her right arm. "If that happens, I imagine I'll figure it out. I ain't as concerned with staying in the old lady's good graces as you are."

"I ain't *trying* to stay in her good graces," Corwyn said. "She just ... I dunno, likes me better than she does you."

"Of course she does—you're the most valuable thing she owns now Antoine's gone."

Corwyn stiffened; it felt like she'd been punched in the chest. She hadn't told anybody about finding Antoine in the alley, not even Gwen. She knew it was likely safer not to. She just didn't like not knowing for sure, nor wondering what direction the danger might be in. "Shut up, Gwen, you're sore and mad at yourself, don't you take your stupid out on me."

"Stupid? Really? At least I ain't the one looking for someone to replace our—"

Well, that was just insulting. "I am not looking for another drunk to beat on—"

There was a knock at the door, and Ioren Gudrunson opened it, seemingly unaware of the morass of argument he was sticking his head into. "Gwen! Can you—"

"Gwen can't do nothing—she knocked her shoulder out of joint falling off a building," Corwyn snapped.

Ioren barely paused. "Can you come, then? I need a lookout."

"She won't go, that'd upset *Mommy*."

"Oh, I'll go," Corwyn spat, grabbing her pants and pulling them on over her drawers, "I'll go and *you* can sit here stewing about where the hell *I* am for once, Gwendolyn." She picked up her boots and stalked out the room.

Ioren closed the door without comment, waiting until she got her boots on.

"All right," she asked, "where are we going?"

"Beatriz d'Souza's. I'm gonna break into her office."

"YOU ARE OUT OF YOUR *goddamned mind,* Ioren Gudrunson!" Corwyn swung down the rope after him to the second floor, too staggered to do anything but follow.

"See, this is why I'd have preferred to bring Gwen," Ioren called over his shoulder.

"You realize Beatriz d'Souza wants Gwen dead, yeah?"

"So? It ain't like we'd get caught. And you're the one actually coming with me, so."

Corwyn pressed the palms of her hands over her eyes and breathed deep. Beatriz d'Souza had come to the Volary shortly after she and Gwen had moved in; it had been a sight to watch the old lady gaze unblinking into the face of Mrs. d'Souza's titanic, curse-laden, but ultimately impotent fury. The protection of the Volary was not something anyone in the Hill would violate: every story about those who did ended with Mrs. Simcote cleaning her pipe with someone's bones.

That said, Corwyn thought she'd caught sight of the borders of Mrs. Simcote's protection, and sneaking into Beatriz d'Souza's Parlor was very likely beyond them. The old lady had opinions on foolhardiness and responsibility. This was pushing all kinds of luck.

"Why do you need to break into Beatriz d'Souza's office, Ioren?"

Ioren paused near the door to the foyer to wait for her. "Because I got a source says she keeps tabs on every gang in the city, so maybe she's got something on whoever killed my grandfather."

"And you think she won't be expecting you to show up?"

Ioren shrugged, looking enough like Gwen that Corwyn had to bite her tongue not to snap at him. "Mostly I don't care."

Corwyn's brain and stomach churned, and she couldn't make heads nor tails of either of them. "Fine. Let's go see if we can get ourselves killed, then."

PEOPLE—GANGSTERS, SHOPKEEPS, brothel owners—came and went steadily from the Parlor. Corwyn and Ioren watched from the rooftop next door. A guard stood watch on the roof—there was a door up there—smoking a cigar as he walked round the edge.

"We've been here at least half an hour, and he ain't noticed us yet," she murmured to Ioren.

"Yeah, he ain't the smartest lug Beatriz's got on hire," Ioren replied.

Corwyn shifted where she crouched to keep some feeling in her legs, cold without even a bit of her rage having abated. "So why are we waiting over here?"

"Shift change. Sooner or later—I think sooner—someone's going to relieve him, then it's another five hours 'til the next guy comes up. So we take the next guy out right after he comes on—"

"That still leaves whoever we find inside," Corwyn observed.

"It ain't a plan if you don't leave enough rope in it to trip yourself on," Ioren said, seemingly without care.

"Or hang yourself with," Corwyn said.

"See, more reasons I'd have rather brought your sister."

"You could have brought Esma and her lockpicking knack," Corwyn pointed out.

"You and Gwen are the only Volary kids I can stand," he replied, distracted.

They waited a while longer. Corwyn, tired of chewing on her fight with Gwen, began reciting as many of the Samson poems as she could remember under her breath. Ioren glanced curiously at her but didn't tell her to stop. Maybe Gwen had told him about all the poems Corwyn knew and why she recited them. Did they talk about their mothers? Gwen barely talked to Corwyn about Mama.

The door to the club roof opened. Ioren rolled up into a crouch. The cigar man headed downstairs. "Stay here 'til I'm done," Ioren said. Corwyn nodded, getting into her own crouch.

Ioren slunk through the shadows like a ferret. He jumped the gap between the roofs, landing with barely a scuff; the new guard didn't even turn from looking down at the entrance. Ioren caught his balance for a moment, pulled something thin and metal from his boot, then murder-walked closer to the man.

It was quieter than Gwen would have been; Ioren's favorite thing was sneaking up on folk, after all. He grabbed the man, pinched something in his neck or shoulder, and slid the blade into his throat. The guard went down with the barest struggle.

Corwyn hadn't realized Ioren was going to kill him, but she reckoned it made the most sense. She stood up and took a running start to jump to the other roof. Ioren, only slightly blood-spattered, wiped his blade on the man's shirt. "You ready?" he asked.

They made their way carefully down the stairs to the upper floor of the Parlor. Muffled music and voices rose through the heavily carpeted floor. The place smelled of tobacco and must, trapped in the dark wood paneling. They encountered no guards, but likely they'd not hear anyone on another part of the floor, anyway. Corwyn moved as fast as she could while keeping her footsteps gentle as she followed Ioren down the hall.

"How do we know which one's her office?" she whispered.

"Hoping for a sign," he whispered back. "Otherwise we start trying doors."

"Tripping length of rope," Corwyn hissed.

There *was* a sign—small, brass, with *office* etched into its surface, attached to a locked door. Ioren dropped to his knees and pulled a small lockpick kit out of his pocket.

"It's charmed," he muttered. "Because of course it is."

"Are we at hanging length yet?" Corwyn asked.

He grunted as something gave way. "Not yet."

"You want me to pick it? I'm good at it."

"No."

Ioren got back to it, muttering a couple of foreign words to the mechanism, at one point licking his thumb and holding it to the lock. Corwyn softly corrected some of the Greek pronunciation—he didn't have much of an accent, but the little he did got in the way of Greek. Finally the lock gave and let them slip inside. Corwyn stayed just behind the door to keep it open enough to see out.

Ioren combed through the desk in the corner as fast as he could. The hallway remained deserted. Corwyn let herself hope that Beatriz d'Souza considered a guy at the stairs and a guy on the roof enough protection for the second floor.

"I didn't know silver wire cost so much," Ioren whispered after a few minutes.

Corwyn glanced over at him; his eyes were glued to the paper in one hand while the other rubbed absently at his blood mark. "Quit wasting time with files and look for ledgers."

"Finally, bringing you along is made worthwhile," Ioren said with a grin. Corwyn shifted her weight and rolled her eyes.

The jumpiness seeped out of her as Ioren went through the shelves behind the desk. She stifled a yawn just as he whispered, "Yes!" and ripped some pages out of a book. He shoved them into his pocket and replaced the book carefully. "Let's go."

That was certainly easy, she thought as she passed through the door. This might have been why, when the man standing flat against the wall next to it reached out and grabbed her by the arm, she wasn't surprised.

She knew two things: she didn't want this goon seeing her face, and she didn't want to get dragged to Mrs. d'Souza. She twisted to keep her back to him, her sleeve bunching around her arm, then slammed her head back into what she meant to be his throat—he ducked his head, though, so she got him right in the mouth. His teeth ground into her scalp; maybe she'd broken a couple.

He was good enough that he didn't let go—he tightened his grip, instead, even as she kicked back into his shin with the heel of her boot. She knocked him off-balance; there was a muted thump and something pulled him backwards. He lost his grip on her.

Corwyn turned partway, face kept low, to find Ioren with the man's head in a chokehold. The thug struggled, reached behind himself toward Ioren's crotch, but Ioren kept his body curved out of his reach until he passed out.

Ioren lowered him to the floor. "Come on."

They didn't slow down until they were three buildings away and back on the street, and they made the trip back to the Volary in silence.

THEY WERE GREETED BY Jouanna.

"Where have you been?"

"Proving potions," Corwyn said. She might as well get whatever use she could out of that excuse while she still had it; she hadn't told anyone but Gwen yet she'd been fired. "Ioren came to get me. What do you care?"

"Ben Brogan got killed," Jouanna replied, like that was an actual answer to Corwyn's question. Corwyn waited for some explanation of what this had to do with her, but Jouanna just gave Ioren's blood-spattered shirt a significant look before she took off to tell the old lady they were back.

Well, nothing for that, then. Corwyn and Ioren headed up to the third floor. It was late, but not so late that the rest of Mrs. Simcote's kids weren't still milling about.

"You want to see what I found?" Ioren asked.

Thing was, Corwyn didn't much care who'd killed Veigar Olafurson. "No," she said. "I think I just want to go to bed." Corwyn's shoulders and chest were all tight up around her neck as she thought about whether Gwen might be asleep—Gwen could sleep when she was mad, a talent Corwyn did not share—or awake and either pointedly ignoring her or ready to yell some more, but she trudged up the bridge to the third floor anyway.

Ioren took a rope to his side of the landing; as Corwyn reached the top she heard him: "What in hell is this?"

She turned to look—a trunk sat just outside his door. Corwyn leaned on the rail as Ioren kneeled and reached out toward it. "Anything in it?" she asked.

He flipped the latches and cautiously opened it. "No." He paused, looking it over. "Is this the trunk from the docks?"

"Is it clean?"

"It is ... ?" Ioren looked across the space between them, bewildered. "She trying to tell me something?"

"What kind of message is a trunk?"

"I dunno, is she kicking me out?" Ioren was gathering an audience of bored kids. Oid Zavcar and Chilo Urrea drifted closer to get a better look.

"The old lady wouldn't give you the option of misunderstanding her," said Corwyn.

"She's secretive, but not like that," Gwen said; Corwyn turned to find her leaning on the wall next to their door. Gwen didn't look at Corwyn.

"That has to be a message, though," Chilo said from the other end of the landing. "Maybe she's close to tossing you out?"

"It's empty," said Oid, peering over the opened lid. "That likely means something."

"Maybe she's making a point about what used to be in it," Corwyn said softly.

"It's clean," Gwen said, and it sounded like agreement, for all that she still wouldn't look at Corwyn. Pointed ignoring, then.

"I cleaned it." Nils leaned out of his cocoon hammock, hair tousled. "Took most of a day—I ain't never seen bloodstains looked like that before. Chunky. Stickier than usual."

Ioren kicked at the trunk suddenly, sending Oid skipping backward to avoid barked shins. "Goddamned harpy," Ioren muttered. "Well, whatever it means, I don't want it." He shoved at it again. Oid swore at him and retreated farther, taking Chilo with him.

Corwyn sighed; she'd been done with Ioren's problems before they even saw the thrice-damned trunk. She shoved herself off the railing and headed to their room. Gwen didn't follow, so she pulled off her clothes, unpinned her hair, and got into bed. She didn't sleep much, and when she did get up the next morning, Gwen was gone, her bed, as usual, unmade.

CHAPTER NINETEEN

It turned out Ben Brogan getting killed did have something to do with Corwyn, after all: Mrs. Simcote locked up the Volary again until whatever storm his murder started died back down.

The sparring started up almost immediately after they ran out of lessons they could do without outside help. The roof filled with kids—even ones without fighting knacks got in on it. Corwyn didn't; she sat to the side and watched Gwen fight Ioren. Even with Gwen nursing a lame arm, he was the only one who could match her, and he showed her ways to compensate for the injury.

There wasn't much any of Mrs. Simcote's kids, past or present, could teach Gwen. None of them could get hold of her, for one thing, and Mrs. Simcote, secretive and unwilling to show her hand to anyone outside her vast network of children, never bothered to find the teachers for Gwen that Veigar Olafurson had found for his grandson.

It was like lightning teaching quicksilver, Corwyn thought. The phrase echoed round her head, souring and tiresome for it, particularly when the lessons worked and Gwen got faster and smarter and just *better*. All the kids did, really, even the ones as just watched or got used as cannon fodder for Gwen and Ioren's battles.

Eventually Gwen and Ioren started taking on two kids, one each, keeping points on who took theirs down quicker. Memno ended up with a cauliflower ear out of it. Gwen won.

Then the real boredom set in. Word from the outside (though, since nobody was allowed outside, it was a mystery as to how anybody got the word) said the Hill was pure-on chaos: fighting, blood, and not a cease-fire in sight. The gossip and the skirmishes they could sometimes see from the roof made the kids with the fighting knacks restless, which got everybody distractible. The old lady, caught between the need to keep her kids safe and her growing rage at every con, plan, and source of income she used those kids for being ground to a standstill, stayed in her office. She emerged only when the occasional scuffle got loud enough to disturb her, and then scared the living hell out of all of them with the merest murderous glance.

Corwyn and Gwen finally holed up in their room after Mattie Singh blew the windows out the lab room downstairs by mixing rubbing alcohol with, it was rumored, butter. They were awkward, but in the face of Mrs. Simcote's wrath and all that broken glass, they found themselves willing to ignore it. Ioren joined them, Beatriz d'Souza's notes in hand.

"He didn't train me to be a *detective*," he groaned, tossing the pages and himself on the end of Gwen's bed. "He just wanted me to be able to kill people seven different ways."

Corwyn put her book down with a sigh. She didn't know if the d'Souza boys were aware the pages were gone, or if Beatriz knew who'd been in her office if so. The lack of relevant rumors was her least favorite part of being locked up.

Gwen looked over the pages. "Beatriz's got a nice hand," she said, flipping the front page to show Corwyn. The whole thing wasn't in code—Veigar's name was written at the top, and in the margins she could see other names: Ioren's, his mother's, one Corwyn didn't recognize but that was clearly not coded.

"That your uncle?" she asked, remembering what Ioren had told her about surnames.

"I guess. My mum never really talked about any of them to me."

Gwen flipped the page back and peered closely at it. "She's not making this hard," she murmured. "Hand me a pencil, Wyn?"

"You think you can read it?" Ioren asked.

"I think I got codebreaking lessons back when we first got here," Gwen said as Corwyn passed her a pencil.

"I don't remember that," Corwyn said, frowning.

"You were otherwise engaged," Gwen said. "The old lady was testing her knack a lot," she replied to Ioren's puzzled look. "She wanted me kept occupied. Most interest she's taken in my education thus far."

"She didn't test out your knack?" he asked.

"I've got a fighting knack; ain't much she needs to know. Finding knack's harder to come by," Gwen said, going back to the page.

"Your fighting knack ain't exactly garden variety," Ioren said, and for a minute Corwyn actually liked him.

Gwen ignored him, opting instead to divide the pages between the three of them. "Find single-letter words and double symbols," she told them. "She's smart enough to skip apostrophes."

"I'd have imagined Corwyn'd be the one good at this," Ioren said.

"Gwen's got the better eyes," Corwyn replied, watching her sister scribbling letters in the spaces over the symbols.

"You just make stuff more complicated than it needs to be," Gwen said without any bite. Then, "It's an Imperial shift! Ha!" She scribbled some more in the top margin of the page, then went back to the text itself with a little humming laugh of triumph. Ioren hovered over Gwen's shoulder; Corwyn wondered how long Gwen would put up with that and whether the length of time it took her to shoo him off would mean anything about the two of them. Gwen still hadn't said a thing about it.

About three pages on, Jouanna knocked on their door and leaned in. "Hey Gwen, the old lady wants you."

"Why? Ioren gave Memno the cauliflower ear, not me."

Jouanna shrugged. "There's a lady in her office, maybe she got you a job?" She left, leaving the door open. Gwen looked dubious—Mrs. Simcote rarely found Gwen work—but put the pages aside and leaned over the bed to get her boots.

"The cypher's at the top of the page," she said. "Corwyn ought to be able to figure the rest out. And be sure you tell me what it says when I get back."

"Be careful of your shoulder," said Corwyn.

"I will be careful of my shoulder," Gwen echoed, singsong. She tied her boots and filled her pockets. "Don't do anything stupid without me, you hear?"

Ioren watched after her with a look of longing that soured the bit of liking Corwyn had mustered for him. "All right," she said briskly, "Let's solve this, then."

THE CANNY OLD BITCH used no names beyond Veigar's and his children's—they were dead, so what was the harm, Corwyn supposed—everybody was a street or an animal, and she'd pay cash money to find out who "the Leshi" was. On top of that were the references to things that might have made sense if they'd had more pages. Or the whole journal.

"Now your problem is a lack of context," Corwyn told Ioren as she handed him her finished pages.

She left Ioren to puzzle over them, settling in to read her book. The Hawk had just been doublecrossed by the gods when Ioren asked, "You know anything 'bout a guy named 'The Devil'? Uses knives?"

Corwyn didn't look up. "I heard about Asmeday Duarte, but he uses those chakram things he stole off the Sikh up by Stolarski Park. The Stigmata hermit used knives, but he's been dead for years."

"No, this guy's called The Devil. The Jersey Devil—maybe he's English?"

Corwyn dropped her book. "Where was that?" she asked, scrambling up behind him to look over his shoulder.

"Up here—Gwen ciphered it. Corwyn?"

"Jersey Devil? Sharp blades, many, many wounds. Too precise for one of those blood monsters. Would also explain how the killer eluded Veigar's."

Corwyn pulled back from hovering over Ioren. "The Jersey Devil ain't a guy," she said.

"What is it, then?"

She reached over and pulled her rucksack from under the bed, then carefully pulled the rag-wrapped bug out of it. "It's one of these," she said, unwrapping the bundle. "I found it in an alley by St. Phil's."

Ioren put out a finger to the wing, pulled it back with a hiss. "Someone's making these to kill gang lords?" he asked.

"There any gangs got an alchemical engineer as a pet?" Corwyn asked.

"Ain't none of them willing to pay what an alchemical engineer'd charge, I'd've thought," Ioren said around his bloody finger.

A drop of Ioren's blood was caught on the silver-wire wing, for all like it was supposed to be set there. Corwyn gingerly soaked it up with a corner of her sleeve. "So one of these things killed your grandpa?"

"Beatriz d'Souza thinks so," Ioren said thoughtfully.

"So whoever set the bugs on Veigar is who you need to kill."

Ioren tilted his head and looked at her. "That enough for your knack?"

Corwyn felt for it, that moment of waking, something inside her head pricking its ears up, curious. Maybe she felt it stir, but it subsided again. "No," she said, looking back at him.

She still hated him, with his puppy eyes at her sister and fighting skills to match her. But if he could satisfy his oath and not die. If he could manage to get back his grandfather's empire. If Gwen could be somewhere safe *and* somewhere she could be happy. Well.

"I know someone we can ask about it, though," she said. "You up to sneaking out to Chaffins Grove?"

CHAPTER TWENTY

Her knack, ridiculous thing that it was, woke up for Cadogan Rentsch.

Ioren peeked out the door. Jouanna and her few friends stalked the Volary, itching to start a row or get someone in trouble. Other kids milled on the bridges and climbed the ropes. The littles played hide and seek; some of them had chalked a hopscotch court on the second floor by the stairs.

"Come on," Ioren finally said. "I can show you, since Gwen's not back."

Corwyn followed him out the door and played along. "I know how to kneecap someone, Ioren Gudrunson."

"Yeah, but Gwen says you ain't good at it, so come on."

Corwyn was half-afraid someone would want to watch Ioren teach her how to take somebody out at the knees—which she was perfectly fine at, thank you—but Jouanna had gotten distracted by Cy Blackburn trying to set fire to Lawrence Booth's discarded shoes, and the littles were all-in on their games.

They went out via the roof into a Hill that was not, in fact, roiling in chaos and blood. No, the windows were tight shut; the carts in front of the grocers' were empty; there weren't many people on the streets; and the ones that were moved fast without looking at anything around them. The air lay still with just the slightest trembling sense to it, as though Cobbler's Hill itself had drawn a breath but had not yet exhaled.

Their footsteps echoed flat off the buildings as they walked. Ioren flinched when he spoke, modulating quickly, "So what were you up by St. Phil's for, when you found that thing? Your knack?"

"The hell d'you care? Enough that I found it." Her knack buzzed between her eyes, misbehaving.

"Just, St. Phil's was Grandfather's. Lots of fighting that way."

"Yeah, well, lots of fighting that day, too, but I found it all the same," she replied.

"What in hell is your problem with me, Corwyn?" Ioren asked. "I can't decide if you like me or hate me. Gwen's got her mind made up, why don't you?"

Corwyn stopped walking, ignored the pulling of her knack, and turned to face him. "What exactly are your intentions toward my sister, Ioren Gudrunson?"

He blinked at her. "My—whats?"

"Your intentions. Oh, don't go all stupid on me, I know you two are fucking. But I see how you look at her, so what are you intending?"

"How the hell should I know? It ain't like she talks to me about anything like that!"

"Just 'cause she ain't talking don't mean you ain't thinking—and you'd best be thinking about what happens if we find whoever killed your granddad." Corwyn poked at his chest with one finger before turning to stalk up the road.

Ioren scrambled to catch up to her. "Now, wait—you don't like me because I like your sister?"

Well, she sure wasn't going to admit to *that*. "I don't like you because I don't know what you plan to *do* about liking my sister. Assuming you live."

"So if I marry her, it'd be okay?"

Corwyn ground her jaw. "No," she bit out. "But it'd be tolerable."

He was quiet for a while, as they trudged north, until finally he asked, "D'you think she'd want that? Would she stay with me?"

Corwyn swallowed down *She would if I talked her into it.* "Hell if I know—there's no predicting Gwen."

"Well, *that* ain't true."

"Oh, it ain't?"

"I am under no illusions whatever as to what would befall me at your sister's hands, were I in any way foolish enough to mess with you, Corwyn Teachout. I'm surprised the old lady's still kicking, to be honest."

"Gwen's not dumb enough to kill a meal ticket," Corwyn said wearily.

Ioren scoffed. "What'd the old lady do to make Gwen hate her so much, anyway?"

Corwyn kept her eyes on her boots. "Gwen overreacts."

"She does not."

"You're just contrary as hell today," Corwyn muttered, then sighed. "Mrs. Simcote got my knack to kick and then locked me in a room to see what'd happen. Gwen took exception to that."

Ioren said nothing for about a block, then asked, "What did happen?"

"I clawed my hands bloody on the door, then knocked myself out. After a while."

"Nine hells, Corwyn."

"I am tough as nails and twice as sharp, what can I say."

He shook his head. "See, now, that would make me leave."

"Well we ain't got that option, and you know why," Corwyn told him.

"You think you two ain't got—" Ioren broke off, then, because they'd just crossed Mars Hill Road; the afternoon sun reflected off the leaves of the clockwork redwood into their eyes. "Is that ... ?"

"Yup."

Ioren gaped. Corwyn thought she'd never seen him look so much like a boy before, all wide eyes and slack jaw, a little dirt and a scab across his cheek, scudding his hand over his face to push his curls off his forehead.

"Come on," she said. He followed her, eyes still on the redwood until he finally tore them away.

"The problem with both you Teachout girls is you lack vision," he said, but Corwyn was finished talking about it and didn't reply.

IOREN SHIFTED INTO Veigar Olafurson's grandson somewhere between the bottom and top steps of Cadogan Rentsch's porch: his spine straightened, his mouth tightened. His knock on the door was a pounding.

"Yes?" Corwyn didn't expect Rentsch to recognize her, but he hadn't changed much—hair as wild as ever, eyebrows as absurd, same goggles atop his head. Fewer bleeding cuts; grayer hair. But still very much the same man who'd nearly got them killed in his basement.

"You Cadogan Rentsch?" Ioren asked.

"I am." He glanced back and forth between them, puzzled. "I'm not looking for apprentices."

"My name is Ioren Veigarson," Ioren said, with the air of a prince reluctantly picking up a crown. "I got some questions for you."

Rentsch did that thing again, that imperceptible thing that turned him from harmless eccentric to dangerous eccentric. "I've had no dealings with the Olafursons."

"Maybe not directly," Ioren replied, and pushed past Rentsch into his house. Corwyn followed, rummaging carefully in her bag to get the bug.

"D'you know who made this?" she asked, handing it over.

"Did *you* make it?" Ioren asked.

"Of course he didn't make it," Corwyn snapped, "it ain't his style—look round the room."

Rentsch took the bug, but his gaze lay on Corwyn with an appraising quality she didn't much care for because she was pretty sure it meant he knew just who he was looking at. "And where'd you find this?" he asked.

"Over by the cathedral. The kids say it comes from up round Jersey Court Road."

Rentsch smiled, slanted. "Someone's been refining their skills, then."

"And selling them to gang lords," Ioren said.

"Maybe," Rentsch murmured, turning the bug over in his hands. The yellow lamplight caught along its body, turning it golden. "Nobody I know of works this fine," he said, a bit louder but no less preoccupied. "That's good wire work—does it fly?" he asked Corwyn suddenly.

"Hell if I know," she said. "I mean, there's no skin or nothing on the wings."

"Good eye. But I bet it does, don't you?"

She nodded, feeling shy suddenly, as Ioren—sounding equal parts desperate and angry—said, "If you got no idea who made it, you got any as to how we can find out?"

Rentsch looked over at him, up and down. "You're the grandson?"

"I ain't got money to pay for information—not now—"

Rentsch waved a hand. "I'm not a witch, you don't always have to pay me. Sometimes the intellectual exercise is enough."

"And other times you get the heir to the Olafurson empire owing you a favor," drawled Corwyn.

She got a full-on smile in response to that. "Indeed." Rentsch took the bug to a cluttered table near one of the front windows, the one that held his lamp. "Alchemical engineers are a vain lot, but we're also not fools—not everything we make should announce its maker to the world. Therefore—" He moved to one of the bookshelves along the back of the room and retrieved what looked like a magnifying glass, but with an extra lens on a metal arm extending from the handle, which was also home to two knobs and a button. He spit on his fingers, rubbed the button, then brought the contraption over and peered through it at the bug. "Therefore," he repeated, turning a knob and bringing the extra lens to bear, "we leave maker's marks on our work. But we hide them."

It took a while; he looked carefully at the body and the head, at the tail and the wings, and finally he let out an "Ah-ha!" and motioned for Corwyn and Ioren to take a look.

"Is that a flower?" Corwyn asked. The mark was tiny, etched onto one wing-wire. She leaned closer in, trying to coax her knack along with thoughts of Jersey Court Road and Veigar Olafurson, Ben Brogan.

"Looks like an oyster," Ioren said. "Whose is it?" Corwyn's knack stirred again, then dropped back down to wherever in her skull it usually lurked.

"Dunno," said Rentsch, frowning. "But I'd certainly like to find out." Ioren looked at Corwyn over his head, eyebrows up. She shrugged, shaking her head there merest amount. "Tell you what," Rentsch said, straightening up, "if I rig it to take you to wherever it thinks home is, will you come back and tell me?"

"Whyn't you go yourself?" Corwyn asked. "You're so keen to know."

"He's keener," Rentsch said, with a nod in Ioren's direction. "And I have no desire to wade through the mess that is currently the Hill."

Of course. Well, it wasn't like he'd specified the information had to be attached to anybody living. Corwyn watched Ioren and nodded when he did, adding, "You're going to pay us for our trouble, though, slogging all the way back up here from Pallasgreen or worse."

"Half up front, half when you come back," Rentsch agreed cheerfully, headed off to another room in the back of the house.

"Actual cash money, not some alchemical engineer's scrip!" Ioren called after him.

Rentsch's voice was muffled, but still cheerful when he called back, "Oh, you *are* Veigar's grandson."

IT TOOK RENTSCH A WHILE to fiddle the bug back to life. He worked at the table with his goggles on and the lamp turned up high. Corwyn found a chair and got her book out of her rucksack, read about the Hawk's doomed campaign against the trickster gods while Ioren paced the room.

She wondered, watching Ioren examine the items on the shelves, what it might have been like to apprentice herself and Gwen to Cadogan Rentsch. Learning to make little people. Maybe building arms and legs, maybe chaining demons into music boxes, maybe making watches that controlled their wearers or any number of things that alchemical engineers were rumored to do, the things that had driven some of the kids at the Home mad. Then again, not every kid went mad, or there'd be no new alchemical engineers. She wondered if Molly and Archulus were still there, in the attics of the rebuilt (and, she hoped, fireproof) Singleton Home, if there were more kids up there with them, now.

In the end, she thought, it would have been an entirely different set of skills she'd have, as an alchemical engineer's apprentice. She couldn't have said if they'd have been better or not.

"Come here," Rentsch finally called, nodding over his shoulder at her. "As will likely come as no shock to you, this thing needs blood. So hold out your hand."

"How come I'm the one gets to bleed?" she asked.

"Well, for one thing it might tie the bug to you a little bit, assuming I do it right." Corwyn sighed and stuck her right hand out. "And," he went on, slicing across the scar on her palm, "I like you better than I do him."

"Lovely way you have of showing your regard, Mr. Rentsch."

He collected the welling blood with a glass dropper and handed her a bandage with his other hand before positioning the bug just so under the light. "You continue to appear on my doorstep periodically without ever introducing yourself, so I feel our relationship warrants unusual demonstrations of regard."

"Corwyn," she said. "Corwyn Teachout."

He smiled at her, his eyes magnified huge and a little crazy by his goggles. "Pleased to finally make your acquaintance," he said, then turned and dropped the blood into a small concavity on the bug's tiny head. It ran from the indentation along tiny crannies that she could only see as the blood filled them. It was actually kind of lovely, the red outlining the bug's silver body like a drawing.

"Whoever they are, they've got an eye," Rentsch said appreciatively. He raised his voice so Ioren could hear, "All right, I turn this on, it's going to take off, so get ready to follow."

He flipped the tiny switch with his nail. With a clacking wheeze, the bug's wings began to flap and pull it unsteadily into the air. Corwyn hurried to the door and opened it. The bug flew over her head though the doorway, ruffling her hair, into the rapidly darkening evening.

CHAPTER TWENTY-ONE

The roar as the Hill exhaled became apparent long before they crossed Jersey Court Road, but it got much, much louder once they did.

The first visual indication of the battle: a kid with a Tong tattoo just under his throat running straight out past them, chased by three thugs whose tattoos Corwyn couldn't see, but who she was pretty sure belonged to the late Ben Brogan. The Tong kid, for all his speed, didn't look particularly scared as he led the Brogan boys toward the docks. The Tongs weren't much for fighting, but they were brutal when they decided to wade in.

Ioren barely noticed, intent on their lopsided clockwork guide.

Corwyn debated for a while about skipping out on him and going back to the Volary, but the idea of encountering Mrs. Simcote without the pass of assisting with familial revenge—along with the appealing idea of an eventual gang lord owing her a favor—kept her trudging along as the crowd steadily thickened.

There wasn't time enough to get their bearings or head to the rooftops: the bug sounded sickly but moved unerringly south. One eye apiece on it, they ducked bricks thrown by kids leaning out tenement windows; they moved quick and gingerly around the gang of men kicking someone or something they couldn't see on the ground. The sun passed behind the buildings, but the street got warmer with the body heat of the fight. The wall of noise, a rumble of feet and violence, laced with the smell of blood and shit, rose around them.

"It's everyone," Corwyn marveled; she saw Brogans, Dockworker's Union boys and their clockwork sailors, some of the Goldberg crew, the d'Souza gang, the Haitians from down by Follett Row, a multitude of others whose tattoos she couldn't make out, and what she swore was the Suarez gang. Corwyn dug the truncheon out of her rucksack, which she swung to hang across the front of her.

A fist came at Ioren, who ducked it, grabbed hold, and broke its owner's wrist. Corwyn broke the nose of a man who lunged at her, teeth bared to show a gap where the four front ones ought to be.

Following Ioren through a gang battle was different from following Gwen. Ioren had a tendency to drop people where they stood rather than tossing them aside and into Corwyn. Folk would make room after that, so they lurched through the crowd in spurts until they came across someone who hadn't seen Ioren use his blade on the last one.

This meant his focus was on the crowd, though, so Corwyn kept eyes on the bug as best she could. A number of the things darted round—she took one out with her truncheon before it could slice her eyes—but theirs stood out, crooked in the air on one track.

A man with a nail-studded piece of wood came at her; she dropped and slammed the truncheon into his knee, kicked his shin and caught up to Ioren. "Where the hell are *your* people?"

He pulled his knife out of another man's throat; blood was scattered across his face like his freckles. "I reckon they're here somewhere. There ain't many of them left."

"That don't bode well for your future prospects," Corwyn said. Someone yanked her around backward by her elbow. Osian Lauredent frowned down at her, arm drawn back to punch.

"Corwyn?"

"Fucking hell," she said, and kneed him solid in the crotch.

Osian folded, looking betrayed. She kicked him in the ribs to keep him down before turning back to Ioren.

Who wasn't there.

She took an elbow to the ear from someone who wasn't even trying to hit her and staggered into a slightly more open space in the crowd. A knot of thugs, keeping together, hurried out of the fight. "Nine goddamned hells," she muttered, casting a fleeting look up to note the direction of the bug. Then she set off after them.

By the time she emerged from the crowd into an alley, she was nursing a shallow knife wound to her arm and probably a bruised rib, while Ioren already had two of the men who'd grabbed him down. Corwyn slammed the truncheon into the third's skull while Ioren bounced the fourth one off a wall.

They stood there, panting and looking at the men's Brogan tattoos—Corwyn was pretty sure only a couple of them were dead, which meant they needed to get moving—until Ioren looked at her. "Dammit, Corwyn, we lost the bug!"

"Yes, well, next time you're snatched I'll leave you to it," she said, not arguing. "I know which way it was headed, so—"

A chugging, off-kilter buzz materialized over their heads. The bug circled above them a couple of times, then wobbled off south again. It seemed Cadogan Rentsch was better at blood magic than he thought.

AS THEY APPROACHED St. Phil's, Ioren's people appeared; Corwyn recognized them from their visits to the Volary. The haggard woman and a couple of big bruisers found and followed them for a while, spitting what Corwyn could only figure was Icelandic at Ioren, who spat back at them in that and Creole.

She guessed he'd explained what they were after, because the Olafursons did their best to keep the bulk of the fight off Ioren. It wasn't easy—the bug led them through the thick of it, where the stench and struggle were worst. She caught glimpses of others she recognized, and some who looked like they had the Olafurson mark on them, but Ioren was right—there weren't nearly as many of them as was needed to win this war.

They came to a standstill in the midst of the crowd, elbowed in the ribs and back and head by the fighters around them, unable to push through the mass of bodies. Corwyn dropped to her hands and knees and yanked Ioren down with her. They crawled through legs like, Corwyn imagined, crawling through a forest. Streams of blood from the mobs' injuries caught in channels on the road and flowed toward the cathedral.

They left Ioren's folk behind as they crawled through the mob. It was hot and close, but they finally found a space in which to stand and weave around the gangsters.

The two of them were filthy, battered, and bloody when the bug finally led them down a side street that emerged back onto Jersey Court Road and the great stone arch that read BROGAN. The bug sailed under the arch toward the house, the pull of its maker apparently now stronger than the tie of Corwyn's blood.

"But Brogan's dead," Ioren said as they made their way under the arch. The bug had disappeared into the shadows. Iorne led the way to the front door. "And he wasn't any kind of alchemical engineer. His son's no genius, either, I think his knack's for growing plants or some such—"

Corwyn's head filled, then—the tool kit in the lighthouse, the smell of oil, the stripped clockwork man; she heard Cristos Katsaros, *I told them Tansa's smarter than she looks* and *Nobody cares about your fucking toys!*

"It's Tansa," she said. "Fucking bloody—it's *Tansa*." Immediately she wanted to find and tell Gwen, not sure if she was afraid or admiring or just wanted to see Gwen's face—

—and her knack woke up and pointed, like *it* was the dog this time, and she knew she wasn't admiring a damn thing, because what in nine hells was Gwen doing in Tansa Katsaros Brogan's house?

CHAPTER TWENTY-TWO

"Gwen's in there," Corwyn said. Ioren, bouncing on his toes in his wanting to *go*, came down flat-footed.

"Why would she—is that who the old lady wanted her to body-guard?"

"I don't think either one of them'd agree to that. We got history with Tansa Brogan."

Ioren knelt and applied himself to the front door lock. "The two of you got history with every damn one in the Hill—come on, ain't like Gwen can't take care of herself."

Corwyn couldn't argue, but she also couldn't fathom why Gwen would be in the Brogans' house to begin with. But it didn't matter, she reflected. She was going in after Gwen anyway.

"We could knock," she suggested. "Maybe we get lucky and Tansa opens the door."

"Because that sort of luck is likely. No, we'd more likely get three or four of Brogan's boys—let's aim for a touch of surprise."

It took some time for Ioren to work through the lock. Once it was sprung, he glanced at Corwyn, then opened the door carefully. It creaked; Corwyn tensed. They walked inside, Ioren first.

The foyer and the living room were empty.

Nobody came thundering down the staircase. They heard no footsteps from the floor above them as they followed Corwyn's knack through the front room into the silent dining room. The table, covered by a heavy, floor-length cloth, wasn't set. The room was neat; it didn't look like anyone had left in a rush.

The smell, though. Blood and shit. As they rounded the table toward the kitchen door, they found the source of it: Allen Brogan, sliced-up bloody dead, arranged neatly parallel to the table, where he and his mess were hidden from the entrance by the tablecloth.

Ioren's eyebrows rose, but he made no sound. Nor did Corwyn; just followed her knack over the body and to the kitchen. This room was deserted, as well, though its tidiness wasn't marred by any corpses.

Still. "I don't like this," Corwyn said in a low voice. They approached a door that, when opened, proved to lead to a basement. A narrow set of raw wood stairs ran down the wall into the dark.

"Here we go." Ioren went first, again. Corwyn dug in her rucksack for one of her glowing rocks and the truncheon.

The rock was more comfort than real illumination, but it kept them from tripping down the stairs. Corwyn's knack went a little fuzzy as they descended, much like descending to Mrs. Simcote's office, but nonetheless it kept her aimed toward *Gwen, Gwen, Gwen.* She stayed behind Ioren as he stepped onto the dirt floor. Shelves containing shadows and dark rose up around them; the basement itself smelled stale, but not as damp as she would have thought. "Over this way," she murmured.

"Is that a door?" Ioren whispered back. The green light showed it was, in an arched doorway.

Upon close inspection the plain wooden door proved to have one hell of a lock on it. Corwyn squatted to inspect it in the rocklight. There were layers upon layers of charms and clockwork lock—not sophisticated, more like discouragement through sheer volume of work. She handed the truncheon to Ioren, pulled her lock-pick tools out of her pocket, and shoved her knack to the back of her head.

The first level went quickly; she felt the mechanics give under her tools, found the charms inside and whispered a few all-purpose bits of Greek to them, then began the second layer of clockwork, then the next layer of magic. It would have been soothing had her knack not been hissing at her.

Eventually she sat back on her heels as the lock, then the door, popped open.

"You are good at that," Ioren whispered. Corwyn shrugged, putting her tools in the case. All told, she thought it'd taken four minutes, but she had been one-handed.

Ioren's cautious step forward landed with a metallic clang. A plate under his foot flipped up, knocked him off-balance. He staggered back. Corwyn lunged out of the way—a grinding hydraulic noise came from above—and didn't think, just scrambled through the doorway and over the plate before a huge metal door slammed down between her and Ioren.

She could hear him, muffled, through the door: "Goddamn you, Corwyn Teachout, do *not* kill that woman!"

Well, at least he knew better than to think she'd wait around for him to find a way through the new door. She stood up, stowed her lockpick kit—still in her hand—in her pocket. She brushed off her knees and hands, then let loose her knack.

HER ROCK LIT A SHORT, low-ceilinged corridor with two doors set in either wall and one door facing her at the end. They were regular plank doors without a lock to be seen on any of them. If her knack hadn't been pulling at her she might have opened one to get some idea of what she was oh-so-carefully walking into, but as it was she kept going. Gwen, it seemed, was behind the door at the end of the hall.

The knob turned easily. She tensed, ready to jump or duck or spring, and nudged the door open. It swung smooth, not even a creak of hinges.

The room beyond was well-lit, so she slid the rock into her other pocket. It looked to be a workroom: shelves, tables to work on with gears and wires scattered over them, tools hung on hooks, a door in the opposite wall, and a huge black box that looked like nothing so much as a coffin on a wheeled platform at the other side of the room. Toward which her knack pulled her.

Corwyn paused inside the door to cast around. A thick metal rod that she could use as a crowbar—why wasn't Gwen banging and trying to get out of the box?—lay on the shelf closest to her; she took it and started across the room.

Tansa Katsaros walked through the door in the opposite wall, sweaty, covered in dirt, a soil-caked shovel clutched in one hand. She stopped when she saw Corwyn and rolled her eyes.

"I told that woman you'd show up here." She sounded more irritated than scared. Corwyn could use that, she was sure.

"Where's my sister?" she asked, even though she knew. She shrugged her rucksack off her shoulder onto the floor.

"In the box." Tansa laid her shovel on it, gave the lid a pat of her filthy hand.

"And she got there how?" Corwyn shifted a tetch, got her weight distributed better.

"I'd have thought you'd be more curious as to why." Corwyn didn't reply. She ignored her knack and the panic slapping at the back of her head. She waited. Tansa Katsaros was a frustrated alchemical engineer; surely she'd want to brag. And after a moment, she did: "The Simcote woman had her red cap drug her as she came down the stairs."

Corwyn couldn't think of anyone in the Volary who wore a red cap. "You talking about Ned Shuluk? He ain't fast enough for that. Ain't none of Mrs. Simcote's kids faster than Gwen."

"It's not a kid; it's a monster. Of a sort I want. I want a monster with claws and teeth and a knack for fighting."

Oh, nine hells. "I guess that would be quite a thing to have," Corwyn said around the lump of panic and knack lodged in her throat.

Tansa smiled. "I'll own the Hill. And then the city. It's not got the obvious poetry of using Veigar's grandson, but the old bitch refused—"

Corwyn threw the crowbar at her.

She meant it at most to be a distraction, but Tansa ducked and Corwyn got her good on her upper arm. Tansa hissed, then whistled.

The tops of all the shelves in the room came alive with movement as maybe two dozen clockwork bugs woke up and started to swarm.

They got in each other's way, flying into one another in a mad rush to get to her. Corwyn took that moment of chaos to bolt for the coffin and vault it, pulling the shovel over with her as she went.

She nearly landed on Gwen, lying on the floor behind the plinth.

The two of them looked each other over; Gwen was sweaty, greenish around her mouth, clearly mad as hell and getting madder.

"That your blood?" she mouthed.

Corwyn raised a hand and tilted it back and forth. *Not all of it.*

"I can't walk," Gwen mouthed.

"Goddammit," Corwyn muttered, and the bugs swept over the coffin.

She rose and got a couple of them with a heaving swing of the shovel, dirt showering into her hair and eyes, but the bulk of them dodged like a flock of birds. Corwyn wiped her eyes on her shoulder and stepped over to cover Gwen as much as she could.

The noise and heat of the clockwork blanketed them. Gwen peered round the side of the coffin; Corwyn couldn't see much as she swung at the cloud of bugs again—she got a couple, the impact running down the shovel to her elbows—but she could hear Tansa moving round on the other side of it. Probably trying to figure out how to get to the coffin without getting cut by her own weapons.

Corwyn got another one. A sharp line of pain along her arm—a bee-shaped bug dodged her swing. Corwyn's blood caught in Gwen's hair.

"Get *closer*," Gwen muttered in a voice made of rocks. Corwyn spun and kicked at a dragonfly that dodged down toward her sister, who didn't notice anything, fiercely focused as she was on what was happening on the other side of the coffin.

The coffin lid smacked Corwyn hard in the back. She heard Tansa—"Where the hell did you go?"—just before Gwen shoved the coffin away from them so hard she fell on her face. Corwyn, balance thrown, hit the floor on her knees, waving the shovel blindly round her head as the bugs took their opportunity to open up slices along her back and shoulders. The lid closed with a meaty thud. Tansa screamed again. Corwyn lurched around, trying to catch sight of Gwen.

Tansa knelt on the floor by the coffin, cradling her right hand. Gwen hauled herself with her forearms across the room, toward the shelves.

A moth dove for Corwyn's face, nearly getting her cheek, and she lost track of everything save the stench of blood and oil and the movement of trying to knock the bugs down. She stumbled toward the coffin, hoping to draw them away from Gwen and make Tansa's life harder. Three bugs down at once; her arms were getting tired, starting to ache, and the wound in her hand had lost its bandage and reopened painfully. One bug moved feebly on the floor; Corwyn stomped on it until it stopped.

There was a sudden shriek of metal, followed by Gwen's inventive cursing—"Bitchshitting fuck-mook *bastard*!"—and all but four of the remaining bugs dropped out of the air around her to the ground, bouncing with a metal jangle. Corwyn wearily wound up to swing at the rest—

A blast of heat knocked her and the rest of the bugs to the floor. She landed flat on her back, stunned, the shovel lost.

"Goddammit," Gwen swore.

"*Gwen!*" Ioren's voice; Corwyn couldn't quite pinpoint which direction anything was coming from. She pushed herself up sitting and shoved her hair out of her face to see.

Ioren stood in the doorway, panting, glaring at Tansa Katsaros Brogan, who stood with her back to Corwyn. She'd set her boot firm on Gwen's neck. Gwen, covered with soot, hands burned-red, struggled under Tansa's foot, her legs barely moving.

Corwyn's head cleared quick. She glanced around herself. Ioren's eyes never moved from Tansa.

"You the one as killed my grandfather?" Ioren asked, in a voice that would have been even had he not been out of breath.

A bug, shaped like a butterfly, lay next to Corwyn's leg. She reached out carefully and wrapped her hand around it, not even hissing when it sliced her palm open again across the wound Cadogan Rentsch had made. She got to her feet silently, imagining the book on top of her head like Mrs. Simcote had had them taught.

Corwyn could hear the smile in Tansa's voice as she said, "I couldn't rule the Hill otherwise."

Ioren made half a lunge toward Tansa, who ground her boot into Gwen's neck. Gwen grimaced, didn't make a sound, but Ioren stopped all the same. Nobody seemed to notice Corwyn, which was, after all, how she preferred it. "You move and I will break her fucking neck," Tansa said, her voice still smiling.

Corwyn hoped that Tansa's face was at least as shocked as Ioren's when Corwyn stepped up and slit her throat with the clockwork bug.

CHAPTER TWENTY-THREE

Tansa's blood flowed warm over Corwyn's hands, spattering her boots as the body thudded onto the floor. Gwen sucked in a wheezing heave of air.

Ioren was on Corwyn before Gwen exhaled. She couldn't have been less surprised.

"She was *mine*, goddammit, it was supposed to be me—" Ioren slammed Corwyn into the wall; her head hit hard enough that she saw stars. "Did you fucking *forget*?"

"No," she said. She'd known exactly what she was doing to him when she slit Tansa's throat. Thing was, faced with that boot on her sister's neck, she didn't care.

Was he crying? "The hell am I supposed to do, now, Corwyn? *Die*? You wanted me dead?"

Had Ioren been less frenzied, he'd have heard the scrape and grunt behind him, but he didn't and Gwen took him out at the knees with the shovel. Corwyn staggered off the wall, eyes streaming, as Gwen hauled herself the rest of the way upright with the shovel. Ioren rolled onto his back.

"Stay the hell down," Gwen told him, her voice a wreck of gravel and squeaks.

Ioren shot her a look made of murder and sat up. Gwen, quicker than she had a right to be, swung the shovel at his head. He looked surprised as it connected, which was likely why she got him.

He dropped hard. Gwen stumbled; Corwyn threw out a wobbly arm and got her round the waist, barely managing to keep them both upright.

They stood in the sweat and blood and gunpowder smell for a while, catching their balance and their breath. Corwyn swayed a little; Gwen coughed. "You okay?" Corwyn finally asked.

Gwen gently stomped one foot, then the other. "I think I can walk," she said. "Maybe not far, but—"

"All right. Good." Corwyn glanced over at Ioren, unconscious on the floor. The blood mark was gonna eat him alive. And that left Gwen ... where? Mrs. Simcote'd sold her to Tansa.

That left Gwen with Corwyn. Who'd killed Ioren, more or less. All of it washed over her in a hot rush.

"Gwen—I'm *sorry*," she said, her voice thicker than even the battered state of her head could explain. "Maybe we can, I dunno, we could haul him out of here somehow? Maybe find his people, see if they'll—"

Gwen snorted, then grimaced. "We're not hauling his ass anywhere. He put his hands on you. He can find his own way out."

"He's gonna die because of me," Corwyn said.

"You think I give a shit? Nobody lays hands on you, Corwyn."

"But—Gwen. I know. Okay? I know."

Gwen shot her a sharp glance. "You know what?" Corwyn said nothing, just gestured to Ioren and raised her eyebrows. Gwen got it, then looked at her like she was stupid. "We've been fucking, Corwyn, yeah. So?"

Corwyn put out her hands, shook her sore head, confused.

Gwen's face turned murderous. "He bounced your head off a fucking wall. I don't care if he rots from the inside out. He's lucky I ain't got the strength to kill him right now." Gwen's expression softened. "Ain't nobody I love in the world save you, Wyn. Don't you know that?"

Corwyn blinked, let loose a breath it felt like she'd held for years, then smiled—not much, it hurt too much. "I guess I do, at that." Ioren twitched on the floor. "And we'd best get out of here before he wakes up."

The tunnel leading from the work room to the yard of the Brogan house sloped upward rather than having steps. Corwyn couldn't decide whether this was a mercy. They left the light of Tansa's workroom behind, so she got out her glowing rock again. It seemed heavy to her overworked arms—getting her rucksack over her shoulder had been no fun, either.

Not many houses in San Xavier had yards, outside of Chaffins Grove. Miss Vadoma had one for her witchy herbs, but Corwyn couldn't think of any others. And Miss Vadoma's yard likely didn't have a big hole dug up along the far side garden wall.

"The hell was she doing?" she asked.

Gwen shrugged, then winced. "She said I'd be the foundation of her empire. I guess she meant the dictionary definition."

Corwyn rubbed a hand over her face. It came back stickier than before. She was sweaty, bloody, stinking, and every part of her hurt. Gwen looked better than before, but still not good. They needed to rest and let the poison work its way out of Gwen, maybe eat something.

Fog spilled over the wall into the garden. "Let's go to St. Phil's," she said. "We'll look at the clock and see if we can steal something to eat from Mr. Katsaros."

Gwen chuckled, an odd creaking noise from her abused throat. "He surely does owe us for our trouble."

CORWYN HAD FORGOTTEN the damn gang war.

The first corpse materialized from the fog, laid out across the sidewalk into the street, just off Jersey Court Road. Corwyn set herself to figuring how they'd get through the mob. Maybe rooftops instead of St. Phil's. Pry down a board or two and sneak into a tenement for a while.

But the mob never appeared. Instead they came across broken glass, chunks of clockwork and flesh, entire blood-soaked corpses, and the occasional, easily-avoided skirmish of winded, bleeding people. The streets were full of detritus both mechanical and physical, blood outlining bricks and stones.

"I wonder who won?" Gwen asked. Her voice echoed hoarse off the silence and the fog. Something rumbled, but it was impossible to tell where in the mist it originated.

"Whoever it was, looks like they'll have trouble scraping together people enough for a respectable gang," Corwyn replied. The only thing lacking in all this aftermath was a fire; she hoped they'd not run across one.

They turned up Saints' Alley. St. Phil's emerged on the other side of it through twists of fog. The rumbling became a low grinding; the closer they got to the cathedral the more Corwyn felt it in her chest. And ...

"Is that music?" she asked Gwen. Off-key and weird, wheezing, a bit like an organ. Or their voices.

"Corwyn." Gwen's hand clamped hard on Corwyn's arm as they came out the mouth of the alley into the space in front of St. Philomena's. "Corwyn, the clock."

The clock tower rose wreathed in fog and lit by clockwork lamps hidden somewhere in its roof. The doors around the tower gaped open; St. Philomena lay in the midst of a mass of clockwork wolves who busily devoured her metal body. Neither St. Phil nor the wolves had paint left, now; they were just plain clockwork automata. Her stomach had little doors in it that they could see, flipped open wide as the wolves dipped their jaws in and out. Clockwork pieces—gears and little things meant, Corwyn thought, to be bone or organs—traveled up and down fine, stiff wires that ran up out of her belly.

The cathedral's sisters and two priests stood on the steps, watching the show with awe, or delight, or disgust. Corwyn glanced round and saw she and Gwen weren't the only folk standing slack-jawed in the street; people leaned out windows, stood near the doors of their stores and houses, all to watch.

It took a good long time before the righteous clockwork fury of heaven sent the wolves back into the spire doors and St. Philomena put herself together. The mechanism pulled her back inside, the music ended, the doors shut. The clock tolled twice.

"I don't think the time's right," Corwyn remarked.

"Still a sight to see, though," said Gwen.

CHAPTER TWENTY-FOUR

"Trenches in the goddamned street to direct the blood to the cathedral," Corwyn marveled. "You think anyone even knew they were there?"

"Could have been the Russians put them there, or the alchemical engineers," Gwen said, lowering herself to the steps of the Cathedral with a groan. "I need something to eat. And drink."

"All right." Corwyn surveyed the street around them. Between the boarded-up windows and the people milling about to assess damage from the gang battle in the light of the still-glowing clock tower lamps, the pickings for easy theft were decidedly thin. The fog might help, though.

She crossed the street to the dry goods store. It looked to be deserted, nobody in it or standing round outside who belonged to it. A couple of kids who might have paid her some attention were too busy going through the pockets of a dead gangster to notice Corwyn loitering.

She waited until the fog closed around her, then, gritting her teeth against the pain from her abused arms, pried one of the boards from the front window loose. The glass was already broken, so she used her elbow to knock out the remains.

Inside she found apples, some jerky, and a water barrel with a dipper. A search of the shelves produced a metal canteen, which she filled and put, along with the rest of her spoils, into her filthy, stained rucksack.

They ate on the steps—Corwyn only ate one apple, cutting the other one into small pieces for Gwen—the faint groan and hiss of the clock tower underscoring the sounds of people looting bodies and stores. The kids she'd seen earlier had abandoned the corpse to use her pulled-off board to sneak into the dry goods store.

Gwen stretched her legs out, one at a time, groaning.

"You feeling any better?" Corwyn asked.

"Yeah. Ugh. You okay? You look like you got dragged through all nine hells."

"I waded through a gang war and killed Tansa Katsaros, so I imagine I do, yeah." She glanced at Gwen, who was rubbing her calf, and asked, her voice careful, "Was it true, what Tansa said? The old lady having you drugged by a monster thing?"

Gwen's hands stilled; she stared at her knees. "I guess. I got grabbed by something, and it wasn't a kid. Slammed me face-first into the wall and put a needle in my neck. Next I knew I was in a box with Tansa fucking Katsaros telling me she's gonna bury me alive to assure her turf or some shit. Empire. That was the word. Bitch."

"How the hell does that work? And I thought she wanted her own monster."

"Alchemical engineers're all mad as rats, maybe it'd do both." Gwen put her head on her knees. "Stupid bitch didn't even lock the box. Lot of damn faith in whatever that shit was they gave me."

"I bet Frank made it," Corwyn said. "Drink some more."

Gwen obliged, swallowing some water. "Been a while since we've had dinner at St. Phil's," she observed.

"Yeah," Corwyn said. She glanced up to watch the fog undulate above their heads. "Lord, remember back when all we did was spar, steal shit, and wait 'til we were both old enough to join a gang?"

Gwen chuckled. It sounded terrible. "I remember I was trying to put that off as long as I could manage. I liked nobody giving me orders."

Corwyn blinked at her. "What? The hell are you telling me, Gwen?"

Gwen shrugged, grinning a little shy. "I dunno, I figured we didn't have much choice, right? We had to do something, sooner or later. But I just ... liked that it was later?" Her grin faded. "Then Lars Hallstrom grabbed you, and fucking Gad d'Souza ..." she sighed. "I reckoned what I really needed to do was make sure you were safe. I thought I could do it myself, but then I fucked it up every single time."

"The hell are you on about?" asked Corwyn. "How d'you think I got away from Lars Hallstrom, Gwen, magic? You taught me how to fight."

"Can't deny Beatriz d'Souza, though, can you?"

"Beatriz d'Souza can go fuck herself."

Gwen snorted at that. "She does seem to have more to worry about right now than us."

Corwyn couldn't argue. All the gang lords were about to have a time rebuilding. This much mayhem might even bring the Jacks into the Hill.

She got that feeling again, like something in the back of her brain was simmering. "You know, all I wanted was for you to be happy. And safe. But ain't noplace really safe, is it? Blood monsters and you got eaten by a house and the old lady sold you to whatever the hell Tansa thought she was—"

"And you came after me, Wyn," Gwen said, trying to reassure her. But Corwyn didn't need to be reassured.

"Yeah," she agreed. "I did. I always come after you. And you always come after me." Corwyn went quiet for a minute, letting that simmer. Gwen, exhausted, sighed, heavy and shuddery, and put her head back down.

"So we go back to the Volary—if we can get into the kitchen we can take some food." Corwyn felt like she was figuring it out as she spoke. "I dunno where we're gonna stay, neither one of us is up to rowing out to Bishop's Light ... maybe Cadogan Rentsch? Did I tell you Ior—um. I went to see him before all this? Anyway, maybe I can talk him round for a night—"

"Wyn?" Corwyn frowned at Gwen. She still had her head resting on her knees, but she'd turned it so she could stare at Corwyn. "What're you talking about?"

"He kind of owes me a favor?" Corwyn replied. "I mean, you have to look at it sideways and squint, but—"

"You're—the Volary?"

And Corwyn figured it out. *Oh.*

"The old bitch tried to kill you, Gwen," she said softly. "I mean, I ain't gonna try and kill her if she's got some monster on a leash that's faster than *you*, but we need supplies and I ain't letting her have our stuff. We ain't staying long, though."

"How'd that be any different than the last time we tried to live on our own?" Gwen asked tiredly, frowning. She had a look about her, though. Like she wanted to be convinced.

Corwyn's mind bubbled over. "We got equipment, for one thing. The old lady gave us some of those gadgets and things outright, so it ain't stealing if we keep them. We know what we're getting into, for another." She leaned forward and pointed at Gwen. "And we ain't living on the street this time, neither. If my knack's so goddamned valuable, maybe I ought to make some real money off it, pay some rent."

"You'd be safer with the old lady," Gwen tried, but Corwyn could see her heart wasn't in the argument. "I'm the one has Beatriz d'Souza after her."

"Who's d'Souza gonna send? Dunno if you noticed—most of the fighting knacks in the Hill just got used to fuel a puppet show." Corwyn waved a hand up and behind her at the closed doors of the steeple. "And so what if she does come after you? We're both grown and you've been trained by Veigar Olafurson's assassin grandson. Who, I might add, is after *me*, unless you killed him with that shovel. *He* ain't gonna care about Mrs. Simcote's protection." Corwyn didn't mention that she was more likely to wait out his mark if he didn't know where to find her.

"You really think we could do it?" Gwen asked.

Corwyn took a deep breath, let it out slow. "I dunno. It ain't gonna be easy, and it ain't safe. The old lady won't just let us go—"

"Fuck the old lady," Gwen said darkly.

"—but ain't nobody in the world I love, Gwen, save you," Corwyn said with a grin. "So, you know what, better to go out together. Be legends or something."

Gwen stared at her for a long moment, then smiled a sweet, broad smile. She took a bite of her apple without straightening up.

"Well," she said, "we're gonna be here a while—that was enough poison for four sailors. So tell me what the hell you did that Cadogan Rentsch kind of owes you a favor if you squint right."

CHAPTER TWENTY-FIVE

Though there was very little chance their absences had gone unnoticed, the Teachouts snuck back into the Volary via the roof. The sky was the dark blue of near-dawn as they crossed the bridge from the boardinghouse to the Volary. Corwyn was too tired to feel anything but sad.

They hoped they might not be seen, but luck had taken her leave of them. The first person to spot them was Mattie Singh, halfway down the ladder from her sleeping sack. She took one wide-eyed look at them and climbed back up, pulling the sides closed firmly. They passed Jouanna and Memno on the way to the second-floor washroom, where they stripped to their slightly less bloodstained underthings to wash the blood and dirt off their skin. Whatever else she might think of the old lady, Corwyn reflected, she'd had the good sense to blackmail someone into outfitting the place with running water—a good thing, as what went down the drains was red and gray, in gallons.

Had she been a little less tired and a lot less sad, it would have concerned Corwyn that nobody bothered them in the washroom. Nobody came near as they headed back to their room, disgusting clothes in hand. A few kids stopped on the landings to watch them, but most everyone else was out of sight.

Nils sat next to their door, which had been defaced by an enormous scrawled Olafurson gang symbol. The still-wet paint dripped down the wood.

"What in nine hells is that?" asked Corwyn.

Nils' face was equal parts exasperation and exhaustion. "He said to tell you it's a message. For both of you. I dunno what you two did to piss him off, but he aims to see both of you dead."

"He'll have to wait in the fucking line, then," muttered Gwen, pushing the door open. Nils followed them in but paused in the doorway.

"The old lady said she wanted to see you, Corwyn, when you got back."

Corwyn took a quick glance at Gwen, who had thrown her clothes in a corner and knelt on the floor to get her rucksack from under her bed. "Just me?" Corwyn asked.

"She didn't say anything about Gwen."

"That don't mean anything," Gwen said, her voice muffled as she pulled a set of boots and three socks from beneath her bed, but her tone still full of warning.

"I ain't going anywhere," Corwyn told Nils. He said nothing, just looked even more worried. She took his arm by the elbow, pulling him into the room. "You go tell her whatever you have to, but Nils—don't trust her."

"None of us trusts her," Nils said, confusion deepening.

"That ain't true," Corwyn said. "Not completely. We trust her to keep us safe. And we shouldn't. You get your legacy and get the hell out, you hear me?"

"What the bloody damn hell did the two of you get into?" Nils asked. "I thought this was about Ioren."

"No," said Mrs. Simcote from the door. She let her skirts drop with a soft thump. Gwen stood up; Corwyn suddenly felt her own bare feet inside her unlaced boots, the air on her shins and neck, as Gwen's chin lifted and her jaw set.

"I take it Mrs. Brogan is dead?" Mrs. Simcote asked Gwen.

"Was that the outcome you were hoping for, Mrs. Simcote?"

"No, but I don't particularly mind it." The old lady's mouth twitched. She turned her eyes to Nils. "Nils, I want the room."

Nils left, but kept eyes on Corwyn for as long as he could. She didn't hear him climbing to his sleep-sack, so she didn't know how close he stuck. But she guessed it didn't much matter.

Corwyn regarded Mrs. Simcote, the lines around her mouth and eyes, the perfect sweep of her white hair to the top of her head, the brooch at her throat, the sagging skin above it. She considered yelling at her. But she reckoned from the old lady's straight spine that yelling was what she expected, so instead Corwyn dropped her own bloody bundle of clothes onto the floor and slipped her still-filth-encrusted rucksack off her shoulder. Most all of her things were in it already; she just needed some clothes and her books.

"Corwyn," said Mrs. Simcote. Corwyn pulled *Farther Shores* out from under her pillow and stuffed it in the bag. "You don't have to leave." Corwyn heard the slight emphasis on "you."

Far too many words at once rushed to Corwyn's mind, but the only one that found its way out her mouth was, "No." She found *The Sad Whore's Privateer* and *A Treasury of Verse* on the shelf under their night table and put them in her rucksack. Gwen, who hadn't moved since the old lady'd arrived, turned to loading her own things into her bag.

Mrs. Simcote took half a step back and let out a long breath. "On your head be it, then," she said, and left the room.

THE VOLARY CHILDREN stood on the top landing, on the bridges and ladders, some on the ceilings of the rooms beneath their sleeping sacks, as the Teachouts left their room. Nils looked troubled, as did a few of the others—Memno, Mattie, Oid, Frank—but nobody looked mad. None of them, not even Jouanna, said a word, but they all watched as the Teachouts, bags over shoulders, left the Volary through the door to the roof.

"This is too easy," Gwen murmured as they ascended the stairs.

"All of them staring at us was no damn picnic," Corwyn replied, shaking herself to get their gazes off her skin.

"No, but—" Gwen paused at the roof door. "Maybe I can see her letting *me* go. Maybe she don't care what I can tell folks about her. But why wouldn't she fight to keep you? Even if your knack weren't of any value to her, keeping you here's a good hold on my mouth."

Corwyn looked for a reason to argue Gwen's point, uneasily recalling Antoine Gregoire's torn-up body in the alley near St. Phil's. "Maybe she knows I'd run off the first time she sent me finding anyone?"

Gwen dropped her head sideways to acknowledge the point. "That's as may be," she said, pushing the door open, "but I'm still placing bets she knows Ioren's on that roof ready to kill both of us."

Corwyn's tired, blood-spattered brain finally put it together, then, and she said, "No, not Ioren."

Over by the bridge between the Volary and the wrecked playground that was the boardinghouse rooftop, a spindly shadow detached itself from the deep dawn-blue murk and made its way—long-limbed and low—toward them.

"HOW THE HELL DID I forget her *goddamned monster*," Gwen muttered. She dropped her rucksack and slid a knife out of her boot. Corwyn fell a half-step behind her, eyes on the creature that came for them delicately across the roof on its long, knobby legs. A sweet scent of copper wafted toward them as it moved; the top of its head caught the sun like a puddle of blood in the street.

It stopped a couple feet in front of them to look them over with its huge green and silver eyes. "You were supposed to be my sister," it told Gwen in a creaking, high voice that Corwyn recognized from the walls and her dreams.

Gwen blinked; Corwyn fought down a sick, jealous urge to get between the two of them. "She's *my* sister," she said, instead.

"I know," said the monster. Its teeth, black and three rows sharp, glimmered as it spoke. "I knew she'd be a good one to me. I saw how well she took care of you."

Gwen closed a hand around Corwyn's wrist as the thing went on, "I was only me for a long time, until the scrob-man made me a brother. He wasn't bad. We played together sometimes. But the metal bugs cut him apart." It paused, then said, "The lady said to kill whoever came up here, but she didn't say it would be you."

Gwen let go of Corwyn's wrist. "You could let us go," she said, but it didn't sound as persuasive as it ought to've. She grinned her knack's grin at the thing in front of her. Corwyn's stomach sank.

The monster didn't smile. "No," it said, and leapt at Gwen.

Corwyn ran for cover behind a chimney. She knew she wasn't a match for anything unearthly without a weapon as had range to it, but pawing through both their bags turned up nothing like that. She glanced up to see Gwen and the monster dancing round each other; the thing had an unearthly grace that nobody Gwen had fought before had ever shown. It went for Gwen quick, clawed the top of her head as she ducked. A little blood curved into the air; the creature swiped its palm and caught it, slapped the hand to the top of its head as it kept after Gwen.

"Goddammit, gods damn it," Corwyn swore, turning back to the bag. Knives, a brick—no truncheon, nine hells, Ioren had that and she'd likely never see it again—not even a bloody slingshot. If they got out of this, they were getting a goddamned armory.

There was nothing to do but watch, trying not to choke on her heart as it hammered in her throat, and keep a hope that there might be an opening for her to help. Somehow. Anyhow.

Gwen stepped, swift and sure, onto the low wall that ringed the rooftop, then launched herself at the monster to wrap her legs round its neck and drop. The thing staggered without falling, and Gwen swung back up again, jammed her elbow into its head-jelly as it slammed her into the wall by the roof door and dropped her. It clawed at her, but Gwen got a boot up to shove it back a couple steps and, winded, dropped to the ground to take out its legs. The thing jumped to avoid the sweep, landing light.

Gwen grinned and sprung back up; Corwyn watched her charge the monster and thought, again, despairingly, that Gwen fighting was the most beautiful thing in creation, even when she could barely damage the thing she was fighting.

Then. Gwen stopped short and fell back a little, bouncing on her feet. The monster, braced for impact, lunged after her; she danced back a little more, cocked her head. Watched even as she evaded. *Nine hells, Ioren Gudrunson, you were right*, Corwyn thought.

The monster wasn't thinking, just attacking, and maybe that worked on regular folks or other fighting knacks, but Gwen was another manner of beast, now.

"Even if you kill me," Gwen said, ragged breaths between the words, "you're going to be alone. The old lady won't make you a sibling. And the others as know how are dead."

The monster paused, staggering a touch. "You don't know. Maybe if I'm good," it said.

"She never did before," Corwyn called. She stood up as the monster swung to look at her. "She don't need two of you. She buried you somewhere—maybe I could find where if I tried—and you became her pet, and she's got her kids to do her work, and she's content. Her empire's set."

"She doesn't trust sisters," Gwen added, and the creature turned again to face her. Gwen's knack was draining out of her, it looked like. "Even if you had one, she'd keep you away."

The monster sagged onto its scrawny frame. There was no reading its face, but its body seemed confused, maybe sad, so Corwyn took a breath and told it, "You saw what all she did to us."

They stood there like a tableau, Gwen's breathing easing, the monster's head swinging between them. Corwyn crept closer even though she didn't know what good it'd do.

The door to the roof scraped open. Mrs. Simcote stepped through and stopped, staring aghast at the three of them. Corwyn caught sight of Mattie, Nils, and Jouanna behind her before the monster lunged.

Corwyn jolted for Gwen and Gwen for Corwyn, but the creature went for Mrs. Simcote, fast, howling cracked and windy. It raked its claws along the old lady's belly before she could take more than a step back to the door, shoved her backwards into Jouanna. The creature fell back, then, sobbing.

The old lady sank to the rooftop, one hand over her bloody stomach, glaring hard. "That make you feel better?" she asked the creature.

"You ain't a nice lady!" the monster accused, sounding wounded.

"No, I ain't, but I'm all you got! I'm all *any* of you got, you hear me?" Mrs. Simcote swung her head around, grimacing, to take in all the kids behind her, her monster, and Corwyn and Gwen across from it all. Jouanna started to kneel to help Mrs. Simcote, but pulled back when the creature dropped to its knees next to her.

Corwyn thought she ought to say something in the face of Mrs. Simcote's dripping blood; in the face of the monster's tears. Hell, she probably ought to say something to Nils' horrified eyes. But the world swayed round her from tiredness—she'd be willing to sleep in Shoemaker's Alley if it meant putting her head down and forgetting everything for a while.

"Go away," the monster said. It looked at them both. "Go away. Stay away and I'll leave you alone. *She'll* leave you alone."

Then Jouanna did kneel next to Mrs. Simcote, whose eyes were closed, though she looked no less rageful. Corwyn put a hand out for Gwen and found her arm. The two of them got their bags, then started across the roof of the Volary as the sunlight spread to light up the Hill, and the monster cried, harsh and barking, over the old lady.

EPILOGUE

Corwyn Teachout, not very much older than the day she left the Volary but a sight better-rested, opened the door to the Pallas-green flat she shared with her sister to find Cadogan Rentsch on the other side of it.

"I found this on my doorstep last night," he said, handing her a box. "It had a note on it."

Corwyn had not had coffee yet. Or breakfast. She held out her hand. Rentsch put a piece of paper and the box into it, then turned to make his way back down the stairs. "Come by tomorrow—I've a thing I want you to see," he called over his shoulder.

"You want me to do more than look at it, you'd better have cash on hand!" Corwyn called back. The box was heavier than she'd expected, with a hollow thud from inside.

"The hell is that?" asked Gwen from the bedroom doorway, bruised from her previous evening's job and rumpled with sleep.

"A present," said Corwyn. The note proved to be instructions for working the lock on the box. "It's probably pretty stupid to follow the directions and open this thing," she said.

"It won't be the stupidest thing we've ever done." Gwen sat herself on the sofa to watch as Corwyn read the paper, licked her finger, fed the lock, then slid the plates on it in the manner illustrated by the diagram before tapping the entire mechanism three times. The lock popped open. Corwyn, Gwen leaning over her shoulder to see, opened the lid.

On the inside was drawn the Olafurson sigil. In the box itself lay their truncheon.

"Well," said Corwyn. "I guess there's no chance Ioren didn't follow Mr. Rentsch here, huh?"

Corwyn glanced at Gwen, and they grinned at each other, somewhere between uneasy and excited. "I'd not bet on that, no."

Acknowledgements

There is truly nothing like writing an acknowledgements page to make you realize how eclectic your community is.

First off, I want to thank Kat Howard, who is an amazing editor and helped me figure out how to make this book cohere.

Annie Dobrin helped me find the first scene with a one-word prompt. David Walker knows a lot of archaic terms for prostitution and fashion history, because of course he does. Erin Rausch and Deanna Sims answered all my random questions about the weather and burying people in California with good grace and only the occasional, "The hell are you *writing*?" Karen Sorenson taught me about structuring a long piece of fiction and the power of swearing in a rough outline, for which I am extremely grateful. Jaxton Kimble's all caps texts as he read the draft made the outlining worth all the swearing.

Ken Price and Gus Davis are my models for what kids are capable of; Olive Allen underscored what I already knew.

I would like to especially thank all the wonderful, weird people on my Facebook, whose response to "Who wants something named after them?" was "I do!" even when it was a corpse or a murder house. My Tumblr peeps, thank you for all the likes whenever I tell you I'm writing; you guys keep me going.

Linda Davis does the dishes and the laundry and never touches my desk, even when I'm sure it drives her up the wall not to tidy it.

The faculty and staff of the Richard H. Rush Library at Florida SouthWestern State College circa 2012-2014 gave me so much research help and support; I can't thank all of you enough. Cover illustration is by kixckcore artwork on Shutterstock.

And finally, thank you to Brandy and Steph, Ann and Sandi, Taylar and Lena, and Judy and Juanita: y'all showed the only child what sisters are like.

Don't miss out!

Visit the website below and you can sign up to receive emails whenever Laura E. Price publishes a new book. There's no charge and no obligation.

https://books2read.com/r/B-A-ZGSCB-CICZE

BOOKS 2 READ

Connecting independent readers to independent writers.

About the Author

Laura E. Price writes fantasy, horror, and the occasional bit of soft science fiction. Her short stories about the Teachout sisters have appeared in *Beneath Ceaseless Skies, GigaNotoSaurus, Translunar Travelers Lounge,* and on her blog. She lives with her family in Florida, in a house that hasn't eaten anybody (yet) and tries to keep her website (lauraeprice.com) updated on the regular.

Read more at https://lauraeprice.com/.